Twists

OF FATE

Joana Starnes

"O, learn to read what silent love hath writ:
To hear with eyes belongs to love's fine wit."

WILLIAM SHAKESPEARE, 'Sonnet XXIII'

New Characters

In addition to well-known and much-loved characters, there are a few others.
Most of them are incidental to the story and are listed below only as a memory aid.

Lord and Lady Malvern: *Colonel Fitzwilliam's parents*

Francis, Lord Leighton; Henry; Lady Amelia and Lady Harriet Fitzwilliam:
Colonel Fitzwilliam's brothers and sisters

Lady Rosemary Sinclair: *family friend of the Fitzwilliams and the Darcys,*
and an influential lady of the highest circles

Miss Beatrice Endicott: *Miss Darcy's closest friend*

Mr Kettering, Mr and Mrs Lyle: *Mr Darcy's Derbyshire neighbours*

Mr Geoffrey Lyle, Miss Cecilia and Miss Flora: *Mr and Mrs Lyle's offspring*

Major Aubrey: *Mr Kettering's nephew*

Mr and Mrs Prescott; Miss Prescott: *Derbyshire neighbours*

Mr Frederick Vincent: *The Bennets' new neighbour*

Miss Eleanor (Ella) Vincent: *Mr Vincent's daughter*

Mr Howard: *Mr Darcy's butler*

Mr Weston: *Mr Darcy's valet*

Mrs Blake: *housekeeper of Mr Darcy's townhouse*

Thomas, Peter, Simon: *Mr Darcy's footmen*

Joseph: *Mr Darcy's coachman*

Norbert: *Mr Darcy's former gamekeeper*

Sarah Parsons: *maid at Longbourn; later Mrs Darcy's lady's maid*

John: *footman at Longbourn*

Susan: *John's intended, maid at the Red Lion in Meryton*

Mrs Valpy: *the owner of the main shop in Meryton*

Lucy: *Mrs Valpy's maid*

Martha: *Mrs Phillips' cook and Lucy's cousin*

᪥ ᪥ ᪥

Chapter 1

"Really, Mr Collins, you puzzle me exceedingly!" Elizabeth exclaimed, glaring at her irksome cousin who stood by her chair – too close, verily towering above her. "If you find encouragement in what I said so far, I know not how to express my refusal in such a way as may convince you that I am utterly in earnest. I thank you for the honour you have done me, but I cannot possibly accept your offer. My feelings in every respect forbid it. How can this be said more plainly?" she enunciated, having long reached the limits of her patience.

That word – refusal – had passed her lips thrice, yet had been like water off a duck's back to Mr Collins every time.

To her deep vexation, the third repetition did not sink in either.

"You are uniformly charming," the infuriating man declared with an air of awkward gallantry – and had the audacity, moreover, to reach out and run a finger down her cheek.

A shocked intake of breath hissed through her teeth as Elizabeth drew back, her recoil so sharp that her head hit the ornamental sphere at the corner of her backrest with a quiet thud.

Undaunted and unapologetic, Mr Collins spoke again, his tone cloying, "You must give me leave to flatter myself, my dear cousin, that your refusal of my addresses is merely words, of course. My connections with the noble family of de Bourgh, my situation in life and my being next in the entail of Longbourn are circumstances highly in my favour. And let us not forget that your small portion can only serve to counter the effects of your manifold attractions, so another offer of marriage may never come your way. Certainly none so advantageous."

Incensed, Elizabeth scrambled to her feet, albeit with some difficulty, for there was not much space between her chair, the dining room table and her heavyset cousin. She opened her lips to speak and let Mr Collins know in no uncertain terms that he thought far too highly of himself, when the bumptious creature spoke again, only to vex her further:

"Therefore I must conclude that you are not serious in your rejection of me, but merely seeking to increase my love by suspense, according to the usual practice of elegant females."

"I do assure you, sir, that this is not the sort of elegance I aspire to. There is no elegance in tormenting a respectable man—" she retorted and took one step sideways, only to find his hand landing heavily on her shoulder.

"I cannot but agree, my dear Miss Elizabeth," he said with energy. "Besides, let me assure *you* that any endeavour of the kind is wholly unnecessary. I already am completely enraptured. Indeed, the violence of my affections—"

"Mr Collins, you forget yourself!" she heatedly protested. But when she jerked sideways once again, his hand slipped from her shoulder to her breast. If it was an accident, he made no apology for it, nor did he shrink back in shock at his own misconduct. The shock was all hers, and the horror, when the hold tightened into a grip, and his other hand clutched her posterior. "Release me, sir!" she gasped, appalled and sickened, and tore the offending hand from her bosom, averting her face to escape yet another offence.

His mouth missed hers by the smallest fraction, and was pressed wetly to her cheek. But before he could impose himself upon her any further, Elizabeth shoved him back with the force of outraged desperation, freed herself and scrambled out of his reach, dragging the fringed tablecloth with her. The blue-patterned pitcher that stood in the middle of the table fell to one side with a loud thump. Water gushed out and spread into a pool under the scattered ox-eye daisies and the sprigs of rosemary and laurel that she and her sister Kitty had lovingly arranged less than a quarter of an hour earlier, but Elizabeth paid no heed to the damage caused, nor to Mr Collins' still unrepentant splutter. She stalked to the door, flung it open and stormed out of the room, then hastened towards the front door almost at a run. She barely broke her stride when Mrs Bennet scurried out of the parlour.

"Lizzy, where are you—?"

"I must see Papa," Elizabeth cut her off, her hand unsteady as she turned the handle.

"You know full well that he is at the parish meeting—"

"Yes, I know," Elizabeth retorted crisply and pulled the oak door open.

"Goodness, child, you cannot march into the *Red Lion* unescorted! The very notion!" her mother blustered, and Elizabeth barely restrained the urge to roll her eyes.

"Of course not, Mamma. I will send word from my aunt Phillips'."

"Hm! Well! But even so, I will not have you scampering off to Meryton and leaving me none the wiser," Mrs Bennet remonstrated. "You had much better come and tell me what Mr Collins had to—"

"Not now, Mamma," Elizabeth forestalled her. "I must see Papa at once." And, without another word, she dashed out of the house, not troubling herself to close the door behind her, for she knew all too well that it would be promptly opened, so that her mother could call after her – demand that she return within.

Her expectations were confirmed. As she rushed around the first bend in the gravelled driveway, Elizabeth could hear Mrs Bennet's voice, shrill with vexation at her disobedience:

"Come back, Lizzy! Why must you—? Oh, that child will be the death of me! Lizzy, come back this instant, do you hear me? *Lizzy!*"

But, head down, Elizabeth kept running, much as she knew that, entail or no entail, her mother's indignation would change direction and scorch Mr Collins if she were to return to the house and reveal what had come to pass. But she needed more than her mother's fit of temper. That would not suffice. She needed her father – his presence – his protection. Now more than ever, she needed his protection and his love.

That was the only reason why Elizabeth barely slowed her pace. She harboured no concern that her mother – or, perish the thought, Mr Collins – would catch up with her. Mrs Bennet's energetic days were long behind her. As for the other, a leisurely stroll had been enough to render him short of breath a couple of days prior.

The passing thought of her repulsive cousin was enough to make her shudder. Instinctively, Elizabeth hastened her steps as she continued on her way, lips pursed, beside herself with disgust and anger, and dangerously close to tears. The impudence of the man! Not impudence, that was nowhere near strong enough. He had been far worse than impudent. He had been vile. Revolting. Loathsome.

'How dare he!'

The fast pace could not serve to calm her, but at least it kept her warm, which was something to be thankful for, once Elizabeth was able to spare a thought for the folly of setting out to Meryton wrapped in a shawl. It was a mercy that the weather was so mild – uncommonly mild for the time of year – for she *would not* go back for her pelisse or some other garment. If she should catch a cold, it would be a small price to pay. No form of sickness could be worse than *that man's* wet lips at the corner of her mouth and his hands on her person – his insulting grip. Painful. Terrifying.

Another shudder racked her, and Elizabeth flinched as she forced the abhorrent episode aside. Enough! Fists clenched around the edges of her shawl, she drew a deep breath, and then another. Enough now. The repugnant creature was not worth another thought. All would be well. It was all over. The worst was over. He would not be suffered to come near her again! Her papa would see to it. She would be with her dearest papa as soon as may be, and all would be well. Not long to go. And thank goodness for the hours she had spent out of doors, walking, running, building her strength and stamina. She was certainly reaping the rewards today. She was not out of breath, and had no need to slow her pace. So she would be in Meryton in no time at all.

⁂

It was not so, to Elizabeth's growing frustration. A while later – about a quarter of an hour later, in her estimation – she was but halfway into the small market town. Yet it was not tiredness that hampered her in her progress. It was the pouring rain.

The first droplets had caught her unawares. She had raised her head to glower at the low-lying clouds and pressed on, choosing to ignore the inconvenience. She kept walking even when the drizzle grew into a shower. But when the light rainfall became a veritable deluge, Elizabeth was forced to concede that she had better seek shelter. Not that she was daunted by a spell of bad weather. She had been caught in the rain many a time, on her daily rambles. But it would not do to arrive drenched and bedraggled in Meryton, and looking decidedly improper. Her cashmere shawl was quite wet by now, and her skirts were hardly faring any better. They were damp, mud-splattered and clinging to her legs – to say nothing of her shoes which, by the looks of it, were already beyond redemption.

Even so, Elizabeth could not regret that she had left the house without her pelisse and in dainty shoes, not boots. It mattered not that she was cold and wet, in ruined shoes, and that her feet ached because the thin soles gave scarce any protection against sharp stones and the hard road-surface. She would gladly endure all this and more, rather than spend another moment in her odious cousin's presence!

There was nothing she could do about her shoes, but at least she was reasonably safe from becoming soaked to the skin, once she found shelter under a clump of hollies. A protruding root gave her a place to sit while she waited for the downpour to abate, so in short order the aching soles of her feet were feeling a little better too. She was still cold and wet. Vigorously shaking her cashmere shawl had made no difference, for the rain had already seeped into it. Yet a glance upwards brought a touch of warmth into her heart. The clusters of bright red berries, standing out in cheering contrast against the glossy leaves, could not but remind her that Christmas was coming. Aye, it would be Christmas in less than a month's time. Her aunt and uncle Gardiner would come to stay – they always did at this time of year – and all would be joy and kindness, just as it ought to be.

A new sound – a clatter of hooves? – caught her notice and distracted her from her pleasing reflections. At first, it could barely be heard over the steady patter of the rain, but it soon grew louder and removed all doubt. Clattering hooves, aye. A rider approaching at a leisurely canter, seemingly in no haste despite the pouring rain. Was it her father? So, he had ridden to the parish meeting, then? For some reason, she had been convinced that he had gone on foot.

'*Oh, well. No matter,*' Elizabeth thought and smiled, reminded of the few times in her girlhood when her dear papa had taken her riding with him, perched before his saddle. With any luck, she would not fall off if she were to return home with him in like manner.

She stood and peeked from behind the interwoven tree trunks, lest it be someone else, not he – and was in equal measure glad that she had taken that sensible precaution and vexed by the unremitting perverseness of fate. For the approaching rider was not her father. It was Mr Darcy.

⚮

"Oh, for goodness' sake!" Elizabeth muttered under her breath and stepped back, eager to conceal herself as best she could.

She was scarce fit to be seen and, more to the point, she was not disposed for conversation. Least of all with *him*. On the previous evening, at the Netherfield ball, their terse exchanges had been enough to put her out of humour. Even if she were in a cheerful and forbearing frame of mind right now, she would have precious little patience with Mr Darcy's singular brand of intercourse. But after the sort of morning that she had just had, no power under heaven would induce her to tolerate his company with equanimity.

'Tolerable, I suppose…'

She snorted at the recollection of his gross incivility at the Meryton assembly. How very generous of him to deem her tolerable! Well, she was not of a mind to say the same of him – and certainly not today.

So Elizabeth took another step back, then another, stealthily assessing his progress as she went, so that she might keep the clump of hollies between them at all times. She reached down to gather her skirts, lest they flap in the rising wind and draw his notice.

What was he doing here, anyway? There were any number of roads and bridleways he might have chosen. Surely he was not on his way to Longbourn to observe the niceties that required gentlemen to call upon the ladies with whom they had stood up at the latest ball!

When she took another backward step, a stick cracked underfoot – awfully loudly, by her reckoning – and Elizabeth froze on the spot when she espied him turning his head towards her. But no, he did not rein in, so Elizabeth released the breath she had been holding and shuffled back a little further for good measure.

And that was when she slipped or tripped – she could not tell. But either way, her feet flew out from underneath her, and the next thing she knew, she was lying on the ground, winded, mortified beyond endurance, and her left foot in agony. Dazed and confused, Elizabeth raised her head, then let it drop against the sodden grass with a strangled groan, not so much one of pain as exasperation.

Those of a superstitious bent claimed that Friday the 13th was inauspicious. For her part, she could not say if there was any truth in that. But she had no doubt whatever that this wretched Wednesday, the 27th of November, was fast becoming the worst day of her life.

that was unmistakably apologetic. He released her foot, drew back and put his unwarranted contrition into words:

"Forgive me. Did I hurt you?"

"No," she whispered and left it at that, although his mien grew puzzled, then questioning. But she was not about to tell him why she was suddenly given to such displays, nor reveal who had injured her – not so much her person as her peace of mind; her pride; her innocence. She flinched, yet clasped her hands together and raised her chin, her lips set into a valiant quirk of determination. Somehow, she must find a way to cease dwelling on *that!*

To her relief, Mr Darcy did not press her for the cause of her tears. But his gaze remained fixed on her for a long moment – a steady, solemn look, oddly akin to sadness. And then he exhaled sharply and darted his eyes away.

"Nothing seems broken," he said at last, yet his voice was solemn too, as though he were declaring the opposite. "So there is no need for anything but…" he added, indicating her attempt at a bandage, and the remaining strips of fine lawn.

He did not complete his sentence, but did finish the work, his fingers nimble, their touch still light, then reached for her shoe and slowly eased it on – thus turning himself into a modern-day Prince Charming, and her into an English *Cendrillon*, Elizabeth thought, the tenuous connection with Monsieur Perrault's tale bringing her to the verge of a nervous chuckle. She timely suppressed it and rolled her eyes at this fresh proof that her emotions were in a dreadful state of flux, rendering her absurdly tearful one moment and giggly the next. Mr Darcy would have reason enough to doubt her sanity. Not that she had ever cared two straws for his opinions.

But this time he was too intent upon his task to notice her reaction. He only glanced at her once he had set her foot down.

"Too tight?"

Elizabeth shook her head. "No. I think not."

He retrieved the hoof pick from where he had left it on the grass, put it in his pocket and asked, "May I escort you home now?"

Sensibly, Elizabeth bit back the instinctive reply that she would not return to Longbourn without her father if her life depended on it. She merely said, "I thank you, no." But then he made to speak, his mien mulish, so she elaborated, "I am not headed home."

"Where, then?"

"Meryton," she tersely owned, and could not help thinking that the answer should have been obvious. Where else might she have gone from here? Meryton was the sole alternative, once she had declared that she was not on her way to Longbourn. Did he perchance imagine she had chosen to live in the woods and become a hermit?

Brow furrowed, Mr Darcy cast her an assessing glance, but did not commit the *faux pas* of asking why she had set off to Meryton in indoor shoes and without so much as a coat, not to mention gloves and a bonnet. But he did not keep silent either:

"Not the best day for a walk," he stated the obvious again.

Elizabeth shrugged with some impatience.

"It was not raining when I left. And I have to see my f— I need to call upon my aunt," she amended at the last minute, vexed with herself and her ungovernable tongue.

"Can this not be left for another day?"

"No," Elizabeth retorted, wishing he would put an end to quizzing her. Yet he did not.

"What is amiss? Something is troubling you. What is it?" he asked, leaning back to rest on his haunches, his scrutiny so intense that she was forced to look away, her frustration mounting.

He had chosen the wrong day to read her rightly. This was none of his concern. Why could he not assume, as he always had, that she was simply traipsing over the countryside like a hoyden?

She could not discuss her troubles with him – could not speak of the repugnant episode with any gentleman of her acquaintance. Not even with someone she had known all her life, nor the amiable and caring Mr Wickham. Most assuredly not with the likes of Mr Darcy.

"Nothing is troubling me. I am weary, that is all."

It was not entirely a falsehood. By now, she genuinely *was* more weary than troubled. Weary of this day, although it had barely begun. Weary of reliving the vile scene, much as she sought to ward off repulsive recollections. Weary of picturing her return home to another dose of ugliness which could not be avoided, even though her father's presence would make it more bearable. And above all weary of the struggle to keep dark thoughts at bay and not permit herself to think of what might happen should they lose him – of the hardships a vengeful Mr Collins would heap upon her and her mother and sisters, once he became the master of Longbourn.

"All the more reason not to walk into Meryton," Mr Darcy said, disrupting her train of thought – which was not a bad thing under the circumstances, and she might have been grateful, were he not so eager to express an opinion on matters which did not concern him.

So she retorted, "I fail to see the difference. This is halfway between there and Longbourn. If anything, my aunt's house is a little closer. And that is where I am going as soon as the rain abates," she concluded blandly.

Mr Darcy's tone was equally matter-of-fact when he made his answer:

"I was not suggesting otherwise. What I meant was that you should not go on foot."

Elizabeth's lips quirked into a little moue at having to explain the matter, yet proceeded to do so regardless.

"You seem to believe that there is another option, but I assure you, there is not. Your horse is not equipped for riding side-saddle, and even if he were, this would not serve me. I hardly ever ride, so I could scarce hope to control a beast the size of yours."

"Perhaps not. But he will obey *me*. And, as you have just pointed out, you cannot use that saddle."

"Precisely," Elizabeth replied, at a loss to grasp why he imagined that what he had just said strengthened his argument, when it clearly supported hers. And then comprehension dawned, and her eyes widened. "You are *not* suggesting I ride to Meryton with you!" she spluttered, but the look he levelled at her told her that this was exactly what he was suggesting. So Elizabeth rolled her eyes and declared, "No, sir, that is out of the question! How would it look?"

"What are *you* suggesting, then?" Mr Darcy countered. "That you walk half a mile or so with that injury and make it worse, or catch a severe cold, just to humour a set of busybodies who had much better mind their own affairs?"

"From what I have noticed, people rarely mind their own affairs," Elizabeth shot back at this further sign that the same could be said of him. "I thank you for your concern and no less for your assistance," she added, gesturing towards her bandaged foot, "but I believe this would be a good time for us to part company."

For the briefest moment, a peculiar expression overspread his countenance, but as soon as she made to remove the coat and return it, the look she could not read gave way to unmistakable exasperation.

"Would you kindly see sense and keep that on?" he rasped. "You may be assured that I am not taking it back. Not yet. And I am not going anywhere," he announced as he rose from his squat, only to drop down next to the nearest tree and lean back against it.

Elizabeth opened her lips to argue the point, but he forestalled her and spoke again with stern determination:

"You may think that the good people of Meryton would have been better pleased had I seen you injured and ridden past, leaving you to your fate, but I cannot oblige them. So I will wait with you until the rain lets up, and then follow you into Meryton at two hundred paces, if I must. But, as I just said, I am not going anywhere until I am assured of your safety. 'Tis the very least I can do."

And with that, he rested his arms on his bent knees and remained still, leaving her open-mouthed and speechless – but not for long.

"That is very thoughtful," she said at length, and largely meant it, "but quite unnecessary. I am virtually on my own doorstep."

"'*Virtually*' is, I think, the salient word here," he pointed out, then his tone softened when he asked, "Are you still cold?"

"No, not at all. But you must be freezing."

He made no answer, just gave a vague gesture of indifference, so Elizabeth could not help adding, "Have you ever been told that you can be too stubborn for your own good?"

"Repeatedly," Mr Darcy said, with a disarming smile that had her staring. It was completely out of character – as was the light-hearted teasing that came a fraction of a second later: "Whereas I imagine that no one has ever said the same of you."

Elizabeth gave a mild chuckle.

"If memory serves, I may have been called obstinate and headstrong once or twice."

"Have you? Astonishing," he retorted, the open smile still in place, then leaned his head against the tree trunk and closed his eyes.

Bemused, Elizabeth sat staring at him for quite some time, and only dropped her gaze when his horse startled her with a loud snort. But Mr Darcy kept his eyes closed, even as he spoke again:

"How is your foot?"

"Happy enough, I thank you."

"I am glad to hear it."

Then he fell silent. So did she. And nothing could be heard but the patter of the rain, and the horse leisurely cropping the wet grass.

Chapter 3

"This is not letting up," Elizabeth concluded a little while later.

"Seemingly not," her companion concurred, without glancing her way. He was no longer leaning his head against the tree trunk, eyes closed, but sat gazing into the distance, absentmindedly toying with a sprig of holly that had fallen on the grass. For the second time in as many minutes, Elizabeth saw him trying to suppress a shiver, which was foolish. As she knew full well, that was an involuntary reaction that could not be suppressed. She had not commented on it before, but now she chose to:

"You *are* cold."

Mr Darcy shrugged.

"That is neither here nor there."

She could not agree. And being held to ransom by the rain was becoming more than a little vexing.

"This is absurd," Elizabeth declared with energy.

"Indeed," Mr Darcy said, and this time did turn his head to look at her, the same sort of disconcerting smile playing on his lips.

For her part, she could not see the humorous side of it.

This *was* patently absurd! Were it not for the turn in the weather, the walk from Longbourn to Mrs Phillips' house would have taken her just twenty minutes. Half an hour at the utmost. Being compelled to wait here for twice that long would have been laughable, were it not so provoking. As for the chivalrous streak she had discovered in Mr Darcy, it was astounding, but was fast becoming somewhat of a nuisance, too. Not necessarily because his society was as uninspiring as ever. If anything, his disinterest in conversation had brought her nothing but relief this time. She could not have borne a chatty companion. But his stubbornness was another matter.

It made no sense at all that Mr Darcy, of all people, should task himself with ensuring her safety. Admittedly, that did work to restore some of her faith in gentlemanly conduct, since this man who clearly had no regard for her was putting himself to so much inconvenience just because she was a damsel in distress. Even so, she profoundly disliked being the cause of someone else's discomfort, and was not of a mind to countenance it for a great deal longer.

But then a sterling notion came to her, and Elizabeth could only chastise herself for not thinking of it sooner.

"It is a ten-minute ride, is it not? Or a quarter of an hour, shall we say?" she asked, and Mr Darcy nodded.

"Aye, about a quarter of an hour at a walk. Possibly less."

"Very well, then. I believe I have a solution."

ഷഇ ഇൟ

"Is that the bridleway?" Mr Darcy asked.

It was the first time he had spoken in the whole of ten minutes – the first time either of them had spoken – and, however quiet, the sound of his voice made Elizabeth sit up with a start.

"Yes. Just there," she indicated, then returned her hand to her lap.

That was her solution: the bridleway that skirted the small town, running behind a number of houses, of which her aunt and uncle's was one. The seldom-travelled, narrow track would serve a vast deal better than the main road into town. It would allow her to gain access into Mrs Phillips' garden through the back gate, with no one any the wiser as to how she might have got there, rather than turning heads and raising brows by blithely riding into Meryton with Mr Darcy.

It was such an obvious answer to her conundrum that she really should have come up with it in a matter of moments, Elizabeth told herself as she endeavoured to ignore the feel of Mr Darcy's knee brushing against her calf when he steered his mount towards the bridleway with a nudge, a pull of the reins and a click of his tongue.

It was a hopeless business. She had not learnt to ignore the feel of his arm around her either, and she had applied herself to that task for considerably longer than the last four seconds.

She could boast of only one achievement: she had subdued the nauseating panic that had gripped her when Mr Darcy had swung himself into the saddle and asked permission to hold her.

It had been a senseless panic. Idiotic. The precaution was strictly necessary. Of course it was! And he had civilly requested her consent. This was nothing like the sordid business at Longbourn. He had *asked her*. And once she had nodded in acceptance and his arm had encircled her waist, the hold was considerably light, for her own safety, not his base gratification.

Even so, she could not ignore it. And the same could be said of his breath on her cheek, or his chest against her shoulder. In essence, other than the fact that she sat atop a very large horse, this particular experience had nothing in common with her girlhood recollections of riding with her father.

A flash of black-and-white plumage caught her eye, and all of a sudden two magpies flapped their way out of the undergrowth and flew across the path with caws and loud screeches. Startled, the stallion shied away from the disturbance, tossed up his head and snorted mightily by way of complaint, but thankfully he neither bucked nor reared, and had the good sense not to bolt. Her panic fully justified this time, Elizabeth could be nothing but grateful that the hold around her waist had already tightened into a fierce clasp.

Yet, for all her fright, a modicum of common sense prevailed, and she knew better than to spook the horse further with a missish cry of alarm. She smothered it and held her breath, releasing the lungful only seconds later – several awfully long seconds – once she found that, through sheer good fortune and thanks to Mr Darcy's fast reflexes, they were not thrown off. His one-handed grip on the reins remained firm as he soothed the startled beast with low, reassuring murmurs, but the tight hold around her gradually slackened – and she almost wished that it did not. Her balance felt unnervingly precarious after the near-mishap, and she could scarce wait to have her feet back on the ground. Elizabeth opened her lips to ask for assistance in dismounting, but Mr Darcy spoke first, manifest concern in his voice and countenance:

"Are you well?"

"I am, yes, I thank you," Elizabeth faltered, then released a shaky little laugh and sought to make light of her alarm and the enduring perverseness of fate that seemed intent on dogging her every step on this irksome day. "It would have been in keeping with the rest of the morning if we should have been unseated within thirty feet of our destination."

"Oh. Are we here, then?" Mr Darcy asked, and for some reason sounded less pleased than he might have been at finding his self-appointed task accomplished.

"Yes. That is my aunt's house, over there," she replied, pointing it out through the spindly branches of the coppiced trees that bordered the bridleway on both sides.

"I see," he said and nudged the stallion forward.

When they reached the gate sunk into a hedge of hazel, dogwood and hawthorn, he dismounted, assisted her down, then offered his arm.

The support was welcome, Elizabeth found, as she tottered across the track, favouring her injured foot. How ever had she imagined that she could walk unaided for half a mile or so?

"Thank you for all your help. And for your coat," she said with a small, conscious smile as she removed it and handed it back – and about time, too. His silk waistcoat offered no protection from the weather, and the drenched shirtsleeves were clinging to his arms like a second skin.

But Mr Darcy did not don his coat. He draped it over his arm and remained motionless, his eyes trained on her countenance in a long, almost unblinking stare that she might have met with a mixture of unease and vexation at any other time. Today, in view of everything, Elizabeth chose to excuse his penchant for staring at people, indifferent to the discomfort he might cause them. Then a second generous impulse came on the heels of the first, and prompted her to extend her hand.

Mr Darcy took it in both of his, and although she had been wearing his coat for over an hour while he had braved the November weather in his shirtsleeves, Elizabeth found that his hands were much warmer than hers. Very warm. For his sake, she hoped he had not caught a fever.

"Well, then," she said, "I believe this is goodbye."

"Yes. It is," Mr Darcy concurred, his voice gravelly. "I leave today."

"Oh?"

"I— It cannot be helped. I must return to town – to duties that can no longer be neglected. Thankfully, I had this chance to see you and take my leave. I wish…" He broke off, and his lips tightened. "If we are not to meet again, I wish you a lifetime of joy."

The solemn finality of his parting words surprised Elizabeth nowhere near as much as his choice to bend down and press his lips to the back of her fingers. He still held her hand as he straightened up – held it for a good many seconds – then slowly released it and bowed.

"Farewell, Miss Bennet."

"Farewell, sir. Travel safely, with my best wishes for your health and happiness," Elizabeth replied in kind, astonished to find the exchange strangely moving.

If anyone had made such a prediction yesterday, she would have laughed and chided them for sporting with her patience. But nay, it was this topsy-turvy day that was sporting with her and her emotions, Elizabeth concluded, and wrapped her arms around herself, uncomfortably aware that she was no longer sheltered by Mr Darcy's woollen coat.

Inexplicably, he made no use of it as yet. Nor did he seem in any haste to leave – at least not until he saw her shiver. He recollected himself then with a swift, "Forgive me. I should not keep you," and turned around to open the garden gate for her.

'It should be a fine thing if it were locked,' Elizabeth could not help thinking. That would be in keeping with Fate's mischievous games too.

But the gate gave way and swung back with a grating squeak, its hinges in dire need of oiling. And when Mr Darcy bowed again, Elizabeth matched his wordless farewell with a curtsy, perfectly unaware that Fate had not quite finished toying with her yet.

⊙⊙ ⊙⊙

"Lordy, just look at them bowing an' curtsying, all prim an' proper, like," the ruddy-faced maid scoffed, clinging to her companion. "As if there weren't a vast muddy patch on her bum, an' his knees in a right old state besides. I'd wager they've been at it too, an' then some. What d'ye reckon, lovey?"

"Who's to say, pet? Who's to say?" her paramour muttered, grinning from ear to ear, and shuffled sideways for a better look through the narrow crack in the door of the barn.

But by then the young woman had already had enough of spying on the others.

"Of all the rotten luck, them two turning up just now!" she grumbled. "What's to be done, George? Can't sit here all morning to wait till the coast is clear. I've got to get back to the shop, an' sharpish, else old Valpy-the-Harpy'll tan me hide."

"Oh, I think she will forget to scold you if you present her with a juicy bit of gossip," Lieutenant Wickham cheerfully retorted, patting her rump in reassurance.

Chapter 4

Mrs Valpy's shop stood at the heart of Meryton, halfway along the high street, but its prominence was not merely geographical. It was the only place in town, with the obvious exception of the church, that received the compliment of regular attendance. Unless housebound or too young to go where they pleased, every local denizen and many of those who dwelt in the vicinity would bend their steps towards *Valpy's* at least twice a week for sundry purchases and the additional delights of conversation.

On the 27th of November, however, the natural order of things was reversed. The plentiful and varied merchandise was wholly ignored by the shop's patrons and, most uncommonly, by its owner too. For Mrs Valpy had it in her power to regale her faithful customers with the most sought-after commodity of all: gripping news – tidings of a *scandal*.

"Aye! Miss Lizzy Bennet and none other than that haughty man staying at Netherfield – the high and mighty Mr Darcy, who turns his nose up at everybody! Well, he didn't turn his nose up at *her*, by the sound of it. And she – oh, she must have thought herself ever so sly and clever to put on such a grand show of indifference and claim that she has not set her cap at him. And then she goes and sneaks out of her home for a secret assignation with the man! An assignation of the basest sort, moreover!"

"Surely not!" gasped Mrs Long.

"Good gracious!" spluttered Mrs Robinson.

"Well, I never!" muttered Mrs Purvis.

"But… are you quite certain?" stammered Mrs Watson.

Mrs Valpy folded her hands before her and gave a grim nod.

"My maid Lucy swears by everything that's holy that she saw them with her own two eyes!"

"Your maid caught them *in flagrante*?" cried Mrs Ashworth.

"As good as, ma'am. As good as," Mrs Valpy sniffed. "Both of them were dishevelled, their apparel marked in the most conspicuous manner. I blush to speak of such things, as you would imagine, and I beg your forgiveness for uttering such words in your hearing, but I believe you should have the full truth of the matter." She lowered her voice to a whisper and resumed, her eyes darting from one of her listeners to another. "I understand that the back of her dress was smeared in mud all over, and lo and behold, so were the knees of his tan breeches. So there you have it. Have you ever heard of such a thing? Frolicking in the woods like the lowest of the low! And she, a gentleman's daughter!"

Predictably, the intelligence was met with cries of horror and a chorus of disjointed exclamations from the flushed and wide-eyed ladies gathered in the deepest recess of the well-appointed shop.

"No!"

"What, that well-mannered girl? I can scarce credit it!"

"Shocking! Truly shocking!"

"Unthinkable!"

"Beyond belief!"

"Precisely. I refuse to believe this of Lizzy Bennet!" the apothecary's wife enunciated – not the sole voice of dissent, but the firmest and most articulate. "Your maid must be mistaken, Mrs Valpy. Or worse still, she made the whole thing up for some malicious reason of her own."

"The maid spoke the truth," Mrs Goulding declared crisply. "I cannot comment on… ahem… on the other party and his attire, but you may be assured, Mrs Jones, that the state of that girl's dress was exactly as described. I have seen it myself."

"Have you, ma'am? When?" Mrs Jones challenged that blunt statement.

"This morning, if you must know, when I was taking tea with Mrs Phillips," Mrs Goulding was quick to substantiate her claim, her eyes glittering with dark satisfaction at her ability to do so. "All of a sudden, Elizabeth showed up in the parlour, and she had not come into the house through the front door, I can tell you that, for I had the main entrance in my sight at all times, from where I was sitting. She must have sneaked in through the back gate, just as the maid said. And the telltale patches of mud and whatnot were there for all to see. Lady Lucas can bear witness. She was there too."

Nine pairs of eyes turned questioningly towards Lady Lucas, but she trained hers upon her cuffs, which she proceeded to smooth with a nervous gesture. She made no answer, so Mrs Goulding prompted, "Well, Lady Lucas?"

"I... Lizzy excused herself and left the room as swiftly as she came and besides, if you remember, my chair was facing away from the door, so I truly cannot say... I did notice her muddied hems, but as we all know, that is a regular occurrence with Lizzy Bennet."

"Aye, because she is suffered to scamper about the country as she pleases, with no care whatsoever for decorum," Mrs Goulding sniffed. "*My* daughter would never dream of making such an exhibition of herself."

"No, indeed. Nor mine," cried Mrs Purvis, while Mrs Ashworth nodded with energy on behalf of her own brood.

"Of course not," Mrs Robinson spoke as well. "Same as my dear Edith, they know better than to expose themselves to ridicule and censure."

"Mrs Robinson, really!" Mrs Jones exclaimed. "Surely you are not suggesting that going for a walk is either ridiculous or warranting censure."

"Not in itself, no," the other countered. "There is nothing objectionable in taking a little stroll with one's friends and relations now and then. But when a young woman is always wandering about unescorted and finishes by looking almost wild, with her hair blowsy and untidy and her skirts six inches deep in mud, that is a wholly different matter. I call it ill-advised at best."

"You are uniformly generous, Belinda dear," Mrs Goulding said, but her tone and the look she cast her lifelong friend made her words sound like a reproof rather than a compliment. "For my part, I call it hoydenish and improper."

"Too true. And asking for trouble," Mrs Ashworth added with another vigorous nod.

"Should we not show a little more understanding and judge not, lest we be judged?" Mrs Long whispered, as though fearful of being heard.

"And above all, let us not judge hastily," Mrs Jones said, her voice louder and far more decisive. "Rather than rushing to believe the worst, we should begin by seeking innocent explanations."

"Indeed. And also remember we were all young once," Mrs King chimed in, twisting her crochet purse in her uncommonly large hands.

"Aye, so we were," Mrs Goulding scoffed. "But some of us were better behaved than others."

"Just *what* are you implying by that, pray tell?" Mrs King demanded to know, her voice no longer conciliatory, but sharp and clearly offended.

"My dear Gertrude, surely you do not imagine I aimed to slight *you* or anyone present!" Mrs Goulding exclaimed with an air of ill-usage. "I only wished to say that the apple does not fall far from the tree. All of us here remember Fanny Gardiner's bold and immodest ways. Oh, except you, Mrs Jones, naturally. You only came to live in Meryton some five years ago, upon your marriage, but the rest of us remember all too well the arts and allurements that Fanny had not scrupled to employ in her efforts to beguile Mr Bennet. The most brazen husband-hunting minx that ever was seen. Neither slyness nor outrageous flirtation were deemed beneath her, and I daresay she stopped at nothing to ensnare her prey."

"I see," Mrs Jones said tersely, more than a touch of cold incredulity in her voice, for although she was a new addition to the society in Meryton, she had heard enough over the years to know that Mrs Goulding – Miss Dorothea Morris as was – had long carried a torch for Mr Bennet.

"I should think anyone can grasp my meaning," Mrs Goulding insisted, "for one only need look at her daughters to see Fanny Gardiner all over again. Not Jane, to her good fortune she takes after Mr Bennet's mother, and poor Mary is mousy and insipid and cares for nothing but her music and her books. But the other three – heaven help us! Hoydenish all, and flirting with anything in breeches. Lydia and Kitty have lost all shame and every pretence to decorum ever since the regiment was quartered in Meryton. As for Elizabeth—"

"Of all the girls, I would say that she is the one who bears the greatest resemblance to Mr Bennet's mother," Mrs King intervened, but Mrs Goulding dismissed that notion with a flick of her hand.

"Her physical appearance is neither here nor there," she sneered. "I was speaking of her conduct. Do you not see how pert and flirtatious she is with any young man she meets?"

"Flirtatious, indeed!" Mrs Jones protested. "I think her ways sportive and charming."

"Yes, well, I wager you would think differently if you had a grown son," Mrs Goulding shot back. "The good Lord blessed me with two, and at one time both Hugh and William were hanging on that girl's every flippant word. They saw sense in due course, thank goodness, so I was spared the pain of seeing the scheming little Jezebel coming between them. And when they ceased beating a path to Longbourn, Fanny Bennet's palpable disappointment was a balm to my fretful heart. I daresay that by then she was already calculating how many years longer Mr Goulding is likely to live and regarded Haye Park as quite her own."

"Whereas she might find better employment in doing her sums and settling her accounts in a timely manner," Mrs Valpy muttered, turning the conversation towards her own grievance against the mistress of Longbourn. "Ever since she had joined the ranks of the local gentry she had conveniently forgot what she had learnt at her father's knee: namely, that those of us who must labour for our daily bread would prefer to receive our dues sooner rather than later."

"Frankly, I would not put it past her to have condoned and indeed encouraged Elizabeth's misconduct," Mrs Purvis chose to have her say as well, her voice lowered to a poisonous whisper. "But they have set their sights too high, if you ask me. And Lizzy Bennet, who prides herself on her cleverness, should have known better. Mr Darcy is too far above her station to have any serious designs on her. Like as not, he is merely toying with her, and indulging his carnal lusts and appetites will gain her nothing."

"So much for not rushing to believe the worst!" Mrs Jones bitterly exclaimed, her accusing glare skewering Mrs Purvis, and then alighting upon each one of Elizabeth's detractors in turn. "Should you not take the time to look more closely at the matter before you appoint yourselves judge, jury and executioner?" And then she spun towards Lady Lucas. "Ma'am, your eldest is Lizzy's closest friend. What does she think of—?"

"I beg you would not bring Charlotte into this! Whatever she thinks, says or does has no bearing on Elizabeth – and the other way around!" Lady Lucas sternly interjected before Mrs Jones could finish, which was not entirely surprising to the latter.

The doting mother must have thought that, at the age of seven-and-twenty, her eldest daughter was already at a disadvantage in the quest for a husband, even without the added millstone of being tainted by association.

Long neglected on the marriage mart herself, until Mr Jones had fortunately crossed her path and found that her inquisitive mind and discerning nature were perfect complements to his own, the apothecary's wife had some sympathy for Miss Lucas. She could only hope that the young lady was a loyal friend, and not as spineless as her mother.

The quick-witted Mrs Jones had no difficulty whatever in taking the measure of all the other ladies gathered at *Valpy's*. She found them as transparent as Lady Lucas. Thus, when her steady gaze travelled once more over them, sparing only Mrs King, the timid Mrs Long and the wavering Mrs Watson, it was not so that she might read their thoughts, but convey her profound displeasure. For their thoughts were clear enough already. Mrs Valpy had petty grievances to air. Mrs Goulding was the embodiment of the old adage about the fury of a woman spurned. As for the others, they heartlessly estimated that Elizabeth's disgrace would ruin the matrimonial chances of all the Bennet girls – by and large, some of the handsomest young ladies in the environs – which would work to the advantage of the horsey Miss Ashworths, the scatterbrained Miss Robinson, and the prettyish but ill-humoured Miss Purvis.

If anything, it was to Mrs Long's and Mrs Watson's credit that they had not hastened to join the evil crowd, one for her nieces' sake and the other to increase the chances of her two unmarried daughters. Mrs King had no need to resort to underhanded ploys. Her father-in-law's recent demise had left her only child handsomely provided for. Miss Mary King was now an heiress with ten thousand pounds to her name, so she would easily find a husband. The challenge would be to detect fortune hunters and drive them from her door.

"Pray, Mrs Jones, look more closely at the distasteful matter at your leisure, if that is your wish," Mrs Goulding spoke again – mightily offended by her glare, Mrs Jones suspected. "But pray give me leave to draw my own conclusions."

"What, from a patch of mud?" Mrs Jones scoffed.

"Aye, that. *And* her father fetched from the parish meeting before it was concluded. And Mrs Phillips ordering the carriage for the pair of them. Who orders the carriage for a one-mile journey – unless they have something to hide?"

"Very well, madam," Mrs Jones replied, heartily sick of Mrs Goulding's vitriol. "Draw your conclusions and act as you see fit. I shall only tell you this: beware, lest the harm you do is visited upon you."

Gasps of outrage came from Mrs Goulding and her coterie, who – not unjustifiably – chose to regard themselves likewise warned. But before they could give vent to their fiery sentiments, the door of the shop opened, and who should walk in but the hapless Mrs Phillips.

"Ah! Well met, my dear ladies," she jovially exclaimed. "I am especially glad to have come across *you*, Lady Lucas and Mrs Goulding, for it gives me the chance to apologise for having to put an early end to our lovely conversation this morning. A small family matter, you understand, but all is well now—"

With a scathing, "Humph!" Mrs Goulding interrupted her friendly effusions, then turned away, leaving Mrs Phillips stunned by a cut direct from one of the ladies who had been drinking tea in her parlour scarcely more than an hour earlier. As for Lady Lucas, she mumbled a few parting words and scurried out of *Valpy's* as fast as her small feet could carry her.

"I believe I have also lost my appetite for shopping. I shall return later, Mrs Valpy, when your shop is not so crowded," Mrs Goulding declared, then curtsied towards her clique, nodded at her opponents, completely ignored Mrs Phillips and swept out of the door.

Left without their spearhead, Mrs Goulding's allies exchanged quick glances, as though torn between making an equally dramatic exit and lingering to see what would happen next. For her part, Mrs Jones was not plagued by indecision. She walked towards Mrs Phillips and laid a comforting hand upon her arm.

"Would you spare me a few moments of your time?" she asked the older woman. "I believe we need to speak in private."

Visibly mortified and baffled by what had come to pass, Mrs Phillips gave a hesitant nod. When Mrs Jones curtsied to *the others* and bade them a terse adieu, she found that the civility was returned, however coldly. Thus, as she escorted her companion towards the door, Mrs Jones' lips twitched in unholy amusement. They could not afford to shun her. Mr Jones was the only apothecary in town.

⚬♋ ♋⚬

In due course, *the others* were granted their own amusements, and they were of an unholy nature too, much as the sanctimonious ladies thought otherwise as they donned the mantle of defenders of decency and honour.

To begin with, they enjoyed the opportunity of revisiting the most gripping narrative of the day without any hindrance, once the outspoken Mrs Jones had taken herself away, and Mrs Long, Mrs King and Mrs Watson soon followed. To their satisfaction, Mrs Valpy thoughtfully obliged them and fetched her maid, so that they might receive first-hand information and quiz the girl at leisure on every detail of interest.

But then, just when there seemed to be nothing left to learn, Mrs Ashworth, Mrs Robinson and Mrs Purvis were uncommonly pleased to be proven wrong. For, as they were preparing to depart, they found themselves perfectly placed to observe the Bennet carriage emerging from the lane that linked Meryton with Longbourn, then driving past the shop and heading for the turnpike.

When they noticed that the sole occupant was an exceedingly grim-faced Mr Collins and that a large trunk was strapped at the back of the vehicle, the three ladies and their accommodating host exchanged nods and telling glances.

"And there we have it: fresh proof of that girl's disgrace, as if further proof were needed," Mrs Purvis voiced the thought of all. "Time and again Mr Collins said that he would stay with his relations until Saturday, yet here he is now decamping as fast as he can, and looking like thunder too. He must have learnt of her heinous conduct and demanded to be put on the first southbound stagecoach."

"Of course he is eager to quit these parts with all possible haste," Mrs Robinson declared. "He was about to offer for that minx. Did you not hear Fanny Bennet boasting of it to all who would listen?"

"Poor man. The agonies he must suffer!" Mrs Valpy commiserated, shaking her head. "For a righteous gentleman, it must be all the more distressing to discover that the one he had chosen as the companion of his future life is so unworthy."

"Aye, the poor man indeed," sighed Mrs Ashworth. "How he must rue the day he set foot at Longbourn!"

The ladies gathered behind the bow window that graced the *façade* of *Valpy's* were in the right on two counts out of three. Yes, Mr Collins was determined to board the first southbound stagecoach, and yes, he did rue the day he had arrived at Longbourn. But, needless to say, they quite mistook the matter as to the reasons behind his tempestuous departure.

Much like his relations, Mr Collins had not the slightest inkling that malicious rumours were circulating in Meryton. Had he but known, he might have taken lodgings at the *Red Lion* to learn more, or at the very least his air of ill-usage might have been brightened by vindictive satisfaction. But nay, Mr Collins learnt nothing at all, except that there was a side to his cousin Bennet which no one knew about – not even Mr Bennet himself.

Long accustomed to regarding nearly everything in life as a pale backdrop to his bookish pleasures or as fuel for his wit, for the first time in above five decades Mr Bennet had been shaken by sentiments so gripping and so fiercely real that they could not possibly fade into the pastel-coloured backcloth of his existence. And those sentiments were wrath and fear. Fear for his daughters' fate when they would be deprived of his protection – and wrath against the one who had sought to prey upon the dearest of them all.

Turning Collins out of the house with the bare minimum of sharp, deadly words and the help of a few efficient servants had been easy work. But now the threat of the entail loomed larger than ever. Thus, once Elizabeth had been entrusted to Jane's tender care, Mr Bennet had repaired downstairs to allay his wife's fears and his own in the only way that suited: by facing reality head-on and beginning to undo the ill effects of ignoring it for three-and-twenty years, ever since Jane had come into the world instead of the son and heir who was meant to join in cutting off the entail and provide for his mother and his younger siblings.

The momentous task was terrifying in itself. Yet, as Mr Bennet set about covering his desk with business letters, old ledgers and all manner of papers, he vowed to keep his daughters safe from his cousin Collins, even if he should have to watch every penny and labour over holdings and investments each waking moment for the rest of his life.

About a mile northeast as the crow flies, at her house in Meryton, Mrs Phillips was not contemplating the rest of her life but the last half-hour as she fought to come to terms with Mrs Jones' revelations about the evil rumour that had raised its ugly head at *Valpy's*.

"I beg your pardon for distressing you so," the apothecary's wife finally broke the too-long silence. "I have not come into your home to sow discord between you and those who, until this very morning, had called themselves your friends. But I do believe that Elizabeth should hear of this and steel herself against such malice."

"Of course… of course…" Mrs Phillips stammered, then choked out a scornful, "Friends! May the Lord preserve us from our friends, eh?" Her voice gathered strength, but still shook with rage as she fulminated, "False friends, I call them, and deadlier than the worst enemy. Malice, indeed! Cruel, cruel malice. Evil. How can they even bring themselves to look one another in the eye and say such a thing of our Lizzy?"

"My thoughts entirely, ma'am. It defies imagination," Mrs Jones said, a grim twist to her lips. "You may be assured that I will work to quash this repulsive rumour by every means possible. I have not had the opportunity to speak with Mr Jones as yet, but I know my husband and can already vouch for his assistance. We can rely on Mrs King as well, I think. And perhaps Mrs Long and Mrs Watson, although I doubt that the pair of them are prepared, or indeed able, to be quite so vocal," the lady astutely assessed the strengths and weaknesses of the defenders' camp. Then her voice and mien softened as she pressed her host's hand in reassurance. "Take heart, Mrs Phillips. Those of us who value Lizzy will speak up for her. And if there is any justice in the world, she shan't be made to suffer."

❧☙

As soon as she had seen Mrs Jones to the door, thanking her again and again for her kindness, Mrs Phillips briefly rested a trembling hand on the back of a chair for support, then tottered unsteadily towards the kitchens, where she was sure to find another resource that could be deployed into battle.

"Give us a moment," she told the scullery maid. "I must have a word with Martha."

"Is there aught amiss, ma'am?" the cook asked, nervously searching her mistress's countenance once she heard her name uttered in a tone that did not bode well.

But Mrs Phillips made no answer. Not until they were alone.

"Yes. There is," she said at last. "Your cousin Lucy has been spreading vile rumours about my niece. So leave whatever it is that you are doing. I shan't have any appetite for luncheon anyway. Go and see the girl and have her retract her falsehoods at once. Do not bring her to me. I have no wish to see the insolent chit, nor hear her apologies. They are of no use to me or my relations. The damage is done, and some will still say that there is no smoke without fire. But this repulsive business has to come to an end. She *must* declare in no uncertain terms that she was mistaken. Now. Today. Have I made myself clear?"

"Aye, ma'am," Martha nodded fretfully. "So you have, to be sure. Clear as day."

⋅৹৫ ৯৹⋅

"Say it were a falsehood? What for? It weren't no falsehood, an' no mistake neither," Lucy declared, her countenance set into a mutinous scowl. "I saw her niece with a man. The stuck-up gent from Netherfield, he was. An' they were sneaking 'round the back of Mrs Phillips' house—"

Not waiting to hear more, Martha pounced upon her cousin like a fury:

"So? What's it to ye? Let them mind their own business an' ye see to yourn. Lord, Lucy, have ye no sense at all? What's gone into ye to work against me lady an' her kin? D'ye want me to lose me place on yer account? Never in me life have I seen me lady so shaken, an' no wonder, once ye've set the cat among the pigeons with a tale such as that."

"Ain't no tale. I spoke the truth, ye hear me?"

"Oh, shut yer trap, girl! What if ye did? Won't do ye any good to crow about it. There'll be hell to pay, I tell ye. There's always hell to pay when ye're angering yer betters."

"Me betters!" Lucy scoffed. "Yer lady's precious niece ain't no better'n me or any other woman who dallies with her man. 'Sides, I'll go up in the world, just ye wait an' see. When George an' me are wedded—"

Martha's hand cut the air in a gesture of irate impatience.

"The butcher's son? What's he got to do with anything?"

Lucy gave a scornful laugh.

"Oh, Martha, ye talk some tripe, ye do," she cried. "As if I'd give a fig for George Hicks. I'm no fool to dawdle with the likes of *him*. How's George Hicks to raise me in the world, eh?" she sniffed pityingly at her cousin, then tilted her chin upwards with no small amount of smugness. "Me *own* George'll make me a gentlewoman."

Martha's eyes narrowed. "The officer? George Wickham? That's who ye've set yer sights on?"

"Aye. Who else?" Lucy sneered.

"Who else?" Martha mimicked. "Ye silly cow! Ye're a damn fool if ye're moonstruck over him. Mark me words, Lucy," she sternly added, "ye ain't be going nowhere 'cept a home for magdalens when yer belly swells an' he's long gone."

"Spiteful witch!" Lucy spat. "He'll marry me by Candlemas. Ye'll see. He's as sweet on me as I'm on him. He comes to me every day, if his colonel can spare him. He was with me this morning, so there!"

"Was he, now!" Martha scoffed.

"Aye," Lucy shot back, triumph in her voice. "I snuck out to meet him. An' he said that if I were to give Old Valpy-the-Harpy a bit of gossip to feast upon, she'd gnaw on that juicy bone an' forget to scold me for going missing when I were supposed to set to work a-scrubbing the floor an' whatnot. An' he were right, me George, weren't he? The mistress couldn't care less about me. Off like a shot she was when a gaggle of women came in. Couldn't wait to tell them all about it."

Martha's eyes widened, as though about to pop out of her head.

"*That's* what set yer tongue wagging? Ye sparked me lady's anger, an' her kin's, to humour yer man an' hide yer own mischief?"

Lucy shrugged with callous indifference.

"Yer lady an' her kin should've kept a close eye on their girls. Then there'd be no talk. An' I care naught for their anger. I've me mistress's favour. I do, aye. Better'n ever. She's right pleased with me now. An' so are half of them women who came to the shop an' heard me tidings."

"As pleased as Punch, I'd wager," Martha growled. "Wicked tattlers an' gossipmongers, all!"

"Now who's smearing her betters, eh?" Lucy retorted, then drew herself up and rearranged her cap with an air of importance. "Ye'd best be off. I can't chatter all day. I've work to do."

And with that, she spun round and darted up the back stairs of the shop, leaving her relation seething in the rear courtyard of *Valpy's*, and mightily afeared too. Little wonder if she *were* to lose her place now, Martha miserably thought, cursing her misfortune of having an insolent numbskull for a cousin. She heaved a deep breath and wearily made her way home to face her mistress and faithfully recount every wretched word that had been said.

✧

To Martha's relief and good fortune, Mrs Phillips was a fair mistress and a kindly sort who did not hold with venting one's spleen on the blameless. The cook kept her post.

As for the manservant, he had scarce driven the landaulet back from Longbourn, saw to the horse and resumed his duties in the house when he was asked to ready the conveyance yet again – for, contrary to Mrs Goulding's firm opinion, if a carriage was ordered for a journey of one mile, it did not follow that it was used for the purpose of concealment. Sometimes such an extravagance was necessary simply because one did not trust oneself to walk.

Chapter 5

"For heaven's sake, Weston, cease fussing so," Darcy exclaimed when his habitually taciturn valet chose to dispense with that commendable quality and resumed muttering in dismay about the state of his apparel – wet through – and pressed him to agree to a hot bath.

Categorical in his refusal, Darcy removed his soaking wet garments, dried himself thoroughly with the large towel his man offered and gratefully donned a fresh shirt and dry breeches. But the dressing gown that Weston held up instead of a coat was met with a stare and an arched brow.

"I thought it might serve you better to warm yourself by the fire for now, sir, rather than go down to a draughty drawing room," Weston explained, undaunted. "The ladies and Mr Hurst are yet to emerge from their bedchambers, so I took the liberty of having the papers brought up, along with a warming drink. When you set off this morning it seemed to me that you were well on your way to coming down with something, and riding for hours in wet clothing could not have done you any favours."

'Indeed? And there was I thinking that it was a panacea,' Darcy irritably thought, but did not go so far as to utter the graceless remark aloud. His man deserved better, and Weston's determination to ensure his comfort sprang from loyal concern for his welfare. Besides, it was not his valet's fault that he was in the darkest of humours this morning.

Truth be told, a hot cup of tea in the privacy of his bedchamber would be welcome – a great deal more welcome than partaking of the same in the drawing room. So he took a seat in the armchair that Weston had placed before the fireplace, and found that the heat of the well-stoked fire was exceedingly welcome too. He was still shivering. His man had guessed aright: from the first hours of the morning he had felt as though he was coming down with a cold, and in all likelihood the hours in the rain had sealed the deal. But that was the least of his concerns. The vastly more disturbing matter was that he was also coming down with the severest case of intractable infatuation.

Why else would he have ridden towards Longbourn on such a wet and miserable morning? He could have simply waited for the others to awaken after the late night and their exertions at the ball to let them know that he was leaving – for he could not be so uncivil as to go without a word, since he had not had the good sense to quit Netherfield at the same time as Bingley.

Darcy scowled and sipped his tea as he belatedly owned that this was precisely what he should have done: he should have accompanied his friend to town. Yet he had not. It was only later that he had decided to take himself away – and even then, even when he had finally acknowledged that it was high time to distance himself from the temptation, he had still chosen to go for one last ride towards Longbourn.

What the deuce for?

To bid his adieus? For one final glimpse of her house, like a besotted mooncalf? In the hope of a chance meeting?

He gave a loud snort of derision as he set the cup back on the saucer. Well, he had had his chance meeting, had he not? And it had left him more wretched than ever.

Elbow on the armrest and chin in hand, Darcy stared into the flames and sighed. If he had any sense at all, he would regard their encounter as an unexpected gift. As Fate's mercy, allowing him to store away a treasured recollection upon which he might gaze fondly in the years to come.

But he had no sense – and could not regard it thus. Because it was the most poignant time they had ever had. An exquisitely private interlude, without vexing company, without interruptions. Alone, together. Caring for her. Holding her – warm, vital and more desirable than ever. Closer than ever as they had ridden through the rain, his arm around her waist, her lips inches from his, each second of their journey a blessing and a torment.

So nay, this could not hope to be a bittersweet memory he would take with him and revisit time and again until he was old and wizened. It was a gut-wrenching picture of what he was forsaking.

"Yes, Weston, what is it?" Darcy asked with morose impatience when he sensed his valet coming to stand silently beside him.

"I thought you should have this as well, sir. Brandy and hot water," his man said, setting a steaming glass of amber liquid on the small table at his elbow.

Darcy grimaced.

"Brandy? At this hour in the day?"

Weston nodded.

"Think of it as medicine, sir. I could not help noticing that you are burning up. Down it in one draught, and I daresay it might be of use, lest you become ill."

"Nonsense," Darcy said with a dismissive gesture. "I am never ill."

"Even so, sir. Prevention is better than a cure."

Too weary to argue the point, Darcy did as bid and downed Weston's purported cure in one draught, then set the glass down and observed, "You do know that you are clucking like a mother hen, do you not?"

Weston allowed himself a little smile.

"That I do, sir, and I am relieved to see you bearing it with equanimity. On that note, might I persuade you to lie down for an hour or so? Read the papers in bed, perchance?" he suggested, as though cajoling a sick child to take his playthings into bed with him.

But there was a limit to Darcy's forbearance, and he did not hesitate to make that plain.

"I have not done so in living memory. Do cease fussing over me, Weston. I assure you I am absolutely fine."

The pain behind his eyes, the shivering ache in his muscles and the enduring headache told a different story, but Darcy was not about to disclose as much to his valet. He drained his cup of tea, and Weston obligingly took the empty receptacle from him.

"Shall I fetch you another one, sir?"

"I think not, I thank you."

"Very well, sir. I shall leave you now, shall I?"

"Pray do. And let me know when Miss Bingley and Mrs Hurst have emerged from their apartments. I imagine everything is in readiness for my departure."

"Of course, sir. Is there any particular time for which you would wish me to order the carriage?"

"You may order it as soon as the ladies come down."

"As you wish, sir," Weston undertook and quietly withdrew, whereas Darcy turned his gaze back to the leaping flames – and, unavoidably, turned his mind to aching recollections.

Was their parting as heartbreaking for her as it was for him? Was that why she had been on the verge of tears while he had tended to her injured foot?

He flinched. Had he betrayed himself, then, with unguarded signs of admiration – with an unwitting and decidedly unwise display of partiality? Had he committed the cardinal sin of making her hope for a shared future, when all such hope must be in vain?

A pain-filled grimace flashed across his countenance as Darcy prayed that he had not done irreparable damage. Let the pain be his – for his was the power of choice, and duty demanded that he choose self-denial. It did not bear thinking that she should suffer too.

God willing, she would not. One as astute as she must know, just as he did, that the disparities between them made their union impossible. She must have understood – and made her peace with it. There was *some* reason to believe as much, for she had seemed to rally by the time they had reached the end of their journey. Almost restored to her habitual self, she had teased and made light of their near-mishap when they had come so close to being overset due to his lapse of alertness, a mistake excusable only in a novice rider, which should not have happened. Which *would not* have happened, had he not been daydreaming, his arm around her, his head full of her.

His head still full of her, Darcy closed his eyes as justice compelled him to own that it would be easier for her if Elizabeth were to resent and despise him for his desertion. For her sake, he almost wished she did, harrowing as it was to envision her alive in the world and thinking ill of him.

But she did not. Generous to the last, she had wished him well. Soft parting words, conveying her best wishes, while he had agonised and sought to commit every detail of her appearance to memory.

Not without success, it seemed. His mind's eye effortlessly conjured up the exquisite picture. Would it remain as clear in the years to come?

Darcy sighed again. Lord knows he should not wish it. He should not spend his days remembering her – regretting her. Even so, just now he could not bear the thought that his memories of her should fade. They were all he was allowed to take with him when he would quit Hertfordshire a few short hours later.

A couple of hours later, when Weston returned for the fourth time to his master's bedchamber, he found Mr Darcy just as he had left him: still asleep in the wingchair set before the fireplace.

With a quiet, measured tread, the valet approached to rearrange the quilt he had draped over Mr Darcy as soon as the fevered sleep had claimed him. Feeling the young master's brow was deemed presumptuous – an opinion with which Darcy would have doubtlessly agreed – but Weston had no need to take such liberties. The flushed cheeks and the heavy slumber told him what he wished to know, so Weston frowned and yet again bemoaned his master's reckless choice to go riding in the rain and return with wet and ice-cold garments.

He cast a glance at the clock on the mantelpiece and found it was nearing half past two. It would be dark in less than two hours. Sooner than that, in this dismal weather. There was no merit in setting off to town at that time of day, and nothing short of dangerous folly for Mr Darcy to travel while so patently unwell.

Thus, Weston resigned himself to bearing his master's displeasure later in the evening and chose not to wake him. The valet stoked the fire, his motions still cautious and quiet, and then he left the room to find the pert young maid who had been sent up thrice so far and inform her – and, through her, all the interested parties – that no, Mr Darcy had not awakened, that he was still feverish, and therefore regrettably unlikely to join the company as yet.

The girl returned in less than ten minutes to seek him in his master's dressing room and ask on the family's behalf if there was anything that could be done for Mr Darcy's comfort; then, half an hour later, a footman was sent up with the exact same message – both instances pointing towards Miss Bingley's resolute persistence, which more than vindicated Mr Darcy's wish to leave Netherfield forthwith.

'*The rest will do him good,*' Weston mused. '*With any luck, he will feel better by the morning, so that he might go home and be assured of peace and quiet.*'

Lest his master's peace and quiet be disturbed when he was not looking, the faithful valet took a seat in the dressing room, on a chair carefully positioned so that he could keep watch over Mr Darcy's chamber. Then he drew the candle closer, opened the slim volume of Mr Hazlitt's essays and began to read.

◦◦ ⊙◦

Every hope of peace and quiet was lost at Longbourn. It had been blasted around two o'clock by Mrs Phillips. She came, still overcome with shock and anger, and requested a quiet word with her sister. She was shown into Mrs Bennet's parlour, but within less than three minutes from her arrival, that room – and indeed the house – became anything but quiet. A wail rent the air, and a moment later the door was flung open and Mrs Bennet burst into the hall, calling for her housekeeper, her second daughter, her husband and her smelling salts, in that order. And thus began the swift descent into pandemonium.

◦◦ ⊙◦

Elizabeth's mind was reeling. This was vile – monstrous! No one who knew her at all would believe such an enormity! Just as *she* would not believe that the instigator of the disgusting rumour was Mr Wickham, or that he was a reprobate, dallying with maids in barns.

But as the daylight hours wore on, hideous tidings kept coming.

First came the proof that the vile rumour was spreading through Meryton like a miasma – from house to house, kitchen to kitchen, parlour to parlour – and that more than one acquaintance was prepared to lend it credence, or at the very least distance themselves from the scandal. Lydia and Kitty, who had taken advantage of a lull in the weather and walked into Meryton less than an hour before Mrs Phillips' arrival, returned distressed and flustered to say that Mrs Rowan and her niece had barely acknowledged their greetings and had swiftly moved away when they had run into them on the high street; that the Miss Bensons and their mother, along with Miss Harrow and her sister Mabel had shunned them at the milliner's; and when they had stopped on the way home to call upon their friend Maria, they had been denied admittance to Lucas Lodge.

The second blow, and just as severe, came from John the footman, who also served as her father's man and occasionally as coachman. He was emboldened to speak out once he had grasped what was going on from Mrs Bennet's and Mrs Phillips' lamentations. It was no surprise that he could overhear well-nigh every word. They were always loud, be it in gleeful moments or in times of grief – and now

39

they were louder than ever. The beasts in the field and the bats in the belfry could hear them.

John solemnly addressed himself to Mr Bennet, but soon Elizabeth had no difficulty in hearing what he had to say because, once they had caught a few salient words, her mother and her aunt fell silent.

"Didn't want to say anything afore, sir, didn't think it were proper, but I reckon ye'd best learn this. I have it from the lass I'm sweet on, Susan, who's just found herself a place at the *Red Lion*. I stopped by to see her when I went to bring the meat from the butcher's, an' she told me she'd caught some troubling words today, when Mr Wickham an' other military men came to partake of ale an' what have ye. The officers were carousing an' slapping Mr Wickham on the back, condoling with him over our Miss Lizzy being *'snapped up by his foe,'* as they put it. But he chortled an' bade them save their pity for them that need it, for he don't. He said that he who laughs last laughs best, an' that he reckons this'll work to his advantage."

"The fiend! The foul beast! To his advantage, is it?" her mother cried, before Elizabeth could even begin to digest John's shocking revelations. Then Mrs Bennet turned upon her husband. "Mr Bennet, this cannot stand! You must meet with him at once and make him undo his vile scheming!"

The habits of a lifetime must have been hard to break – for, despite the severity of the situation, Mr Bennet's tone was not devoid of its customary note of sarcasm:

"I thank you for pointing out my duty, madam. Now, how do you propose I do that? I trust you are not suggesting I call him out. For if you are, I shall have to observe that, as an officer, he must be reasonably handy with both sword and pistol, and little as I should wish to appear a coward, I daresay I should not tempt fate. At least, not until I have had the chance to set my affairs in order."

Elizabeth flinched. He should not say that, not even in an instinctive display of mordant irony. Yet she was compelled to own that although some things might never change, others most noticeably had. Every trace of scornful levity had been starkly absent from her father's manner a short while earlier, when her mother had rounded on her with an impassioned admonition:

"Oh, Lizzy, *why* did you go traipsing to Meryton this morning? None of this would have happened if—!" Mrs Bennet had exclaimed, wringing her hands, but she had not been suffered to continue.

"Enough, madam! *Not another word!* You know perfectly well just why Lizzy had felt the need to leave the house. So you will oblige me and never revisit the subject, nor presume to lay the blame on her, lest I have *my* say about your choice to let that interview take place when my back was turned, and your most particular insistence that Lizzy stay and listen!" Mr Bennet had enunciated, his voice ringing with unprecedented sternness.

The look of acute remorse in her mother's countenance had been unprecedented too – yet nowhere near as astonishing as finding herself clasped in a fierce embrace and presented with a tearful apology. *That* had verged on the extraordinary, for her mamma was not given to tears, nor to violent displays of affection – and, if memory served, had never acknowledged being in the wrong.

A strangled cry cut her musings short, and Elizabeth darted her eyes back to her mother when Mrs Bennet forcefully began to vent her horror, and also demonstrate that she was not about to turn humility into a habit:

"Call him out? Of course not! Mr Bennet, I beg you to show some compassion for my oppressed spirits and never mention anything of the sort again! Call him out! An officer! A trained marksman! Heaven forbid you do anything so reckless, sir! I cannot even bear to think about it!" she wailed, fanning herself with her kerchief although the room was anything but warm. She fumbled for her smelling salts, inhaled and gave an exaggerated sob at their sharp odour, then wiped her eyes, dropped one hand into her lap and proceeded to gesticulate vigorously with the other:

"I would never suggest you call him out. But you must meet with him. Make him desist and have him and his hussy retract their repulsive slander. Nay, wait!" she cried, as though Mr Bennet were already on his way to the door to obey her. Then her countenance smoothed into relieved satisfaction. "I have a much better notion: you should go straight to Netherfield and consult with Mr Darcy. He will know how to act. *And* will have better means of coercing those two into submission."

"Mamma, there is no cause for that!" Elizabeth protested.

"Of course there is," Mrs Bennet countered. "His honour was impugned as well."

Elizabeth gave a little sigh of exasperation.

"Be that as it may, there is nothing to be gained from Papa going to Netherfield," she declared, and swiftly added by way of explanation when her mother made to argue the point further: "Mr Darcy will have left by now. He said he would return to town today."

"Oh. That is inconvenient," Mrs Bennet grimaced, then glanced back at her husband. "In that case, my dear, you must follow him to town forthwith."

"Whatever for?" Elizabeth asked, but her mother ignored her.

"Hmm, let me see," Mrs Bennet pensively muttered. "What did Mr Bingley say?" Suddenly, her mien brightened. "Now I have it! Yes, I remember now. Berkeley Square – that is where Mr Bingley said his friend's townhouse was. You must leave directly, Mr Bennet, and—"

"Mamma, do cease going on so," Elizabeth urged. "There is no need whatsoever to involve him."

"Nonsense, child," Mrs Bennet retorted with the air of one who had just struggled to arm herself with patience. "He is already involved in this sad business. And now there is but one thing to be done: your father must bring him back to Hertfordshire to marry you."

"Yes, indeed!" Mrs Phillips cried, her firm agreement drowning out Elizabeth's splutter.

⊱⊰

A low but irksomely persistent murmur of voices and strong, obtrusive light drew him from heavy slumber, and Darcy groaned, struggling to fully rouse himself.

It turned out to be a challenge. His head ached as though a hundred demons were beating muted drums inside it, and his throat felt raw and parched. He blinked and squinted, only to be forced to close his eyes once more against the assault of the bright light coming from two Argand lamps placed on the nearest bedside table. And then he could make sense of one voice, at least.

"…when darkness fell, I sought to persuade him to move from the armchair to the bed," he heard his valet say. "He dropped off back to sleep almost immediately, and scarce stirred these two hours."

Darcy grimaced, vexed in equal measure by the excruciating headache, the soreness in his throat and by his man not only allowing strangers into his bedchamber, but also regaling them with details on the duration of his sleep and with tales of cajoling him out of the armchair – which must be true, for now he was abed, much as it had felt like a confusing dream or a feverish illusion at the time.

He squinted yet again and raised his hand to shield his eyes, which was of some assistance in the matter, for now he could spot Weston and a middle-aged man whose countenance seemed vaguely familiar. Yet he was nowhere near as successful in his attempt to chide his valet for speaking out of turn. All he could utter was an inarticulate, hoarse croak.

"Ah, there you are, sir," Weston greeted him with unwarranted good cheer, as though he had just returned from a journey rather than simply waking up. "This is Mr Jones, the—"

"The apothecary," Darcy rasped, and thus achieved two feats in one by compelling his disobliging vocal chords to do their office, and also by recognising the newcomer from the day, a fortnight prior, when Mr Jones had arrived at Netherfield to attend Elizabeth's eldest sister. "Confound it, man, why did you summon him?" Darcy remonstrated with his valet, only to find his sharpness punished with a long, racking cough.

As soon as the bout of coughing ceased, Weston hastened to defend himself.

"It was Miss Bingley who sent for Mr Jones of her own accord, sir," his valet informed him, and this time Darcy made no effort to suppress a snort of exasperation.

"It was unnecessary. A pity you were troubled for no purpose," he said to the medical man. "There is nothing wrong with me. Except perhaps a head-cold," he reluctantly acknowledged in response to the apothecary's level look, for doubtlessly Mr Jones could tell as well as he that his cough and his hoarse, nasal voice were no indications of good health. And then three loud sneezes came in quick succession and put the matter beyond any doubt.

They also sent stabs of pain through his temples, so Darcy groaned as he reached for one of the two neatly folded handkerchiefs left on the bedside table.

"Well, sir, as I am here, perhaps you will allow me to examine you," the visitor suggested. "Your man has just told me that you were laid low for quite some time today."

Darcy rolled his eyes, ungraciously wishing the pair of them at Jericho. So, he had slept heavily for a few hours. What of it? Bingley's confounded ball had kept him awake long into the night. And it certainly was no one's affair but his that he had chosen to walk through his friend's gardens for above an hour before he had taken himself to his bedchamber for a short and fitful sleep. As for the ride in the rain and its consequences, that was his own affair too.

But then Darcy eased himself up a little higher against the stack of pillows and privately allowed that he was being churlish. After all, Jones had come all this way on a wet and windy evening, so he should be permitted to go ahead and do whatever he deemed necessary.

"Very well, sir. You may do your worst," Darcy said, and at that Mr Jones cast him a faint smile.

"Rest easy, sir, I shall not trouble you unduly," the apothecary promised, but for his part Darcy was inclined to disagree as the older man peered, prodded, tapped his chest and listened to his breathing.

Then Mr Jones straightened up and gave his verdict:

"I am pleased to say you were in the right, sir. It seems to be naught more than a cold. And for that, rest is the best medicine."

"Good to know," Darcy muttered. "Even so, Weston, you should have woken me. I had matters to attend to," he added with another cough and a peevish glance towards his valet, his displeasure at having been treated as a child not entirely abated.

Weston tilted his head sideways in silent apology. It was only Mr Jones who spoke:

"No doubt, sir, no doubt," he said soothingly. "But, that aside, you should have a care for your health and not tax yourself too soon. Neither you nor Miss Elizabeth will be served if the cold settles in your lungs. True, you are young and strong, but you ought not rely excessively on that. Lung fever has claimed many a strong young man, in my experience."

Whatever the apothecary said after Elizabeth's name fell on deaf ears. Concern easily overrode common sense, and Darcy could not help asking, "Miss Elizabeth Bennet, you mean? Is she unwell too?"

The apothecary forced a smile.

"All things considered, I should be very much surprised if she were bright and cheerful, but nay, she is not suffering from any bodily ailment, to my knowledge. I was not summoned to attend her.

Nothing came from Longbourn today but a request for the usual prescription for Mrs Bennet's nerves."

Darcy stifled a huff. Without a doubt, a sizeable proportion of the apothecary's earnings must be owed to Mrs Bennet and her nerves.

"I see," he said, then gave a tired sigh. "Well, there we are, sir. If there is nothing else you would advise, then I thank you for your troubles and I bid you good evening. Weston, if you would…" he gestured towards his man by way of requesting that Mr Jones be recompensed for his efforts and then escorted out.

But instead of recognising his words for the courteous dismissal that they were, the apothecary fixed him with a steady gaze and solemnly made his answer:

"'Tis not for me to advise you, sir. This is a matter for your conscience. But since you ask, I trust you will do what is right."

The pronouncement surprised Darcy quite as much as Weston's intervention and the valet's stern tone of voice, bordering on the uncivil:

"You were brought here to give an opinion on medical matters, sir. Kindly restrict yourself to that."

"Very well, if I must," Mr Jones said, patently offended. "I shall prepare some draughts for the fever and a linctus for the cough, and send them tonight. With any luck, this should not worsen into a lung fever. But I should be summoned at once if the patient develops any difficulty in breathing or experiences sharp pains in his chest when he coughs. And, needless to say, until the fever breaks bed rest is essential."

"Oh, come now, sir! I will not be mollycoddled, so pray do not encourage my man in that regard," Darcy spoke up, his irritation mounting at the pair of them speaking as though he were not there, or had no say in the matter. "Bed rest!" he scoffed. "That is out of the question. I must return to town as soon as possible."

Eyes widened in outrage, Mr Jones spun round to face him.

"You are aiming to quit Hertfordshire, sir?"

"At first light, aye, if it can be arranged. I have tarried for too long as it is," Darcy retorted, out of patience with being told what he could or could not do.

To his indignation, the apothecary had the impertinence to glower. And then the man compounded that offence by snarling, "I see. The code of my profession gags me, Mr Darcy, but this much I can tell you: I hope you live to rue this day and the damage you have caused. And which you stand to worsen with a rushed— Nay, with a cowardly departure. Good day to you, sir," he spat, then turned on his heel and headed for the door.

Tutting in vexation, Weston made to follow, but Darcy would have none of it.

"Mr Jones! What the devil do you mean by *that*, sir?" he asked, incensed beyond measure, only to regret raising his voice when his sore throat made him pay dearly for the display of temper.

The apothecary opened his lips to answer, but Weston spoke first as he turned round, his countenance darkened into acute discomfort.

"Do not concern yourself with it for now, sir. Scurrilous gossip, that is all. You will address it when you are recovered."

Eyes narrowed, Darcy growled, the sore throat be damned:

"*What* scurrilous gossip?"

Chapter 6

Mrs Phillips had long returned to her own abode. Mr Bennet steadfastly refused to stir from his. To his wife's growing despair and frustration, he maintained that he ought not and *would not* go begging to Mr Darcy's house in Berkeley Square.

Despite the grave unrest that ruled over the genteel part of the house, the cogs turned – sluggishly, yet they still turned – in the kitchen and the pantry, and thus dinner was served at more or less the usual hour. It was taken up largely untouched.

Mrs Bennet might have chosen to retire early and seek solace in tea, laudanum, and in finding employment for the full complement of household servants. Yet she remained downstairs, walking from room to room as she heaped blessings on Mrs Jones, invoked all imaginable curses upon false friends and the architects of her family's misfortune, and regularly burst upon her husband in his study, to interrupt his efforts in sorting out his papers and ask just *what* he proposed to do about Mr Darcy and Mr Wickham.

The messenger arrived shortly after seven, and he was attired in Netherfield livery.

"What is it? Mr Bennet, what is it? What news? Who is the note from?" a frantic Mrs Bennet demanded to know.

Her husband darted his eyes over the contents of the letter and entrusted the Netherfield footman with the briefest verbal message:

"Very well."

Then, as soon as the young man took himself away and Mrs Bennet's tremendous agitation permitted him to speak, Mr Bennet observed dryly, "I finally have something to offer in response to the question you have been asking me all evening. As yet, I cannot say what is to be done about Mr Wickham, but Mr Darcy has written to request an audience on the morrow."

"He has?" Elizabeth exclaimed. "So… he is still at Netherfield?"

"Of course he is!" her mother beamed. "Oh, the wonderful man! Upright – mindful of his duty – everything that is charming. And he is coming on the morrow to offer for you! I always knew how it would be!"

The old refrain was exceedingly familiar. Mrs Bennet always knew how everything would be, either after the event or whenever matters appeared to proceed in accordance with her wishes. But this time her mother's claim was so preposterous that Elizabeth could not let it pass.

"Mamma! You know nothing of the sort! He most certainly *is not* coming to offer for me – and if he is, it would be for the very worst reasons. This cannot be! I will not have it!"

Her protest made no difference. The brightness of Mrs Bennet's countenance remained undimmed.

"Lizzy, you do not know what you are saying. I tell you he is coming to offer for you, and of course you will have him, there is no other way. Oh, I daresay he will stay for luncheon. He must, he *shall* stay for luncheon. Let me speak to Hill and see what can be contrived. Hill! Where are you? Hill?" Mrs Bennet cried, her voice shrill enough to rouse the dead.

As soon as her mother vanished from her sight, but most certainly not from her hearing, Elizabeth cast a weary grimace towards Jane, ignored her younger sisters' inquisitive chatter and made her way into her father's study.

"Close the door, Lizzy," he said as Mrs Bennet's voice continued to reverberate through the entire house, and Elizabeth did as bid, then leaned against it with a sigh.

Mr Bennet cast her a reassuring smile.

"I imagine you would wish to know what he has to say," he quietly observed, and Elizabeth nodded. "There you go, then. See for yourself," Mr Bennet said, handing her the sheet of hot-pressed paper.

She unfolded it and found just seven lines penned in an even script:

Sir,

This evening I was made aware of rumours of the basest nature concerning Miss Elizabeth Bennet and myself. As you may imagine, they are wholly without foundation. Nevertheless, the matter must be addressed. To that end, pray allow me to call upon you at ten hours in the morning.

Yours etc.

Fitzwilliam Darcy

Ever so carefully, she folded it back and returned it to her father.

"Well?" Mr Bennet asked. "Short and to the point, do you not think? There is much to be said for brevity."

Elizabeth winced. For once, she could not bear her papa's air of feigned nonchalance, which he often assumed when matters of great import caused him to feel uneasy. She made no pretence of matching it.

"Papa, surely you must see that this… that whatever Mamma said is just… not possible. Not sensible at all. We have done nothing wrong. It was a kind gesture on Mr Darcy's part. An offer of assistance. And he would rightly resent being punished for it – resent *me*. He *will* finish by resenting me, if he does not already."

Mr Bennet leaned against his desk, folded his hands together and, of all the rushed words his dearest daughter had just uttered, he alighted upon a single one:

"Punished?"

"Just so," Elizabeth confirmed with energy. "If he were to offer – which I strongly doubt – this would be far removed from the sort of marriage he aspired to. He is meant to marry his very wealthy cousin, if Mr Wickham is to be believed."

She grimaced as she said that, as did her father. Once they had exchanged a telling glance, Mr Bennet voiced what both of them were thinking:

"Well, by now we can agree that Wickham's words are not the gospel truth."

Elizabeth pursed her lips and shrugged.

"Even so, if Mr Darcy were to offer for me, it would be out of necessity. Out of a misplaced sense of duty. And that cannot be agreeable to either one of us." She warmed up to the subject as she continued. "'Tis not to be contemplated. It would be the most ludicrously disproportionate response. A marriage of convenience – and what for? Because I injured my toes on a root!" she exclaimed, teetering on the thin edge between tears and hysterical laughter.

She nervously ran her hands over her still-dry cheeks, as though expecting to find them damp with tears, then took a couple of deep breaths in an effort to regain her composure. When she felt she had attained at least an appearance of it, Elizabeth looked up and sought her father's eyes.

"All this… excitement will blow over," she said at length in a voice of forced calmness. "In due course, our acquaintances will find something else to occupy their minds. And until they do, I can always go and stay with my aunt and uncle Gardiner and—"

"No!" her father countered, pushing himself away from the desk and making her start with the sudden, uncommonly forceful exclamation. Then his voice softened. "My dearest child, that is the last thing you should do. There must be no suggestion that you have gone into hiding. If you leave Longbourn, it would be seen as an admission of guilt."

Brow furrowed, Elizabeth murmured, "Why? I do not understand…"

And then she did. The deep discomfort that overshadowed her father's countenance as he stepped closer to take her hand and wrap his other arm protectively around her gave her to understand precisely what her father could not bring himself to put in plain, stark words: if she were to leave Longbourn, it would be seen as a means of hiding her supposed shame and… its consequences.

"*Oh.* I see," she mumbled, a hot blush flaring in her cheeks. And then her voice lost the meekness that came from mortification, and turned defiant. "Very well. In that case, I shall stay where I am and stare them down. Or better still, I shall take care to show myself in Meryton once a fortnight, but otherwise forswear their acquaintance altogether, sit with you and help you with this," she said, her free hand moving in a half-circle to indicate the fearsomely untidy heap of papers and ledgers on her father's desk.

Mr Bennet squeezed her fingers, then brought them to his lips.

"A delightful prospect for *me*, dear girl, but you must agree that it would be a sad waste of the bloom of your youth. Now then, Lizzy," he resumed when she made to answer, "let us not be drawn into fruitless speculations. First, we had better see what the young man has to say."

◦⊙⊙◦

The young man in question had no coherent notion as to what he would say to Mr Bennet in the morning. In fact, he had scarce any coherent thoughts at all. From the moment when his profoundly uncomfortable valet had temporarily escorted the apothecary out of the room, closed the door and returned to his bedside to acquaint him in a few terse words with the abhorrent rumour that one of the maids had brought from the servants' hall, Darcy's much-prized capacity for coherent and rational thought had been blown to smithereens by unconquerable anger.

How dare they! Those… those… vulgar – crass – coarse – uncouth – worthless – *small people!* Small-minded people. Foul-minded. A host of low-born, revolting boors attributing disgusting connotations to a perfectly justified—

How *dare* they spread such repulsive tales – impugn his character – his very honour as a gentleman with such base calumnies?

Their perverted notions of moral rectitude would have been satisfied if he had left her by the side of the road, Darcy scoffed, refusing to acknowledge that prudence *would* have served him a great deal better. A prudent gentleman would have offered Elizabeth his coat and ridden for assistance. He would have reached Longbourn at a gallop in a matter of minutes. Or he could have sought assistance at her aunt's house in Meryton, since she had so patently preferred that.

He scowled. They would have found reasons to snicker even then, no doubt – petty-minded halfwits always did – but there would have been no room for scurrilous allegations that he had debased her and himself by—

Blood rose to his head, worsening his pounding headache.

How dare they besmirch his name – and hers!

The note to Mr Bennet had been penned and sent in no time at all. In truth, Darcy's first impulse had been to go to Longbourn forthwith. It was imperative that the matter be addressed as soon as possible – his honour and Elizabeth's good name demanded it.

Predictably, that scheme had found instant opposition, both from his man and from Mr Jones, once the latter had garnered that he was not about to act the part of a dishonourable coward. Mr Jones had actually offered to deliver the note into Mr Bennet's hands himself, and yet again launched into recommending prudence and care for one's health.

Yet it was not the medical man's exhortations that had carried the day. Darcy could not care less that he was so ill he could scarce stand. He would rally, since he had to. That had always been one of his guiding precepts. Nor was he concerned that he lacked full command over his faculties, which might render him unable to express himself with ease.

The difficulty – and the reason why he had conceded that the interview was best left for the morrow – was that he could not determine exactly *what* he was to say to Elizabeth's father.

Hours later, long after he had sent Weston to his rest despite the loyal man's protestations, the matter was still undecided, and the fever-induced headache did not help. Darcy had taken several doses of the draughts Mr Jones had sent, but still shunned the laudanum, much as the apothecary had insisted on the merits of a good night's rest.

Stupefying himself with laudanum was out of the question. This was not the time to sleep. So Darcy had paced back and forth to keep himself awake, to keep himself thinking, until intolerable weakness, sneezes and frequent bouts of coughing had made him curse the monumentally mistimed illness – all the more aggravating to one who was hardly ever ill – and sent him to the wingchair by the fireplace. But he could not possibly allow himself the luxury of simply sitting there, staring at the soporific play of flames. He had yet to choose the way forward – and he was running out of time.

No doubt, on the morrow Mr Bennet would insist on having his daughter's good name restored – and, for his own part, Darcy wished for nothing less.

But… how? Marriage?

His lips tightened. For days on end, for weeks, he had laboured to remind himself that a connection with the Bennets – and through them to country-town attorneys and Cheapside merchants – would be a degradation. In that respect, nothing had changed. And it could not but rankle – of course it rankled! – to have his hand forced by a herd of gossip-mongering rustics.

Marriage would be a highly disproportionate response to the mishap that had caused the contemptible furore. Frankly, had it not involved Elizabeth, he would not have so much as considered it. Had he happened upon Miss Kitty Bennet in the woods or her friend Maria Lucas or any of the other local misses, he most certainly would not have contemplated shackling himself for life to any one of them. Of course, he would not have offered to convey any of them to Meryton on horseback, nor would he have lingered to explore the state of their ankles. Which brought back the issue of his own unguarded conduct, and his lack of prudence.

But the material point was this: if the incident had involved anyone except Elizabeth, he would have agreed to nothing but some sort of financial reparation, however minimal his fault in the matter, or some other mutually agreeable arrangement. An acceptable alternative, perhaps – the young vicar of Kympton or some other impecunious but respectable acquaintance.

What was he to offer now?

Sluggish from fever and the confounded headache, his brain would not rise to the challenge. As though that were not bad enough, a wave of nausea suddenly surged from the pit of his stomach at the mere thought of Elizabeth wedded to his vicar or some other acquaintance.

The nausea passed swiftly, because such notions were utterly preposterous – nothing but trespassing wisps of thought devoid of reason – for of course he would not orchestrate her marriage to anyone he knew. He had not lost his senses to fix her anywhere near his circle, and least of all at the Kympton vicarage – forever in his life, but never his.

Yet as soon as the nausea passed, a raw ache took its place as other imaginings flashed before him, a vast deal more vivid: Elizabeth's eyes brimming with tears earlier that morning, on what was supposed to be their last encounter – and the likely turn of her countenance, were he so lost to every proper feeling as to insult her with the suggestion of financial reparation or any other arrangement of the sort.

He flinched. She would rightly hate him for such callousness – not that he thought himself capable of it anyway. He *could not* bring himself to ride roughshod over her pride and, worse still, over the affection she might have grown to feel for him.

Another salvo of sneezes intruded, and they were too much of a nuisance to leave Darcy at liberty to think that he must be cutting a terribly foolish figure, handkerchief to his nose and the other hand to his aching head. But when he leaned back with a weary groan, he had reason to inwardly scoff that the violent sneezes must have rattled his brain into place, for the conclusion to his disrupted musings was now self-evident: her views on their predicament should carry quite as much weight as his.

So he would have to learn how Elizabeth wished to proceed, and explain his own position: his sentiments; his duties; the stark difficulties arising from the disparities between her world and his;

and lastly his relations, who always prized good judgement above inclination, as rational, dispassionate onlookers are wont to do. She should be forewarned that they would frown at a connection brought about by the threat of scandal. Yet, conversely, the scandal would make them bow to the inevitable. They would understand that his sole recourse was to offer for her, once both his inclination and his gentlemanly honour were engaged.

Darcy knew he had made the right decision by the sudden sense of relief that washed over him. An oppressive weight seemed to have been lifted from his chest, leaving his heart lighter than a feather, and the equally oppressive weight of conflicting thoughts dropped away too, setting him free. There: his course of action was mapped out.

It was a profoundly liberating notion.

So, a smile on his lips despite the persistent headache, Darcy stood from his armchair, banked the fire and took himself to bed. And, for all the inconveniences of a severe head-cold, in less than twenty minutes he was fast asleep.

Chapter 7

"He is not coming! Oh, the awful, prideful, wretched man! He has changed his mind and is not coming!" Mrs Bennet exclaimed, just as she had every four or five minutes, with minor variations on the theme, ever since ten o'clock had come and gone, yet had brought no sign of Mr Darcy, and no word from Netherfield.

Although closeted with her father in his study, Elizabeth had no difficulty in hearing her. Closed doors had never made much difference in that regard. She folded the piece of paper she was holding and spoke, struggling to keep her voice even:

"This one pertains to Wheatlock Farm, Papa. In which pile shall I put it?"

"Hmm?" Mr Bennet muttered without looking up from the ledger he had been perusing for an inordinately long time. "Oh, that one, I believe," he carelessly indicated towards a stack of papers which, upon closer inspection, was shown to contain correspondence regarding the upkeep of the parish church and a couple of other letters from the vicar.

It served as sufficient proof that her father was as distracted as she, so Elizabeth mildly suggested, covering his hand with hers, "What do you think, Papa, shall we leave this for now?"

This time he looked up and forced a smile.

"Not a bad notion." Then he cast a glance outside. "Is it raining? I cannot tell."

"No. It has not been raining for a goodly while. Shall we take a turn in the garden?"

"Perhaps later," Mr Bennet said, closing the ledger.

Silence fell, as both of them waited for Mrs Bennet to bewail Mr Darcy's tardiness yet again. Four minutes later almost to the second, she did not disappoint.

࿔ஒஒ࿔

Needless to say, Darcy had not changed his mind. Nor had he overslept. He had been delayed, however, at the very gates of Netherfield, just as his coachman was slowly negotiating the turn from the gravelled avenue into the lane.

Agreeing to travel to Longbourn in his carriage had been Darcy's sole concession to the vexing head-cold and to Weston's excessive fretting about his health and comfort. But all sense of comfort vanished when a rider intercepted him at the gate. For that rider was Wickham.

"Good morning, Darcy. Well met. I was just coming to Netherfield in search of you," the fellow smirked, and had the impudence to tut as he dismounted. "By the looks of it, I caught you just in time. I must say, I am staggered. Not like you to turn tail and run."

"No. That is *your* way," Darcy scoffed, and raised his voice to instruct his coachman. "Drive on, Joseph."

"Wait!" Wickham called and flung the carriage door open.

For his part, Darcy wished that the blackguard had caught his sleeve in the handle, only to be dragged along by the moving vehicle, but that did not come to pass. In any case, the carriage was not moving fast enough. As for Joseph, he had been at Pemberley for decades, so he knew that his master and the former steward's son had grown up together, but – just as it should be – he had not the slightest inkling of Wickham's vile attempt to elope with his master's sister. So, vexingly but predictably, he assumed that Mr Darcy would oblige his boyhood companion with conversation, and allowed the carriage to draw to a halt.

"Thank you," Wickham genially cast towards the coachman and added, affability oozing from his every pore, "Now then, Darcy, I was hoping we might have a quiet word."

"Did you, now!" Darcy shot back, and cursed the cough that came and spoiled the haughty disdain befitting his retort.

"Dear, oh, dear. You caught a cold, did you?" Wickham remarked with the most provoking air of false concern, only to lose the cordiality under taunting smugness. "Well, I cannot say I am surprised. In fact, I have a fair notion as to how you came by it. Which is precisely what I wish to speak to you about."

"I have nothing to say to you," Darcy declared, but Wickham shrugged, undaunted.

"I did not come to hear you talk. But it might serve you well to listen."

Darcy's eyes narrowed at the implied threat.

"What is it that you want?"

"Straight to the point, as always," Wickham grinned. "Very well. Then oblige me with a few minutes of your time and come to stretch your legs along the road. Dear old Joseph is an excellent fellow and loyal to the teeth, I'm sure, but take my word for it, this ought to be a private conversation."

Darcy checked his pocket watch. It was coming up to half past nine already. He scowled. He had timed his departure so as to ensure perfect punctuality – but he had not bargained for Wickham. What mischief was the devil brewing? He had to learn *that* at least, little as he could afford to tarry.

"You had better make it short. I can scarce spare you five minutes," Darcy muttered as he put the watch back in his pocket and alighted from the carriage.

"Is that all? I was hoping for a little longer, but there we have it. As you know full well, I have already learnt that beggars cannot be choosers," Wickham sneered, driven as always to harp on about his grievances and the living at Kympton.

Darcy ignored the jibe and glanced at his coachman.

"Draw up next to the wall and wait. I shall not be long," he instructed, although the lane was quite deserted, then strode away to distance himself from the conveyance without waiting for Wickham to wrap his mount's reins around the railings of the wrought iron gate and join him. Nevertheless, the other caught up with him soon enough. At the sound of Wickham's approaching footsteps, Darcy spun round.

"Speak," he ordered, then added by way of a terse warning, "And you had better not sport with my patience."

"Perish the thought," his foe smirked, hooking his thumbs in the pockets of his breeches. "Then I shall astound you with my forbearance and not comment on your recent notoriety. A pity, for it would have made for a fitting introduction to what I came to say. But if you want me to be brief, I shall. Believe it or not, I am here to assist you."

"Assist me," Darcy said flatly. "How?"

"First, I should retract my untoward remark—"

"What remark?" Darcy snarled.

"The intimation that you would turn tail and run from the scandal. Now I can see that there are no trunks at the back of your carriage. But I daresay I should have known better, anyway. Of course you would not make yourself scarce. Too much of a gentleman for *that*," Wickham drawled, somehow succeeding in making the complimentary phrase sound like an insult. His sly grin widened as he resumed, "I shall not enquire too closely into the sort of reparations you are prepared to make, but I believe it is safe to say that your prejudices will not permit you to form any matrimonial designs on her. You and I know that your precious Pemberley deserves better than a portionless young woman with connections in trade. So, seeing as you will not countenance acquiring relations whose condition in life is so decidedly beneath your own, here is what I am proposing: make it worth my while, and I shall take the delectable complication off your hands."

Suddenly lightheaded, Darcy could barely sense the tremor in his muscles, reminiscent of last night's bodily response to illness and fever. The molten lead in his gut was new, as was the wisp of incandescent heat that ran down his spine, urging his gloved hands to tighten into fists. The soft leather stretched, but not enough – it was not meant to accommodate outbreaks of fisticuffs – and its resistance made him aware of the almost painfully close fit over his protruding knuckles. He slowly unclenched his fists, spread out his fingers, flexed them again, and focused on their movements – flexion… extension… flexion… – as he marshalled the chaos in his head into one coherent thought: he had been on the verge of inflicting violent physical harm upon Wickham.

Still was, in fact. But by now the voice of reason, however thin and weak, was able to break through and make itself heard.

Not worth it. The blackguard was *not* worth it. Hard to credit now – aye, too true, it was impossible to credit – but a vicious outburst of rage would not make him feel a vast deal better. And he would come to regret it. Not for the vermin's sake – Lord, no! For his. He was better than this. He *would not* stoop to brawling! Least of all in his coachman's presence, and possibly under Miss Bingley's eyes or whoever might have been watching from the windows of Netherfield.

Raising his head, Darcy took a deep breath, then another, and the voice of reason gathered strength and grew louder – but, blithely unaware of how dangerously close he still was to having his nose broken, Wickham continued:

"If our… shall we say, turbulent past blinds you to your interest, I shall approach her father and I do not doubt that he will oblige me, once the scheme is laid out for him with rather more *finesse*. But I trust you will not add insult to injury and leave this burden to Mr Bennet and his meagre resources, so I venture to hope that the pair of us can let bygones be bygones and come to an agreement. Ten thousand pounds should do the trick. You see, I am prepared to be reasonable. 'Tis poor form to be greedy, so I shall only mention in passing that fifteen would suit me better. You may settle the capital on her if you prefer, but pray have the goodness not to tie it up in stipulations. And fear not, I shall not ask you to make provisions for her firstborn. Regardless of the tittle-tattle, I know you well. You are too honourable for your own good, and too fastidious into the bargain. Not like you to rut with her in the woods of Longbourn, so I am fairly certain that she is still as pure as driven snow, and her firstborn will be mine. But feel free to surprise me and let me know if you have succumbed to her nubile charms—"

The strike was lightning-fast. Aimed with deadly accuracy at the solar plexus, it served the purpose. As Wickham fell to his knees, struggling for breath, Darcy spun on his heel and headed for his carriage, with no regrets that the voice of reason had been overruled.

At the sound of his footsteps crunching loudly on the gravel, the coachman cast a glance over his shoulder, but had too much sense to comment on the fact that his master's boyhood companion was kneeling in the middle of the road, clutching his chest. Once Darcy had regained his seat in the conveyance, slammed the door behind him and ordered, "Drive on!", he was obeyed with due alacrity.

Joseph obeyed just as promptly a while later, when they were about half a mile beyond Meryton, and Mr Darcy demanded that he stop the coach. They were running late, by his reckoning, but with the wisdom of his fifty years of age and all the loyalty of a longstanding retainer, Joseph held his peace, asked no questions and offered nary an opinion when his young master strode to a clump of hollies growing by the roadside, leaned against one of the tree trunks and stood there, breathing deeply, for an uncommonly long time.

಄಄಄

With a tender gesture, Jane needlessly smoothed a wrinkle in the sleeve of Elizabeth's spencer and pressed her arm in reassurance, then opened the front door.

"Come, Lizzy. A breath of fresh air will do you good."

Elizabeth nodded, the ghost of a smile on her lips. This was almost word for word what her dearest sister had said a short while earlier, when she had come to entice her out of their father's study and persuaded her to take a stroll around the garden. Sweet Jane! Her kindness and goodness shone through, every day – and all the more so in times of trouble. Dear Jane had watched over her all morning, and throughout the night. For the first time in years, they had shared a bed, and Jane had stroked her hair, whispering words of comfort, and held her as she wept. For Elizabeth had wept bitterly in the hours of the night – something she had not done in a fair while, if ever. Dissolving into tears was not her way.

Nay, the very phrase was ill-fitting, she inwardly scoffed. Dissolving into tears was what nervous damsels did when they were thwarted in their wishes or fearful for their future. That was not why she had wept at all. The future *was* gloomy and uncertain, but she had not abandoned herself to apprehension. She had wept in anger at evil tongues, false friends and her own unpardonable folly of trusting in the goodness of the world.

Now she wished she had had more sense than to shed tears over that. Her powerless anger made no difference to her detractors. No puffy, smarting eyes for *them*. They had slept soundly.

Elizabeth pressed her lips together into a grimace and tossed her head back, firmly refusing to dwell a moment longer on the worthless rabble. The bracing wind that met her on the threshold was refreshing, and she breathed in greedily, relishing the prospect of a walk. But a glance along the drive was enough to do away with that promise of innocent enjoyment, so she released a huff and said flatly, "Oh. He is come."

"Who? Who is come?" Mrs Bennet cried, rushing out of the parlour, and Elizabeth could only marvel yet again at how exceedingly sharp her mother's hearing was, whenever it suited her.

"Mr Darcy, of course," she tersely replied. Who else were they expecting? Indeed, who else would grace their doorstep now, except dear Mrs Jones and Mrs King – neither one of which possessed such a luxurious carriage.

"Is he? Oh, thank goodness! He is here at last, that is all that matters, so I shall not grumble that he kept us waiting," Mrs Bennet beamed as she came to join them in the doorway. "Oh, gracious me, just look at that!" she exclaimed, clapping her hands together in delight. "Arriving in that elegant carriage of his, as befitting the occasion. What a fine gentleman, Lizzy! Now, *that* is what I call good breeding and gentlemanly behaviour!"

Elizabeth barely suppressed the urge to roll her eyes. Not long ago, in the drawing room at Netherfield, her mother had used almost the same words to praise Sir William's conduct in contrast to Mr Darcy's.

"I daresay we should—" she began, yet a fraction of a second later her mother's full attention was upon her.

"Oh, Lizzy, do take that dreadful spencer off!" Mrs Bennet cried as she closed the front door. "Gracious, is that what you are wearing? Goodness, child, could you not have chosen another dress? No time to change it now, more's the pity, but take my shawl, it will enliven it a little. Here. Here you go. 'Tis the finest cashmere, and look, it does make a difference. And pinch your cheeks, dear. This will not do! You are as pale as Death."

"Why, thank you, Mamma," Elizabeth said crisply, yet was not chided for her sauciness.

Her mother's high hopes regarding Mr Darcy might have had something to do with that. Or else it was her youngest sister's interference:

"Oh, she looks lively enough for the likes of *him*. My future brother, the spectre," Lydia scoffed. "If only he were to wed you tomorrow, Lizzy, so that we can go back to the way we were. 'Tis monstrously unfair, if you ask me. You always reproach me for my conduct, yet 'tis yours that is now making us suffer," she grumbled with excessive petulance, even for her, only to jump when Mr Bennet's voice rang forcefully behind them.

"Enough, Lydia! Go to your bedchamber – *now!*" he commanded in a tone of voice that brooked no opposition, which made Lydia's eyes widen, although it was impossible to tell whether it was in alarm, mortification or vexation.

But Mr Bennet was very far from finished:

"Go up, I said, and do not dare stir until I come to fetch you. And this shall be a regular occurrence if your mouth runs away with you again. In fact, nay: as of this morning, you are not to stir from your chamber unless you can prove you have spent at least two hours in a rational manner. Silence, girl! I do not wish to hear a single word!" he forestalled her when she began to protest. "And the same goes for you, Kitty. Some sensible employment shall not go amiss. But we shall speak more of this later. Off you go with Lydia, and make sure she obeys me," he instructed, leaving Kitty both flattered and startled by the request to supervise a wilful sister who had always led the way. "Now, madam," Mr Bennet continued, turning towards his wife, "I shall not presume to order you to your chamber as was the case with our unruliest offspring, but pray find an occupation in the parlour upstairs. A tranquil one, for I require a quiet house. To the same end, Mary, oblige me and interrupt your music practice. Go with your mother and read Fordyce's sermons or whatever takes your fancy. Jane— Hm. Well, I see I need not ask you to look after your sister," he said, his voice considerably softer at beholding his eldest daughter clasping Elizabeth's hand, one arm wrapped protectively around her shoulders. "Run along now, all of you. I shall have to meet with our visitor."

No sooner had he finished speaking than Mrs Bennet took charge:

"Upstairs, girls! You heard your father. Hush, Lydia, not another word! Up you go. And you, Kitty. Never mind Mary, she is coming. Unlike the pair of you, she can be trusted to do what she is told. Goodness, Lizzy, where do you think you're going? Your father did not tell *you* to go up. Did you, Mr Bennet? Nay, of course not," she answered her own question, without giving her husband the opportunity to answer. "You are to wait in the parlour. Mr Darcy will want to see you once he has finished speaking with your father. And Jane will keep you company. Hill!" she called, then caught herself and lowered her voice, so that the second and third calls came in a strained, loud whisper. "Hill! Hill! Ah, there you are. As soon as you hear the knock, let the gentleman in and show him into Mr Bennet's study. Everything is in readiness for luncheon, thank goodness, but you are not to lay it out until I give you word. No traipsing back and forth along the corridor for now – your master and Mr Darcy are not to be disturbed. But be sure to see to the coachman.

The poor man should not be left out there for hours. Or if he has instructions to stay with the horses, have Sarah take a warm drink to him. There. Heavens, I hope I have not forgotten anything of consequence!" she fretfully exclaimed, then pinched Elizabeth's cheeks, yet it was anyone's guess if it was for luck or because Elizabeth had not complied with the instruction to pinch them herself. With that, she repeatedly flapped her hands to shoo a still mutinous Lydia up the stairs, and when Lydia finally obeyed, Mrs Bennet followed her with a haste and agility she had not displayed in upwards of ten years.

Affectionate amusement in her countenance, Elizabeth followed her mother's progress with her eyes, then her attention returned to her father when he patted her arm and urged her and Jane into the parlour with quick, flapping gestures which, by accident or design, seemed modelled after Mrs Bennet's.

Elizabeth tarried only for one moment to stand on tiptoe and press her lips to his cheek before she did as bid. Her sister silently matched her compliance. They walked into the parlour holding hands, closed the door and sat, whereupon Jane chuckled, "It must be decades since Longbourn was so free of noise and bustle in the middle of the day."

Grateful for this attempt to coax a smile from her, Elizabeth obliged, for the house *was* absurdly quiet. Thus, when it finally came, the rap on the front door was all the more resonant for it.

Chapter 8

To his surprise, once he had gained admittance to Longbourn, Darcy found the house exceedingly quiet. Eerily so. He would not have imagined that anything of the sort was even possible under a roof that sheltered Mrs Bennet. Perhaps she was from home. Or perhaps the wretched situation he had come to redress was responsible for the gloomy pall of silence.

He darted his eyes around the hall as he removed his hat and gloves and set them on the small table by the entrance. Closed doors on all sides, and not a living soul in sight except the housekeeper. No sign of Elizabeth. How was she?

"This way, sir. Mr Bennet is expecting you," the housekeeper said, and Darcy squared his shoulders, channelling his thoughts towards the task ahead.

The master of Longbourn offered a solemn greeting, then a chair and a glass of brandy. The latter was tempting, but Darcy did not touch it. He needed a clear head. More confident of his command over his faculties or having no reason to feel under scrutiny, Mr Bennet sipped his own brandy and said nothing, manifestly waiting for Darcy to speak. So Darcy did. It was not his way to shrink from what had to be done, however challenging.

"It is unfortunate that we meet today under such circumstances," he said by way of an opening, and as Mr Bennet tilted his head in agreement, it occurred to Darcy that, over the course of the month spent at Netherfield, he had but seldom been in company with Elizabeth's father, and when they *had* met, they had exchanged nothing but cursory greetings. With hindsight, now he wished he had exerted himself more in that regard.

"I must say that—" he made to admit as much, but Mr Bennet raised a hand and stopped him with both word and gesture.

"No need, sir. I shall not require your version of events. I have it from my daughter, and it will suffice. I have no cause to mistrust it."

Although he had been interrupted before he could even begin to make his point, Darcy nodded in appreciation of Mr Bennet's rightful trust in his most deserving daughter. Besides, the remark brought no little relief at his own reprieve. He most certainly *was not* looking forward to that part of the discussion.

"Indeed. But what I was about to say is that I wish we have had more meaningful conversations in the past," he resumed, only to hear Mr Bennet give a bark of mirthless laughter.

"And you think it would have made the present situation any less awkward?"

Darcy's lips twisted into a grimace.

"No. I should imagine not. Before we go any further, pray allow me to apologise for my tardiness. I set off at the appropriate time, but I was… waylaid. And after that particular encounter I had to pause halfway between Meryton and Longbourn for a while. I was not—" He was about to say *'I was not master of myself,'* but the expression struck him as trite, pretentious, and woefully inadequate in describing his murderous fury. So he replaced it with, "I was not fit for company."

"Ah." Mr Bennet took another sip of his drink, then set the glass down and repositioned it just so, as though its place on the desk were of some considerable import. And then he said, "I believe I can guess of whom you are speaking. So, have you just heard of his involvement, or were you aware of it already?"

"His involvement, sir?" Darcy echoed, then scowled as he shifted in his seat. "No, I have not heard of it. But it does not surprise me that he would say anything to add to that abhorrent rumour."

"He was its instigator," Mr Bennet said in a flat, even voice, yet his quiet words propelled Darcy out of his chair with all the force of an explosion.

He did not see Mr Bennet start, nor did he deliberately command his feet to carry him across the small, ill-lit room. But as he ran his hand over his mouth and chin, he found that he was standing by the window, looking out into the garden.

Darcy clasped his hands behind his back and turned around to face Elizabeth's father.

His lips almost too stiff to form the words, he owned, "I did not know *that*," although by now this must have been readily apparent.

"So, what did he want? Payment to retract the rumour?" Mr Bennet asked, then his hand sliced the air in an angry gesture. "'Tis too late for that. The gossipmongers have served him all too well. The tale has spread beyond his control—"

"He is not seeking to control it," Darcy interjected tersely, and neglected to apologise for the interruption. "He wants ten thousand pounds to marry your daughter. From me, or from you."

"Is he out of his mind?" Mr Bennet exclaimed, pushing himself up from his chair. "Or does he think *me* mad enough to entrust Lizzy to— Nay, *sell* her off to the very man who had worked to slander her?"

"Oh, he would have come as her knight in shining armour," Darcy retorted, his voice dripping with dark sarcasm. "He would have ranted and raved about the depth of his devotion to her and lamented his circumstances, blaming me for his inability to offer her the comforts she deserved, until your purse was substantially lightened."

"Too late for that performance too," Mr Bennet snarled. "After his spell in the metropolis, he seems to have forgotten that everybody knows everybody in a small town such as this, and no scheme remains concealed for very long. Within hours, I heard from two reliable sources that he was behind it. And now I get to learn the rest. So come, sir, out with it, if you please. Precisely *what* did Wickham have to say?"

The overwhelming fury Darcy had fought so very hard to conquer under the clump of hollies that grew halfway between Meryton and Longbourn – *their* hollies – rose again, choking him, but he forced down the bile and spoke with fierce determination:

"You will forgive me, Mr Bennet, but I shall not repeat what he said. Not to anyone, least of all her father. I have not come to give you an account of—" Darcy rasped, and words suddenly failed him, blown away by abhorrent mental pictures that sprang from the vermin's sickening outpourings. Elizabeth's firstborn – *Wickham's?* Not while he had any breath left in his body!

Perversely, the breath that he had drawn in a forceful gasp left his body in an uncontrollable cough, and a long, exasperating bout followed, which prompted Mr Bennet to turn towards the drinks tray and pour some other liquid – a cordial of sorts this time, not brandy. But Darcy refused that too with a shake of his head and a quick, decisive gesture, and resumed as soon as he could speak.

"Forgive me. This confounded cough is very vexing. But no matter. What I came to say is that this foulness and malice must be kept at bay at all cost and not suffered to touch her. None of those who have presumed to cause her pain should be allowed to repeat the offence, nor come within a mile of her with impunity. This is what I came to offer: my name, and the protection that is in my power to give. You have my word, sir: *no one* will injure her again!"

In the silence that followed, Darcy's breathing settled, and the onslaught of emotions settled too – at least in part – giving him a moment to reflect on the discrepancy between last night's resolution and what he had just said.

A moment was enough for that inconsequential detail to be dismissed. Last night's resolutions were now meaningless. They had lost all substance from the moment when Wickham's repulsive monologue had thrown the starkest light upon a truth he should have acknowledged long ago: that the very notion of her belonging to another – lying with any man but he – was past bearing. Nothing short of agony. So offering for her was not just a possibility to be contemplated and discussed. It was the only option he could live with.

Moreover, the explanations he had resolved to give could no longer pass his lips. Not now. Not ever. He could not mention the disparity in their stations, nor the imbalance between the worth of her connections and his, without hearing Wickham's words on those subjects. And he would cut his own tongue before he willingly echoed Wickham!

Mr Bennet's quiet voice drew him from his disordered thoughts:

"That was a fine response, Mr Darcy, gentlemanlike and honourable, and I greatly appreciate your chivalry. But I fear you are taking too much upon yourself."

"I beg to differ," Darcy countered. "This is not chivalry, but accepting responsibility. Wickham's malicious scheme was aimed at *me*, in retaliation for our past disputes. Your daughter is an innocent victim caught in the crossfire."

"I see," Mr Bennet muttered, silently indicating that they should resume their seats, and Darcy did as bid as he continued speaking.

"I hope you do see by now that he has no scruples about twisting facts to suit his purpose. Even so, in this instance I shall insist upon you having my version of events – that is to say, the truth of the matter."

Mr Bennet made no answer, just gave a slight gesture by way of an invitation to proceed, and Darcy lost no time in doing so.

"Knowing Wickham, he must have shared his tale of woe with all who would listen, so I should not be surprised if snippets of it have already made their way to you," he began, while Mr Bennet leaned back in his chair and steepled his fingers, his lined countenance giving no hint as to whether he had been served a sample of Wickham's lies or not.

But it made no difference, either way. Given the blackguard's latest proof of moral depravity, there was no reason why Mr Bennet should credit Wickham, and not him. Soon, the account of their connection and past dealings was duly given. Out of consideration for his sister's sentiments and the dear girl's good name, Darcy forbore to disclose the fiend's sins against her, but everything else was laid out clearly and succinctly: his sire's attachment to the worthy steward and the steward's undeserving son; the stipulations in his father's will – the legacy of one thousand pounds and the family living destined for Wickham as soon as he took orders; Wickham's choice to relinquish a career in the church in exchange for three thousand pounds; and lastly the rogue's impertinent demand for the Kympton living, once the capital was squandered in three years of idleness and dissipation.

"As you may imagine, I refused to comply with his entreaty, and resisted every repetition of it," Darcy supplied just as concisely, more than a little eager to be done. "Yet there is no limit to his impudence. Reproachful letters kept coming for many months afterwards, testament to his growing resentment. Thus, I have no doubt that, whatever else he hoped to gain from the slander, his chief object was to revenge himself on me. So I trust you can see my meaning now, sir, as to E— Miss Elizabeth being caught in the crossfire through no fault of her own. This… situation *is* my responsibility – and so must the remedy be."

His fingers still steepled, Mr Bennet lowered his gaze as if to assess the movements of his thumbs tapping against each other in a slow, rhythmic motion. And then he folded his hands and looked up.

"I do see your meaning, Mr Darcy, and as I said, I appreciate your stance – and now your motive. But whether we are to call it chivalry, responsibility, duty or anything else in the same vein, I hope we can both agree that necessity is not a solid foundation for a marriage."

Of all the remarks Darcy had imagined the older gentleman would make in response to his disclosures, this was highly unexpected. Necessity would have sufficed for the man's wife, if one was to judge by Mrs Bennet's cross comments at the ball the other night, about her daughters being thrown in rich men's paths.

But then Darcy chastised himself for falling into the trap of tarring Elizabeth's parents with the same brush. Although Mr Bennet had married a grasping woman of weak understanding and illiberal mind, it did not necessarily follow that he shared her views in everything. In fact, one ought not be surprised if he did not agree with her on any count whatever. After all, Elizabeth must have learnt her principled way of thinking from one of her parents – and evidence suggested she had not acquired it from her mother.

Thus driven to harbour some respect for Mr Bennet – not least for finding him interested in all aspects of his daughter's future welfare, beyond matters financial – Darcy's reply was warmer and more candid than it would otherwise have been:

"No, sir, it is not. But I believe that your daughter's sterling qualities and my admiration and regard for her do form a solid foundation. And it would be an honour to task myself with her happiness and safety."

He could not have put it any better, even if he said so himself, Darcy thought – but, to his mild frustration, Mr Bennet did not seem quite as pleased as he should have been. Instead, Elizabeth's father chose to play devil's advocate.

"Handsomely said, Mr Darcy, but the fact remains that the pair of you have been acquainted for... what? A month? Five weeks, perhaps? Time enough for you to learn whether the other favours a plain dish over a *ragout* and *Vingt-Un* over *Commerce*, but not much else."

"Not so, sir," Darcy retorted. "For my part, I also came to see that Miss Elizabeth is one of the most charming ladies of my acquaintance, delightfully quick-witted, with engaging manners and an amiable and sunny disposition. I believe that in our short acquaintance I have learnt as much of the essentials as I might have discovered, had I been allowed the privilege of studying her character for a twelvemonth."

But, yet again, the reply vouchsafed him was dissatisfying.

"As her doting father, I am gratified by your discernment," Mr Bennet said, his voice smooth and quiet. "Even so, with her felicity in mind, I must speak plainly: I doubt she thinks she has studied *your* character for long enough."

Darcy sat up in his seat, hard-pressed to harness the sharp surge of displeasure. It did not spring from the reminder of what Elizabeth herself had said two nights earlier about the illustration of his character and her attempts to make it out. Whether or not she had been in earnest, whether or not she felt she understood him, she cared for him. Yesterday morning, her eyes had filled with tears at the prospect of their parting. It was something else entirely that raised his hackles: namely that Mr Bennet, an obscure gentleman of modest means and undesirable family connections, should bring *his* character into question.

But then the older man had the good sense to speak again and give credit where it was due, which served to mollify him, to some extent at least.

"That being said, it would also be fair to note that the length of the acquaintance is but one of the many factors in the equation, and that we have learnt more of your character in one day than could be ascertained in the course of an entire month."

Darcy bowed his head in silent acknowledgement, and thought it only fair to reciprocate with his own admission.

"I understand why you would regard a longer acquaintance as preferable. But I fear that, all things considered, this is not an option now."

"I expect not," Mr Bennet muttered, and said nothing further, but remained deep in thought, staring at his folded hands.

In the ensuing silence – the overlong silence – Darcy kept his gaze fixed on the other man as he wondered with no little impatience and mounting frustration what on earth there was to think about. It should have been perfectly clear by now that he and Elizabeth must marry as soon as may be.

It was astounding – nay, to be frank, it bordered on insulting – that his readiness to answer the dictates of both sentiment and honour was not met with due satisfaction, nor was it promptly rewarded with parental sanction and the opportunity to speak with Elizabeth alone. But surely Mr Bennet's fatherly affection was not so selfish and misguided as to make him insist on a delay that would go against his own daughter's interest – against the interest of his entire family. For everyone's sake, the scandalous gossip should be countered and quashed as soon as possible. So why the hesitation?

Darcy's jaw tightened when it eventually occurred to him that Mr Bennet might take parental devotion to preposterous extremes and see fit to reject his offer.

Panic was his first response. Indignation – the second. Surprise came last, at finding that his own perception had undergone so material a change in a matter of days – nay, hours. Less than a day ago, a parting of ways had seemed the only option. Now it felt like a catastrophe to be avoided at all cost.

But Darcy refused to dwell on fruitless reflections and leaned forward, his hands clasped together on his knee.

"May I have your answer, Mr Bennet?"

The crisp question brought the other man from his trance with a start. Mr Bennet looked up and exhaled, shifting in his seat.

"'Tis not for me to give it, sir," he said at last. "True enough, in days of yore the decision was entirely the father's, but I, for one, am glad that times are changing, for it is not the father who has to live with that choice day after day." With another sigh, Mr Bennet pushed his chair back and stood. "Allow me to thank you on Elizabeth's behalf for the honour of your proposal, Mr Darcy, and pray make yourself comfortable. I must speak with my daughter. You shall have her answer as soon as may be."

Darcy nodded in appreciation of the older man's enlightened way of thinking and, as the door closed quietly behind his host, he allowed himself a faint sigh of relief. So, it would be Elizabeth's decision – thankfully. Then the matter was as good as settled.

At that happy thought, Darcy's guarded countenance softened into a smile.

Chapter 9

"There, Lizzy. Now you have the full account of what we have discussed," Mr Bennet quietly concluded, and at long last Elizabeth turned her head and met his troubled gaze.

"Thank you, Papa," she whispered, then fell silent and trained her eyes on her folded hands.

Nothing else was said for quite some time, as Elizabeth sat huddled between her sister and her father. There was more than enough space left on the sofa, yet neither Jane nor Mr Bennet seemed willing to make use of it. Instead, they remained just as they were, as though intent on shielding her. Comforting her. Or perhaps seeking a measure of comfort for themselves as well in that uncommonly close proximity.

"So, what do you think, Lizzy?" Jane suddenly asked, and Elizabeth darted a quick glance towards her, startled to find that the dire circumstances had done away with her sister's angelic patience, so that even Jane – sweet, forbearing Jane – could no longer hold her peace, but pressed her to share what was on her mind.

Yet how was she to do so, when her mind was in such turmoil that she could scarce separate one thought from another? She was shocked, sickened and beyond enraged that Mr Wickham should presume to wreak ruin upon her for his own ends – use her thus, shamelessly and without scruple. He, who in mere years had frittered away so staggering a sum as four thousand pounds, had worked to destroy her reputation so that he might profit from extortion!

And she would have aided and abetted him! She would have given him credence, and hastened to work against herself. She would have been her own worst enemy!

That was the most dreadful truth of all. If she had not heard all the corroborating evidence against him – if her aunt Phillips' cook were not related to that foolish maid, his plaything and instrument –

if John the footman were not betrothed to one of the serving girls at the *Red Lion*, or if John's Susan had gone to serve a different set, at some other table – if the vile schemer should have come to Longbourn as her champion and saviour – why, then she would have welcomed him with open arms! She would have dismissed Mr Darcy's disclosures to her father as malicious slander, and would have chosen to place her confidence in Mr Wickham. She would have trusted him with her fate, and followed him to her doom! Just as she had oh-so-eagerly believed all the lies he had spun on the first day of their acquaintance, simply because he had simpered and smirked, and had favoured her with his attention.

Good heavens, how could she have been so easily deceived? So vain and gullible? Nay, not gullible. Downright stupid! A stupid, shallow girl who had unquestioningly sided with a villain because he was plausible and charming and quick to flatter her.

She frowned as it occurred to her that Mr Darcy was quite wrong to assume full responsibility for their predicament. He might have been the one who had attracted Mr Wickham's malevolence, but she – *she* had drawn the target on herself with her own hand by hanging on the blackguard's every word like an empty-headed ninny. Of course Mr Wickham would think her ready and willing to join her fate with his, had he arrived at her door posing as her knight in shining armour, as Mr Darcy had put it.

And yet, now that the damage was done and her reputation was in tatters, the one who had come to bona fide offer his name and his protection was the latter. So she might very well say that her knight in shining armour was Mr Darcy.

The notion conjured an absurd picture of medieval splendour complete with pennants, a long lance, and that gentleman's stern countenance under a gleaming visor.

Under normal circumstances, the mental picture would have made her laugh. But these were not normal circumstances, and she was not disposed towards laughter in the slightest.

With a sharp intake of breath, Elizabeth clasped her hands together in her lap in an unconscious gesture of supplication and turned towards her father.

"Papa, what am I to do?"

Mr Bennet's lined countenance creased further into something of a flinch.

"Dearest child, I cannot presume to tell you that!" he protested. "As I told Mr Darcy, 'tis not my choice to make."

On impulse, Elizabeth reached for his hand and brought his fingers to her lips.

"Thank you," she earnestly said. "Not many fathers would have taken that view in so grave a matter. I know you would neither coerce nor coax me. But I set great store by your opinion," she whispered, keeping his veined hand in hers. "Yours too, Jane," Elizabeth added in the same breath, glancing over her shoulder at her sister, then left her seat to draw a stool, so that she could sit facing them both yet still close enough to hold their hands.

To an onlooker, they would have formed an affecting picture as they sat huddled together at this time of momentous decisions. But no one else was there to see them or distract them from their purpose, which was just as well, for Elizabeth's dearest relations already were more than a little uncomfortable with the role of advisers that had been thrust upon them.

Nonetheless, Mr Bennet spoke, quick to recognise his duty:

"Voicing opinions has its dangers too, Lizzy," he said, his mien a study in affectionate reluctance. "I should not wish to sway you towards any course of action that might make you unhappy. Yet it would be remiss of me not to speak of the very real peril that now comes from the entail. I failed you grievously in this, failed you all—" he grimly owned, but was not allowed to finish his sentence.

The truth of the matter notwithstanding, his daughters interjected in one voice:

"Oh, do not say that, I beg you!"

"Papa! You are too severe upon yourself!"

"Hush, girls. We all know that it must be said," he replied, patting Jane's knee and squeezing Elizabeth's hand. And then, as was his wont, he once more resorted to the forced lightness he employed whenever his demise became the topic of discussion. "Now, I flatter myself that I am of strong constitution and shall not shuffle off this mortal coil anytime soon. God willing, I shall be around for many years to come, to impose uncommonly harsh standards of economy and provoke your mother with my newfound parsimony. So, with a grain of luck and a long-overdue dose of common sense, I might have some success in raising our fortunes. That being said, I cannot expect to see a long line of suitors beating a path to our door, thanks to our friend Wickham and the trouble he has stirred," he added darkly, "which is unfortunate, for I wish there was adequate protection for you all when I am gone. Much as it pains me to put it plainly, Lizzy, *you* should not be left defenceless before Collins. There is only so much that your uncles could do, should they survive me. Whereas distance and one of the largest fortunes in Derbyshire would be a decided safeguard. Of all the things I can say in Darcy's favour, to my mind this is the most noteworthy: few men have it in their power to defy him – and Collins is not one of them."

With her shoulders hunched and her gaze lowered, Elizabeth had listened to her father speaking of the deeply distressing subject of his passing and found that sort of talk as unbearable as ever. But she darted a startled glance towards him when he mentioned his repulsive cousin, horrified by the gruesome image that his words had just forced into her head: she, in mourning, in the agony of loss – and beset by Mr Collins fired up with vengeance over his thwarted lust.

Elizabeth released her relations' hands and wrapped her arms around herself to suppress a shudder. No! Nothing could be worse than that. And no price was too great for her deliverance.

So she sought her father's gaze and quietly prompted, "You said '*Of all the things…*' What other things did you have in mind, Papa?"

Mr Bennet's brow furrowed.

"Pardon?"

"What other things would you list in Mr Darcy's favour?"

Her father leaned back in his seat as he gave a little shrug.

"Well, I shan't sport with your patience by speaking of the obvious. No more than I already have, that is. But I will own that I am beginning to warm up to the fellow. On account of his honourable conduct, of course, but mostly because he has the good sense to appreciate your worth. Or, in his own words, your sterling qualities."

'*He did say that,*' Elizabeth mused. Her papa had already told her – and had also revealed that Mr Darcy had followed it by declaring his admiration and regard for her.

She shook her head in a mixture of bemusement and exasperation. He had the strangest way of showing his admiration and regard, seeing as he had scarce said a word to her of his own volition.

Yet when her father spoke again, he gave her to suspect that he had drawn the wrong conclusion from the shake of her head.

For what he said was, "Of course, that is neither here nor there. My warming up to him has no bearing whatsoever, if *you* cannot say the same."

Elizabeth pursed her lips.

"In truth, I have not given it much thought. That was foolish, on reflection, but there we are. I have not seriously considered that Mamma might be in the right about Mr Darcy's purpose in coming here today. But Mamma *was* right — which in itself is a sobering notion," she sought to jest, only to instantly abandon the feeble and unfilial attempt at humour. Instead, elbow on her knee and chin in hand, she applied herself to the weighty matter in earnest, and voiced her thoughts as they were formed. "I cannot say that I have warmed up to him, not as such. But I expect that in due course I shall. After all, my dislike of him had sprung from a frivolous reason, and was fed by Mr Wickham's lies—"

She did not have the opportunity to pursue that logical line of reasoning any further. With a strangled sound, Jane slipped from the sofa to kneel beside her stool and wrapped her into a tight embrace.

"Oh, Lizzy, it breaks my heart to hear you speak thus," she tearfully choked out. "See you so… so emotionless and practical. You used to say that nothing but the deepest love would ever induce you into matrimony!"

Dangerously close to tears herself, Elizabeth put her arms around her sister. It could not escape her that not once had Jane so much as hinted that, if left unchecked, the scandal stood to taint her by association – if not in Mr Bingley's eyes, then in his sisters' view, and that of his wider circle. Nor had Jane pointed out that Elizabeth's marriage to Mr Bingley's best friend would make a second marriage a great deal more likely.

Of all the reasons that demanded she accept Mr Darcy's offer, this was the one that spoke the loudest to Elizabeth's heart. But she knew better than to say as much. Jane would be appalled to hear she was considering it from that perspective. To her, it would amount to sacrifice – to her sister's happiness traded for her own.

So Elizabeth merely pressed her lips to Jane's cheek, then drew back and put a false cheer in her tones as she airily replied, "Oh, pray do not hold me to all the naïve nonsense I used to spout. Naught but girlish fantasies that have no place in the real world. In such cases as these, a good memory is unpardonable."

Jane winced – a clear sign that the bravado had been a poor choice, and had not served its purpose. Quite the opposite. Moreover, her father took it badly too. Pained determination in his countenance, Mr Bennet leaned forward and firmly spoke:

"No, Lizzy! I will not have it! If that is how you see a union with Mr Darcy, as the end of your best hopes, then this is the last you shall hear of it. I will go and tell him that it cannot be, and send him on his way. Fear not, we shall deal with the gossip one way or another, until it dies a natural death. And if the young men hereabouts choose to stay tied to their mothers' apron strings and are too dull-witted to see the truth when it stares them in the face, then let the loss be theirs. You shall find your deepest love elsewhere. We can spend the greatest part of each year in places where the scandal cannot touch us: Bath, Weymouth, Cheltenham, Eastbourne, Ramsgate – any and all of the above. There, Lizzy, that is what we shall do. And nothing more need be said about it."

That was bravado too – a string of valiant, generous falsehoods – and Elizabeth readily recognised it as such. For the gossip would not die a natural death. There would always be those who would say that there was no smoke without fire. And they could not afford to flit about the country in this fashion so as to keep their distance from the scandal. Mere moments ago her father was speaking of frugal living and harsh new standards of economy!

But she could not distress him with such comments, so she voiced the only argument that she felt at liberty to make:

"Dearest Papa, forgive me, but that is unsound. Who can gain any real knowledge of a person's disposition, character and circumstances in Ramsgate or Bath or some other watering place? Whereas we can safely say that Mr Darcy is honourable, dependable and of good standing. And then there is his close friendship with one as amiable as Mr Bingley, which speaks highly in his favour," she added and cast her sister a repentant smile as she clasped Jane's hand again. "You said something to that effect last week, dearest, did you not? I should have seen the logic of it, but I was too headstrong to pay heed, and too enamoured of my own convictions. Now I must beg your pardon for blithely ascribing your sensible opinion to your unwillingness to think ill of anyone."

Misty-eyed, Jane gave a little flourish of her other hand as though to indicate that no apology was necessary, but said nothing. The sole reply came from Mr Bennet, and he did not seem appeased:

"So – now what?" he asked. "Are you suggesting that all your hopes for a marriage of affection are of no consequence, and you are resolved to grit your teeth and have him?"

"No, Papa. Nothing of the sort," Elizabeth countered, endeavouring to put a hopeful ring into her even tones. "I am not discarding my hopes. Merely seeking to ground them in reality. I am saying that it is nonsensical to wish for a *coup de foudre*, and in truth I believe I never had. A *coup de foudre* can be severely misleading. And less likely to last than the love that comes from a journey of discovery."

Mr Bennet grimaced.

"That, I cannot fault you for," he muttered, "and I should be glad to hear you speak so wisely." He sighed. "But the deuce of it, dear girl, is that I am not glad at all. In fact, I am tempted to agree with your sister," he owned, tilting his head towards Jane. "When clear-headed wisdom makes its way into talk of marriage, it leaves too little room for sentiment for my liking. And I was hoping that you would fare better."

The tremor in her father's voice brought a fresh sting of tears to her eyes as Elizabeth raised her hand to stroke his cheek.

"That is because you love me," she said simply. "So you wish the very best for me. In fact, I shall hazard to say that you wish me to fare better than anyone can reasonably expect. But let us favour reason for a moment, now that you and Jane already think me wise and practical. I hope we can all agree that there are far worse fates than being Mrs Darcy of Pemberley. So I need not grit my teeth, Papa," she argued, purposely curling her lips into a smile. And then, because she was her father's daughter and had learnt at his knee to resort to quips whenever the subject under discussion was too serious for comfort, she finished with, "Speaking of which, there must be a host of young ladies, Miss Bingley included, who would give their eye-teeth for that privilege."

"Yes, well, you are not Miss Bingley," came Mr Bennet's gruff retort, and Elizabeth obliged him with a little chuckle.

"No, indeed – and I give daily thanks for that. Although I should not speak thus of Jane's future sister."

Then she smoothed her skirts and stood.

"I should go and see him now," Elizabeth said with a vague gesture in the direction of the study, but Mr Bennet scrambled to his feet and spoke to detain her.

"You need not decide this very moment!" he urged, clearly overcome by the finality of it. "Would you not prefer I went and asked him to give you a day or two to think about it?"

Elizabeth's lips tightened. What was there to think about? They must marry. That was as plain to her as anything. So, with some determination, she smoothed her countenance into a semblance of good cheer and evenly said, "If something is worth doing, it should be done sooner rather than later."

"I would not know. 'Tis not a precept I have ever followed," Mr Bennet mumbled, which could not fail to put a spark of genuine amusement in Elizabeth's eyes, for what he said was true. "But never mind that now. You must tell me this: *is it* worth doing?"

Elizabeth held his gaze and nodded.

"Yes, Papa. You know it is. And so do I."

Chapter 10

As soon as she closed the door behind her, Elizabeth's shoulders slumped and her air of confidence vanished. It had been naught but a brave front she had put on to spare her dearest relations' feelings and, for their sake, she hoped that it had served its purpose. Hoped that, if they had seen through her – and they must have done, for both of them loved her dearly and knew her ever so well – then they had not seen too much evidence of her consternation and misgivings.

Two days ago the world made sense. She had her family, her friends, and her beloved home, which she had not imagined quitting anytime soon.

Now most of her so-called friends were shown to be false-hearted and all too eager to believe the worst of her. Her nearest and dearest were made to suffer alongside her, even though they were as blameless as she. The unmerited disgrace that had befallen her and her entire family was the work of a man she had trusted and favoured. Longbourn could not remain her home for much longer. She would have to leave and make a life with the one whom, until very recently, she had regarded as the very worst of men. The last man in the world whom she could ever be prevailed upon to marry.

Or so she had thought. But then she had been given proof that Mr Darcy was not the villain of the piece, so the picture she had formed of him had perforce been discarded.

She had nothing to replace it with. No reliable likeness, just the beginnings of a sketch. She knew so little of him. And yet he would be her husband. Because rejecting his offer would be selfish and irresponsible in the extreme.

She was no dunce. Once her father had acquainted her with the fine details of his conversation with Mr Darcy, her keen wit had already indicated the way forward. She had recognised it as the sole rational option long before she had endeavoured to persuade her dear papa that she was sanguine about it. Now she needed to persuade herself. She needed reassurance that she could be happy with the choice she had to make. And she had little expectation of finding that reassurance in the study.

Her gaze still fixed on the closed door, Elizabeth tugged at her mother's shawl, needlessly rearranging it around her shoulders. She blinked as the distance to her father's study seemed to grow. Never before had she hesitated going into that room, nor regarded the prospect with such trepidation. How preposterously missish of her to loiter here now, Elizabeth chided herself with growing vexation.

'Oh, for goodness' sake! Go in and get on with it!'

She cast her eyes down and took a steadying breath – only to glance up with a start when a loud cough rang from behind *that door*.

The notion that sprang to mind a fraction of a second later was but an excuse to defer the unnerving interview, and well she knew it. So much for telling her father that when something was worth doing it had better be done without delay, Elizabeth inwardly scoffed, disgusted with her own cowardice. Even so, she quietly limped towards the kitchen.

⸙

"Miss Lizzy!" the housekeeper exclaimed when Elizabeth stepped into Mrs Hill's domain – an uncommon occurrence over the last eight years or so. "Is there anything you need?" she asked, hastening to wipe her floury hands on her apron.

Her cowardly excuse at the ready, Elizabeth nodded.

"Yes. Tea for Mr Darcy, if you would."

"Of course," the older woman said, then her mien grew apologetic. "Beg pardon for not seeing to it already. I thought of it, but didn't wish to interrupt. I'll brew some in a trice and fetch it."

"You need not step away from what you are doing," Elizabeth replied with a slight gesture towards the ball of dough that the housekeeper had been kneading. "Sarah can come back with me and carry the tray."

Surprise flashed across Mrs Hill's countenance at Elizabeth's intimation that she would wait in the kitchen for the tea to be brewed, but all she said was, "As you think best, Miss Lizzy. Sarah, fetch the caddy, will you? Here's the key. And get yourself a fresh apron while you're at it."

The housemaid, a steady, cheerful girl some six or seven years Elizabeth's senior, bobbed a curtsy as she hastened out of the room to do the housekeeper's bidding, while Mrs Hill cast an assessing glance at the chairs lined up against the wall, then offered:

"I'd ask if you'd care to sit, Miss Lizzy, but there'll be flour or wet patches or goodness knows what else on these, so best not risk it, lest your skirts be marked. What of the seat in my parlour?"

"No need. Do not trouble yourself," Elizabeth demurred, by now increasingly aware that her presence in the kitchen was an untoward disruption. She ought to leave, but could not bring herself to do so. Not just yet. Instead, she drew out of the way and self-consciously added, "Pray do not mind me. I should leave you to your work, I know, but this is… very welcoming."

The housekeeper cast her a warm smile.

"I'm glad you think so. Then I hope you'll keep coming back, just as you used to do when you were a little girl."

A tomboyish little girl, romping in and out of the kitchen, the pantry and every other room in the house, affectionately indulged by everybody and chided by no one but her mother. It was a wonder that she had not grown insufferably spoilt, Elizabeth thought, her countenance brightening in amusement. But her recollections ended in a sigh. The carefree days of childhood were gone, more was the pity. Life had been blissfully uncomplicated then. No knowledge of difficulties or evil, and nothing more irksome than grazed knees and the odd scratch from Mrs Phillips' surly cat.

Yet the aura of untroubled times still lingered here, in Mrs Hill's warm kitchen. A very soothing aura. Tranquil. The glow of the fire gleaming in the copper pans arrayed in neat rows upon the shelves. The scent of cinnamon and cloves and orange peel and ginger – Christmas and childhood in *potpourri*. The muted chatter in the scullery, where the maid-of-all-work, Ruth, and young Nell, the scullery maid, were going about their business. The homely sight of Mrs Hill kneading the dough, pausing now and then to add another sprinkling of flour.

As Elizabeth stood to one side, taking everything in, a sense of comfort slowly began to settle over her. For here, where she had gained a respite from the imminence of a life-altering decision, she had also found the leisure to reflect on promising notions, and carefully count all her valid reasons for trusting that Mr Darcy was a good man underneath his prideful manner and uniform reserve. Not communicative nor lively, but a good man, and reassuringly appreciative of those two aforementioned qualities. His longstanding friendship with Mr Bingley stood testament to that as well.

Elizabeth's gaze was drawn towards the door when Sarah rushed in with the tea caddy. Quick to follow instructions, she had already changed her apron for a long, freshly starched one, and had donned a pristine cap as well, which earned her a brief nod of approval from the housekeeper.

Perhaps Mr Darcy would not be averse to learning some liveliness from his wife, Elizabeth pondered as she idly watched Mrs Hill warming the teapot, then preparing the beverage. Or perhaps that was too much to hope for. After all, if he had not acquired liveliness from Mr Bingley in the whole course of their acquaintance, he would not learn it from her either. A pity, if that should be the case. She would have liked to think that she might bring at least that little something to their marriage. Besides, a lifetime with a taciturn man, however kind, would be a challenge for one of her disposition. Would it not? Still, there was the old adage claiming that opposites attract…

"How many cups, ma'am?" Mrs Hill asked, disrupting her musings. "Four? Two?"

"No. Just one, thank you."

In short order, the requested cup and all the accoutrements were placed on a silver tray, so – out of excuses, but reasonably at peace with that – Elizabeth left the kitchen and Sarah followed with the tray, the one cup rattling softly on the saucer.

There was no reason to expect that they would encounter anyone on the way, but when Elizabeth rounded the corner into the entrance hall, she found her father standing near the closed door of the parlour, just as she had done a short while ago. She met his eyes and they exchanged rueful smiles, both sheepishly aware that they had been caught out: he displaying nervous impatience and she delaying the requisite interview despite her declarations to the contrary.

By way of explanation, Elizabeth stepped aside and gestured towards Sarah and the tea things, before meeting him halfway to press his arm.

"All will be well, Papa," she whispered, then made her way into the study.

⁘

"My apologies for keeping you waiting for so long," Elizabeth offered, once Sarah had bobbed a curtsy and vanished, having set the tray on the desk, and Mr Bennet had come close enough to the door to pull it shut, thus giving a tacit indication of his consent to their complete privacy. "I thought a cup of tea would not go amiss. I fear you have caught a chill after all."

A wry quirk in his lips by way of confirmation, Mr Darcy said, "I thank you, a cup of tea would be most welcome," so Elizabeth poured it, with just a dash of milk and no sugar as she vaguely remembered that he took it, then handed it to him, while noting without rhyme or reason just how uncommonly tall he was. So tall that the top of her head seemed to reach no higher than his chin – if that. She turned away as she suppressed a grimace. That this should be the first time she had paid heed to such details was utterly ridiculous.

She wordlessly invited him to sit and, by force of habit, chose to go and lower herself onto the cushioned window-seat where she often curled up on wet days, when she and her papa happily kept each other company. How strange that the beginning of her married life should be decided here! She had never imagined that her future husband would propose in her father's study. And yet she suddenly found it deeply comforting.

Even the fact that he fixed her with a solemn and unwavering stare as he drank his tea no longer felt unsettling. She did not stare back, but lowered her gaze to her folded hands as it occurred to her to wonder if she had misjudged him in this too: had he always stared because he admired her, and not because he disapproved?

⁘

He had never been drawn to her more than now, when admiration for her efforts to show strength before adversity was heightened by heart-wrenching pity. Because he had never seen her thus, Darcy was distraught to note. Pale and subdued, her countenance pinched, her eyes devoid of their adorably impish sparkle. There was nothing that he wanted more than to see her restored to her cheerful self – nothing that he needed more than to protect her.

Darcy pressed his lips together as he owned that his understandable reluctance to sound like Wickham and echo the fiend's words was of little import now. His own views notwithstanding, he could not have brought himself to say anything to her of the disparities in their condition in life. He could not have injured her pride with the honest confession of the scruples that had long prevented him from forming any serious design on her. Not now, when he could scarce hold back from striding across the room to wrap his arms around her and tell her that he would keep her safe, and that henceforth she need not fear anything.

Perhaps it was too soon for such a liberty. But he was damned if he would still struggle to keep his distance!

So Darcy set his half-empty cup on the desk and rose to his feet. He crossed the room towards her, drew a chair next to her window-seat and lowered himself into it, then reached for her hands and gathered them in his.

⚜

He had excessively warm hands, Elizabeth noted. Perhaps the chill *had* brought on a fever. There was a feverish glint in his eyes too, she found, when she raised her head and met his gaze. But this time she did not look away, despite the sudden flutter of nervousness at his proximity. She ignored it, and allowed herself to acknowledge something she had always known: that he was a handsome man. Very handsome. In truth, *that* had been her first thought of him upon their initial encounter, before his uncivil comment at the Meryton assembly had goaded her into resentfully welcoming every critical view of his person, and the full set of lies that Mr Wickham had concocted.

Her sin in believing them without any evidence, simply because they vindicated a dislike born from that offence, was certainly greater than his incivility in declaring her merely tolerable but not handsome enough to tempt him. So she would not be so childish and petty as to bear him a grudge for it.

A faint stirring of mischief prompted her to think that although she was ready to forgive the transgression, she might still tease him over it, given the opportunity. But for now, her natural penchant for archness could not distract her from a very different thought: it *was* a relief that she found him attractive. Then marital duties should not be a hardship. Which was something she never could have said of Mr Collins.

Heat flared in her cheeks at her immodest reflections, and Elizabeth darted her eyes downwards, hoping against hope that Mr Darcy had not already read in them precisely what it was that she was thinking – that this was not the reason why he leaned forward in his seat with a sharp intake of breath. But he came no closer – merely ran his thumbs over the back of her hands.

The light caress sparked comparisons too, much as she loathed her cousin's intrusion in her thoughts at any time, and now more than ever. Yet she could not help comparing one instance with the other, and blessedly found that there was a world of difference between *this* and the travesty of a marriage proposal she had received from Mr Collins. Just as there was a world of difference between Mr Darcy and that vile excuse of a man – in every way.

She exhaled slowly, noting in passing that she had not realised how taut her every muscle, nerve and sinew had been – as taut as bowstrings – until now, when the tension seemed to ebb. Even her hands had been rigid, she discovered, when she felt them going slack and resting almost limply in Mr Darcy's warm clasp, as his thumbs kept brushing back and forth over her skin.

Elizabeth blinked. She had not expected tenderness. In truth, she could scarce tell what she had expected, once her preconceptions had been overturned – but not that. His voice was uncommonly soft too, when he finally spoke.

"How are you faring?"

"I am quite recovered, I thank you. It turned out to be a trifling injury," Elizabeth replied and looked up, but not for very long. It would be very strange indeed if she were to stare at him from less than an arm's length.

"I am very glad to hear it, but that was not my meaning. I was wondering how you were faring on the whole."

"Oh. Of course…" she faltered, then gave a faint shrug and chose honesty over the niceties of polite conversation. "Well enough, I daresay. That is, when I am not dwelling on perfidy, unprovoked malice and my inexcusable credulity."

"Let us not call it thus, but ignorance of evil," Mr Darcy countered, yet his voice lost its warmth as he continued. "I rather thought as much the other night, at the ball, when I detected Wickham's poison in some of your remarks—"

"And so there was. I owe you an apology for letting it hold sway," Elizabeth cut in, determined to make a clean breast of everything. Unwittingly, she curled her fingers around his as she added, "I should have known better."

She darted a self-conscious glance towards him, only to find that the turn of Mr Darcy's countenance rather suggested he was in agreement – she *should* have known better than to lend an ear to Mr Wickham's spiteful talk. But he scrupled to say so. Instead, he civilly replied, "Pray do not make yourself uneasy. You could not have known that he lies as he breathes."

"Yes. I can see that now," Elizabeth retorted, her voice low and bitter, but before she could say anything else, Mr Darcy spoke with nothing short of quiet ferocity:

"I would gladly tear him limb from limb for that. And make all the Meryton gossipmongers pay. Coarseness and insolence are common enough in those of their station, but their readiness to turn on you, when they have known you all your life, is unforgivable."

Elizabeth's lips tightened. She had found this deeply objectionable too: his obvious disdain for her acquaintances. She could not fault him for it now. On reflection, perhaps she should have made allowances for it sooner. Why should he not hold them in contempt, given the manner of his reception in the area? He must have heard the whispers at the Meryton assembly, just as she had – their ill-mannered chatter about his affairs and his person; and the report, which was in general circulation within five minutes after his entrance, of his large estate in Derbyshire and his ten thousand a year.

"There *is* a coarseness about them," she acknowledged with some asperity, "and a littleness, which you saw and I did not, even though I grew up among them."

"I will not make a merit of seeing through them. I have lived in the world for a few years longer than you, that is all," Mr Darcy replied, a faint quirk at the corner of his lips. "Time enough to grow circumspect. Or jaded."

"Which is one of the reasons I *detest* this wretched business," Elizabeth retorted, her voice still quiet despite the sudden vehemence. "You have every reason to resent them for forcing your hand. I should not wish you to resent me by extension. And for suggesting the bridleway in the first place."

Mr Darcy's shock was readily apparent – and no less reassuring – when he shot back, "Resent *you*? You must not think that! How could I possibly resent you? You have been maligned through no fault of your own. I would wager that you have uniformly shown them civility and kindness, and never injured a single one of them. And yet they had no qualms about injuring you. I would dearly wish to have their sins visited upon them, but sadly there is not much I can do except put distance between you and their malice, if you are in agreement. Are you? Will you let me take you away from all this?"

Elizabeth raised her head, lifting her gaze from their joined hands to his face, and for once it did not seem discomfiting or unnatural to stare at him from such close quarters. She searched his countenance, looking for answers to her as-yet-unspoken questions.

And then she put those questions into words:

"Why would you give yourself the trouble? Because they maligned you too? To prove that you are not a rake?"

Under her very eyes, his mien softened almost beyond recognition.

"Only a fool would marry to spite others or to prove anything to anyone," Mr Darcy said with somewhat of a chuckle.

Yet a fraction of a second later he released her hands and startled her by turning abruptly in his seat. Perplexed, Elizabeth watched him rummaging in his coat pocket, but her confusion vanished, replaced by mild amusement, when she saw him hastily producing a handkerchief and sneezing loudly into it – twice, in quick succession. Then he put his kerchief away and cast her an engagingly self-deprecating grin.

"Forgive me. So much for a dignified proposal."

She flashed him an understanding smile in her turn.

"Do not concern yourself. Dignity can be overrated. So, you were saying…?"

"Just that I am not seeking to prove anything," Mr Darcy resumed, gathering her hands in his once more. "I am asking you to be my wife because I have good reason to believe we shall be happy."

That answer was unexpected too.

Did he genuinely think so? Or was that his way of saying he wished they would make the most of the hand they had been dealt? Or was it just plain courtesy?

Clearly, he had offered for her out of necessity, otherwise he would have spoken sooner. But he had not. He had made plans to quit Hertfordshire. He would not be here, were it not for the scandal. *That* was the fact of the matter, even if he was too gentlemanly to say so.

Nonetheless, Elizabeth could not dismiss his words as common courtesy, for the look in his eyes did not suggest he had merely uttered a requisite civility. As to her other speculations, she could not determine which one came closest to the truth, but in a flash a more pressing notion leapt to the fore: was he about to kiss her?

If so, she was not sure how she felt about that, either. Nervous? Curious? Uneasy that her first kiss should be here, in her father's study? Breathless? Dizzy? Not surprised? Definitely not surprised. Was that not part and parcel of a betrothal?

In the end, it mattered not how she might have felt about it, for Mr Darcy did not kiss her. Instead, he pressed his lips to the back of her hand – warm lips, yet their touch sent a sort of tingling shiver coursing over her skin. An astonishing response, unaccountable but not unpleasant. Quite delectable, in fact. And then he raised his head to ask, "Will you marry me, Elizabeth?"

Another novelty there. Not the question itself – that particular question had been hanging in the air ever since she had joined him in her father's study – but Mr Darcy addressing her by her Christian name, and the timbre of his voice as he did so.

A part of her mind – the part that was not distracted by sundry novelties – diligently laboured, cataloguing sensible thoughts and peculiar sensations, and in due course presented her with the conclusion that she had been wrong in thinking she would not find reassurance in her father's study this morning. That is to say, in her interview with Mr Darcy. For his gentleness *was* reassuring. As was her own response to it. To his closeness. To him.

There was but one answer she could give to his offer of marriage, and they both knew it. But by now Elizabeth had sufficient cause to hope that, despite the hand they had been dealt, they might make a good life together. Thus, her smile was shy rather than forced when, with one word, she pledged herself to him in a low whisper.

Chapter 11

Once the glad tidings were made known to her, Mrs Bennet was too elated to mind that her future son-in-law had already left, so she and Mrs Hill had gone to great trouble for nothing in her endeavour to impress him with an excellent luncheon.

Later that day, Miss Bingley was equally unable to contain her glee – but, unlike Mrs Bennet's, hers came from blissful ignorance. While travelling apace to town with her sister and Mr Hurst, their carriage barely keeping up with Mr Darcy's, Miss Bingley was verily bursting with joy at finding him so eager to quit Hertfordshire. To her, this was the best proof that her rival's machinations had come to naught. She had learnt the scandalous piece of gossip from her lady's maid that very morning, and had not doubted for one second that the rumours had been industriously circulated with Eliza's consent and her family's assistance, for the sole purpose of trapping Mr Darcy into marriage. But he would have none of it, and had wisely chosen to take himself away, leaving the brazen hussy to reap what she had sown. And, to Miss Bingley's way of thinking, this was precisely as it should be.

꩜

A couple of days later, Darcy was travelling in the opposite direction, this time without a second vehicle hurtling behind. Henceforth, Miss Bingley would have no cause to pursue him, literally or otherwise. She was firmly settled in her sister's house in Grosvenor Square, in the foulest humour from the moment she had learnt from her brother that her matrimonial ambitions had been blown to smithereens.

Not surprisingly, it had not even crossed Darcy's mind to take Miss Bingley and the Hursts into his confidence when he had returned from Longbourn an engaged man. It was his sister who deserved to be told first. The second should be Bingley. All things considered, Darcy felt he owed him that.

The tidings had come as a great shock to both – and both conversations had been awkward.

His greatest challenge had been to speak to Georgiana of Wickham. Not in detail, of course. Giving his sister an account of their foe's role in bringing about his precipitate marriage was unthinkable. Under no circumstances would Darcy have distressed her with such revelations. Having to inform her of the blackguard's presence in the area had been bad enough. However gentle the delivery, there had been no mistaking her sadness and disappointment at learning that, because of Wickham, she ought not travel to Hertfordshire to attend the wedding.

Yet Darcy knew that there was a deeper cause for the dear girl's dismay: Georgiana had wished him to marry her best friend. She had never said it outright, of course – no girl her age, least of all one so shy, would have presumed to meddle in her older brother's affairs – but he had suspected for a while that both she and Miss Beatrice Endicott treasured hopes of that nature.

He had not encouraged them, but he had considered the possibility with great care and arrived at the conclusion that, in the fullness of time, he might oblige his sister, for Miss Endicott *was* a prudent choice. Although not especially well-dowered, she was well-connected. She was also mild-mannered, accomplished, and had a pleasing countenance. More to the point, the bond of friendship between her and Georgiana spoke highly in her favour. But Miss Beatrice was full young – just a year or so older than his sister – and, however much Georgiana might have hoped for the connection, Darcy could not bring himself to propose marriage to a girl barely out of the schoolroom. It seemed far more reasonable to let matters rest and revisit that option later, should Miss Endicott not form an attachment in the interim and receive a different offer.

But then Fate had intervened and placed him in the highly enviable position of being not merely allowed, but honour-bound to wed his heart's desire. Georgiana's silent consternation pained him, and he was uneasy about Miss Beatrice and her disappointed hopes, but it could not be helped. And it was comforting to know that Elizabeth and Georgiana were bound to grow close, once they came to spend time together. Georgiana would love her as a sister. As for Elizabeth, she was the embodiment of kindness and had all the patience in the world – even with that hoydenish pair, Lydia and Kitty – so she could not fail to appreciate Georgiana's good sense and gentle nature.

It was a pity that they would not meet before the year was out. Georgiana had requested his permission to remain in town with Mrs Annesley, her new companion, rather than travel to Pemberley later in the month with their cousin Richard for an escort, as Darcy had suggested. She had insisted that she would be perfectly content to spend Christmas with their Fitzwilliam relations at Lord and Lady Malvern's house in Grosvenor Square, allegedly to allow him and Elizabeth some tranquillity at the start of their marriage. Yet, as Darcy knew full well, there was more to it than that. First and foremost, Georgiana was seeking to escape the misery of recollections.

They had gone to Pemberley after the Ramsgate near-disaster, and the self-imposed seclusion had done more harm than good. It had afforded her too many opportunities for solitary reflection – too much time to blame herself for faults that had never been her own.

His efforts to assure her that the blame should be laid squarely at Wickham's door – and also at his, for entrusting her to the conniving Mrs Younge – had been for naught. Georgiana would not be persuaded. She had given all the right answers, but it had been plain to see that she had merely told him what he wished to hear. And nothing he had said or done had made any difference to her state of mind.

Darcy had eventually cajoled her into travelling to their house in town and, once in London, she had revived a little, thanks to Miss Endicott, and Bingley's cheering presence, and that of their Fitzwilliam cousins – only to become unbearably subdued as soon as they were left alone. Thus, it could not be denied that, instead of helping her to recover, his company had only served to fuel her mistaken belief that she had failed him. So, much to his distress, Darcy had been forced to own that she might fare better in his absence – which had been his sole reason for agreeing to travel into Hertfordshire and stay with Bingley for a while.

He had secretly hoped that Georgiana might be enticed to join them, but to no avail. She had rejected Bingley's invitation, thus demonstrating that her need for time alone – or, more to the point, for some time away from her brother – had outweighed any joy she might have hoped to find at Netherfield. So Darcy had complied, difficult as it had been to show his devotion in a way that suited *her*, not him. If he loved her – which he did, deeply and devotedly – he should allow her the freedom to make her own choices, and let her see that he trusted her judgement as to how she was to mend her broken heart.

Those arguments had lost nothing of their strength during their time apart. If Georgiana chose to remain in town in the company of trustworthy friends and relations who would raise her spirits and help her forget the wretchedness of Ramsgate, then so be it. She *should* seek her own sources of happiness, and richly deserved to find her peace at last.

Once he had assured his sister that he was in full agreement with her wish to spend Christmas in town, Darcy had endeavoured to do his duty by Bingley – the second awkward conversation of the day.

It could not possibly sit well with him to tell his friend that he was contemplating a happy union for himself, and then reveal his firm conviction that Bingley would not find the same in Hertfordshire. Because, in his opinion as a careful and cool-headed observer, Miss Bennet's heart had not been touched. Her manners were cheerful and engaging and she had received Bingley's attentions with pleasure, but also with the serenity of amiable indifference, and no sign of peculiar regard.

His heart on his sleeve as always, Bingley had made no secret of his dismay. He thought himself in love, and had imagined that Miss Bennet returned his sentiments. To Darcy's relief, his friend had naturally finished by heeding the voice of experience – yet Bingley's readiness to rely on him for guidance in all things, from the weighty to the trivial, could not fail to taint the relief with mild exasperation.

For goodness' sake, how long was he expected to play nursemaid? Of course, his friend had an undisputed claim to his affection. Bingley was the kindest man he knew – warm-hearted, sincere, and selfless to a fault – but his inherent goodness rendered him apt to think well of everyone around him, and endow them with all the good traits under the sun. In many ways, Bingley's generous candour matched Georgiana's, which was what had endeared him to Darcy in the first place. So of course he wished to guard his friend from errors with far-reaching consequences. But it was high time Bingley learnt to tread through life without assistance. High time to outgrow his propensity to leap from one boyish infatuation to the next, and conduct himself like a grown man.

With any luck, the latest disappointment would prove salutary, and nudge him onto the right path at last. Still, Darcy could not bring himself to conclude their conversation on that note, so he had opted for a more supportive manner – not that he expected his words to make a vast deal of difference. Words brought no healing, and precious little comfort. What Bingley needed now was time, and a more fortunate attachment.

Their adieus had been brief – too much had been said already. Thoughtful as ever, his friend had offered him the use of Netherfield, but in the same breath apologised for not returning with him to attend the wedding. Bingley had openly acknowledged that it was beyond him to encounter Miss Bennet at this point in time – and Darcy could only commend him for that decision. Without a doubt, it was the most sensible one.

Thankfully, the practical reasons for travelling to town had posed no difficulty. His attorney had been instructed to prepare the marriage settlement, and the efficient Mr Stratton had obliged. The licence had been procured as well – so, praise be, he could return to Hertfordshire.

And now he was on his way at last, travelling at full speed. Darcy consulted his watch, then returned it to his pocket. They were making good time. There was no reason why he should not reach Netherfield by three hours in the afternoon.

⚜

The shuttered building appeared into view over an hour later than envisaged. Once his carriage had quitted the main thoroughfares, Darcy's patience had been taxed by rutted roads showing evidence of heavy rainfall and rendering his progress maddeningly slow.

Even so, no sooner had the mud-splattered conveyance pulled up at the door than he requested that one of the mounts left in Bingley's stables be saddled and, leaving his valet and his footmen to nudge his friend's people into action, he rode towards Longbourn at a canter.

As he approached along the drive, light shining in several of the ground floor windows gave him to suspect that this might not be a good time. The Bennets were presumably keeping country hours, so they could very well be at dinner. But when he dismounted at the entrance, Darcy could hear the sound of a cheerful tune played on the pianoforte, along with a clear voice, singing. Elizabeth's voice. Unmistakably. An overwhelming sense of homecoming washed over him, and startled him with its intensity. He was still reeling from it as he walked forth to employ the knocker.

The maid who had brought the tea tray into Mr Bennet's study the other day answered the door and curtsied, then stepped aside with an uncommonly chatty, "Right this way, sir. Mr Bennet is just here, in the parlour, but the mistress is from home. She went to see her sister in Meryton, along with the young misses. Still, they'll be home before too long, I'd wager."

Darcy gave a brief nod of unconcern at the intelligence. He had not come to call upon Mrs Bennet.

The sense of homecoming returned in force when the maid opened the door into the parlour and revealed the most heart-warming picture: Elizabeth at the pianoforte, bathed in the soft glow of candlelight, a song on her lips and the old sparkle in her eyes.

His entrance brought an end to her performance, and a charming blush to her cheeks. Tearing his eyes from her was a challenge. Thus, several seconds passed before he remembered to bow, to say nothing of his tardiness in acknowledging Mr Bennet's surprised greeting.

The maid vanished, and Mr Bennet invited him to sit.

"Come, sir, make yourself comfortable. You find us quiet and content here, Mr Darcy. Jane has just gone to negotiate with our housekeeper as to what sort of cake we might have with our tea. In fact," he added as he left his chair by the fireplace, "I should send word for another cup. And perhaps something more substantial than cake should be contrived for you on a tray, in case you have journeyed on an empty stomach."

So he had, but that was immaterial.

"Pray do not trouble yourself, sir. I thank you, but there is no need," Darcy said, and belatedly noted that Mr Bennet was headed for the door, and not the bell-pull. So he must have considerately aimed to use the offer of sustenance as a convenient excuse to allow them a few moments' privacy.

Pressing his lips together, Darcy could have kicked himself for being so slow in gathering as much – and rather suspected that the older gentleman had some inkling of his thoughts, for there was a droll turn to his host's countenance as Mr Bennet sauntered back to the fireside with a quirk in his brow and a smooth, "As you wish."

Not in the least amused by the surmise that his future father-in-law found him so transparent, Darcy bent his steps towards a small sofa that would afford him an unimpeded view of the pianoforte, only to discover that Elizabeth decided to abandon the instrument and the lively performance. That was a pity. Yet his mild regret vanished without trace when she approached and chose to sit beside him.

"I am pleased to see you are feeling better," she said with a little smile that curved the corner of her lips but slightly, yet lent a warm glow to her gaze and rendered it utterly bewitching.

"Pardon?" Oh. The confounded cold. He had completely forgotten about it. "Yes, I am, I thank you."

"You returned much sooner than I thought possible," Elizabeth observed, and Darcy acknowledged the truth of that with a vague gesture.

"Everything that had to be done was done, and I had no wish to tarry. I would much rather be at hand and keep an eye on Wickham." And be with her. But he was not about to say that with her father in attendance.

His forbearance was ill-rewarded when Mr Bennet quipped, "You did not think me able to hold the fort in your absence? I am sorry to hear that. As you can see, I managed well enough."

Darcy suppressed a grimace and evenly replied, "I did not doubt it for one moment. Even so, I preferred to return as soon as may be."

The opening door saved him from yet another witticism and, rather glad of it, Darcy rose to greet Miss Bennet with a bow. The housekeeper followed bearing a cake dusted with sugar, and then the maid with the tea things, the last in the domestic procession.

She was not sent for a fourth cup. The girl had seen to that already. And when Elizabeth filled his and brought it to him, Darcy found some consolation for so doltishly missing the chance of a few private moments. The light brush of her fingertips beneath the saucer was preposterously stirring.

The next words that passed his lips — or at the very least, their timing — could only be called doltish too.

"Needless to say, I have the marriage licence. Nothing remains now but for you to choose the date."

"Oh? I… Very well," Elizabeth faltered, adorably nonplussed at the abrupt introduction of the topic, and the turn of her countenance went a long way towards reconciling Darcy with his *gaucherie*.

She resumed her seat and asked, "Do you have any preference?"

"No, none at all," he said — a necessary falsehood. The truthful answer was, *'Yes. Tomorrow, if that could be arranged,'* but by then Darcy had regained his senses, and a measure of control over his tongue.

"I daresay it need not be decided now," Mr Bennet intervened. "We should give it some thought, and also consult with the vicar."

Elizabeth's father was well within his rights to have the final say, and Darcy acknowledged that, albeit with no pleasure. There was nothing he could do at this juncture but bow his head with a bland, "Of course."

True to form, it was Elizabeth who graciously sought to rekindle the conversation, as soon as the cups of tea and the slices of cake were distributed, and the door closed behind the housekeeper and the maid.

"Did you come with a large party?" she asked.

"Oh, no. I came alone."

"Alone?" Her quiet exclamation denoted disappointment, so Darcy hastened to reassure her, lest she perceive it as a slight.

"My sister would have dearly liked to come. But it was not—" He was about to say *'not possible,'* yet at the last minute replaced it with, "It was not advisable."

He could not tell her of Georgiana's history with Wickham. Certainly not in the others' presence. In fact, he saw a great deal of merit in not informing her of that wretched episode at all. At least not until Elizabeth had become acquainted with his sister and had grown to understand her gentle and principled nature. It would not do to taint her views of Georgiana before they had even met. Much as disguise of any sort was his abhorrence, a half-truth was in order.

He frowned. He would have preferred to talk about plans for the future when they were alone. But then, it could be worse. At least they were in company with the decorous members of her family.

So Darcy shifted in his seat so that he could face her and endeavoured to speak almost as openly as he would have done in private – the necessary half-truth notwithstanding.

"I would much rather she travelled in greater safety than with just a footman, a coachman and her elderly companion. She would have had to return to town in this manner, and I find it unadvisable. Georgiana is to spend Christmas with my uncle and aunt's family in Grosvenor Square, whereas I was thinking that the pair of us might go to Pemberley after the wedding. That is, if you have no objections," he civilly added for form's sake for, truly, what cause would she have to object?

And Elizabeth did not, just as he had expected.

"Not at all. It is a pleasing prospect. But could your sister not have returned with Mr Bingley? Or is he aiming to stay in Hertfordshire for some time, once he arrives?"

"Bingley has no plans to come to Hertfordshire. He is to remain in town for the foreseeable future," Darcy replied, darting a glance across the room to the spot where Miss Bennet was sitting with her slice of sponge cake. Perfectly unruffled, she turned away to set her plate down and lowered her gaze as she brushed a crumb or something from her lap, patently more concerned about the state of her skirts than the present topic.

It would not do to pry, so Darcy looked away, content to be proven right in his advice to Bingley – not that he required further confirmation. Frankly, of the two, it was Elizabeth who seemed affected by the intelligence he had just imparted.

"Oh," she said, fresh disappointment evident in her voice and countenance. "I thought he would come and stand up with you as your groomsman."

"Sadly not. But it cannot be helped."

Elizabeth's brow furrowed.

"Have you…? Forgive me, but have you and Mr Bingley had any… disagreement?"

"No, nothing of the sort," he said swiftly, touched by her concern, now that he grasped that her troubled manner was on *his* account. "We are as close as ever, I assure you. My friend has various engagements in town, that is all."

Another half-truth, that, yet this time Darcy was not sorry for it. Bingley did have a life in town. It was the Hertfordshire interlude that was the aberration.

"I see," Elizabeth said. "Then if he means to be but little at Netherfield, he might as well give up the place entirely."

Darcy gave a gesture of agreement.

"I should not be surprised if he were to give it up, once presented with an eligible offer. In any case, I think it unlikely that he will come to stay for very long in future. He has many friends, and he is at a time of life when friends and engagements are continually increasing."

"Would you care for a fresh cup of tea, Mr Darcy?" Miss Bennet intervened. "Or perhaps another slice of cake?"

"I thank you, no," he said, glad of the interruption, as well as her lack of interest in the subject. He had not come all this way to speak of Bingley. Nor did he wish to dwell on his friend's disappointed hopes.

Elizabeth seemed to have lost all inclination to pursue that conversation too. She stood and asked her sister, "Will you come with me for a moment? I need your opinion on something."

Whatever that might be, Darcy could only hope it would not keep her out of the room for very long – and then Jane Bennet rose considerably in his estimation when she countered, as though she had guessed his thoughts:

"Oh, it can wait, Lizzy, can it not? I think it should. Besides, I was just about to ask if you would play the last piece again. I missed it when I went to speak with Mrs Hill, and I should dearly like to hear it."

Elizabeth cast her a hesitant look.

"Are you certain?"

"Oh, quite," Miss Bennet airily replied.

"I hope you will indulge us," Darcy added his own entreaty. "I heard some of it when I arrived, and it would be a privilege to hear the rest. You played that song so beautifully."

"Not very beautifully," Elizabeth demurred, "and not faithfully at all, I fear. Had you arrived a few moments sooner, you would have heard me fudge and slur my way through the difficult passages."

"That, I find very hard to believe," Darcy said with a warm smile. "Well-nigh impossible, in fact. In my experience, everything you do is done exceedingly well."

He could not regret speaking his mind, nor the uncommon impulse to make daring declarations in company, when he found his choice rewarded with a delightfully bashful laugh.

"I should not wish to disabuse you of that gratifying notion, but your gallant speech deserves my full honesty. Very well, you shall hear the entire piece, along with all my flaws in its execution, and I can only hope that you can bear the disappointment."

Darcy flashed a quick grin towards her as he set his cup down.

"'Tis poor sportsmanship to accept a challenge when I already know how it will end, but there we have it. May I turn the pages for you?"

"And deprive me of the only excuse I might supply for my faltering performance? By all means, if you wish," Elizabeth replied, but the glance she cast him told Darcy what he already knew: that she was jesting. So he did not hesitate to follow her to the pianoforte and take his place beside her on the padded seat.

It was a great relief to find her spirits rising to playfulness again, and see that, free from the dejection which had rendered her so painfully subdued a few days ago, she was once more disposed to tease him as she used to. But that relief was a tame and placid sentiment, easily subsumed into the heady mix that claimed him as they sat in deliciously tormenting proximity, and she began to play.

He could not care less whether or not there were flaws in her performance – and, in any case, Darcy noticed none. Her intoxicating closeness filled his senses, and he could scarce follow the notes' quick succession on the staves, so as to timely turn the pages. And Elizabeth played on, weaving pure enchantment with the fluid movements of her fingers; making him forget the others – her father, her sister – and feel as though she played for him, and him alone.

Chapter 12

Elizabeth had not resorted to a subterfuge when she had asked her sister to come away with her. Aye, she had tried to give Jane an excuse to leave the room after the distressing tidings of Mr Bingley's caprice and inconstancy, but Elizabeth had genuinely wished to garner Jane's opinion on a particular subject.

Once Jane had discreetly but insistently indicated that their private conversation should be deferred, Elizabeth had complied. Thus, her question was set aside until later, at bedtime, when she sought Jane out and asked, "Will you let me speak to Mr Darcy? He will be your brother ere long. And I think he should know that his best friend is well on his way to breaking his new sister's heart. I daresay he will be able to do something about it."

With a weary sigh, Jane set her brush down and dropped her hands into her lap.

"What will you have him do, Lizzy? Should Mr Bingley offer for me simply because he has to?"

"And why not? It seems to be the fashion."

Jane shook her head and gave a little tut.

"It pleases you to be flippant, but we both know that our circumstances are quite different. You heard what Papa said: Mr Darcy had spoken quite forcefully of his admiration and regard. Whereas Mr Bingley had never made any declarations of the kind – which, frankly, is my greatest comfort now. I have no broken promises to reproach him with. I was spared that pain, thank goodness!" Jane fervently exclaimed, then lowered her voice to add with calm deliberation. "'Tis infinitely better, and easier to bear, to know that it was nothing but an error of fancy on my part. My own vanity deceived me into taking his open, cheerful manner and his amiable nature and embroidering them into a false picture—"

"Not so!" Elizabeth disagreed. "We have all seen his attentions to you. His marked, unguarded attentions—"

"Lizzy, we must not expect a lively young man to be always so circumspect and guarded," Jane sensibly argued. "Women fancy admiration means more than it does."

"And men take care that they should," Elizabeth retorted, then gave a resentful huff and resumed with no little asperity, "The more I see of the world, the more I am dissatisfied with it. There is malice and lack of honour everywhere I turn. In fact, I believe—"

She stopped short, appalled by her own thoughtlessness. She had very nearly blurted out, *'I believe I am about to marry one of the few honourable men in existence.'* That might be true, but it would have been horribly callous of her to say so to Jane, today of all days.

Elizabeth flinched, only to dart a guilty glance towards her sister when Jane prompted, "Yes, Lizzy? What do you believe?"

"Nothing of consequence," she dissembled, lowering her gaze. "You know I speak without thinking when I am angry."

Jane's countenance grew very solemn.

"Pray do not pain me by imputing malice or lack of honour to Mr Bingley. Let us be fair," she urged, then concluded softly: "I do not blame him for my disappointment, Lizzy. Nor should you."

"What I do blame him for is his want of attention to your feelings. And for that he deserves the severest censure!" Elizabeth said with unbridled resentment. But the pained look in her sister's eyes brought her up short, and her declaration ended in a sigh as she reached to hold and press Jane's hand. "Forgive me," Elizabeth whispered. "I should not distress you with fruitless talk."

"You know me well," Jane murmured. "Aye, it *is* distressing to hear that he has sunk in your estimation – that you think him… what? Thoughtless? Careless? Callous?" Jane winced and bit her lip. "I would much rather you did not," she resumed, her voice low but by no means lacking in firmness. "I am not ashamed of having been mistaken. Or rather, the shame is slight, and the pain of disappointment is nothing in comparison to what I would feel, were I obliged to think ill of him. No, Lizzy, you must let him live in my memory as the most amiable man of my acquaintance. But that is all. The rest shall— The rest *must* be forgot."

"How?" Elizabeth mournfully whispered in her turn. "My marriage will throw you constantly together."

Twists of Fate

"Not constantly," Jane countered with the ghost of a smile. "I think I can trust you to give careful consideration to who should visit you and when. I fully expect we shall meet on occasion. I know it cannot be helped. And that gives me all the more reason to be glad that he is unaware of my feelings. How could I face him, Lizzy, if he knew?"

Elizabeth bit her lip and cringed at a different question: how was Jane to face him when Mr Bingley married and brought his wife to future gatherings at Pemberley?

She jumped when Jane gasped, as though her sister had just read her thoughts. But Jane had not – how could she? When her sister spoke, Elizabeth discovered that Jane had a more immediate cause for concern on her mind.

"Goodness, Lizzy! Mamma! We forgot about Mamma! I must speak with her – beg her to be guarded in what she says, lest she says too much. Oh, that was a stroke of luck, Mr Darcy taking his leave so soon after Mamma's return from our aunt Phillips'," Jane sighed with a faint measure of relief, then her brow furrowed. "But I must persuade her that henceforth she must be doubly careful. Perhaps the safest choice would be for her not to speak of Mr Bingley at all."

There was truth in that, Elizabeth inwardly acknowledged: it would be easier to persuade their imprudent mamma to avoid the subject altogether than teach her to approach it with caution. Also, Elizabeth was quite certain that luck had not come into it, and in fact Mr Darcy had quitted Longbourn precisely as a result of the commotion caused by her mother, Lydia and Kitty – with no help from Mary, naturally; however sanctimonious, Mary was generally quiet.

She found that, strictly speaking, she could not blame him for that choice – not after the peaceful time spent with just Papa and Jane. Elizabeth could only hope that he would eventually deem the others *tolerable* too.

"Let me come with you to seek Mamma," she offered and, squeezing her hand by way of thanks, Jane silently agreed.

They found Mrs Bennet at the top of the stairs.

"Ah, Lizzy! I was just coming up to speak with you. This way, come. Come into my chamber, we have much to discuss. You too, Jane. You always give good counsel. Now then, Hill and I have just had a good rummage through the pantry, the larder, the meat safe and the cellar to see what could be done about tomorrow's dinner. Mercy me, I did not imagine that Mr Darcy would return so soon!

103

The shock I had when I came home and found him in the parlour! All I could think of was the ox cheek! There was no time to rustle up anything better, not at half an hour's notice, and there I was, struck dumb, with this spinning in my head: how am I to ask *Mr Darcy* to sit down to ox cheek and dumplings? I thought I should faint dead away when your father invited him to stay for dinner, with nary a notion of consulting me beforehand! Praise be, Mr Darcy had the goodness to refuse. I expect he saw me blanch. Oh, girls, this is the mark of good breeding: a gentleman from the highest circles never puts his hostess on the spot! Well, there we are. With any luck, by tomorrow night I will have done better than ox cheek. Thank goodness, we still have a good supply of fine wines, port and brandy, cheeses, dates and candied pineapple, for I shall not spend another farthing at *Valpy's*. It will be inconvenient to send John further afield, but so be it. Never again shall that woman have my custom! Nor shall I waste my breath speaking of her and her confounded shop. Let us concern ourselves with things of significance. So, tomorrow's dinner: there will be a saddle of lamb, and partridges, and venison – is Mr Darcy fond of venison, Lizzy, do you know? And what sort of fish does he favour? Oh, no matter," she said with a wide flourish of her hand when Elizabeth could not oblige with an answer to either question. "We shan't be able to procure it for tomorrow anyway. John brought back some carp this morning. I hope Mr Darcy is not averse to carp, if it is properly dressed. Though goodness knows if Hill can prepare it to his satisfaction. I suppose he has two or three French cooks at least."

'Heavens, never mind his cooks!' Elizabeth thought with growing impatience. Yet, mindful as ever of what was owed one's parents, she checked her exasperation and evenly said, "You keep an excellent table, Mamma. No one can find fault with it, however many French cooks they might have. But pray let us set aside tomorrow's dinner for the moment. There is something that Jane and I think you should know."

∾๑ɢ ɢ๑∾

"He is *not* coming back? But is it certain? Absolutely certain?" Mrs Bennet spluttered.

"Yes, Mamma. Quite certain," Jane woodenly repeated and, to make things easier for her, Elizabeth saw fit to intervene.

"Mr Darcy said so, Mamma, and left no room for doubt."

"He did?" Mrs Bennet grimaced. "I wish I had been at home to hear it all myself. What did he say, exactly?"

Jane parted her lips to answer, but Elizabeth pressed her hand and patiently gave her mother the word-for-word account that Mrs Bennet had requested. Then, to spare Jane as best she could, she proceeded to carefully explain to their tender-hearted but eminently thoughtless parent why her sister dearly wished that Mrs Bennet did not speak of Mr Bingley to Mr Darcy.

"Speak of him?" their mother cried. "Who wants to speak of *him*, when we have a wedding to arrange? So, your father said that Mr Darcy had already obtained the licence. That was quick. So efficient! But then, I expected nothing less of him. Oh, Lizzy, what a treasure you have brought into the family!" she exclaimed, pinching Elizabeth's cheek. "You shall be married on Wednesday," Mrs Bennet declared, barely stopping to draw breath. "You know what they say: *'Monday for wealth, Tuesday for health, Wednesday is the best day of all.'* You must and you shall be married on the best day of all, and as soon as possible. This coming Wednesday, not the next. We must not let grass grow under our feet. First things first, we must find a moment with the vicar tomorrow, after the service, and fix the day. And then all the preparations. There is so much to be done, Lizzy, so much to be done! The wedding breakfast – Hill and I must speak about the wedding breakfast. And we must see to the wedding clothes, of course. There is no time to make you a new dress, but the one you wore at the ball the other day should do nicely. Hill will have it looking as good as new, and we shall add some blonde lace to the neckline and the sleeves. Take my word for it, you shall look a picture. Oh, how I wish we had the time to go and stay with my brother and make our purchases at the best warehouses in town! Still, there are a few good ones in St Albans. They will have to do. We shall go on Monday, and—"

"Mamma, what purpose will that serve?" Elizabeth spoke to stem the effervescent flow, as soon as she had recovered from the shock of her wedding being planned for as early as the coming Wednesday. "There will be no time to have new garments made. Not even if we were to wed next week, or the one after that – which, by the bye, would be a great deal more sensible."

"What, wait as long as that? Nonsense! We must strike while the iron is hot, I tell you. Besides, would you give all those evil tongues more time to wag? No, of course not!" she promptly answered her own rhetorical question. "You must be married as soon as may be. As for new garments, you are sure to find seamstresses in the North, and a good dressmaker and whatnot, so I shall send you with plenty of stock for the linen cupboard, and several dress-lengths, and fine fabrics for new spencers, and also for a pelisse or two. I will not have it said that Mr Darcy took you with nothing but the clothes on your back!"

As her mother's tirade continued with scarce any pauses for breath, Elizabeth could not but grow self-conscious and distressed for her sister. It felt profoundly wrong that Jane's troubles should be ignored on account of her own upcoming nuptials. Yet, as oftentimes before, Mrs Bennet was quick to remind her of the old adage: *'Be careful what you wish for.'* Her mother turned to Jane, stroked her cheek and spoke with the firmest conviction:

"And never you fear, dear girl, you shall have your turn. You are to move in the highest circles now, thank goodness, and with your beauty, you shall have your pick of Mr Darcy's friends. I should not be surprised if you were to have both wealth *and* a title. Would that not be grand? I do not doubt that your future brother is acquainted with many a titled gentleman, and one of them is bound to take a fancy to you. So do not repine, my sweet. Mark my words, this is a blessing in disguise. You shall do so much better than five thousand a year! That Mr Bingley, he thinks too highly of himself. How dare he spurn you! Well, I say good riddance. Who needs him now, when you can set your sights upon a baron, or a viscount, or even an earl's son?"

◈◈◈

Mrs Bennet might have been given to extraordinary flights of fancy, but she was also an eminently practical woman who knew full well on which side her bread was buttered. Not to mention that, material advantages aside, on the following morning Mr Darcy obliged her greatly – and endeared himself to her into the bargain – by not merely joining them at church for the Sunday service, but coming to Longbourn to escort them on foot, and walking arm in arm with Lizzy for everyone to see.

It was a pity that the vast majority of their detractors worshipped in Meryton. Still, Mrs Bennet had ample reasons for contentment.

Once the service had come to an end, they spoke with Mr Newell, the vicar, and the date of the wedding was set for the coming Wednesday, in perfect accordance with her wishes. Mr Darcy had readily supported her in that – another point in his favour. And then Mrs Bennet was thrilled to see her future son-in-law glaring most delightfully at Lady Lucas when the latter took hold of Charlotte's arm, patently seeking to prevent her from walking up to them. But, to her credit, Charlotte paid no heed and came to greet Lizzy with a warm embrace, so Mrs Bennet bestowed her best smile upon her daughter's loyal friend, then strode past Lady Lucas with so small a nod that the tall feather on her bonnet scarcely fluttered.

Several hours later, Mrs Bennet was pleased to find that dinner was a success. Mr Darcy ate little, but with gusto. He praised the venison – and well he might, for it was roasted to a turn – and acknowledged that the partridges were remarkably well done.

He did not speak much, but that did not surprise her. Mrs Bennet knew well enough by now that such was his way. She could only hope that, since he was not one for talking, he did not find it awkward that there was little conversation around the dinner table. For her own part, she did not venture to speak to him, unless it was in her power to offer him any attention, or mark her deference for his opinion. Lizzy, bless her, must have been dazed by the speed of change, for she was uncommonly quiet. So was Mary, but that was to be expected – she had been told in advance to refrain from pontificating. Lydia and Kitty had received their instructions too. Mr Bennet had told them both in no uncertain terms to be civil and speak sensibly, or else hold their tongues – and when either of them appeared to have forgotten about their father's injunction, Mrs Bennet was swift to remind them with a glower or a well-aimed prod under the table.

Thus, it was mostly her husband and dear Jane who sought to encourage conversation, and Mrs Bennet could not but beam at her spouse with delighted gratitude at finding him so willing to exert himself for once.

And then there was tea and coffee in the parlour, and the necessary forming of plans for the days ahead, at which point Mrs Bennet was distraught to find that she caused Mr Darcy some considerable disappointment with her proposed shopping expedition to St Albans.

But of course! He would not wish to be separated from his betrothed for the entire day. So she was quick to offer, "Would you like to join us, sir? Your company would be greatly appreciated."

Yet Mr Darcy seemed startled by the suggestion.

"I thank you, no," he promptly negatived. "I would be in the way. But pray allow me to offer you the use of my carriage, and my footmen for an escort."

The generous offer was accepted in a trice. And as she mused with great anticipation on the rewarding prospect, a fresh notion came to Mrs Bennet. It was so magnificent and so immensely gratifying that she would have kissed him, had she dared take such liberties with her future son-in-law.

⁓ﾟﾟⵊ

The following morning, the emblazoned carriage drew to a halt before *Valpy's* at Mrs Bennet's particular request. Remarkably well-trained and resplendent in their livery, the tall and handsome footmen were at the vehicle's doors in seconds, ready to assist them.

"We should all go in," Mrs Bennet declared, and although Elizabeth shook her head in mild reproof, her lips were twitching in an indulgent smile, and she silently obliged her.

Jane followed, as did the younger three, and, as though previously instructed – which, for all Elizabeth knew, they might have been – they ambled towards the entrance in their most dignified manner. One of the footmen hastened ahead to open the door for them and, linking arms with Elizabeth, Mrs Bennet stepped in. She cast a cursory glance around her, looking through the other patrons as though they were made of glass, and paused briefly to examine a bolt of sprigged muslin. She lifted a corner of the fabric and peered at it, only to let it drop with an audible, "Humph!" Then she released Elizabeth's arm and walked up to Mrs Valpy, who seemed unable to decide between sheepishness and boldness. But Mrs Bennet was not prepared to wait until the shopkeeper settled upon one or the other. Opening her reticule, she produced a folded note.

"Your dues, madam. Payable in full at Mr Garrett's bank." And then she spun round and headed for the door with a brisk, "Come along, girls, no more time to waste. We have a staggering amount of things to purchase."

Mr Darcy's impeccable footman held the door once more, then followed to assist his counterpart in handing them in.

A few minutes later, as the conveyance took to the road, Mrs Bennet rearranged her bonnet, her lips pursed into a moue of perfect smugness, then patted Elizabeth's knee and gleefully muttered, "It had to be done, Lizzy. It just *had* to be done."

⁓ॐ ॐ⁓

Shopping with her mother and younger sisters had always been a taxing experience for Elizabeth, but she did not find it so today. There was a certain bitter-sweetness in knowing that things would never be the same. Thus, she threw herself into the cheerful expedition with gusto. Her only challenge was to persuade her mother not to purchase all the lengths of fabric that Mrs Bennet deemed absolutely necessary.

They returned to Longbourn tired but content, to discover that Mr Darcy had left less than two hours earlier, having spent the day shooting with Mr Bennet, then discussing the marriage settlement.

The intelligence that the latter was extremely generous revived Mrs Bennet. She requested that the trunks be brought from the attic, and proceeded to superintend their filling with the new purchases, as well as with the rest of Elizabeth's belongings, which were to be sent to Pemberley by carrier, ahead of the soon-to-be-married couple.

It was a momentous task. For her part, Elizabeth would have put it off for as long as she could, expecting to find it deeply unsettling. Yet it was not so. Her mother's choice to turn it into a family affair blunted the painful edge of their imminent parting, and smothered the wistfulness under boisterous activity. The whole endeavour felt as though they were preparing for a journey to the Lakes.

They could not possibly finish in whatever was left of the day. But, with her energies replenished overnight, Mrs Bennet roused them early on the following morning and spurred them into action, so before breakfast all the trunks were packed, except the one which Elizabeth was to take with her on the journey to her married home. Then the waggoner was summoned, and an hour later, when Mr Darcy came to call, the ruddy-faced fellow and his lanky son had just finished loading the trunks onto the waggon and were covering them with a thick canvas to protect them from the weather, under Mrs Bennet's keen-eyed supervision and her second daughter's steady gaze.

Elizabeth curtsied as her betrothed dismounted and handed the reins to the stable lad. Once he had joined her onto the rounded porch, Mr Darcy did not bow over her hand, but wrapped his gloved fingers around hers and stood beside her in silence, as though he understood how poignant this moment was for her. And, in all likelihood, he did. Given what she had learnt of him over the last few days, Elizabeth had enough reason to believe that. So she squeezed his hand and glanced up towards him with a misty smile.

In the end, Mrs Bennet could not find another fault with the manner in which the trunks had been covered. She sent the waggoner on his way, with a general instruction to be careful. As the sturdy vehicle was set in motion, Elizabeth wrapped her arm around Mr Darcy's and walked with him into the house.

The morning had begun with spells of wintry sunshine, but soon grew windy and wet. Had the weather remained dry, Elizabeth might have given in to the temptation of going a-wandering one last time over the familiar countryside. She could not help thinking that, were she marrying for love, on this, the morning before their wedding, she would have found great if bittersweet delight in acquainting her beloved with her favourite places, which she was about to quit to follow him. But then, had this been a love-match at the end of a thrilling period of courtship full of promise and anticipation, her betrothed would have been well-acquainted with her favourite places already…

As matters stood, being seen wandering over the fields with Mr Darcy would have merely served to fan the repulsive gossip. The morrow's ceremony would quash it, naturally. But, for now, mitigation was still the order of the day, Elizabeth discovered with far less surprise than exasperation, soon after her belongings had commenced their journey towards Derbyshire. When Mr Darcy began to speak of a visit to the Meryton bookshop, she assumed that he was seeking to save himself from the bustle that reigned supreme in her mother's parlour. Yet, before long, she learnt that he was not to go alone. Nay, this was to be a family outing arranged on the previous day with her father – one over which Mr Bennet fully intended to preside.

Thus, the purpose of the foray into Meryton became clear to Elizabeth: it was meant as a public demonstration of parental sanction. No ride along deserted bridleways, this, but a parade along the main street. A blunt statement that there was nothing clandestine about her association with Mr Darcy, since her own father's presence on the outing counted as the seal of his approval.

They would travel in the carriage – the rain had decided the matter – and Jane and Mary would join them, but not the others. Lydia and Kitty were not in the least inclined, while Mrs Bennet welcomed the chance to recover from the recent flurry of activity and prepare herself for more of the same. Not just the forthcoming nuptials and the wedding breakfast – that very evening, there would be a dinner engagement at Mrs Phillips' house.

While she and her betrothed waited in the porch for the other three to join them, Elizabeth felt compelled to say, "I must thank you for your forbearance."

"In what respect?"

"My father's scheme," Elizabeth clarified, gesturing towards the carriage, "and tonight's dinner, for that matter. From what Miss Bingley had to say about your extensive library, I doubt that the Meryton bookshop holds much interest to you. And I expect you do not make a habit of dining with your apothecary, either in town or at Pemberley."

"I do not," Mr Darcy acknowledged. "But Mr Jones and his lady were commendably vocal in your defence, which entitles them to my gratitude and esteem. As for the scheme you mentioned, it was mine."

Brow furrowed, Elizabeth settled a puzzled look upon him.

"Yours?"

"Just so."

"But... we are to leave tomorrow. Why should you care what the townsfolk are thinking?"

"Their small minds and petty lives are of no interest to me," he shrugged, then lowered his voice as he added, "Yes, we are to leave all this behind on the morrow, thank goodness. But your relations are not going anywhere. And what happens here after our departure is not a matter of indifference to you."

"No, it is not," Elizabeth said softly and straightened her shoulders, her spirits buoyed by the discovery that warming up to her considerate betrothed was easy work indeed.

She brushed a stray lock from her temple and greeted another cheering thought with a warm smile: this chaotic se'nnight must have played havoc with her powers of perception, for there she was, squarely in the middle before she even knew she had begun.

Chapter 13

"Dearly beloved, we are gathered together here in the sight of God…"

The words had a solemn, yet gentle cadence, and Mr Newell's voice – the vicar who had known her ever since she was a little girl – might have had a soothing quality to it, if anything could soothe her now.

Elizabeth doubted it as she kept her eyes trained on the well-worn Book of Common Prayer that lay open in Mr Newell's hands. She swallowed hard at the next words he uttered – "…to join together this man and this woman in holy Matrimony…" – for the wording brought to mind thoughts that were very far from holy. Disconcerting thoughts born from her mother's teachings, imparted the previous night.

Until then, Elizabeth had fancied she had a fair understanding of the world and the generalities of married life. But a half-hour with her mother had been enough to disabuse her of that notion. The plethora of details made known to her on the eve of her wedding had made her see just how naïve and uninformed she was. Or had been, rather.

Elizabeth almost wished that her mamma had told her nothing at all. Or, better still, that she had gained that knowledge from her aunt Gardiner. Her mother had never had a way with words, and the previous night had been no exception. Something told Elizabeth that her dearest aunt would have addressed the matter with delicacy, and would have concluded with something more uplifting than the assurance that women grew to bear the demands of the married state quite cheerfully, once they became accustomed to them.

But Mrs Gardiner was not there to share words of wisdom. Two days prior, Elizabeth had learnt with no little sadness that her aunt and uncle Gardiner would not attend her wedding. Her uncle was from home, pursuing his affairs in Bristol, and her aunt could not find a way to leave the children and travel to Hertfordshire at such short notice.

Instead, Mrs Gardiner had conveyed her best wishes in a deeply affectionate letter that had warmed Elizabeth's heart. But as to the voice of experience, the only one that had made itself heard was Mrs Bennet's, leaving Elizabeth to wonder what was the salient point of her mother's summation: that one must learn to bear the demands of the married state – or that one grew to do so cheerfully?

She could not bring herself to request clarifications, mortified beyond endurance by the stark fact that the actors in the mental pictures conjured during the profoundly uncomfortable conversation were her *mother* and *father*.

Imagining the… scene – for want of a better word – played out between herself and Mr Darcy was no less discomfiting. In fact, it was the very opposite. Now she could not so much as look him in the eye without blushing scarlet.

Elizabeth drew an uneven breath and endeavoured to be thankful that her mother had left *that talk* to the very last minute, else she would have blushed and stammered and acted like a perfect ninny each time she had laid eyes on him since their betrothal. And there she was thinking that the last se'nnight had been excessively fraught already!

Not the previous evening, though. The dinner engagement at her aunt and uncle Phillips' house had surpassed her expectations. It had provided a most welcome contrast to the one and only time that Mr Darcy had dined at Longbourn, when she had been on pins and needles from the first minute to the last, lest she be mortified by tactless, crass or unmannerly remarks from the unguarded contingent of her family. But last night she had been able to set that concern aside. Her immediate relations had already given proof that they could avoid exposing themselves to ridicule and censure. Mrs Phillips had been too busily engaged with her duties as a host to be vulgar and intrusive. Mr Phillips had never caused unease. As for the others, they had brought nothing but pleasure.

Thus, it had been an agreeable evening spent with family and loyal friends – the same ones who had gathered this morning to attend the ceremony: Mr and Mrs Jones, of course; Mrs King and her daughter Mary; Mrs Long and her two nieces; Mr and Mrs Watson and their daughters. And dear Charlotte, who had defied her mother and accepted Mrs Phillips' invitation, then this morning had braved the muddy lanes on foot to be with her on her wedding day.

Mr Darcy had made precious little contribution to the conversation around Mr and Mrs Phillips' table, if any. But, before dinner was announced, he had spoken at some length with Mr Jones and his lady, Elizabeth's most stalwart champion, and then had crossed the room to join her and had walked with her from group to group while Elizabeth had endeavoured to spend some time with each one of her friends in turn.

In fact, with the exception of the brief separation of the sexes after dinner, Mr Darcy had remained at her side all evening – which, given his options, had not been overly surprising. However, during the musical diversions, as they had stood together arm in arm listening to Mary King's performance, Elizabeth had felt compelled to quietly observe, "We are among friends here. No one is disposed to pry or judge. So there is no need for you to lavish me with your attention throughout."

The light touch of his fingertips tracing a circle over the back of her hand had jolted her pulse into a delectably new rhythm, yet that was nothing to the flurry of bewildered butterflies that had burst into flight and risen all the way to her throat when Mr Darcy had leaned closer to whisper in her ear, his warm breath making her ringlets and her senses flutter, "Even so, I have no wish to do otherwise."

"Ahem…? Elizabeth…? Wilt thou?"

The vicar's discreet cough and gentle prompting had her darting her eyes towards him, her cheeks blazing more fiercely than ever. Good grief, how embarrassing! She had been standing here caught up in girlish daydreams, and had missed her first cue in the ceremony!

"I— I will," Elizabeth stammered, and from the pew behind her, where her mother was sitting, came a perfectly audible sigh of relief.

Elizabeth pressed her lips together, lest she disgrace herself further – this time with an immoderate chuckle – and looked down, endeavouring to conceal the ill-timed merriment. What had she been thinking, her poor, warm-hearted but wildly nonsensical mamma? That she had changed her mind and would cry off right here, at the altar? Heavens, the very notion! No one but her mother would imagine *that*.

The thought was utterly preposterous, but Elizabeth struggled to bring herself to order – for, if it would not do to chuckle, it most certainly would not do to snort, shake her head or give some other sign of incredulous amusement.

She was reawakened to the solemnity of the occasion when Mr Newell asked, "Who giveth this woman to be married to this man?" and, in time-honoured fashion, her father granted his ultimate, formal consent to the union with a tenderly spoken, "I do." Then Mr Newell placed her right hand in Mr Darcy's, and Elizabeth resolved to keep her thoughts from wandering, for she *would* be sorry to walk away with but the scantest recollection of the pair of them exchanging their vows. There would be other times for butterflies and daydreams.

Yet, for such whimsical and ephemeral forms, the butterflies were remarkably strong-willed. She could not command them. Nor could she possibly ignore them when Mr Darcy began to repeat after the old vicar, his resonant voice sending their flutter into an absolute frenzy.

"I, Fitzwilliam, take thee, Elizabeth, to my wedded wife, to have and to hold from this day forward, for better for worse, for richer for poorer, in sickness and in health, to love and to cherish, till death us do part, according to God's holy ordinance. And thereto I plight thee my troth."

Her gaze locked with his, Elizabeth wisely chose to abandon the losing battle, savour the moment and concede that, in truth, the butterflies did not detract from it. All she could hope now, when her turn had come, was that they would oblige and let her speak without faltering.

And, most commendably, they did.

⌾⌾ ⌾⌾

"Lord, how dismal!" Lydia's plaintive cry could be heard when the wedding party was reunited after the signing of the register. "I declare that the church would not be half so cold if it were not so empty," she grumbled, briskly rubbing her arms, then cast a glance around her. "What a queer little gathering we make! I shan't speak for Lizzy, but I shall be miserable if I do not wed during an ordinary service, when all my friends can see me."

Elizabeth grimaced. It was to be expected that Lydia's unguarded nature would prevail and give rise to some thoughtless, impertinent or foolish remark.

She looked away, opting for selective deafness, only to read in her father's countenance that he was not minded to be as forbearing.

Her dear papa made to speak, but her new husband was there before him:

"Thankfully, all your sister's friends are here today. As for the rest of your acquaintances, I would urge caution. If they have turned against her, chances are that you cannot trust them either."

"Precisely! There, Lydia, you had much better listen to your brother," Mrs Bennet seconded him with vigour, then moved away to urge the guests towards the house and warmly insist that Mr Newell join them, leaving Lydia wide-eyed with indignation at finding that her own mother, who had heretofore supported her in everything, had just sided with Mr Darcy against her – publicly, too – and expected her, moreover, to heed him as one would an older brother.

To Elizabeth, the prospect of Lydia ever doing so was as unlikely as it was diverting.

By the time they had covered the short distance between the church and the house, the mischievous amusement had given way to milder feelings, but the good cheer remained. And, as the morning wore on, good cheer still gilded Elizabeth's last few hours in her childhood home, although bittersweet wistfulness came to alloy it, which could not be helped.

Several other sentiments claimed their share too. Surprise, for one, at Mr Darcy repeatedly calling her by her Christian name. Not in everyone's hearing, of course, but whenever he spoke privately to her. The appellation could not fail to jolt her into a strange state of heightened awareness every time she heard it coming from his lips. Coming effortlessly, it seemed, and casually, too. As though it were natural. And perhaps it was. *'Mrs Darcy'* felt decidedly unnatural. Some of those present had already addressed her thus – Mary King, both of Mrs Long's nieces, the Miss Watsons and their father – and each time she had barely suppressed a start. She was rather glad that Mr Darcy had chosen not to follow suit. However strange it was to hear him calling her *'Elizabeth,'* at least it did not make her feel that she had just lost herself into a new name – a new life – a new state of being. Even so, she could not but wonder at the ease with which he had exchanged the requisite *'Miss Bennet'* for *'Elizabeth,'* and was compelled to inwardly own that she would not accustom herself quite so swiftly to calling him *'Fitzwilliam.'*

And this was not the greatest change to which she was to grow accustomed.

That thought had been with her all morning, burning at the forefront of her mind. But the original unease – not panic; it had never brought panic – had subtly given way to something akin to smouldering anticipation, ever since the ungovernable butterflies had become her friends. They resurfaced time and again after the return from the church – in fact, she doubted that they stilled themselves completely even for one moment – and flew into the same frenzied flutter at the slightest provocation. Whenever their fingers brushed, for instance, which happened often. And whenever she felt his hand in the small of her back – that happened often, too. And whenever he bent his head and lowered his voice to a rumbling timbre to quietly speak with her. And whenever she saw him cast surreptitious glances at the clock on the mantelpiece.

Once she had noticed him dart the ninth such glance, Elizabeth found that she was not of a mind to wait and count to a round number. She set her cup of coffee down and closed the small distance between them to ask, "When should we leave?"

A warm smile curled up a corner of his lips as he thoughtfully replied, "Whenever you wish," as though he had not kept a close watch on the arms of the old-fashioned clock for upwards of an hour.

The butterflies turned a concerted somersault when he wrapped his hand around hers and ran his thumb along her forefinger.

'*Where are we to spend the night?*' Elizabeth very nearly blurted out, yet checked herself and timely chose a different wording.

"How far are we to go?" she asked instead.

"Not far. Just under thirty miles. A very easy distance." And then he answered her unspoken question, as if he had read it in her eyes in the long, charged moment when he had seemed to search them. "I have commissioned my people to make arrangements at the *Swan* in Bedford. Do you know the place?"

Elizabeth shook her head.

"No, not at all. I did travel through Bedford with my uncle and aunt Gardiner a few years back, but we only stopped to bait the horses at a small inn on the way to Goldington."

"The *Swan* is just beyond the bridge. You might have driven past it. I know it well. Georgiana and I have broken our journey there on occasion. 'Tis happily situated on the riverbank, in a rather picturesque location. I ventured to hope you might like it."

The warmth that had crept into her cheeks a little while ago gave no sign of subsiding, but Elizabeth refused to let it distract her.

"I believe I shall," she said softly. "It seems a lovely place, from your description." And then there was the silent intimation that a fair amount of thought had gone into choosing it, which was very pleasing too. So she resumed brightly, "Let me find Sarah to assist me. She will notify your people. I daresay we should be ready to depart within the hour."

Elizabeth might have found it at the very least unnerving to consider that, with those words, she had just set the final limit to her time in her father's house. But she did not dwell on it. And nervous reluctance could not be further from her mind as his thumb traced its way back along her finger and he whispered, "Very well."

♦♦♦

Sarah was quick to see to the appointed tasks. She hastened to the servants' hall to convey the message to Mr Darcy's people, then followed Elizabeth upstairs to help her change into her travelling apparel. Jane must have caught the signs of imminent departure, however discreet, for she soon joined them too, and the obliging maid and Elizabeth's dearest sister tenderly proceeded to aid her in preparing to set off into her married life.

There was very little to be done: the dress was fastened; the shawl placed about her shoulders; the odd disarrayed curls pinned back into place; the wedding finery packed into the trunk along with the last remaining items; the trunk closed and secured.

"I'll go and get John to take it to the carriage, shall I?" Sarah offered.

"Yes, pray do. Then take some time for your own preparations," Elizabeth said, for Sarah was to come with her as her personal maid – her lady's maid, for all intents and purposes. It had been her papa's suggestion, so that she would have at least one familiar face in her new home.

"Much appreciated, ma'am, but I packed my box last night. I only need to fetch it and bid my farewells," Sarah beamed, then bobbed a swift curtsy and was gone, patently unable to conquer her excitement at the advancement to a prestigious position, or the chance to travel further than she had imagined, or very likely both.

No sooner were they left alone than the sisters embraced, each striving to stem her tears to spare the other's feelings.

"Travel safely, Lizzy. And write often," Jane whispered, and Elizabeth nodded as she lost the battle against tears.

"I shall. Oh, Jane, I wish…!"

"I know, dearest. I know…"

Elizabeth fell silent and pressed her lips to her sister's cheek. Aye, in all likelihood, Jane did know precisely what she was thinking. That she wished Pemberley were not upwards of a hundred and fifty miles away. And that they were not about to be separated at the very time when Jane needed her the most. Throughout the day – in fact, for several days together – Jane had bravely put on an air of good cheer, not wishing to detract one jot from the celebration of her dearest sister's nuptials. Even now, she persisted in her effort, so that her own disappointed hopes would not overshadow Elizabeth's special day.

"All will be well here, Lizzy, just wait and see," she valiantly claimed. "Above all, pray do not fret on my account. You must see it my way: your happiness and our family's peace is enough for me—"

"That is because you are truly angelic," Elizabeth countered, but Jane shook her head.

"Not so, dearest. Fear not, though, I *shall* endeavour to be wiser. And not so easily misled by my own wishes."

Elizabeth's brow furrowed as she bit back another protest. She would have wanted to say that Jane's heartbreak could not be imputed to lack of wisdom, but to Mr Bingley's inconstancy, and that her beloved sister deserved a great deal more than to nurture fond thoughts of him and derive her joys from their relations' contentment. Jane deserved the deepest love, and a family of her own. Yet she said nothing, lest she distress her sister with remarks that could only be injurious in their futility, however well-meant. She merely held her, until a knock at the door disrupted their privacy.

"Come," Elizabeth called, and stepped back, releasing Jane from her embrace and clasping her hand instead.

It was John, come to collect her trunk. The young man walked in and picked it up.

"Is that it, ma'am? Nothing else, is there?"

"No. Nothing else," Elizabeth confirmed, with one last glance around her.

The room seemed conspicuously bare, now that it was not to be her bedchamber any longer. But Elizabeth raised her chin and refused to be maudlin. She exchanged a brief smile with her sister and, still holding hands, they silently walked out.

They had barely reached the first landing when Jane gasped, "Goodness, I quite forgot! Give me a moment, Lizzy. I shall return directly." And with that, she turned on her heel and darted back upstairs.

Mildly intrigued, Elizabeth followed her sister with her gaze, yet continued on her way, once she espied her father keeping watch in the entrance hall. A film of tears blurred her vision, but she blinked them back. This adieu should not be maudlin either.

"I just saw your young man walking out to speak to his people, so there we have it. Time to go, I expect," her father observed as she descended the last flight of stairs.

She nodded and walked into his embrace. Her father pressed his lips to her upturned brow, then murmured in a suspiciously thick voice, "Then go, my dearest girl, and be happy."

"Thank you, Papa. For everything," Elizabeth whispered and, tightening her hold around his waist, she rested her cheek on his lapel, dangerously close to losing the battle against tears once again.

Yet, when their tide was stemmed all of a sudden, Elizabeth could not be glad of the interruption that had just dispelled the bittersweet tenderness of the moment. She cringed when her mother's words reached her from the drawing room, seemingly in response to some subdued remark, which she had not heard. But, unlike everyone else, her mother was loud – mortifyingly so – and her voice carried:

"Aye, to be sure, and I shall savour it! This was on my mind only yesterday, when we were about to join you at my sister's house. I can think of no greater joy than to see them humbling themselves and contriving to regain my favour, once they learn how far above them we have risen. Oh, I shall be gracious and receive them with more civility than they deserve, but they shall not be suffered to forget who is the victor. Oh, aye, each time they lay eyes on me, they shall know I bested them. None of their daughters can boast of such a catch, nor do those simpering misses have the slightest hope of marrying so well. Triumph is sweet indeed, my dear, and so is revenge! Sweeter than this wine. So let us raise another glass to my Lizzy's good fortune."

Frowning, Elizabeth drew back from her father's arms, finding modest consolation in the intelligence he had imparted a few moments earlier: namely, that Mr Darcy was outside making arrangements for departure, and not in the drawing room listening to her mother's raptures, now that sweet wine and thoughts of sweet revenge had put paid to Mrs Bennet's efforts to be on her best behaviour.

But then the sound of hurried footsteps on the stairs did away with such reflections, and Elizabeth spun round to greet her sister's return.

"What have you forgotten?" she asked, but Jane's sole reply was an eager, "Come, Lizzy. Come with me."

"Where to?"

"The still room."

"Why?"

"You shall see."

Elizabeth pressed her father's arm to silently excuse herself, only to be met with a faint shrug and a rueful mutter:

"Yes, yes, go. Run along, the pair of you," – more or less the same words with which he had acknowledged their closeness and granted permission for all manner of girlish pursuits on many an occasion, and it was deeply moving to hear him do so now, for one last time.

Elizabeth could not but find her sister's thoughtfulness deeply moving too, when Jane's purpose was made known to her. Once they had gained the still room and the door was closed behind them, Jane loosened the strings of the small velvet pouch she was carrying and produced a silver cylinder decorated with a delicate pattern of leaves, tendrils and flowers. She pressed a tiny ball, and the lid sprang open to reveal a cut-glass bottle.

"'Tis a scent bottle for your reticule," Jane explained, although by then the clarification was unnecessary. "I saw it in Mr Rosen's shop and thought you might like it. I distilled a fresh batch of your favourite scent too, but in all this excitement I almost let you go without it," Jane added with a self-deprecating laugh, and went on to remedy that oversight at once.

She removed the faceted receptacle housed in the cylinder, unstoppered it and carefully filled it from a dark brown bottle retrieved from one of the shelves, while Elizabeth silently watched her at work, comforted by the familiar scent that now filled the air, and no less by the familiar proceedings.

The still room had long been their private domain, hers and Jane's, and they had gladly taken on the task of mixing floral-scented preparations for everyone in the household. Who would assist Jane with those tasks from now on?

That was another maudlin thought, so Elizabeth sought to silence it as she kept her eyes on her sister's handiwork. Jane set the brown bottle down and sealed it, trapping the scent within, then did likewise with the other, returned it to its silver case, and the case to its pouch.

"There, Lizzy," she said softly. "For good luck."

"Thank you. I shall carry it with me always," Elizabeth promised, tears blurring her vision as she placed the exquisite gift into her reticule.

"Oh, you need not do *that*," Jane tenderly protested, pressing her arm. "But it might be of use on your journey. And… tonight."

"I… I expect it might," Elizabeth faltered, darting her eyes upwards to meet her sister's glance, and both of them blushed.

Jane stroked her shoulder and asked in a timid whisper:

"Are you nervous?"

"A little," Elizabeth shrugged, then gave a conscious laugh and answered truthfully. "More than a little, to be honest, but… I believe all will be well."

"Yes," Jane said – a quiet declaration, yet uncommonly firm – only to resume in the same breath. "You are leaving with a good man, Lizzy. We must remember that. 'Tis my only— 'Tis my greatest comfort," she amended. "You married a good man, and he will treat you well."

Elizabeth nodded, a warm smile on her lips.

"I think so, too," she murmured. "He *is* a good man, and I am quite fortunate. We all are. 'Tis a happy conclusion to our troubles – much more so than I could have possibly imagined when I stormed out of the house a se'nnight ago. Goodness," she chuckled softly, brought up short by the notion. "It *was* but a se'nnight ago. How extraordinary…"

Yet Jane did not join her in marvelling at the incredibly short time in which such great changes had been wrought. Eyes narrowed into a dark look of resentment that was exceedingly unlike her, she spoke in low, hard tones:

"If there is any justice in the world, that base creature will pay! I hope his revered patroness makes his life a misery if she ever hears of his role in the affair."

Jane knew everything, of course – she knew every detail of the wretched business. Her dearest sister had always been her confidante, her fount of wisdom and prime source of consolation. Now the sheer vindictiveness of Jane's harsh whisper was starkly out of character as well, yet Elizabeth knew without being told that nothing but sisterly affection could have prompted Jane to depart from her forgiving ways. And although established patterns were highly reassuring, sometimes there was comfort in deviations, too.

"That would be a gratifying form of poetic justice, would it not? Even so, in your heart of hearts you will be glad to hear that I refuse to be the architect of his misfortune. Not even if I could bring myself to speak of his objectionable conduct – which I cannot. Heavens, Jane, can you imagine the mortification?" Elizabeth exclaimed and shuddered, then gave a flourish of her hand. "Nay, I am prepared to wager that he will reap what he has sown, one way or another. For one thing, he had not bargained for this outcome any more than I, and if he should rue the day, he only has himself to blame. None of this would have happened, were it not for his brazen presumption. A simple *'No'* should have been enough for any man! He should have taken it with as much grace as he could muster, and left me be..." She flinched, then drew a sharp intake of breath. "But no more of that sickening business! I cannot bear to dwell on it for one moment longer!" she declared with fierce determination, even as her countenance crumpled at the loathsome recollection of Mr Collins' hands on her, and those terrifying moments when it had seemed that she could not fend him off – until she had been blessed with the strength of desperation and had broken free from his vile, demeaning grip.

'The first blessing of many,' Elizabeth told herself as she took another calming breath – a slow and very deep one this time, then another. That was what she must do: count her blessings, each and every one of them. And, in time, the repulsive memories would fade.

Uniformly counted as one of her greatest blessings ever since Elizabeth had gained the capacity to think, Jane put her arms around her and gathered her close.

"Forgive me, Lizzy," she tearfully whispered. "What a fool I was to bring this up!"

"You did not. *I* did. *I* spoke of storming out of the house," Elizabeth murmured by way of reassurance as she nestled into Jane's embrace and returned it with equal warmth.

"Even so, I should have known better—"

"Hush, dearest. Hush," Elizabeth said softly to stem Jane's needless self-recriminations, and they remained thus for a long, tender moment – bittersweet, yet healing – deriving great comfort from each other, just as they always had.

And both of them found a measure of rueful amusement in the fact that this, their last special moment, was brought to an abrupt end in the same fashion as many before it: the door burst open and their mother cried, "Lizzy, Jane, there you are! I have been looking everywhere for you!"

జుుం ౨ు

Soon after Elizabeth's withdrawal to ready herself for departure, Mrs Bennet's loud voice and moreover the nature of her effusions reaching him from across the hall had given Darcy ample reason to quit the dining room, and then the house. Yet, to his growing irritation, a fair while later he could still catch more of her gloating than he would have wished, even from outside. Her triumph over the gossipmongers. Her kin's elevation in the world. Sweet revenge. What a catch he was, and that the simpering local misses had not the slightest hope of marrying so well.

With a grimace, Darcy privately acknowledged that he had expected nothing better from her. If anything, it was a wonder that she had not launched into that sort of vulgar boasting sooner, and he found her all the more contemptible for holding back and feigning good behaviour until now, when the deed was done and the catch was netted.

Not for the first time, he marvelled at Elizabeth growing up with such a mother, yet becoming the flawless creature that she was. Doubtlessly, much was owed to Mr Bennet, who must have devoted himself to his eldest daughters' upbringing. A pity that he had lost the will or the energy to do the same for the rest of his brood. As for curbing his wife's excesses – the least said, the better.

Mrs Bennet must have found herself another willing listener, or perhaps a fresh victim, for Darcy could hear her recommencing her reprehensible performance *da capo*. He frowned. If he could hear her, then so could his people. It was to be deplored that they should be party to their new mistress's mother making such an exhibition of herself. If the confounded woman was to visit them at Pemberley or, worse still, in Berkeley Square, she would *have* to acquire a smattering of manners – or at least learn to hold her tongue, lest she shame both Elizabeth and him before his relations and everyone of his acquaintance.

But that concern was for another day, Darcy resolved, and went on to distract himself – and likewise his people – with final instructions for departure. The second footman, Peter, was told that he would begin by riding postilion. Weston was asked to countenance travelling at the back of the coach with Simon, the third footman, so as to leave the seat beside the coachman to Elizabeth's maid. Then, at the first inn on the Luton turnpike, his valet was to hire a post chaise for himself and the girl – an extravagance perhaps, but fully warranted. No price was too high for privacy. Not today.

That one thought instantly did away with Darcy's irritation and put Mrs Bennet from his mind. Because, at long last, he and Elizabeth *would* have their privacy. Very soon, they would be on their way.

"Pardon? No, I have no further instructions. You may go and attend them, of course," he said, once Peter and Joseph had brought him from the clouds with their attempt to excuse themselves and see to the trunk that the Longbourn footman had just brought. Hard on the fellow's heels came the new girl, Elizabeth's maid, with her own modest box.

The trunk was Elizabeth's, Darcy discovered, having noticed the initials on the lid. A smile tugged at the corner of his lips at the thought that they were obsolete. E. B. They would have to be amended.

He drew a lungful of the bracing air, yet that did little to temper his impatience. Even so, he forbore to ask the maid – what was her name, Sarah? – how soon Elizabeth was likely to come down. He would not rush her. She should take all the time she needed to bid farewell to her relations and friends, and likewise to her girlhood and her former home.

For his part, he would make his adieus when the wedding party came to see them off. However juvenile, his current state of feverish anticipation was too delectable to be relinquished in favour of more time with Mrs Bennet. So he bent his steps along the paved walk that rounded the house, thinking in passing that the loud matron had presumably chosen to restore her strength by partaking of refreshments or had simply taken her gloating to a more distant room, for – mercifully – her grating tones could no longer reach him.

Thus, Darcy was allowed the questionable luxury of uninterrupted musings that could only serve to fuel his impatience. Such as the fact that they would reach Bedford in a matter of hours, five or so, maybe less – the first stage on the carefully planned journey that would take them home to Pemberley. A leisurely journey. No need whatsoever to make haste. In fact, if Elizabeth was in agreement, they could begin by spending a few days in Bedford. The elegant apartments at the *Swan* should be in readiness by now, just as he had instructed. They had already been bespoken, and his butler was to stop there briefly on the way north, to ensure that everything was in order. Thomas, the first footman, was to accompany Mr Howard from town, then remain in Bedford to take charge of the entire operation after the latter's departure, and supervise the transport of whatever accoutrements the butler and the housekeeper had deemed necessary. Mrs Blake had even mentioned the household linen. But Darcy had not involved himself in such details. Instead, he had left her and Mr Howard to it. With any luck, they would not see fit to include the family silver.

A boyish grin fluttered on his lips at the last notion, but in truth their solicitude was touching. No efforts spared for a good start. It was as though they had guessed his thoughts and wishes.

And then his thoughts and wishes leapt wildly to the night ahead as he rounded the corner and squinted in the wintry sunlight slanting through the bare trees – for the sun was conspicuously low; already lower than the treetops. Not many hours left till nightfall.

Hands clasped behind his back, Darcy drew to a halt beside a bushy evergreen and gave free rein to unruly thoughts, unwise as it might have been to court outright indiscipline. After all, he would still have to make it through some six or seven hours more, until his red-hot imaginings would be fulfilled.

Even so, he willingly indulged them – and when the soft murmur of a disembodied voice reached him, he was disposed to think it yet another flight of fancy born from overwrought impatience, for the voice seemed to be Elizabeth's.

Darcy blinked and looked up, then gave a silent chuckle once he had taken stock of his surroundings. No, he had not lost his grasp on reason. The murmur seemed to come through the small open casement above the overgrown shrub that blocked his path. So Elizabeth must have been in there, somewhere, speaking with goodness knows who. He did not seek to ascertain what it was that she was saying, or to whom. He had no desire to eavesdrop. Yet as he turned on his heel to leave, her voice rose sharply and came loud and clear:

"Heavens, Jane, can you imagine the mortification? Nay, I am prepared to wager that he will reap what he has sown, one way or another. For one thing, he had not bargained for this outcome any more than I, and if he should rue the day, he only has himself to blame. None of this would have happened, were it not for his brazen presumption. A simple 'No' should have been enough for any man! He should have taken it with as much grace as he could muster, and left me be… But no more of that sickening business! I cannot bear to dwell on it for one moment longer!"

In the wake of the thunderbolt, silence fell. Heavy, icy silence. Then other murmurs, inaudible. Then the sound of a door thrown open, and a shrill, "Lizzy, Jane, there you are! I have been looking everywhere for you!" – the first salvo in the pandemonium that Mrs Bennet had such a knack for creating.

Yet this time it went unheeded, devoid of all power to vex him.

For it was nothing to the pandemonium in his head.

Chapter 14

"Take your seat next to Joseph. The maid is to travel within," Darcy brusquely told his valet when Weston made to perch himself at the back of the coach, in keeping with the original instructions.

They had to be discarded, now that everything had changed. Privacy was the last thing he wished for once the shock had given way to anger – livid anger that was not abating. Quite the opposite. He was so incensed that he could scarce speak. Thus, he had nothing but terse thanks and mechanical bows for the small crowd gathered at the entrance for the final scene in the wedding-day charade, while Mrs Bennet's voice rang above the cacophony of empty felicitations as she harassed her footman with directions about warming bricks and the hamper for the journey.

Eventually, they took their seats in the carriage, the doors were closed, and Darcy ordered his coachman to drive on.

No sooner had the vehicle passed through the gate than he abandoned himself to the raging pandemonium. So, she blamed *him* for their predicament and their rushed union – the utter disaster that it was? Of all the evil and the malice she had met with, she had singled *him* out as the one to blame? His brazen presumption! *Presumption*, was it? His fury mounted. He could not bring himself to take 'No' for an answer – could not leave her to fend for herself, alone and injured in the rain – and she saw it as presumption! Called the whole affair a sickening business!

Darcy glowered at the passing landscape. The wretched business *was* sickening indeed. She— She was no better than *her mother!* Concealment and artifice throughout! *Why* had she not dealt honestly with him – told him that she resented this outcome? Another solution would have been found. Something. Anything.

Anything but this!

He tightened his hand into a fist. He had given everything – had sacrificed his duty to his lineage – married beneath him – *and for what?* To find himself saddled with a reluctant bride and a host of reprehensible connections!

And he had thought her *glad* to join her fate with his! Not merely grateful to be rescued from the scandal, but glad to follow him. As drawn to him as he was to her. Fool that he was, he had gone so far as to believe he had read the telltale signs of affection and physical attraction in her eyes, in her teasing, in her blushes! He had deceived himself throughout the course of their acquaintance, and all the more wilfully since the day of their betrothal, like the veriest clod. Like a callow youth with no understanding of the world. Like Bingley!

Good grief! To think that he had secretly looked down on Bingley for falling prey to self-deception – and then had gone and done the same! Illusions of affection and attraction conjured up from nothing – worse than nothing. That speech of hers had overflowed with resentment at being trapped into an unwanted union. That she should resent *him* for it was an absolute outrage, and his indignation swelled, but could not prevail. He was too angry with himself to dwell on anything but this: she resented him – yet in seven days he had caught no warning signs whatever! So much for his pride in his good judgement and his powers of perception.

How could he have been so blind?

The question was foolish too, and moreover pointless, for he already knew the answer: he had allowed lust to blind him. The oldest mistake known to man, and the most contemptible to boot. Not one he had ever imagined making. Yet there he was: shamed by his own folly – trapped by it, too – and powerless.

It was an alien and explosive combination.

Darcy pressed his eyes shut, struggling for composure, or at least the semblance of it. He *would not* make a spectacle of himself before a servant, which was the reason he had wanted the maid there in the first place: as an added incentive to keep himself in check, and an excuse for silence or bland, brief exchanges, until he had had the chance to bring himself to order and decide what was to be done.

At that thought, the foreign sense of powerlessness choked him yet again. What *was* there for him to decide? It was too late now. *Too late!* Matrimony was a life sentence. She should have spoken while they still had their freedom. What the *deuce* had she been thinking?

He dearly wished to ask her that, and the grain of common sense that he could still command told him to be glad of the maid's presence, which precluded quite so much forthrightness at this point in time. Of course, they would have to speak without reserve, eventually. The boil had to be lanced, repulsive as that prospect was. But not while they were caged together in a carriage bound on a lengthy journey!

Caged together! Lord almighty! They *were* caged together for life! And all he wanted was to vanish and lick his wounds in private. But he could not order Joseph to make an about-turn and head back to Longbourn to leave her in her father's house. That would have heaped the greatest amount of fuel on the gossip he had aimed to quell. He could not shorten this nightmarish journey to half a day and travel to Berkeley Square instead. He *would not* take his humiliation to his family and his acquaintances in town – worse still, to Georgiana, who already had severe misgivings about the change in their lives. He could not hide away for a while – somewhere; *anywhere* – and send his wife to Pemberley with his servants for an escort. If nothing else, he was responsible for her safety. As matters stood, there was but one option he could think of: bringing the speediest end to this ghastly journey and reaching Pemberley as soon as might be.

And then what?

For goodness' sake, *what* was he to do next?

No answer came. Just the continuous, mocking rattle of the coach as the vehicle carried them inexorably forward.

A movement caught from the corner of his eye had him darting an involuntary glance towards her. She was producing something from her reticule, a silver receptacle of sorts, and Darcy's lips tightened. What now? Was he to be treated to another hidden resemblance to her mother, and discover that she made a habit of reviving herself with smelling salts?

With a quiet sigh, he grudgingly allowed that a woman's unwanted wedding day was a fair excuse for nerves.

And then it struck him, the starkly vivid recollection of that long pause at the start of the ceremony – her hesitation – her faltering *'I will'* – and he flinched under the sudden assault of pity. It sapped the anger, much as her misguided silence as to her real sentiments had doomed them both. Poor, foolish girl! What consolation was he to offer now?

Even so, Darcy made to ask if she was unwell – a useless platitude – yet the words died on his lips when the phial within the silver cylinder was unstoppered, releasing not the sharp smell of ammonia, but the scent he had long associated with her. Jasmine and gardenia. Hauntingly sweet, and beyond alluring.

Breath caught in his chest as Darcy turned his head to stare unseeing out of the window. Heaven help him, he still wanted her! No change there, even if everything else had changed. If anything, he wanted her more than ever.

He straightened in his seat and squared his shoulders. He *had* to escape the confines of the carriage! Somehow. With any luck, before he lost his mind!

⸲◌℗ ℗◌⸲

"How far to the nearest inn, do you know?"

At her new husband's abrupt question, Elizabeth looked up, puzzled that he should need to ask.

"Half a mile or so to the *Red Lion*?" she replied nevertheless, her inflection rising a little at the end and unwittingly making the reminder sound rather like a question of her own.

Mr Darcy answered it with a crisp, "I beg your pardon. I meant the nearest one on the Luton turnpike. The *Red Lion* will not serve."

'Will not serve for what?' Elizabeth wondered in passing, but did not press him for that particular detail. It had no bearing. She was not disposed to stop in Meryton either.

"In that case, the next would be the *Harrow*, some three miles from here."

"I see."

He made no other comment, so Elizabeth redirected her attention to her sister's gift. Although the phial contained her own favourite scent, it would always bring Jane to mind.

Elizabeth sighed. She had retrieved the thoughtful offering from her reticule on an impulse which she now regretted, for it made her miss her dearest sister more, not less.

She examined the stopper to ensure that the small bottle was properly sealed, then closed the silver lid and endeavoured to suppress another sigh as she ran her fingertips in a light caress over the subtle pattern.

When she glanced up again, she found Mr Darcy's gaze fixed on the small case in her hand. It was not an inquisitive look – in fact, it could have been called brooding – yet she explained, regardless:

"'Tis a parting gift from my sister Jane."

"Oh," he said, then held his peace.

And the three miles to the *Harrow* were covered in complete silence.

⸙⸎⸙

As soon as the carriage had drawn to a halt, Darcy threw the door open and burst out, as though the padded seat were on fire. He drew a deep breath, now that the four walls of wood and glass were no longer closing in on him, then spun round and considerately asked, "Would you like to go in and have a cup of tea or refresh yourself?"

"I thank you, no," she replied. "I am quite at ease. After all, we have barely left Longbourn."

"Very well," he said, and strode off to do what he did best – that is to say, apart from brooding: he threw himself into activity and arrangements. "Simon," he called out to the youngest footman, "you are to take our horses back to Berkeley Square. If need be, a stable lad can be hired to assist you."

"Don't give yerself the trouble and expense, sir. I'll manage on me own," the fellow obligingly replied, and Darcy nodded.

"Good man. See to them then, and ensure that they are fed and watered before you set off. Once you return them to our stables, you are to take the first coach to Grantham to catch up with us."

"Grantham, sir?" the young man echoed, and Darcy could not wonder at his surprise. Grantham was not on the route originally planned.

It was not his habit to justify himself to his people any more than it was theirs to question him, but this once clarifications were in order.

132

So Darcy supplied them:

"We shall not travel through Leicester after all, but head towards the Great North Road from Bedford."

That choice would add several miles to the journey, yet would still shorten it by some considerable time. The Great North Road was by far the fastest route in the country.

"As you wish, sir," Simon bowed, then went to do his bidding, while Darcy continued to deliver the new set of instructions:

"Peter, go in and see to a fresh team, will you? And a riding horse as well."

"At once, sir. You'll want me to ride ahead and bespeak post horses at the next stage, I reckon?"

"No. I want you to remain with the carriage," Darcy said tersely. "*I* shall ride ahead." Which was why the *Harrow* served the purpose — and the *Red Lion* would not have. The last thing he wanted was to make it plain to the whole of Meryton that he could not bear to ride beside her in the carriage.

"Very well, sir," Peter replied, visibly as nonplussed as Simon. But, better trained than the younger footman, he did not say another word.

⁂

The apartments at the *Swan* in Bedford were the most elegant that Elizabeth had ever seen, and the dinner arrangements nothing short of splendid. Exceedingly formal too, which was unexpected. She had not imagined that they would dine attended by the pair of footmen throughout, one standing to attention at her end of the table, the other behind Mr Darcy's chair — solemn and obliging statues springing into action to serve them at the slightest indication of their wishes. It was a novel experience to her, and more than a little unnerving.

Elizabeth could only hope that this was in honour of the occasion, and not an established practice — or, if the latter, that it could be changed. She would prefer more privacy in future. But for now she schooled herself to appreciate their efforts and concede that it was Mr Darcy's place to dismiss them, and not hers.

He did not dismiss them, not until the very end, leaving her to wonder how he failed to see that their presence was an impediment to openness in conversation. Although, upon reflection, perhaps she ought not be overly surprised. Reserve was in his nature.

She hoped for some changes in that regard as well.

As matters stood, Mr Darcy spoke little and ate less. And then, once he had dismissed the footmen, he rose to his feet and thoroughly astounded her with a clipped, "Good night. I shall see you in the morning." And with that, he bowed and left the room.

Half a minute later, Elizabeth was still in her seat, staring dumbfounded at the door.

⚜

The river flowed noiselessly under the bridge, its surface smooth, almost oily in appearance. There was no wind. Just the chill of winter. And the chill within.

Darcy looked up when a bird cried close by, somewhere in the barren trees that lined the southern bank. Then, of its own accord, his gaze drifted across the wide stretch of water. The inn was still bustling with activity. A coach at the door – a late arrival. Ostlers milling about. Lights everywhere – not least in the furthermost bay window on the first floor. She was not asleep, then.

Eyes narrowed, Darcy looked away, still seeking answers – still finding none. He scoffed. Not quite how he had imagined he would spend his wedding night.

He scowled at the dark waters beneath and bent his steps towards the far end of the bridge, yet in due course thought twice about it. He would feel no better if he were to pit himself against the cutpurses of Bedford. Or the cutthroats. Returning to his chambers was the sensible option. So, although he had apparently parted ways with common sense, this time its dictates were obeyed.

⚜

The bedchamber that would be hers for the night was ludicrously large, to Elizabeth's way of thinking – and so was the bed. An expanse of pristine white, against which the vibrant splash of colour was all the more eye-catching: a camellia placed on the nearest pillow, its velvety petals deep rose in hue.

Sarah had left it where it was when she had turned down the counterpane. Then the dear soul had dropped a hurried curtsy and, with an awkward smile, had mumbled, "Sleep well, ma'am," and vanished, little knowing that her newly married mistress was to sleep alone. That this was to be a wedding night like no other.

The best part of an hour later, as she sat warming herself before the cheery fire, Elizabeth had yet to ascertain her own feelings on the matter. Relief might have been the sensible response, but by the looks of it she had bidden adieu to her famed common sense, for she felt no measure of relief.

She was homesick, weary and confused. For the circumstances were at the very least perplexing. To put it plainly, they were disappointing. The very formal dinner – and now this! Why ever had they travelled in such haste to Bedford, if not for the… well… the intimacies of the wedding night?

The journey had been disappointing too. The promising moments over the last se'nnight had led her to expect a great deal less reserve from her new husband. Nothing quite so blatant as Mr Darcy holding her as they rode away from Hertfordshire – heavens, no, nothing of the sort! Just… some form of closeness. Smiles? Glances? Holding hands?

But, much like the footmen hovering over them at dinner, Sarah's presence in the carriage had made reserve a must. Naturally, for the dear girl's sake she was glad that Mr Darcy had considerately spared her maid the discomfort of a four-hour spell in the cold, perched up on the coachman's seat. But, for her part, Elizabeth could have done without scrupulous decorum and the artificial distance. She would have very much liked to speak with him in peace – build intimacy – ask about Pemberley and the sights to be seen on their journey. As for his choice to take to the saddle from the *Harrow* onwards to bespeak post horses at the following stages, that was another disappointment. Could he not have sent his footman ahead to see to that?

With a little huff, Elizabeth uncurled herself out of her snug spot in the armchair by the fire and stood. She might as well go to bed, even if sleep was likely to elude her. A pity that she had not packed a book into her trunk. That might have taken her mind off bittersweet thoughts of home and all manner of unanswerable questions.

But then she made a little moue that was both wry and sheepish. Who would have imagined that she should supply herself with reading matter for her wedding night?

She carefully banked the fire, then put out the candles, all but the one on the bedside table, then draped a shawl around her shoulders over her dressing gown and ambled towards the bay window. She parted the curtains by a fraction and peeked out, deciding that the river must make for a majestic sight in daylight. At this time of night, all she could distinguish was the outline of the trees on the opposite bank and, to her right, the vast bulk of the bridge, now free of the earlier throng of carts and carriages, just one solitary figure walking across, barely visible in the faint glow of the oil lamps.

Elizabeth gave a little sigh and let the curtain drop. Unerringly, and with no little frustration, her thoughts circled back to the conundrum that was her husband and his notable absence. A thoughtful gesture, to give her time to grow accustomed to this new life? She grimaced. He might have taken the trouble to ask her if this was what she wanted.

She walked to the bed and reached out for the rose-coloured camellia left on the pillow. Cradling the bloom in the palm of her hand, she examined it from one angle, then another, as though the answers to her mystifying questions were hidden among the petals. And then she lowered the long stem into the glass of water set alongside the candlestick on the bedside table, divested herself of her shawl and dressing gown, blew out the candle and slipped into bed. The sheets were crisp and cold, but pleasantly scented with lavender. Elizabeth tucked the corner of the counterpane under her chin and, as was her wont, methodically worked to empty her mind of fruitless speculations and let the morrow look after itself.

Her tried and tested method was successful.

And dreamless sleep was her reward.

•ᘓᘚ ᘓᘚ•

The lovely bloom was the first thing that Elizabeth saw when she awoke on the following morning. On impulse, she took it with her when she repaired to their private parlour as soon as she was dressed.

Mr Darcy was within, and she greeted him with a bright, "Good morning," followed by a gesture towards the floral offering and a vaguely conscious, "I thank you for leaving this on my pillow. 'Tis exquisite. And it was a… most agreeable surprise."

He stared blankly at the camellia – then at her.

"Oh. I—" he muttered, then cleared his voice. "Hm. No matter. I am glad it pleased you," he said in a flat tone as he pulled a chair for her. "Would you care to sit?"

She did, and that was when she noticed that while her plate was in pristine condition, his was not.

"Have you sat down for breakfast already?" she asked – a pointless question, for she had the evidence before her.

"I have. I thought you would not mind having as much rest as possible. There is a long journey ahead. Speaking of which, I must beg you to excuse me. Arrangements must be made."

"Of course," Elizabeth replied, quite as tersely as he, and dropped the flower on the table to pick up the napkin and spread it over her lap with jerky little movements, testament to her growing irritation.

Likewise, the butter knife was employed rather too vigorously later, once the door was closed behind him and Elizabeth found herself venting her frustration on her toasted muffin. Pressing her lips together, she set the knife down. With a coachman and so many footmen in his employ, one might think he need not involve himself quite so much in the arrangements. And one might begin to think that he was purposely avoiding her.

◈◈◈

He *was* avoiding her!

Each passing hour brought fresh proof of that, until there was no more room for doubt. Elizabeth barely saw him as they continued their journey northwards – she in the coach, he tearing ahead on horseback from one stage to the next. If he partook of refreshments, it must have been while he was waiting for the carriage to arrive. He only joined her once, for a light repast in Wansford. All the other times when they stopped to change the horses – a regular occurrence every ten miles or so – if Elizabeth felt inclined to step into the coaching inn to warm herself by the fire or have a cup of tea, Mr Darcy tasked his footmen and her maid with attending her, while he remained without, his commanding presence spurring the stable hands into brisk activity.

And then they would set off again, to bowl along the Great North Road at unimaginable speed. This was, without exception, the fastest that Elizabeth had ever travelled in her entire life, and in the greatest comfort too, for the carriage was remarkably well sprung. She could not help thinking that she might have taken pleasure in the novel experience – found it thrilling, even – were it not for her disquieting musings.

In a matter of hours, all her good impressions had been overturned, and her sanguine anticipation had been replaced with severe misgivings. Belated misgivings, woefully belated, for she was bound to him, and there was nothing she could do about it now.

Mere days ago, in her father's study, he had spoken of a happy life together. Had inspired her with the hope that it *could* be so. Yet now it appeared that his notion of felicity in marriage was very different from hers. Either that, or he had been disingenuous – and she could not fathom why he should have given himself the trouble of making the prospect seem rosier than it was. He had no need to cajole her into marriage. He must have known full well that the scandal had left her with few alternatives, if any.

Either way, this was not the man she had gradually warmed up to of late, and her misgivings mounted at seeing him make no further effort to be amiable, now that he was secure of her.

His lack of interest in her company was disquieting too. As for his choice to stay away from her bedchamber on the previous night, by now it had begun to look less like thoughtfulness and a great deal more like lack of interest in her person. The thought made her blush, yet Elizabeth pursued it nonetheless, much as the discomfort was accentuated by a growing sense of injury. If he still deemed her merely tolerable – and patently not handsome enough to tempt him – then… what next? This was a marriage of necessity, and they both knew it. But if he had meant it to be a marriage in name only, he might have done her the courtesy of allowing her to make an informed decision at the time of his proposal. And what of an heir for Pemberley? He wanted an heir, surely. Or was that aspect of their marriage meant to be a matter of necessity as well? A perfunctory business, for the sole purpose of procreation?

Elizabeth flinched. What sort of cold, withering arrangement had she entered into?

Despite the electrifying speed of travel and the brightness of the day, such grim thoughts could not fail to oppress her spirits. Still, with stern determination, she sought to keep herself from leaping to conclusions. She had misread him once, and it would not do to repeat that error and wilfully misapprehend his reasons yet again. Was it possible that there was some other explanation for the dramatic alteration in his manner?

She mentally reviewed the previous day, teasing out each detail, but nothing drew her notice – except her mother's raptures. Had he overheard those ill-judged effusions after all, in part if not in full? He might have. But... what of it? Her mother had already made grossly mercenary comments in his hearing. Such as the disgraceful monologue at the Netherfield ball, when she had enumerated all the pecuniary advantages she expected from having Mr Bingley for a son-in-law, not least her other daughters being thrown into rich men's paths.

Elizabeth cringed at the mortifying recollection, and as she measured it against her mother's outpourings during the wedding breakfast, it occurred to her that Mr Darcy might have one good reason to be disgusted by the latest display and find it all the more objectionable: *he* was now the son-in-law, and thus in the line of fire. For all she knew, he might have gone further and begun to think *her* mercenary too. *'Like mother – like daughter'* was a common enough assumption.

It was distressing to suppose him so quick to think ill of her. She was *not* her mother, and could scarce wait to tell him so. Likewise, she could scarce wait to address all her misgivings, and hopefully clear them. But that was not the sort of conversation they might have in the courtyard of a country inn, or over a brief luncheon halfway through the day's travel. Perhaps not even over dinner – that is, assuming that this time the footmen might be dismissed sooner.

"When are we to reach Pemberley?" she asked Mr Weston, her husband's middle-aged valet, who had complied with her request and joined her and Sarah in the carriage, although his very formal air showed that he did not hold with this departure from the norm.

"Tomorrow afternoon, ma'am, if this dry spell holds. If not, by tomorrow evening," he said and Elizabeth thanked him, privately thinking that the man's reserve and brevity were an excellent match for Mr Darcy's.

She could not say the same of her own disposition. Tight-lipped reserve was not in her nature. Nor was endless patience. But her conversation with her husband should be private – so she *would* be patient. Until tomorrow night.

Chapter 15

The spell of dry weather did not last. The morning brought rain, light but unremitting, yet even that was deemed preferable to her society, Elizabeth discovered with very mixed feelings, of which indignation began to hold the upper hand.

However, just as the carriage was preparing to depart from the third coaching inn beyond Nottingham and follow Mr Darcy, who had already ridden away at a gallop, the heavens opened with such fury that Elizabeth was not surprised to see him return, his greatcoat already drenched.

In short order, the hired mount was handed back, and Mr Darcy bowed to the necessity of resorting to the carriage, whereupon his valet was swift to give fresh proof that, the inclement weather notwithstanding and despite his elevated position in the household, he regarded himself on the par with his master's other servants, not his master, and promptly said, "I should return to my seat beside Joseph, sir."

But Mr Darcy dismissed that notion with a flick of his hand and a clipped, "Nonsense, Weston. Not in this downpour. You had much better stay where you are."

Thus, the coach took to the road with just one change in the seating arrangements. Her private frustrations aside, as they rounded the corner into the lane, Elizabeth reached for the rug that was still left folded on the seat and silently offered it.

Mr Darcy shook his head.

"I thank you, no. You might need it later. I would only make it wet."

There was a measure of thoughtfulness in the refusal, but by then Elizabeth had grown too piqued to appreciate it.

"Very well." She dropped the rug back on the seat and rather testily added, "I hope you can bear the tedium of this speed of travel."

He shrugged.

"Needs must, as they say."

Lips pursed, Elizabeth found herself more than willing to match his terseness. She turned towards the window with a crisp, "Indeed."

❧ ❧

The speed of travel *was* tedious. Excessively so. Even to her. The Newhaven turnpike was nothing like the Great North Road. In Elizabeth's estimation, their progress was but half as fast as on the previous day. Also, since Joseph could not push the horses along the muddy road, there was no need to stop so often to replace them.

The company was tedious too. Over the last couple of days, Sarah had felt at liberty to comment on the sights that caught her notice and, by virtue of the easy ways at Longbourn, she had continued in that vein even once Mr Darcy's valet had joined them. But she was silenced most effectively when the vacant seat was occupied by the gentleman himself.

Just as Elizabeth had expected, he had not come disposed towards conversation. He said precious little, and only when necessary. Not that he could speak freely in their attendants' presence. But, with a frown, Elizabeth decided that she had endeavoured to make excuses for his unaccountable conduct for long enough. She fixed her gaze out of the window, and silently steeled herself for the final stretch of the long journey – in more ways than one the longest that she had undertaken in her life.

❧ ❧

At the *King's Head* in Matlock, Elizabeth learnt that this was to be the last change of horses. Thus, once they took to the road again, if she turned to stare out of the window, it was with interest rather than resentment. But dusk was falling rapidly, so she could see little of the surrounding countryside – just hilly contours outlined against the leaden sky. Soon, the distant hills vanished from her sight, swallowed up by darkness, and Elizabeth could no longer distinguish anything of what lay beyond the stone walls bordering the road. Barely illuminated by the glow of the carriage lamps, the walls kept dimly passing before her eyes, the monotony soporific. Before she knew it, she had drifted off to sleep.

She could not tell for how long she had been lost to the world, nor what it was that had awakened her, but the next thing Elizabeth saw was a compact cluster of lights in the distance.

Pemberley?

Aye, so it was, she found when the conveyance drew to a halt before the house. It was vast, far larger than she had imagined – a looming bulk, scarce softened by the cheery lights shining in many of its windows.

Mr Darcy left the carriage and came to hand her down.

"We are here, then," she needlessly observed.

"Yes. Welcome to Pemberley," came his crisp reply, and as she stepped out and drew a lungful of the cold night air, Elizabeth could not help thinking that she wished he had said, *'Welcome home.'*

◦◦◦

The entrance hall was palatial – daunting in both size and grandeur. Yet that was where, for the first time in two days, Elizabeth was afforded a heart-warming surprise. The one responsible for it was a diminutive old lady, whom Mr Darcy introduced as Mrs Reynolds, the housekeeper. However deferential, her curtsy lacked formality, and so did her greeting, in stark contrast to the very solemn bow from her counterpart, the butler.

"Thank goodness you arrived in safety!" Mrs Reynolds beamed. "The weather took a frightful turn today. I have not seen the likes of it in weeks. What wretched luck that you were caught in it. We were not expecting you until next week – were we, Mr Howard? Yet, praise be, here you are, safe and sound. Might I escort you to your chambers, ma'am? You must be weary and chilled to the bone, but we'll have you warm and cosy in no time," the kindly woman said, gesturing towards the great staircase, and Elizabeth saw no reason to object.

She walked up with her guide, pleased to find that the housekeeper was so affable and chatty. She had imagined that the high-ranking servants would be on a par with Weston – stony-faced and rigidly civil – and although the butler was shown to be an uncanny mirror of her expectations, it was a relief that Mrs Reynolds was nothing of the sort. Seemingly cast in the same mould as dear Hill, the genial woman was the one member of the Darcy household who put her entirely at ease.

'Just as well,' Elizabeth thought with a wry smile. It would have been a fine to-do if she were discomfited by her own housekeeper.

"This way, ma'am," Mrs Reynolds indicated, then opened the first door on the right and revealed a room that could have easily accommodated Elizabeth's bedchamber at Longbourn, along with Jane's and at least half of Mary's. The housekeeper closed the door and offered, "Shall I assist you with your outdoor apparel? It was too cold in the hall, so I thought you'd best keep it, but a fire has been burning here for several hours each day. Hopefully, 'tis warm enough by now."

"It is indeed," Elizabeth replied – a civil falsehood. The chamber of her girlhood would have been considerably warmer if the fire had been burning for a mere half an hour, she thought, and her lips quirked into a grimace. Such was the price of grandeur.

She removed her bonnet and allowed her amiable companion to help her out of her pelisse, then Mrs Reynolds urged, "Take a seat by the fire, ma'am, and warm yourself a little. I'll bring some tea in a trice, but let me light the other candles first. And the oil lamps likewise."

"Oh, that will not be necessary," Elizabeth said, and this time meant it. For now, the glow of the fire and the candelabrum on the dressing table would suit a great deal better. Excessive lighting would only serve to bring the lavish furnishings into sharper focus and make the room appear even more imposing. And colder, for that matter, given the pale aquamarine of the *décor*.

Whether or not she understood her reasons, Mrs Reynolds gave a compliant nod.

"As you wish, ma'am. Is there anything I might do for you before I go and see to a hot drink?"

"No, nothing at all, I thank you."

Once left alone, Elizabeth made her way towards the fireplace, but did not sit. Arms wrapped around herself, she slowly looked about, examining the room at leisure.

It was hard to imagine that she would ever feel at home in a room so sumptuous – so grand. Her troubled gaze travelled over the entire chamber, then returned to the exceedingly large bed, almost as wide as it was tall, its canopy and curtains covered in a leafy pattern that shimmered in the candlelight in shades of silver against the sea-green background. She bit the corner of her lip, and could not fail to wonder if this was where she would become a wife in *that* sense of the word.

With a slight grimace, she owned that she would have preferred the not-so-lavish but more welcoming bedchamber at the *Swan* in Bedford. If nothing else, there had been anticipation then…

All of a sudden, her eyes flicked to the door across the room, beyond which a voice rang – Mr Darcy's voice – barking a curt order. So, the return to Pemberley had not cured him of his ill humour. And then he spoke again, this time in a low mutter, the words too quiet to be overheard, but his tone had an apologetic ring to it.

Lips tightened into a severe line, Elizabeth reflected grimly that the hapless individual who had just borne the brunt of his temper – Weston, presumably, or one of the footmen – might be satisfied with a perfunctory expression of regret, but she would not be. She was not minded to tolerate his unaccountable ill temper with any measure of equanimity!

But… what other options had she? Were there *any* options left to her, now that she had placed herself wholly in his power?

The chilling thought caught her unawares, and in a flash the chill swelled into alarm. Husbands held all the power. Wives had none. All claims to the contrary were as hollow as the empty promise that formed a part of a man's marriage vows: *'With all my earthly goods I thee endow.'* That was false – a mockery. Marriage had given her no say in his affairs, no rights over his property. It had given *him* full rights over *her*.

Without warning, she was overwhelmed by the deepest need to be home – unmarried – safe in her father's house. So what if there were foes in Meryton? At least they were predictable. But this… this was beyond endurance! She had no certainties. Just the sickening suspicion that she had traded her freedom for a gilded cage. And that suspicion grew as she darted another glance at her oppressively luxurious surroundings.

Panic rose to her throat in a suffocating grip which felt horribly familiar, although almost a decade had elapsed from the time when she had accidentally locked herself into Jane's closet in a game of hide-and-seek. The latch had fallen into place, and could not be dislodged – there was no handle on the inside. The sense of being trapped without escape had sparked the wild, senseless fear that the tight space was growing even tighter – that the walls were drawing nearer and were pressing down on her. And now she felt the same, even though she was in a vast bedchamber, not a narrow closet.

Likewise, her bodily responses were no different: she became light-headed; her palms damp; her breathing fast and shallow; her heart pounding frantically in her chest.

Yet, with considerable effort, Elizabeth endeavoured to remind herself that she was a grown woman now, not an impressionable child, and while she was unable to control the fast beatings of her heart, she certainly could regulate her erratic breathing and take slow, calming breaths instead. Think calming thoughts, too. The room was not becoming smaller, was it? The walls were not moving. More to the point, she might long for the safety and comfort of her childhood home, yet it was fair to say that Mr Darcy had not given her any cause to feel unsafe. Confused – aye. And disappointed. And resentful. But she would not cling to her resentments like a headstrong little girl. Little girls grew up, acquired a degree of sense and employed their wilfulness for better aims. Such as discovering the roots of their difficulties, and not resting until they were dug out.

Elizabeth's gaze returned to the closed door on the opposite side of the room and listened carefully, but all was quiet now. Her outburst of panic seemed to have quietened too. There – good sense always served. It would behove her to make more use of it.

So she sought to do just that, and guided her thoughts towards encouraging and logical musings. Not long ago, the road ahead had appeared promising. She *had* felt safe with him. Quite safe – and understood – and, if anything, looked after. Besides, she was not so vain as to imagine herself blessed with irresistible allurements, so she had no reason to suppose that Mr Darcy had made himself agreeable just so that he might coax her into marriage.

With petulant resentment and injured feelings cleared out of the way, justly prized logic indicated that if their future life had seemed appealing a few days ago, and now it did not, then something must have happened in the meanwhile. At the wedding breakfast, to be precise. And she was determined to discover what that was.

Now? Or after dinner?

Elizabeth shuffled uneasily on her feet as she felt heat rising in her cheeks. It had naught to do with the roaring fire. Just her propensity to blush at the most inconvenient moments.

She gave a forceful shrug and raised her hands to press her palms to her traitorous cheeks as though she could force the blood back into her veins, and keep it there.

She could not, naturally. But, her maddening blush notwithstanding, her mind was made up. A great many things had changed or must change soon, but at heart she would remain the same. Resolute and strong. A creature of impulse, perhaps, but certainly one who would not be intimidated into drawing back from what had to be done. And one who firmly believed, moreover, that if something was worth doing, it *should* be done sooner rather than later. So she would speak with Mr Darcy *now*. Even if she had to seek him in his chambers.

Her blush flared all the more fiercely as Elizabeth approached the closed door, which rather served to demonstrate that the anticipation she had given up for lost was still there, somewhere, beneath layers of conflicting sentiments. But she refused to ponder on that now, lest it distract her from the task in hand. She strode to the door and knocked, unwilling to allow herself sufficient time to think of reasons to delay this conversation. She did not wish it delayed. She had waited long enough.

There was no answer, so she counted slowly to fifteen, then knocked again – and, to her shock, the somewhat bolder tap was enough to push the door open. It came slightly ajar, and Elizabeth froze – only to jump like an absolute ninny when she heard another knock behind her, on her own door, the one leading to the corridor.

Blood draining from her cheeks, she stood rooted to the spot, wide-eyed and flustered, as though she had been caught sneaking around the house. And then she scoffed. Good gracious, she was utterly ridiculous! She had just been brought to Pemberley as its mistress. She was within her rights to go anywhere she chose.

Except into Mr Darcy's apartments without his invitation, she sensibly conceded. Heavens, what if the door had swung back fully, and she had found him in a state of undress?

The blush returned as swiftly as it had disappeared, and she reached out to pull the door shut. Quietly. Discreetly. With any luck, he had not noticed it being either opened or closed. She pressed down the handle and pulled the door in all the way to ensure that the latch was properly engaged this time, then turned away and bade, "Come," her voice barely loud enough to be heard from the corridor.

Still, it must have sufficed, for Mrs Reynolds entered, bearing the tea accoutrements on a tray.

"There, ma'am. I have always found that a cup of tea works wonders," she said as she busied herself with preparing the beverage.

"As have I," Elizabeth smiled, and finally availed herself of a seat by the fire, then took the cup that Mrs Reynolds offered. There was truth in that: most things had a way of looking a little better after a cup of tea.

"Shall I ask the girls to bring up hot water for a bath before dinner?" the housekeeper obligingly suggested.

It was a marvellous thought, after so many days of travel.

"I thank you, yes. A bath would be wonderful. That is, if there is enough time."

"Of course, ma'am," Mrs Reynolds replied, a faintly surprised ring to her voice. "We shall keep dinner waiting for as long as you choose."

The experience was both novel and slightly discomfiting, that dinner should be kept waiting at her pleasure. Although, in all fairness, it ought not be for her pleasure and convenience alone.

"What is Mr Darcy's preference?" she considerately asked, only to find that it was the housekeeper's turn to look discomfited.

And then she learnt why: the older woman had ill tidings to impart.

"The master shan't be in for dinner, ma'am. He sends his apologies, but he had to leave."

"Oh. Then I would appreciate a bath, and dinner soon afterwards," Elizabeth said with as much composure as she could muster. But as soon as Mrs Reynolds excused herself to make the arrangements, all pretence was discarded. She set down the delicate cup and saucer with a rattle, and stood from her seat.

This was beyond the pale! That he should continue this abominable… contemptible… whatever this was! And without a word to her! Not even the common courtesy of letting her know himself, but sending a message through the servants!

Tears pricked her eyes, and Elizabeth gave them free rein as she paced back and forth about the room. They were not tears of sadness, but of anger and humiliation. How could he! Not the scantest sign of— Never mind affection, if that was too much to ask for, but not even a shred of consideration! No regard for her feelings. No regard for her at all!

The room no longer seemed so wide as she furiously paced from one side to the other. This was beyond insulting. It was indefensible –

insupportable – unconscionable – callous! Not one word to her of where he was going. Or for how long. Or *why*.

At that, she gave a quiet growl, her indignation overpowering any and all distressing sentiments, such as the aching sense of injury and rejection. Oh, she had had her fill of speculations – of devising excuses for his conduct – of meeting him halfway. If this was the sort of marriage he desired, then so be it!

For the fourth time, her pacing took her all the way to the door that led into his rooms. Or perhaps it was the fifth time – she did not know, and did not care; she was not counting. But that was when her gaze fell on the key in the lock. Lips white and eyes narrowed, Elizabeth turned it. Twice.

Chapter 16

Norbert, his father's gamekeeper, greeted him with understandable surprise, but asked no questions when Darcy arrived at the hunting lodge that had also served as the old man's home for many a year. He did not even ask if Darcy was to spend the night – that was a fair assumption, given the lateness of the hour. He simply offered to go up and make the bed, with an apologetic mutter about the good linen, which had not been aired for some time, and would likely be musty.

"No matter," was Darcy's sole reply. Musty bedsheets were the least of his concerns, and in any case he had no hope of sleeping – hence his arrival on old Norbert's doorstep. He would be damned if he would willingly subject himself to the agonies of a sleepless night one door away from her bedchamber.

That cursed door had been the final straw.

He had not fooled himself into believing that rushing to Pemberley would improve matters – just into thinking that they could not grow any worse. And yet they could. There had been layers of separation at the *Swan* and at the *Angel* in Grantham. The dining parlour. His footmen, his valet, her maid. But if he were to lie awake in his bedchamber at Pemberley, the knowledge that there were but a few footsteps and a door between his bed and hers would have driven him to distraction. And rendered him all the more incapable of deciding what was to be done.

That question had gnawed at him for two days together, yet he still had no answers. Thoughts of an annulment were gut-wrenching. Besides, it was virtually unattainable, and if it could be achieved at all, it would only serve to amplify the scandal a hundredfold. Worse still, the gossip would no longer be contained in the *cloaca maxima* that was Meryton, but would reach the highest circles – would affect Georgiana's prospects. A distasteful business that would do more harm than good.

Which left the pernicious prospect of staying married to a woman who had accepted him out of mere necessity. The irony of it was monstrously hard to stomach, seeing as not long ago he had been one of the most eligible bachelors on the marriage mart. More fool him not to have gone where he was wanted, and seek instead to do right by her. A cursed fool, moreover, for finding relief in having his hand forced – in seeing his gentlemanly duty go hand in hand with his desire.

And now he had the just deserts of lust-crazed dunces: marriage to a woman who did not want him. If all the disappointed misses of the *ton* and their aggrieved mammas had congregated to devise a way of wreaking collective vengeance, they could not have possibly contrived anything worse!

Dark thoughts of the same bent – dark demons – continued to plague him long into the night. Norbert had retired to his berth hours ago, once he had brought up a modest supper of bread, cold meat and cheese, which Darcy could not touch. Instead, he made liberal use of Norbert's other offering: a bottle of rum silently left on the dresser by the door with all the wisdom of one who had seen enough of the world to know that young men who had been driven from their beds might seek oblivion in a bottle.

That choice Darcy had previously scorned, and he had despised its proponents for weaklings and pitiful wretches. Now he could see that there was a tenth circle of hell, purposely designed for the self-righteous – and justly so.

He toasted that newly acquired knowledge with another measure of rough spirits, little as he found rum to his taste. But he only had himself to blame in that regard as well, he thought with harsh self-derision. Knowing what sort of a night awaited him, he should have taken the precaution of bringing along a supply of brandy.

Darcy drained his glass and stretched his long legs towards the fireplace, his stare fixed on the leaping flames. There was no other source of light in the sparsely furnished room; the candles had long guttered out. Nor was there much comfort to be had at the hunting lodge – but, galling as it was to have felt compelled to quit his home and leave all the comforts of the house to *her*, he could not think of another option. Not as yet.

Still, a solution must be found. He was not minded to absent himself from Pemberley indefinitely. Somehow, he *must* find a way to grapple with this hell of his own making – and hers.

151

Glowering at the fire, Darcy clenched his hands into rigid claws around the armrests. It was beyond offensive that she blamed *him* for the debacle and considered herself wedded to him under duress, but it was the disguise that filled him with abhorrence. If she was loath to marry him, she should have damned well said so!

ഏൟ ൟ

"Would you wish me to give you a tour of the house, ma'am?" Mrs Reynolds asked shortly after breakfast, and a fair dose of curiosity and no less appreciation for the older woman's thoughtfulness prompted Elizabeth to agree.

"Yes, I would like that very much."

Of course, she would have liked it a great deal better if that task had not been left to the housekeeper. It made her feel like a mere visitor. Yet she could hardly fault Mrs Reynolds for that.

There had been no sign of Mr Darcy all morning, nor any word from him. But, as the tour progressed, his name was on his housekeeper's lips at every turn:

"…and this is the music room. The pianoforte has just been tuned, as Mr Darcy had requested. Indeed, it was due a tuning, for it is quite new. It came down three months ago, to please Miss Georgiana. I expect my master has told you that his sister is exceedingly fond of music. She plays and sings all day long. Around that time, he also had one of the sitting rooms fitted up for her, just because she had taken a liking to its situation. This is always the way with Mr Darcy: whatever can give his sister any pleasure is sure to be done as soon as may be. There is nothing he would not do for her. Speaking of sitting rooms, shall we go this way now? Ah, there we are. This book-room had served as Mr Darcy's study while his father was alive, but last week he wrote to request some alterations – that this lighter *escritoire* be brought in, for instance, and the easy chairs in the alcove – so that you might use it as your own sitting room, if you wish. Mostly because it is quite close to the library. My master wrote that you are a voracious reader," Mrs Reynolds added, to Elizabeth's surprise at learning he had shared that information. "Of course, if another room should catch your eye, you only need to say so and I shall make the arrangements directly. But if this one is to your taste, we should restock the shelves. Mr Darcy sent instructions in that regard as well. He said that you would prefer different subjects and a greater variety than can be found in the current selection, and I daresay he is in the right, for most of these books are to do with estate management and farming and the like. Even so, we have left them just as they are for now. I thought it would be best to wait until you have had a chance to spend some time in the library, and then you will tell us which books should be moved here. We can go there now, if you wish."

Much as she was tempted, Elizabeth declined, and with good reason, which she did not hesitate to share:

"I thank you, but perhaps that would be best left until the end of our tour. I do take great pleasure in reading, just as you were told, and I have heard much praise for the library. If it is as enticing as I imagine, I might not be persuaded to leave it anytime soon."

Mrs Reynolds gave a little chuckle.

"Even if you were to devote all your time to reading, ma'am, I expect you would be hard-pressed to go through all the books therein. They are in their thousands. So it must be a good thing that you favour livelier pastimes too. Mr Darcy wrote that you are also very fond of walking. I hope the grounds will please you. I daresay they are best explored with a cheery and energetic companion, and I may have a suggestion to offer in that regard, if you will permit me," Mrs Reynolds said with a private little smile. "But as to the library, I believe you may find it even more enticing than you thought. Knowing my master, he must have given you but half the picture. Not one to boast of his possessions, is Mr Darcy, and he is even more modest about his own achievements," she added, which could not fail to put a quirk in Elizabeth's brow. 'Modest' was one of the last words she would have chosen to describe him.

Nonetheless, she held her peace, of course, and allowed Mrs Reynolds to guide her towards the great staircase. As they went up, the housekeeper resumed:

"My master always claims that the library is the work of many generations, and that may be so with respect to the contents, but its present state is largely Mr Darcy's work. Reorganising the library was the first task he applied himself to after his father's passing, and I would like to hope it was a comfort. My late master's illness and demise hit him hard, you see. But I daresay he told you that as well."

He had not. He had barely told her anything – had shared so few of his thoughts with her – which was one of the deepest roots of her resentment. But before Elizabeth could even begin to reconcile that resentment with the surge of compassion brought by her companion's disclosures, she followed the housekeeper into the picture gallery – and came face to face with the gentleman himself. Not in person, but in a large portrait that was arrestingly lifelike. So much so that Elizabeth was unwittingly brought to a halt, and she stood several minutes before the painting, in earnest contemplation of the handsome features that the artist had so skilfully depicted. The resemblance to the original was striking, and so was the faint smile that brightened the painted countenance. A smile that was decidedly familiar – she had seen it playing on Mr Darcy's lips sometimes, when he looked at her.

A light touch tore her from her musings, and Elizabeth darted her eyes towards Mrs Reynolds with a little start when the housekeeper said softly, patting her arm in reassurance:

"He will keep himself safe, ma'am. You need not fret. And he will return to you as soon as possible."

Elizabeth forced a small, self-conscious smile. What was she to say to this kindly woman who had just spoken to her as one would to a new bride consumed with worry on account of her beloved? She pressed her lips together and suppressed a shrug. What else was the dear soul to think? More to the point, what was *she* to make of Mr Darcy?

All she could safely say was, "Thank you." But, unbecoming as it was to probe and seek to extract information from his servants, Elizabeth could not help asking, "Does this happen often, your master leaving the house at such short notice?"

"No, ma'am. Not often, thankfully. But it has happened now and then. The timing is unfortunate on this occasion, most unfortunate, but I daresay it could not be helped. He never neglects his duties," the older woman said, and Elizabeth felt compelled to nod, although she had no doubt that this time Mr Darcy's duties as a landlord had naught to do with his precipitous departure.

But Mrs Reynolds was not quite finished.

"My old master, may he rest in peace, suffered greatly in his final year. As you probably know, his illness was unforgiving. But it was plain to see that he drew great comfort from knowing that he was leaving all his earthly concerns in such capable hands. His son is just like him – the best landlord and the best master – and Miss Georgiana could not have wished for a more devoted brother. Not like the wild young men nowadays, who think of nothing but themselves. You will soon see, ma'am, that there is not one of his tenants or servants who would not give him a good name. Some people call him proud; but I am sure I never saw anything of it. To my fancy, 'tis only because he does not rattle away like other young men."

'In what amiable light this places him!' Elizabeth thought, just before Mrs Reynolds spoke again and delivered the most extravagant praise, which went wholly against her own impressions:

"If I was to go through the world, I could not meet with a better master. But I have observed that they who are good-natured when they are children are good-natured when they grow up; and he always was the sweetest tempered, most generous-hearted boy in the world. I have never had a cross word from him in my life, and I have known him ever since he was four years old."

Elizabeth almost stared at her. Never a cross word! That was an extraordinary claim, which could not be reconciled with the evidence of her own ears. On the previous evening, she had been given proof that there was at least one member of the household who could not say the same. So either Mrs Reynolds was prone to exaggeration, or the special treatment she enjoyed was reserved for those who had known him from his boyhood.

And then the housekeeper's smile grew misty and rather sheepish.

"Indeed, ma'am, this might be the sole excuse I have to offer for speaking so freely. I hope you will forgive me, and that you will not take it amiss if I conclude by saying that it is a great relief to us all, regardless of our length of service, to see that Mr Darcy has finally found a helpmeet and a source of comfort in you. I believe I can speak for the entire household when I say that we wish the pair of you every happiness."

"Thank you," Elizabeth whispered, touched by the housekeeper's obvious devotion for her master, which went beyond a servant's loyalty.

It was to Mr Darcy's credit that he had inspired such sentiments in his people. But the good wishes only served to sadden her. For they spoke of the sort of union Elizabeth would have wished for, while he patently did not. Whatever he was expecting to find in their marriage, it was not a helpmeet. Nor did he come to her for comfort.

And nothing changed as the day wore on – a wet and windy day that augmented Elizabeth's frustrations by keeping her indoors. Mr Darcy remained absent. So the door between their chambers remained locked.

∞⦿ ⦿∞

Since he could not exorcise his demons, Darcy sought to tire them into submission. He spent the best part of his first day at the hunting lodge rewarding his stallion with a long, vigorous grooming as compensation for the inconveniences of an unfamiliar stable. And then he found a grimly satisfying outlet for his angry energy in the lean-to where Norbert's winter fuel was stored.

He came upon the old man chopping wood for the fires and, to his retainer's wide-eyed astonishment, Darcy insisted on offering his services. His singular request met with self-conscious protest, but to no avail, and in the end Norbert stepped aside and let him have his way.

Wordlessly grateful, Darcy removed his coat and set to work. He swung the heavy axe in a welcome release of accumulated fury, and as the wood split under the blade, he could not but wish it were as easy to cleave his way through all his troubles. He lifted one of the halves, placed it back on the chopping block and swung the axe again – and in due course, mercifully, the workings of his anguished mind were silenced for a while. Raw force was what was needed now, and Darcy gave his all as raw force flowed through his taut muscles, and the heavy axe kept falling – again – and again – and again.

Daylight turned murky, but he scarce noticed. Not until Norbert's discreet cough drew him from the cleansing trance.

"I reckon that's me sorted till February, sorr," the old man sheepishly muttered with a tilt of his chin towards the vast heap of split logs. "Much obliged, Mr Darcy, sorr. Much obliged indeed. Now, wouldn't ye want some dinner? An' I've just brewed a pot of tea."

Darcy wiped his brow with the back of his hand and nodded. Dinner would not go amiss, however modest the fare. And tea would serve. With any luck, he might get a wink of sleep without resorting to Norbert's rum tonight.

⁊⊙ ☙ↄ⊙

He slept. Just for five hours or so, but that was three hours more than on his first night at the hunting lodge.

The second day was overcast but dry, so Darcy took his mount for a long ride, which earned the noble creature another diligent grooming upon their return.

On the third day, he took himself for a punishing walk to the top of the ragged tor that stood guard to the east of the cottage.

On the fourth day, he pitted himself against the northern neighbour of that rocky eminence.

And in the early hours of the fifth day, he finally came to his senses.

It began inconspicuously enough, his long-overdue return to sanity: as he sat before the fire in his bedchamber – tired, but not tired enough to sleep – he wondered what Elizabeth was doing. And this time he made no effort to banish that question from his mind, as he had for four days together.

He did not doubt that his people had seen to her comfort. He had left instructions in that regard and, truth be told, even without instructions, he fully trusted Mrs Reynolds to do everything that needed to be done. But he was under no misapprehension that Elizabeth was faring much better than he.

Nor had she fared any better on the journey. For the most part, she had been exceedingly sombre and subdued, even by recent standards, and Darcy frowned, belatedly wishing he had not been quite so self-absorbed, and had paused to think that this was not easy for her, either.

In fact, the more he dwelt on that, the bleaker the circumstances seemed, when viewed from her perspective. He had but rarely considered how matters looked to another – but this was not some inconsequential person with whom he had happened to cross paths. It was *Elizabeth*. And, now that his first flush of anger had subsided and he took the time to ponder on how she might feel, his endeavour to put himself in her place – see the world through *her* eyes – painted an oppressive and deeply distressing picture.

157

If the journey north had been utter hell for him, how much worse must it have seemed to *her!* At least he was headed home – whereas she had quitted hers; had quitted everything familiar and set off into the unknown, full of misgivings and foreboding, which he had done nothing to assuage. Quite the reverse. If she had left Longbourn with low expectations, they must be nothing short of grim now, once she had travelled halfway across the country with him at his worst.

Darcy sighed, wishing he had not kept his distance throughout, and that he had nurtured less resentment and a great deal more compassion. And now that he allowed it to take hold, compassion overwhelmed him, heartbreaking in its intensity. If he felt trapped, powerless and threatened by a bleak future, how much more threatening the future must seem to her! Men held all the cards in marriage, just as they did in everything else. Most women had precious little to rely on except faith in their men. They put themselves in their husbands' power hoping that there was enough affection – or, failing that, enough fairness and kindness – to ensure that they would be treated well.

He flinched, achingly aware that he must return to Pemberley as soon as may be – speak with her – reassure her that she had no reason to be wary, and that he was neither so unfair nor so unkind as to mistreat her. However much he resented being blamed for their predicament.

Darcy's lips tightened. It would be a falsehood to claim that he was no longer aggrieved by the injustice, or that it did not pain him. It pained him more than he could say. But the bitterness and the sense of ill-usage had faded, once he had grown reasonable enough to concede that she was not wholly in the wrong: none of this would have happened, had he taken her *'No'* for an answer and left her be. And he had no cause to fly into another fit of pique and call it *'abandoning her to her fate'*. He might as well own that he *could* have ridden for assistance.

And, now that he had begun to listen to the voice of reason, he would do well to acknowledge other uncomfortable truths. Such as the fact that it was no wonder she had kept her own counsel, once the damage was done.

How was she to tell him that she did not wish to marry him, when her remaining options were so dismal? Shunned in Hertfordshire – or sent to town to live with her merchant uncle and his wife as a glorified governess to their children, and be married off eventually to some lowly clerk or some tradesman in their circle.

How was she to know that he would have never let that abomination come to pass? That he could not have left her obliged to throw herself away on some boorish creature who did not deserve her, but would have done his utmost to ensure she had the means and the freedom to choose a better lot in life? Of course she did not know! They had barely spoken of his sentiments. He had never bared his soul to her – never told her that he loved her – nor that he would do anything to secure her happiness.

Darcy sat up with a start, then leapt to his feet to pace about the room when *that* truth, which had long smouldered undetected, hit him at full blast. *He loved her.* This heart-wrenching agony was unrequited love, not thwarted lust. Even though thwarted desire did come into it – of course it did. He wanted her. He ached for her with every fibre of his being. But, above all, he wanted her to be happy.

His feverish pacing came to an abrupt halt, and Darcy raked his fingers through his hair as he choked out a muted oath. Of all the confounded dolts in Christendom! He had not seen it! *How* had he not seen it? He had ranted and raved and resented her for marrying him without affection, but was there any wonder that she did not love him? He had not courted her – had not declared himself – had not even *known himself* until just now!

How was she to understand his feelings, if he had not?

Still dazed by the discovery, and still staggered that it had taken him so long, Darcy dropped back into his seat and leaned forward to rest his elbows on his knees and his chin on his folded hands.

It was too late now to devise ways of giving her the freedom to choose. True freedom no longer was something he could give, and with no little shame Darcy was forced to own that he was selfishly glad of it. In fact, upon reflection, his selfishness had been very much a part of the equation, else he would have begun to consider the matter from her perspective a great deal earlier than this.

But if it was not in his power to set her free, he *could* strive to make her happy. Court her. Lavish her with affection. Was it so unreasonable to hope that, in time, she might come to love him too?

Darcy leaned back in his seat, and his lips curled up into a faint smile. It was an engaging prospect, courting his own wife.

The fact that he had never courted anyone was dismissed as immaterial. He had no reason to believe that it would be a challenge and, however vain this sounded, he had no cause to doubt himself. Throughout his time on the marriage mart, he had received more than his fair share of attention without the slightest effort – or, to put it plainly, he had received ample attention while actively working to discourage it. So, false modesty aside, why should he not succeed when his heart was in it? When he would do anything to please the one and only woman worthy of being pleased?

Chapter 17

"Good day to ye, sorr!" Norbert said brightly when Darcy joined his ancient retainer in the common room, his skin still tingling from ablutions in ice-cold water, which he had found invigorating this morning, instead of counting it as yet another punishment.

The man set aside the harness he was mending and limped towards the fireplace.

"'Tis grand to see ye've had a decent rest fer once. Ye've slept fer hours," he grunted as he hooked the kettle over the open fire.

"Did I? What time is it?"

"Comin' up ter midday."

And so it was. Darcy's own pocket watch confirmed it. No wonder, then, that he felt better than he had in days. Refreshed. Ready to act on his decisions. And more than eager to be gone.

"If that is for coffee," Darcy said with a tilt of his head towards the kettle, "then pray do not trouble yourself. No need. I am leaving now."

"Are ye? Then I'll be off too. Didn't want to go afore ye awakened, but I'd best get meself t'Lambton now, else there'll be no meat fer supper. Slim pickings at the butcher's of a Wednesday, but I 'spect he'll oblige us as best he can."

Darcy's brow furrowed.

"Today is Wednesday?"

"Aye, sorr. Wednesday, to be sure," Norbert evenly replied – as though it were the most natural thing in the world that his master, a man some forty years his junior, should lose his bearings to the point of needing that reminder – then turned away without another word to take the kettle off the fire as instructed.

But Darcy was no longer paying him any heed.

So – today was Wednesday. A week ago, almost to the hour, he and Elizabeth had just walked out of Longbourn Church, man and wife.

Then what the blazes was he still doing here listening to old Norbert talking of slim pickings at the butcher's shop?

He shook his head as though to clear it and took a deep breath.

Time to go home. High time, by Jove, and no mistake!

"I meant I was about to return to Pemberley," he told his host. "There is no need for you to go to Lambton for provisions. I will have Mrs Reynolds search the pantry to replenish your reserves. A lad will come up later today." He looked around for his hat, spotted it on the windowsill and strode across the room to retrieve and don it. "My apologies for saddling you with a troublesome companion," he ruefully said to the man who, along with his father, had taught him all there was to know about shooting game on the estate. "You will have your peace and quiet now. And I thank you for your hospitality."

"Gladly, sorr. Ain't been no trouble. No trouble at all. It were a pleasure to have ye, sorr. So come back whenever it takes yer fancy. Ye'd be right welcome, sorr. Right welcome any time."

'Heaven forbid!' was Darcy's natural response, as prompt as it was instinctive. It did not bear thinking that he should feel the need to seclude himself at the hunting lodge again. But old Norbert deserved better than to hear him say it. So he nodded his thanks and held his peace.

⁕⁕⁕

Samson was well-rested too and doubtlessly longing for a gallop after the many hours spent cooped up in the small stable. He whinnied, stamped and snorted at the sight of the saddle, shaking his head with energy, but had the common sense to temper his excitement and submit to the necessary preparations for departure.

As soon as they were on their way, the stallion's manifest impatience was channelled into a fast and steady gait. As always, the noble beast understood his master's wishes before they were spoken or otherwise conveyed, so Darcy readily gave him his head, although it was impossible to tell if the mad gallop was quelling or fuelling his own impatience.

They reached Pemberley within the hour, and once he had dismounted, Darcy affectionately patted his mount's neck, then handed the reins to the stable lad who had rushed out to attend him.

"He deserves a good grooming. I have done my best by him while we were away, but he will appreciate his own stall and his customary brushes," Darcy said to the young fellow, then lost no time in making his way towards the house.

He let himself in through the side entrance – only to startle his butler with his sudden appearance. But, true to form, Mr Howard was quick to regain his poise and all his dignity.

"Mr Darcy. Welcome home, sir," the older man greeted him with a bow. A firm proponent of a bygone age and its ways, the butler rarely departed from punctilious formality, yet this seemed to be one of the occasions. A hint of a warm smile softened his impassive countenance as he added, "Grand to have you back, sir, if I may say so."

"Thank you, Howard," Darcy replied, acknowledging the subdued warmth and the longstanding loyalty behind it, then asked, "Mrs Darcy is within, I hope?"

The question echoed in his ears, and it occurred to him that this might have been the first time he had referred to her as Mrs Darcy. Yet the appellation had rolled effortlessly off his tongue and, despite all their difficulties, it had rung as anything but hollow. She *was* his wife. And, God willing, their marriage would be set on the right course before too long.

"Of course, sir," Mr Howard evenly replied, and the older man's words somehow sounded as an encouraging conclusion to his own reflections. The butler relieved him of his hat, gloves and riding crop, then added, "You will find Mrs Darcy in the library, along with the Miss Lyles and their brother. They came to call a little while ago."

"Oh," was Darcy's sole response to the intelligence, and he was left to quietly digest it once Mr Howard took himself away with another bow.

At any other time, he would have said that Geoffrey Lyle was a welcome visitor, and so were his sisters. He was fond of them, and likewise held their parents in his affection and esteem. The elder Mr Lyle and his lady had belonged to his own parents' circle of close friends, and while he could not claim the same degree of intimacy with their offspring who were at least eight years his juniors, he had always received them with great pleasure.

Darcy's lips tightened. Today he could not vouch for that. He had not expected callers. He had returned home to see *her*. Speak with her. Alone, naturally. The delay he was now facing could not be regarded as anything but an irksome imposition. Yet a few moments later he gave a resigned huff. There was nothing to be done. And perhaps it was not the worst thing, upon reflection. A set of friendly buffers might help rather than hinder on this, their first encounter after the fraught journey north.

He welcomed that notion as he headed towards the library in long, purposeful strides, yet at the door he paused, tugging a trifle consciously at his coat and waistcoat. It was unfortunate that he had only taken two spare shirts and neckcloths with him on his self-imposed exile at the hunting lodge, but he was not minded to brook the delay of going up to change. What bothered him more than the imperfect state of his apparel was the sudden nervousness. It was utterly absurd. And the same could be said about hesitating on the threshold of his own library, Darcy told himself and frowned.

So he squared his shoulders, pressed the handle and pushed the door open.

He was allowed a mere fraction of a second to note that Elizabeth was halfway up one of the ladders, a pile of books under her arm; that Geoffrey Lyle was holding her ladder so that it would not slide away; that Miss Flora stood beside him; and that their elder sister was nowhere to be seen. And then, without any warning, an astounding racket broke the stillness.

Its source was instantly revealed: the exceedingly loud yapping came from an incongruously small ball of russet fur, a wiry-haired terrier not much larger than a cat. But the noisy creature could not hold Darcy's interest when a cry of alarm had him darting his eyes towards the others and he saw Elizabeth losing her footing as she attempted to climb down.

Another cry rang out. One of dismay. Lyle's. And, at almost the same time, Miss Flora's panicked splutter:

"Goodness, Geoffrey! Catch her!"

His own sharp intake of breath came out in a relieved rush when Elizabeth grabbed hold of the side rail and regained her balance. It was just the pile of books that fell to the floor.

The other mercy, as far as Darcy was concerned, was that he genuinely *was* fond of Lyle and knew him to be a decent sort, otherwise the sharp displeasure roiling in his gut would have been a vast deal stronger at having to witness Elizabeth descending the remaining rungs with the man's arm wrapped around her waist. But once her feet were firmly on the floor, he could not but find his friend's solicitude excessive. To his way of thinking, the steadying arm remained in place for three seconds longer than strictly necessary, and only fell away when Lyle made some quiet enquiry into her comfort, instantly echoed by his sister.

"I thank you, I am fine. Just fine. The little monster startled me, that is all," Elizabeth assured them and gave an airy little chuckle which Darcy found achingly familiar. "Hush, rascal. You nearly made me fall," she chided the aforementioned monster without turning. "Whatever has got into—?"

Her cheerful admonition came to an abrupt halt and Darcy saw her lips round into a silent *'Oh'* when she glanced over Lyle's shoulder and her gaze locked with his. A wordless bow was all that he could offer under the circumstances, while Lyle turned towards the door as well, presumably prompted by Elizabeth's truncated question. And thus, she was no longer screened by their guest's tall frame, and Darcy had the doubtful privilege of seeing her clearly as she greeted him with a subdued curtsy, which he found as dismaying as the alteration in her manner.

A moment ago she was smiling – laughing. Wholly unaffected by his absence, by the looks of it. Receiving callers. Filling her time with any number of diversions.

Gall simmered at the unavoidable conclusion: he had pined for her for five days together, and all this time she... she had not missed him at all! Worse still, his arrival brought no pleasure, if that frosty greeting was any indication.

"Ah! Darcy! 'Tis very good to see you," Lyle exclaimed, affable as ever, and predictably went on to congratulate him on the occasion of his marriage – ill-timed as the customary phrases might have been.

Miss Flora readily echoed them. She chimed in to offer her own good wishes, her greeting neighbourly and warm – certainly a great deal warmer than Elizabeth's. And throughout all this the terrier kept yapping, darting his way time and again, then leaping backwards as though propelled by the force of its shrill barks. Slipping and sliding over the polished floor, the creature barred its teeth at him, the yaps interspersed with a great deal of growling as the pugnacious little beast seemed intent upon mustering enough courage to come closer and sink its fangs into his boots.

That possibility was of no concern to Darcy. The thick leather would have been no match for a pup's teeth, however sharp. The mongrel's impertinence was another matter. It was beyond vexing that the furry fellow should presume to bark and growl at him as if *he* were the intruder.

"Hush, rascal!" Elizabeth called again, sternly this time. "Enough. Come here and behave."

Wagging its tail at her, the belligerent pup showed some signs of compliance and retreated, but did not cease growling. In the end, it was Lyle who stepped in to end the conflict with some decisive action, once he had collected the books that Elizabeth had dropped. He set the volumes on the nearest table and crouched again, this time to scoop up the pup, tuck it under his arm and hold it there with some determination.

"Come now, let us take all this fuss and bother elsewhere, shall we?" he said to the wriggling creature, rubbing its neck to still it as he rose to his feet. Then he glanced towards his younger sibling. "Shall we find Celia? She must have begun to wonder what has become of us," he suggested, and with a quiet, "Ma'am. Darcy," he shepherded Miss Flora out of the library under the considerate pretence of seeking their elder sister, quick to grasp their hosts' need for a few moments' privacy.

Despite her young years, Miss Flora readily saw wisdom in obliging her brother without question. As for the troublesome pup, it still made no secret of its hostility. If anything, its growls were even louder, now that the mongrel was safely ensconced in trusted arms. Yet, for all its manifest reluctance to cede the field, Lyle held fast and bore the noisy little beast away.

Thus, silence was restored – and Darcy was prodigiously glad of it. He was no less grateful for his neighbour's tact and delicacy. Yet the incipient sense of comfort left him when silence endured and grew into an almost tangible third presence in the room. Conspicuous, heavy silence ringing in his ears. And he could not think of the best way to break it.

In the end, it was Elizabeth who did so:

"Have you just returned?" she asked. But her tone was bland, her air indifferent, and she would not even look at him. Instead, she repositioned the books that Lyle had gathered off the floor, stacking them into a neat pile with the utmost care, as though nothing else — and no one — was worthy of her attention.

Injury and disappointment put unwonted sternness in Darcy's voice.

"Yes," he confirmed tersely, then heard himself adding, "This will not do. You could have done yourself an injury. I wish you would remember that you are the mistress of this house. There are several maids and footmen who can do your bidding."

With that, he gained her full attention, Darcy discovered. Her hand fell away from the confounded books and, tossing her head back, she raised her gaze to his. Yet that was not something to rejoice in, for her eyes were shooting daggers.

"Ah. I see you have returned with more of the same," she acidly observed. "Then give me leave to say that by now I would have grown accustomed to being a married woman and the mistress of this house, had I not been dropped off here like a parcel and left to my own devices for nigh on a se'nnight. Welcome home, sir. Now, if you would excuse me, there are visitors waiting."

She did not pause to listen to his protestations that he most certainly *had not* returned for more of the same bitterness between them, but spun on her heel and stormed into the adjacent morning room, closing the door behind her.

⁘

Cursing the architect who had designed quite so many doors leading out of the library would have served no purpose, so Darcy forbore to do so. Not that it would serve him any better to curse himself for his ineptitude and his mortifying blindness.

For one who prided himself on being a *connoisseur* of human nature, he had just demonstrated a shocking inability to read her perfectly natural reaction. Or rather, he had allowed his injured feelings to blind him to hers. The subdued manner of her greeting had *not* signified displeasure at his sudden arrival. She had merely waited to see how he would behave and take her cue from him.

And he had soured their reunion with a display of temper, as though he were a hot-headed youngster in his teens, not a rational man of eight-and-twenty!

Darcy drew his hand over his mouth and chin, wishing he had followed her out of the library and cleared the air forthwith, much as reason claimed that he had been in the right to resist that impulse. The explanation should come in a private conversation, not in the visitors' hearing. And it *would* come. Later today, as soon as Lyle and his sisters left them.

The corner of his lips quirked into a rueful grimace. At least now he knew what she was thinking, once she had been provoked into stating it plainly. She was not displeased at his return – she was angry with him, lividly angry, for having left her to her own devices for several days. For having dropped her off at Pemberley like a parcel, as she put it.

That, he could understand – her anger.

And, frankly, he preferred it to indifference.

As to whether she had missed him, more fool him to torment himself with that premature question. Last night he had seen sense and allowed – had he not? – that it was no wonder she did not love him. He had returned home to alter that, not rant and rave against the present circumstances. Need he remind himself every God-given hour that patience was the first and foremost answer to the challenges ahead?

"Apparently," Darcy muttered.

Learning patience stood to be the most challenging task of all.

⁓⁓⁓

When he stepped into the drawing room at last, Darcy was not met with a fresh round of yapping, so he assumed that Lyle must have entrusted his loud-mouthed terrier to his coachman or his footman. Bringing a misbehaving pup on a morning call could only be described as singular, but his neighbours' choices did not trouble him unduly. The matter of immediate concern was Elizabeth's absence.

"I thought Mrs Darcy was with you," he remarked, once he had greeted Miss Lyle and civilly made all the right answers to her congratulations and best wishes.

"She was," Miss Flora informed him. "She only went up a few moments ago to retrieve something."

"I see," Darcy said and offered her the three books Elizabeth had taken out of the bookcase then dropped when she had nearly fallen off the ladder. "I thought I ought to bring these along, should any of you still wish to peruse them."

"Oh, yes," Miss Flora laughed. "Elizabeth and I were about to look up some verses in Mr Dryden's poems and Mr Pope's, but we quite forgot in all that excitement."

Elizabeth? That was a surprise, after a few hours' acquaintance, Darcy could not help thinking.

His astonishment must have been readily apparent, for Lyle observed with a mild chuckle, "As you can see, Mrs Darcy and my sisters already are on the very best of terms."

"Indeed," Miss Lyle cheerfully concurred. "We are well on our way to fulfilling Mamma's prediction. Last Sunday after church, she said that it would not surprise her if the three of us should be as thick as thieves by Candlemas, and that Elizabeth would be the—"

"You met at church?" Darcy intervened, fresh astonishment prompting him into committing the solecism of interrupting a young lady, but Miss Lyle did not seem to mind.

"Yes," she casually replied. "Mr Davies kindly introduced us."

"Oh. I am pleased to hear it," Darcy muttered – a civil falsehood meant to cover his unease at the intelligence. So, on her first Sunday at Pemberley, Elizabeth had gone to church and met his neighbours, awkward as it must have been to do so with his steward for an escort, and not him. His lips tightened. It had been a brave choice on her part. And another failing of his – a discovery which could not possibly please him.

But Miss Flora had something to say as well, so Darcy struggled to attend her.

"Celia and I should confess that we have pestered Geoffrey mercilessly to bring us to Pemberley. But we were both eager to know your wife better, so… here we are."

The demands of neighbourly civility, drilled into him from his boyhood, compelled Darcy to say, "You are most welcome." Likewise reminded of his duties as a host, he added, "Would you care for fresh tea? Let me ring for it."

"No need. Pray do not trouble yourself," Miss Lyle was quick to stall him. "As you can see, we are well supplied with refreshments," she said with a vague gesture towards the sideboard where the tea and coffee accoutrements stood, alongside serving plates laden with a fair number of palatable choices.

Palatable to those who could swallow a bite, Darcy inwardly amended. But, that aside, perhaps he would be well advised to pour himself a cup of coffee. It might help him gather his wits about him when the time came to see Elizabeth alone.

No sooner had the thought occurred to him than the door opened and she made her entrance. And what an entrance it was. Darcy's jaw dropped – literally – as he stared.

She had chosen to give more than a little indication that she knew she was a married woman. Her beautiful hair was now covered with a matron's cap – the most elaborate concoction that could ever be imagined. A starched, double-tiered structure of muslin and lace adorned with a profusion of ruffles which, he could scarce doubt, evinced her mother's taste, or rather lack thereof. Moreover, he was absolutely certain that the highly conspicuous item had been deliberately chosen in order to make a point – and the look she cast him, along with her arched brow, only served to add the unnecessary confirmation.

His eyes crinkling at the corners, Darcy pressed his lips together as he rose to his feet along with Lyle, and it was only with the greatest effort that he stifled the chuckle that threatened to burst free. He gave her a smiling nod, acknowledging the hit. *'Touché, Madam.'* And such an elegant hit it was! A vast deal more so than her mother's hideous choice of headdress.

Once Elizabeth had chosen a seat, he ambled towards the sideboard and allowed himself the widest smile as he poured a cup of coffee after all. Their life together might be beset by any number of difficulties, but, by God, it would *not* be dull.

The grin was devilishly hard to conquer, so Darcy was obliged to linger by the sideboard for a good two minutes longer than was necessary in order to prepare a beverage. Yet all the effort of schooling his features into civil blandness threatened to be undone when he turned around to rejoin the others and found the visitors at pains to fix their eyes on anything except Elizabeth's most peculiar cap.

Not unreasonably, Darcy was disposed to think himself able to keep his countenance in most circumstances, so he valiantly sat across from his wife – only to find that not staring at her *outré* headdress was the easiest thing in the world. Her expressive features unerringly drew his gaze time and again, as did the delicious mischief that had banished her first look of defiance and now sparkled in her eyes whenever they met his. And if the cap should occasionally intrude upon his notice and make his lips twitch, it was of little consequence. His cup of coffee could easily conceal traitorous smiles. Besides, her lips twitched too, every so often, as she chatted with Miss Lyle and Miss Flora about some passage or another in the volumes he had brought.

Whatever had originally prompted them to speak of old poems during a morning call, Darcy could not fathom, but he took another sip of coffee and smiled at the heart-warming notion that he would see her discussing books with his own sister before long, when Georgiana joined them at Pemberley. Elizabeth would know just what to say and do to draw the dear girl out of her shell. Few, if any, were better placed or better suited to teach his beloved sister to trust in the goodness of others yet again, and rise above misery and heartache. Just as few were better suited to help Georgiana overcome her inborn shyness, made so much worse by the wretchedness the sweet girl had endured.

Cold fury chilled him as the loathsome reason for his sister's wretchedness forced its way into his thoughts. Yet, with firm determination, Darcy closed his mind to those dark reflections. The vile beast had no place in this hopeful moment and, by Jove, the fiend *would not* taint it! So he straightened in his seat and redirected his attention to the ladies.

"Oh, I see your meaning," Miss Flora said with energy. Although she was some four months Georgiana's junior, she never evinced anything like his sister's shyness. "I have not thought of this before, but seeing them together makes all the difference," she added, her hand darting with a flourish between the volume she was holding and the one that lay on Elizabeth's lap. "Just as you said, the themes are strikingly alike. And Mr Pope does put it better."

"I envy your memory, Elizabeth," Miss Lyle owned. "Our governess quite despaired of mine. And yet you have no difficulty in remembering such details. I must say, Mr Darcy, your wife is quite extraordinary," she cheerfully addressed him without warning – yet, although mildly startled by her sudden choice to include him in the conversation, he found no reason to regret it.

Nor could he find any reason to dissemble.

"Yes. That, she is. Quite extraordinary," he said softly as his gaze sought Elizabeth's and his lips curled up into a smile.

Chapter 18

"Shall we?" Darcy gestured towards the drawing room, once Peter, the second footman, had noiselessly closed the great oak doors behind the departing visitors, and at Elizabeth's small nod of agreement, they returned to the now quiet room together.

"Another cup of coffee?" Elizabeth asked, but Darcy shook his head.

"I thank you, no," he said as he escorted her to the main cluster of sofas and chairs and remained standing, waiting for her to resume her seat.

Yet she did not. She retrieved her empty cup and went to refill it, but there was every reason to believe that she had merely done so to stall for time, as the full cup was set aside on the table at her elbow when she finally lowered herself into her armchair.

She glanced his way when Darcy chose the seat that had been Miss Flora's – for he could not see why they should be separated by more than half the width of the vast room – but, all too soon, she lowered her gaze to the small plate of sweetmeats she had fetched from the sideboard along with her fresh cup of tea. She selected one and nibbled it, then absently tucked a stray lock under the ruffles of her cap – and that was when Darcy's forbearance failed him, and he flashed her the wide grin he had suppressed for above an hour.

"If I may be so bold, that is… a remarkable creation," he said, at long last allowing his smiling eyes to rest at leisure on the formidable structure on her head.

The look she cast him was adorably disconcerted – much like the stunned, questioning one she had darted at him earlier, when he had unabashedly paid her an overt compliment in their visitors' presence. But, true to form, she regained her poise in a matter of moments.

"I am thrilled to find that you approve," Elizabeth shot back, but the twinkle in her eyes and the twitch of her lips told their own story even before she lost the battle and chuckled. And then she gave up the pretence altogether, tugged the starched edifice off and set it on her armrest.

"I must confess that it was a gift from my mother," she said, her lips still twitching.

"And I must confess I thought as much," he cheerfully retorted, then reached for her hand and added without thinking, "Thank you. Coming home to you is utterly delightful."

Her hand quivered in his, but she did not withdraw it, even as colour rose in her cheeks and the merriment faded from her countenance, giving way to an almost solemn air.

"Would you tell me why you left?" she quietly asked.

Darcy dropped his gaze to their joined hands and brushed the back of her fingers with his thumb.

"A… complication I had to address," he said without looking up.

"And is it now resolved to your satisfaction?"

"No. Not as yet. But I hope it will be resolved soon," he replied matter-of-factly and raised his head as he shifted in his seat and gave her her due without equivocation. "Pray allow me to apologise for my abruptness in the library. It was uncalled for. And I should likewise beg your pardon for leaving you when you had just arrived at Pemberley." He frowned. "I should have stayed, regardless of—" He broke off, then quietly repeated, "I should have stayed."

She made no answer, just settled a long look upon him, so Darcy added, "I hope my people made you feel at home. Mrs Reynolds, Mr Davies and Mr Howard in particular."

He forbore to mention that his housekeeper, his steward and his butler had been given express instructions in that regard, with the expectation that his orders would filter down to every member of the household, just as they always had. It would not do to sound as though he was purposely asking for her thanks for, in truth, there was nothing she should thank him for. The entire household's deferential welcome for their new mistress was her natural right, not some granted privilege. Besides, she would have every reason to point out that it was not his upper servants' place to make her feel welcome in his home. It was his place – his duty, more than anybody's, and well he knew it.

Yet Elizabeth said nothing of the sort. She merely nodded, then elaborated, "Of course. Everyone was most helpful. Especially Mrs Reynolds. The dear lady is kindness personified. She would make anyone feel welcome. We have already fallen into a pleasant routine. Truth be told, I had not expected—"

But Darcy was not to learn precisely what it was that she had not expected. A knock on the door heralded an interruption, which could not fail to vex him, not least because Elizabeth withdrew her hand from his as she bade the newcomer enter.

It was Sarah, her maid from Longbourn, carrying the russet ball of fur that had caused so much noise and mischief in the library. The fox terrier was quiet now but, ears pricked forward, the small creature raised its head and eyed him with suspicion. Brow arched, Darcy inwardly allowed that the sentiment was mutual.

"Beg pardon," the maid said, darting a hesitant smile from Elizabeth to the wiry-haired fellow in her arms, "but he just won't sit still without you, Miss Lizzy. Whiny, restless, scratching at the door. Thought I'd ask if you wanted him back. Or should I have one of the lads tire him in the garden?"

"Thank you, Sarah," Elizabeth replied. "I daresay he can stay for now. I shall tire him myself later."

No sooner was the wriggling bundle released from the maid's arms than it hurtled towards Elizabeth, almost comically unable to keep its balance on the polished floor. The terrier paused for a few moments at her feet, panting adoringly, tongue hanging out, then glanced at Darcy with a low growl and cautiously came to sniff at the tips of his boots.

"And who might this be?" Darcy asked. "I thought it was Lyle's little beast."

The creature growled louder, then barked, as though in protest at the appellation.

"No. He is my little beast," Elizabeth countered, and on her lips Darcy's petulant mode of address became a term of endearment.

It was readily recognised as such. Wagging its docked tail with energy, the terrier scampered back to her and leapt up to lay its front paws on her lap. The impudent little fellow released a couple of loud barks, which instantly gave way to plaintive whines as its furry head came to rest upon her knee in a shameless bid for attention.

The claim met with the desired result. Elizabeth stroked the wiry muzzle, then ran her fingers over the dog's back.

"I see," Darcy muttered. "And where did it— Hm. Where did he come from?"

"Mrs Reynolds brought him to me on my first morning here. She said that Mr Davies had him fetched to Pemberley a few weeks ago to be trained in catching vermin and whatnot, but she thought he might be better employed as my companion. I hope you do not mind. As a rule, he is not allowed in the reception rooms, and never suffered to sit on the furniture," she explained, then smiled at the bundle of fur before her as she added, "Except when he lies down on my lap."

Darcy suppressed a grimace. For his part, he favoured large dogs who showed some dignity – and who knew better than to bark and growl at him – but there was only one answer he could give her. His mien softened as he promptly spoke:

"This is your home. You need not ask permission to keep him."

Elizabeth cast him a vague smile.

"I was not asking permission, as such. Still, I could not help thinking that my former home was nowhere near as grand, and yet it had not crossed my mind to keep a dog indoors at Longbourn. I thought it would not be the done thing at Pemberley either, but Mrs Reynolds set my mind at rest. She said that there used to be dogs in the house in your father's time, so I imagined you would not object to them."

"No, of course not," Darcy reassured her, and forbore to mention that the last dog to be kept in the house had been his father's favourite, who had pined away, sickened and died within three months of his father's passing. The faithful soul had not been replaced. The old master of the house was gone, and the new master was not ready for such steadfast devotion. It was not likely that he would meet with an untimely end, God willing. But if he did, no one should curl up and die because he was no longer living.

With somewhat of a start, Darcy brought himself back from sombre musings and looked up.

"Well, since we are to share a house, the little fellow and I should become acquainted. What is his name?"

"Mrs Reynolds and I puzzled over that for the best part of an hour, and in the end settled upon Rufus. On account of the uncommon colour of his coat, you see. But then we found that he responds just as well to Rascal."

The terrier was quick to prove her point. Yelping softly, he pricked his ears forward and wagged his tail again, which could not fail to make them laugh.

"I should not wonder if he becomes known as Rascal after all. He has heard that sobriquet often enough," Elizabeth observed with a wide smile, and Darcy returned it.

"I believe I can vouch for that already. He has heard it at least twice today, if I am not mistaken," he replied, disposed to look with some amusement upon the incident in the library. And then he leaned forward, resting his elbows on his knees. "How do you do, sir," he jovially said to his four-legged new acquaintance. "I see you are otherwise engaged, so you may wish to let me shake your paw later. The pair of us did not get off to a good start, so let us do a little better from now on, shall we? Ah. I hope this means you are in agreement," he chuckled mildly when the small dog tentatively flicked his tail twice and turned his beady eyes upon him from underneath exceedingly bushy brows. "From what I remember," he said to Elizabeth, "my father's pointer, Hector, used to favour some rock-hard rusks made from bran flour, marrowbone stock and I know not what. I expect Mrs Reynolds might be able to locate the recipe. But until she does, one of these should do," Darcy decided, and selected a sizeable biscuit from the plate of sweetmeats Elizabeth had brought from the sideboard.

He stretched out his hand and offered it. The terrier eyed him for a moment, then dropped down on his fours and approached to cautiously sniff at his fingertips. The offering was investigated in like manner, and finally accepted. The small creature returned to curl up at Elizabeth's feet and, holding the biscuit between his front paws, began to gnaw at it with relish.

"We have a truce, by the looks of it," Darcy observed with some satisfaction. "Or the beginnings of one, at the very least."

"So it seems," Elizabeth concurred and reached down to stroke the terrier's head, who briefly paused from his employment to lick her hand, then returned to the biscuit with no little interest.

She straightened in her seat, then her gaze found Darcy's.

"Thank you for your patience with him," she said softly.

His reply was prompt and earnest.

"Not at all. I am glad that Mrs Reynolds thought of bringing him to you, and that you had the little fellow for company. I…" Darcy's voice trailed off, and his lips tightened into a wistful grimace. "Were you very lonely?" he whispered at last, reaching across the narrow space between them to cover her hands, crossed together in her lap.

Both of them jumped when the terrier went berserk. He leapt to his feet with a loud growl, the peace offering entirely forgotten, and lunged forward with more growls and yaps to defend his mistress and his territory, in a most provoking repetition of the scene in the library.

His patience severely tested, Darcy withdrew his hand and released a forceful huff. It was but meagre consolation that Elizabeth was distinctly unamused as well. She leaned forward and wrapped her arm around the terrier's wiry chest to draw him back as she admonished, "No! Hush, now! Hush and sit. Behave!"

As it turned out, her reproofs were an utter waste of breath. The stubborn animal would be neither pacified nor silenced. So, with a tut of vexed impatience, she scooped him up and took him out of the room, just as Lyle had done earlier. But, unlike Lyle, she returned in no time at all. She resumed her seat and offered with a conscious smile:

"I apologise for his appalling lack of manners. Peter will ask the lamp boy or one of the porters' sons to take him outside and have him expend his energies elsewhere until I can take him for a proper walk. He will learn to behave and not treat you so disrespectfully," she said in an obvious endeavour to make light of it, then offered in mitigation, "But for now, everything is very new to him."

"Yes. Just as it is to us," Darcy chose to voice the thought which surely must have been on her mind as well, not only his. Then he forced himself to say with a reassuring smile, "No matter. Do not concern yourself."

It was not entirely a falsehood. Of course, he would have greatly preferred that the mouthy little fellow did not presume to defend his wife from his touch, nor make him feel like an unwelcome visitor in his own home. But it would be a strange state of affairs if he should be so childish as to be cross with a mere pup – who, in all fairness, had been beside her all this time, while he had spent his days at the hunting lodge, sulking.

"Were you very lonely?" he asked again, but this time did not reach for her hand, as though her little Cerberus was still in attendance.

Elizabeth gave a little shrug.

"I am accustomed to living with a large family in a small house. And I am used to a great deal of company at this time of year."

Darcy's features tightened in remorse and compassion. Of course. It was but a fortnight until Christmas. How had he been so self-absorbed as to not even consider that?

"Do you wish to go back?" he asked, but Elizabeth surprised him with a forceful shake of her head.

"Not yet. Not for Christmas, anyway. It would not be the same."

He reached for her hand then, and cradled it between both of his.

"No, I expect it would not," he sombrely concurred. "I am exceedingly sorry that this year Christmas at Longbourn would have been... tainted," he added after a short silence, knowing full well that it was a bland and useless platitude.

But he had nothing else to offer.

Elizabeth raised her head and shaped her lips into a semblance of a smile.

"Thank you," she said with determined cheerfulness. "Things will mend. My neighbours and so-called friends will forget, I will learn to forgive, and all will be well. Eventually. In the meanwhile, I am making amiable new acquaintances. The Miss Lyles are very pleasing company, and so are their parents and their brother. I found them welcoming and kind. And their directness is refreshing."

"Ah, yes, directness and uncompromising candour," Darcy said with a wry twist of his lips. "You will find that in abundance in the north. A surfeit of it, even."

Elizabeth matched his smile with an arch one of her own.

"I hope you are not under the impression that those of us who hail from the south are unaccustomed to either," she airily replied, catching him off guard with her remark.

It was startling and decidedly unwelcome – a stark reminder of a certain lack of candour that begged to be discussed. The overhearings at Longbourn loomed large, giving rise to more than one question.

And all those questions burned on the tip of his tongue. Yet, with no little effort, Darcy bit them back. This was not the time to open Pandora's box with queries that would sound so much like reproaches. It would do nothing but lend weight to her misapprehension in the library: that he had returned with more of the same bitterness that had poisoned the air between them.

He had not. He had come to court her, not reproach her. And they had barely begun to recapture some of the hopeful tenor of their earlier exchanges. He *would not* tear down bridges with ill-timed questions, Darcy resolved, so he forced a smile as a wordless answer to her comment, as if he regarded it as no more than a passing jest.

It served the purpose. The thorny subject was abandoned when Elizabeth spoke again:

"What I have yet to grow accustomed to is the rich variety of ground. It should not have come as a surprise, yet it still does, even after three days of lengthy rambles," she said with a little smile, and Darcy could be nothing but grateful for her willingness, and indeed her skill, in furthering conversation with an innocuous and welcome topic.

He smiled back.

"I am very glad to hear it. I was hoping it would please you."

"How could it not? Rufus and I have already discovered several fine prospects, although it would be fair to say that I appreciated them more than he did, seeing as he is so easily distracted by anything that moves. Speaking of which, I ought to take him for his walk, lest he makes mischief in the ornamental gardens. I imagine we shall return in about an hour," she said, rising to her feet, and Darcy was quick to follow.

"I would be happy to escort you, if I may," he tentatively offered.

She had not expected that – he could easily ascertain as much from the fleeting glance she cast him. Nevertheless, she smoothed her skirts and simply said, "Of course."

❦

The walk proved to be a sterling notion. Everything seemed a vast deal less fraught out of doors. Even the silence was companionable rather than unsettling. Moreover, it was often broken for, without much effort, both of them could find topics for untroubled conversation.

Darcy pointed out garden features and told her a little of their history: his mother's rose garden; the tree-lined avenues so favoured by his great-great-grandfather; the Temple of the Muses, commissioned by his grandmother because she had been so taken with its counterpart in His Grace of Rutland's grounds.

For her part, Elizabeth asked about the layout of the garden; the stages in the building of the house; the follies perched atop the wooded hillside; the concealed and now secured entrance to the tunnel dug in the early years of the Reformation at the behest of a distant ancestor who had steadfastly kept the Old Faith.

They walked further than Darcy had originally thought they would, simply because it was such a relief to discard the cloak of discomfort that had stifled them within. Once they had crossed the gated bridge over the ha-ha and ambled into the extensive parkland, there were several other landmarks patiently waiting to be pointed out: the spire of St Michael's Church in Lambton and the smaller one of Kympton Church; wind-carved gritstone outcrops; the glistening surface of Heatherdale Pool, and the tors in the distance.

"Stunning…" Elizabeth breathed, her eyes wide with wonder as they glided over the surrounding landscape, her manifest delight filling his heart with joy and instantly making the long-treasured scenery all the more precious because it was his gift to her – and she revelled in it.

"I take it that you have not walked this way before," Darcy quietly observed, and she shook her head.

"Not this way, no. As a rule, Rufus chose to scamper towards the stream or beyond the walled garden, and I let him have his way. The pair of us found some very pleasing vantage points, but none quite so spectacular."

The casual disclosure could not fail to bring a measure of concern.

"Just the pair of you?" Darcy asked. "I was hoping you might have had Peter or Thomas for an escort."

"Oh, no, there was no cause for that," Elizabeth promptly dismissed the notion. "I am accustomed to solitary walks – and looking after myself, for that matter."

Darcy pressed his lips together and thought better of belatedly arguing the point or dwelling on fresh contrition. What was done was done. He was home now. And it was his privilege to walk with her – look after her. In every sense, not just on her rambles.

So he merely said, "Nevertheless, I am relieved that you have not walked along this path unescorted. It reaches a very steep ravine in about a quarter of a mile. Quite treacherous, should you lose your footing, or if Rufus should rush heedlessly and find himself in need of your assistance. Having said that, he has not caused any mischief so far," he added, compelled by both tact and fairness, "so perhaps I should give him more credit."

"Perhaps you should," Elizabeth smilingly concurred, and said nothing further.

Neither did he, although Darcy was tempted to observe that he was rather glad of the small terrier's propensity to be easily distracted. Throughout their walk, Rufus had gleefully darted this way and that, too caught in all manner of explorations to keep a jaundiced eye on him and guard Elizabeth from his very presence. So the meddlesome creature was a great deal more tolerable out of doors, Darcy reflected with a touch of wry amusement, little knowing that before too long Elizabeth's boisterous companion would oblige him beyond imagination.

It happened an hour or so later, when they were making their way back towards the house because dusk was falling and, rewarding as the walk had been, they could not linger on the moors forever.

The circular route Darcy had chosen took them down the narrow footpath that meandered through countless clumps of rhododendrons. They were descending the steep incline, step by cautious step, and he was about to let Elizabeth know that, come April, the entire hillside would burst into a riot of colour, when all of a sudden Rufus darted between them and crossed the path in wild, uncoordinated haste, tripping her as he did so.

Darcy barely had the time to spin round and catch her. He instinctively anchored his heels in the soft, damp soil, lest they gracelessly tumble down the slope together, and the terrier's shrill barks rent the air as Rufus gave chase to some hapless woodland creature and vanished in the undergrowth.

The small dog and his quarry might as well have fallen off the edges of the world. Darcy could not spare them another thought. He stood stock-still, lost in her gaze – lost in the gloriously unexpected moment – until a strange tightness in his chest reminded him to breathe.

He did. Air rushed into his lungs, and it was intoxicating. Because they had never stood so close. Close enough for him to find the heady fragrance of her skin in the very air that he breathed.

He drank deep, letting it flood his senses, even as wisps of reason urged him to slacken his hold around her waist. They could barely make themselves heard, those wisps of reason, yet they were irksomely insistent, so he cursed them and complied.

Light-headedness set in when, for all the slackened hold, she made no move to withdraw but remained where she was, her hand on his shoulder, her shimmering eyes never veering from his. Dark brown eyes flecked with gold, a warm glow in their depths. A glow that filled his world when Darcy dipped his head and touched his lips to hers.

He could not have drawn back if his life hung in balance when a puff of air brushed his face, and her slender frame, tense with the shock of the near-fall, loosened into abandon. Closing her eyes, she kissed him back – and it was all that he could do not to give in to the fierce onslaught of desire. By dint of sheer will, he kept the kiss light. Soft. A tender caress against her lips that deepened slowly, with gentle pressure, much as it begged to flare into ravenous possession as passion surged and burst into a blaze. Resisting it was nothing short of agony – exquisite agony, too sweet to be relinquished – and it was only when he felt his self-control inexorably slipping that he forced himself to cease playing with fire and drew back a little. A very little. But it was still beyond him to let his arm drop.

Her eyes fluttered open and, to his relief, Darcy found that they had lost nothing of their glow. If anything, they seemed to have gained an impish glimmer.

"Thank goodness for squirrels, I suppose," Elizabeth said with a breathless little chuckle, "or whatever it was that Rufus was chasing. I should not have wished him to acquaint you with his fangs just now, if he happened to mistake the matter."

She lightly stroked his lapel as she said that, the touch burning him through her gloves and his layers of clothing. So he could not forbear brushing her lips with his again, and his smiling eyes flicked back to hers as he whispered, "Worth it."

True to that view, Darcy nonchalantly stood his ground when loud barks forewarned him of the imminent return of Elizabeth's self-appointed protector.

It was she who stepped back and put distance between them. But she ran her hand along his sleeve as she did so, and linked her gloved fingers with his. And did not let go, even when she bent down to stroke the terrier's back, once Rufus had reached them.

"What have you been up to this time, eh? Now here is a new notion for you: what if you were to leave those poor squirrels be?" she asked.

Predictably, there was no sympathy for the squirrels' plight in the yaps she received by way of an answer. Panting happily and looking very much like he was grinning, Rufus seemed supremely unaffected by the mild reproof. He scurried away, sending dead leaves flying, and returned with a stick, which he dropped at Elizabeth's feet in the clear expectation that she should throw it.

"Oh, very well," she conceded, and Darcy was more than a little pleased to find that she did not withdraw her hand from his when she obliged her little companion, then cautiously resumed her descent down the slope.

Perhaps she was only seeking support, Darcy was quick to tell himself, lest he read too much into it. Even so, walking hand in hand with her was no less enjoyable.

No sooner was the stick sent flying than Rufus darted after it in hot pursuit, claws digging into the mud and ears flapping, and brought it back in no time at all. It was thrown again, and retrieved just as swiftly. When the pattern was repeated for the fifth time, Elizabeth gave a rueful chuckle.

"Now he will not tire of it. And you will say I spoil him."

Darcy stroked her hand and countered, "I most certainly shall not. That would be uncivil. Or churlish. Or both. Not to mention that I would much rather not quarrel with you."

Her lips twitched as she glanced up towards him.

"I am pleased to hear it."

Thankfully, she did not say, *'That makes a change,'* Darcy reflected. Whether or not she was about to say anything else remained a mystery, for Rufus returned, as boisterous as ever and not in the least inclined to abandon his game.

"May I?" Darcy asked and stretched out his free hand, just as Elizabeth made to raise the stick above her head and throw it.

"By all means," she agreed, only to tilt her head sideways with a quirk of appreciation in her lips when, albeit left-handedly, he threw the stick a great deal further than she had.

Yet Rufus was singularly unimpressed. He did not chase after it, but turned his head to look at them, as though disappointed or at the very least perplexed by Elizabeth's choice to include a third party in their game. When he did saunter along the path at last, it was with the air of one who was reluctantly doing them a favour. And once he found the stick, he stretched down and began to gnaw at it.

"I see. Who is churlish now, sir?" Darcy chortled. But seeing as they had emerged from the wooded dell and stood in the open, where they could easily be seen from the house despite the fading light, he thought better of using the terrier's distraction to his personal advantage. Although fiercely private, this time he was not overly concerned if he should be spotted stealing a kiss or two in his own shrubbery. They were newly married, after all. Besides, his people would have better things to do than to stare out of the window. Yet Elizabeth might be of a different mind, and it would not do to discomfit her. So, of necessity, he contented himself with carrying her gloved hand to his lips and said, "Thank you. I greatly enjoyed our walk."

"So did I," Elizabeth reassuringly replied, then gave a little gasp as she peered at the clock above the entrance to the orangery. "Goodness, is it that late? I thought the dark clouds were to blame for the poor light. As it is, we might have to delay dinner."

Darcy nodded.

"By an hour, shall we say?" he suggested. It would have made no difference to him under normal circumstances, but after the spell at the hunting lodge he would much rather allow sufficient time for a hot bath.

Elizabeth gave a vague gesture of agreement.

"Of course. Or even less. I can ready myself sooner. I should not wish to give them the inconvenience of keeping the food warm."

Her thoughtfulness was touching, so Darcy thought better of pointing out that it was his people who should concern themselves with her convenience, not the other way around.

"They will not mind," he said instead. "In fact, I am prepared to wager that Howard and Mrs Reynolds have already made arrangements. They have always had a way of steering the best course before they are even asked."

"Yes. I came to see that too," Elizabeth observed with a little smile. "Dinner in two hours, then," she concluded. "Oh, by the bye, I have chosen the smaller dining room so far, but if you prefer the main one…"

"No, not at all," Darcy assured her, quick to reject the cold formality of the pair of them spending the evening at opposite ends of the twenty-foot-long mahogany table. After his father's passing, that stately piece of furniture had been in use only on the rare occasions when he had bowed to the neighbourly necessity of opening Pemberley's doors to guests. Never when he had dined alone.

He drew a deep breath.

As of tonight, he would never dine alone again, God willing. And soon – how soon? – he would no longer sleep alone either.

Darcy ran his thumb over the back of her gloved fingers, still linked with his, and glanced her way as he said softly, "I would also choose the small one. It is better suited for a quiet family dinner."

Elizabeth did not look up, so he could not see her face – the brim of her bonnet concealed it. Her gaze still lowered, she smoothed her skirts with her free hand and replied, "Indeed."

Several yards ahead, Rufus scrambled to his feet at their approach. He rubbed his muzzle with his paw and sneezed, then took the gnawed stick between his teeth and, head high and tail in the air, he boldly pranced towards the entrance.

For his part, Darcy was not given to prancing. But it was only with determined effort that he kept his pace sedate as he walked hand in hand with his bride towards the house.

Chapter 19

The dressing room was very quiet. Nothing could be heard but the crackle of the fire and a quiet *swish-swish-swish* – Weston sharpening the razor blade. At any other time, the soft melange might have been soporific as Darcy leaned against the tub, eyes closed, relishing the heat that loosened the tension in his muscles. He was not likely to succumb to sleep anytime soon, now that a different sort of tension was keeping him vibrantly awake, but he did find the familiar sounds relaxing as he mentally reviewed the day and found it satisfying. Encouraging, too. Aye, it had been a good day, all in all. And a promising evening lay ahead. More than a little promising. The awkwardness between them, so painfully obvious on his arrival, had melted away little by little. Especially on their walk. They had spoken almost as freely as they had in Hertfordshire. Not as much, but almost as freely. The sense of treading on eggshells had abated too – because she had not shied from him. And he had found neither unease nor wariness in her when he had kissed her.

That ardent recollection was more than apt to jolt him into full alertness, and on its heels came another thought, no less potent: was she in her own dressing room just now – three doors away – readying herself for dinner – bathing…?

Darcy sat up with a loud splash and rinsed his face with a handful of water. At the far end of the room, his valet looked up from his employment.

"Shall I fetch your towel, sir?"

"Thank you, Weston. Aye, do, if you would."

◦◦◦◦◦◦

The freshly sharpened blade produced better results when wielded by his practised and dedicated valet. For one thing, it left his skin intact, which Darcy could not say of his own perfunctory efforts while he was away. Clean-shaven and refreshed, he dressed with uncommon care – and could not fail to smile in a measure of amusement at his overriding sense of anticipation that verged on the giddiness of a callow youth who was going a-courting. And what of it? It was fitting. He was about to spend the evening courting his bride. The most appealing sort of courtship, truth be told. In their own home. In absolute and delectable intimacy. Far from swarming crowds of strangers. Safe from prying eyes. No troublesome relations – hers – his. No meddling and no malice from interested parties. No chaperones. And no fear of interruptions.

Brows knitted in concentration, his man assessed the fall of his neckcloth, tugged once more at his lapels and stepped back.

"Will there be anything else, sir?"

"No. I think not."

"Then may I bid you a pleasant evening, Mr Darcy," Weston said and bowed, mien impassive and voice bland, after the manner of the perfect servant, as if this were yet another ordinary evening.

Or rather, as though Weston did not know quite as well as he that the evening was anything but ordinary, Darcy reflected and thanked his valet with a nod.

As he left his chambers and headed for the stairs, he cautiously acknowledged that all signs did point to a pleasant evening. He could only hope that it would be a great deal more than that.

∞◈∞

The small dining room looked as welcoming as he would have wished. A merry fire burning in the hearth. The table already laid – naturally – the glasses and the small silver epergne glinting in the candlelight. He was early, but Darcy already knew as much, even before he glanced at the *or moulu* clock on the mantelpiece. Fourteen minutes early. And glad of it. Not just because it would have been uncivil to keep her waiting. The short interval of solitude was welcome in and of itself.

As a chance to settle his nerves?

The notion made him chuckle. It brought to mind histrionic females reaching for their smelling salts, and any parallel between them and himself easily accounted for his silent amusement. Still, such absurdities aside, Darcy was compelled to own that he appreciated a few quiet moments to draw breath and mentally prepare himself for the hours ahead. Not to plan his course of action – not as such. This did not lend itself to planning. Besides, planning held undertones of scheming, and he instinctively rejected that.

This evening was not about scheming his way into her favour. It was about building bridges. With tenderness and patience. A great deal of patience and understanding.

Darcy brought his hand to rest on the edge of the mantelshelf and stared into the flames as he reminded himself that the other night – his last night at the hunting lodge – he had endeavoured to do precisely that: understand her. It would serve him well to continue in that vein. In truth, it already had. In the course of just one day – half a day, rather – once he had taught himself to pay heed, he had been given enough reasons to hope that the distressing overhearings at Longbourn had been but a reflection of her fear of the unknown.

So the answer was simple: he must cease to be an unknown quantity to her. Make her see she was loved. Cherished. And then the intimacy he craved would naturally follow. The true intimacy between husband and wife, that went beyond the carnal.

His hand tightened into a fist around the polished wood. Aye, he desperately craved that level of intimacy too, but it could not be suffered to become the crux of the matter. Tonight was about *her*. Her readiness, not his. Her wishes.

The muted sound of the opening door and the faint rustle of fabric caught his notice, and Darcy turned around – only to find himself hard-pressed not to gape. She was exquisite. A vision in shimmering silk, her cheeks a rosy hue as she stepped into the room and walked towards him, her simple but exceedingly flattering gown wreathing her slender form in amber and gold and all the colours of the sunset.

"Good evening," Darcy said at last, his mouth dry, and remembered to bow.

Elizabeth matched his greeting with a curtsy that might have given a formal air to any other woman. But not her. Everything about her spoke of the sort of vitality and sparkle that had nothing to do with stiff formality. She was a vibrantly alluring picture of perfection, from the fetching nest of curls that crowned her head to the tips of her satin slippers. And he would have dearly liked to say so. But commenting on a lady's appearance was simply not done, and much as besotted husbands should be given special dispensation – and presumably they were – perhaps he should not hasten to claim that privilege. Not yet, at least.

So he merely gestured towards the table with a quiet, "Shall we sit?"

She nodded, and he went to pull the nearest chair for her, glad to note that their places had been set close together, with just the corner of the table between them, and not at opposite ends. It must have been Howard's doing, Darcy assumed, duly grateful for his butler's thoughtfulness and worldly wisdom.

He was about to ask Elizabeth if she would like him to tug the cord and let his people know that dinner could be served, when a light tap on the door made that query redundant. The newcomer was Mr Howard himself – timely as ever, not just thoughtful.

Permission was sought and granted, and in short order Mr Howard ushered the footmen within, and the first cover was laid out. Once glasses were filled and their first choices were arrayed upon their plates, Mr Howard tactfully gestured Thomas and Peter out of the room and likewise made himself scarce, leaving them to their own devices – or rather leaving Darcy to belatedly wish he had used his time of solitary reflection better. Namely, that he had made a mental note of things to talk about.

Improvidently, he had not – and now it was just the crackle of the fire and the quiet clink of knives and forks against the china that broke the silence, and that would not do. He reached for his glass of wine as he racked his brain for a neutral topic, and cursed himself when he could think of none.

A notion did come to mind as he sipped his Rhenish wine, but it was instantly dismissed. Toasting the one-week anniversary of their wedding was nothing short of idiotic, he irritably thought. It would only remind her of their first dismal dinner at the inn. Why the deuce would he do *that*, when –praise be – however quiet, this one was manifestly better?

But thankfully one thought led to another, and an innocuous subject came to mind:

"How does your maid Sarah? Is she growing accustomed to the change?"

The glance Elizabeth cast him seemed to be one of surprised pleasure; and then she spoke and confirmed that encouraging impression:

"'Tis kind of you to ask. She is, yes. Much like myself, she has found a warm welcome in the household."

"I am very glad to hear it." For her sake more than the maid's, but for now Darcy thought better of saying so. He helped himself to the perch in parsley sauce and added, "If you should wish to engage a lady's maid already trained for the purpose, that could be easily arranged."

Elizabeth toyed with the food on her plate as she filtered another glance towards him.

"Was that a veiled way of saying that you do not think Sarah equal to the task? I hope there is nothing severely wrong with my appearance."

"Goodness, no! Nothing at all," Darcy exclaimed, horrified at the wretched turn of the conversation. "I did not mean to suggest anything of the sort."

Elizabeth set her knife down and, to his astonishment, reached out and lightly pressed his hand.

"My apologies. I was jesting," she confessed with a rueful smile, before returning to her dish of herbed chicken and glazed parsnips.

"Oh..." Darcy said, feeling a little foolish, his hand still frozen in place at the delectable surprise of her all-too-brief touch. And then it occurred to him that this was as good a time as any to voice what he had been thinking, so he leaned back and made his own confession. "In point of fact, I have been looking for an opportunity to say that you look utterly ravishing tonight."

At that, she darted her eyes towards him once more with a whispered, "Thank you," a most becoming blush rising in her cheeks, and Darcy could not possibly regret his intrepidity.

She was all the more charming when she blushed.

He ought not stare, as he knew full well, yet he could not help it. A good many seconds later he was still staring, mesmerised by the subtle glow of her skin, and no less by the long, enticing ringlet that trailed down from her temple and caressed her cheek with every move she made. But reaching out and twirling it around his finger was not an option at the moment – nor was stroking her face, for that matter – so, with considerable effort, Darcy forced himself to drop his gaze to his plate.

Declaring himself over his half-eaten perch fillet was not a sensible option either, so he was faced with the same conundrum yet again: how on earth did he propose to court her, if he could not even decide on topics that would be neither hazardous nor dull? Heaven forbid that he should find himself speaking of the weather just for the sake of saying anything at all!

And then she spoke – and did precisely that.

"Does this part of the country see much more snow than the south? Or is it rain-rain-rain for most of the winter months?"

"Last winter was particularly harsh," Darcy replied, as soon as he had swallowed his morsel. "There was snow on the ground, and a fair amount of it, from late November all through to February. But I daresay the rest of the country saw its share as well. Hertfordshire too, I imagine. I know that the Thames froze last January."

"Oh, yes. My aunt Gardiner did say so."

That would be the wife of her tradesman uncle, Darcy recalled. Well, if it came to that, he could even speak of her Cheapside relations. It was better than silence. He was about to ask if she had received any communications from her aunt in town, when she spared him that task and, far more adept in the art of conversation than he, brought up a different topic.

"The food is delicious," she observed, then chuckled. "This reminds me. Mamma was greatly unnerved about the prospect of hosting you for dinner."

"Was she? Why was that?"

Elizabeth set her glass down and gave a little flourish of her hand towards the array of choices on the table.

"On account of your being accustomed to sophisticated fare, of course. She supposed you to have two or three French cooks at least, and that anything served at Longbourn would pale in comparison."

At one time, Mrs Bennet's undue interest in his domestic arrangements might have struck him as yet another proof of her lack of breeding. Now it did not even cross his mind to take objection. Nor did he have any recollection of the fare served at Longbourn. Even so, Darcy felt he was no less truthful when he civilly replied, "Pray assure your mother that I found it a most enjoyable dinner. As for French cooks, there is just the one."

Elizabeth cast him a little smile.

"Yes, I know that now. I made Monsieur Gustave's acquaintance on Monday, when I wished to give him my compliments for an especially flavoursome roast lamb. But, most undutifully, so far I have neglected to set my mother's mind to rest in that regard."

Darcy returned her smile and, as undutiful a son-in-law as any, readily dismissed Mrs Bennet from his thoughts.

"Allow me," he swiftly said when Elizabeth made to help herself to another dish – but, to his acute mortification, he very nearly overset his glass of wine in his haste to come to her assistance.

He caught it by sheer chance and fast reflexes, and as he set it down on the other side of his plate, Darcy barely suppressed the urge to roll his eyes. For goodness' sake! Whatever had got into him? He had not been this clumsy since his boyhood. He must have been a gawky lad of twelve the last time he had overturned anything at the dinner table.

Yet whether or not Elizabeth was diverted by his antics, she kindly gave no sign of it.

"I was wondering what this might be," she spoke as though nothing had happened, so he endeavoured to do likewise.

"Which do you mean? Oh. Liver and port terrine, at a guess. But I feel I should give you fair warning: it is an acquired taste. Personally, I cannot abide it." A cheerfully questioning glance was cast his way, so his lips twitched as he added, "You must wonder why it was served. It so happens that this dish is a great favourite with my sister, and for some reason Mrs Reynolds is under the impression that I share that view. I did not have the heart to disabuse her of that notion."

"I see," Elizabeth replied, her lips twitching too. "Well, I am excessively curious by nature, so I shall take my chances with it," she said as she helped herself to a small slice from the serving plate he was holding for her. She cautiously tried a bite, then glanced up to cast him an adorably impish smile. "I fear I shall have to side with your sister. I cannot find anything objectionable about the flavour. Quite the opposite, in fact."

"Georgiana will be pleased to hear it. And Mrs Reynolds too," Darcy said and matched her smile as he set the serving plate back on the table without oversetting anything this time.

He helped himself to beef and horseradish as Elizabeth returned to her terrine.

"It seems to me that you are the only one at a disadvantage in this," she observed.

"Am I? In what way?"

"You will have to see it brought to the table even when your sister is absent."

"No change there, then," he airily replied, gesturing towards the dish in question. "Pray do not let that trouble you. I flatter myself that I can bear it."

"Is there anything else you would not touch to save your life?" she asked with an engagingly arch smile that made it quite difficult for Darcy to focus on her actual question.

Even so, he pondered and eventually said, his eyes crinkling at the corners, "I do not think I feel quite so strongly about anything else except pilchards. And dishes involving cabbage."

"And is Mrs Reynolds aware of this?"

"She is, to the best of my knowledge," Darcy replied, leaning back in his chair, thoroughly enchanted with everything about her, not least her admirable patience with a conversation that bordered on the nonsensical. He had been struggling to find topics that would appeal to her sharp wits – yet there they were talking about cabbage and pilchards!

"Very well. If by any chance she does not know and you cannot bring yourself to set her to rights on that score either, I am prepared to let her think that the objection is all mine. I am not fond of them myself, so rest easy, I hereby declare that neither pilchards nor cabbage will ever be served at dinner," she concluded with an air of mock gravity, which was when Darcy finally grasped that there was nothing nonsensical about their conversation. Rather, *he* was the one lacking in sense.

They were not speaking of pilchards. They were speaking of him – of the pair of them. Of her sitting with Mrs Reynolds to make decisions as the mistress of this house.

"Thank you," he said, the long, smiling gaze he settled upon her a great deal warmer than it would have been, had he still imagined that they were talking about food.

"Your sister, is she much like you?" Elizabeth asked a little later, once Darcy had helped her to a round of veal and some of the asparagus and celeriac gratin.

"There *is* a strong physical resemblance between us, but I expect that was not your question," he replied, only to see her shake her head, so he resumed, "I think we are alike in many ways. But you will form your own opinion when she joins us in January. I hope the pair of you will be friends."

"I am sure we shall. It will be good to have a sister's company," she said without hesitation, her thoughtful answer as touching as her implied admission that she missed her own sisters. Of course she did. They had formed a significant part of her life – even though, much like the liver and port terrine, some of them were an acquired taste, to say the least. But he would not comment on it.

"It will be very good for Georgiana too," Darcy said instead. "She needs female guidance – needs a sister. And, to my way of thinking, she could not have done better than you."

It was plain to see that his instinctive homage pleased her even before she voiced her quiet thanks.

"Not at all," he earnestly replied. "Your liveliness and generosity of spirit will do her a world of good. My sister is—" He stopped short and cleared his voice. "Georgiana is more than ten years my junior, and has not had many companions her own age. Not as a child. This must be one of the reasons for her growing up to be so very shy."

Excessively shy – cripplingly so. But that, he did not say. Nor did he permit himself to dwell on the monstrous blight upon Georgiana's gentle nature. Tonight of all nights, he *would not* think of Wickham!

Unwittingly, Elizabeth rescued him from grim thoughts when she spoke again, and he blessed her for it.

"Not something you would say about yourself, then," she observed, and Darcy's gaze lingered on her beloved countenance – the surest antidote to bile and hatred.

"No," he said at last. "Reserved, yes. Perhaps distant. Aloof and unsociable, my cousin Richard claims whenever he is inclined to reform me. But certainly not shy."

Elizabeth gave a mild chuckle.

"Reform you? In what way?"

Darcy shrugged.

"He is an expansive sort, and would like me to follow his example. But that has never been my way."

"Do you have any other cousins?" she asked, and for a moment Darcy was astonished that she did not know already.

But of course she did not. They had not spoken of his relations. In fact, ever since their sudden betrothal, they had barely spoken of anything except the essentials. Their vexing predicament. Immediate plans. Arrangements for the wedding. So how in heaven's name had it come as a surprise to him that they had yet to form a true connection?

"Six altogether on my mother's side," he supplied, and then elaborated. "My aunt has only one daughter – Anne. Richard, the expansive one I spoke of, is my uncle's second son. He is a colonel in His Majesty's army. Then there is Henry, his younger brother, and their sisters, Harriet and Amelia. And Leighton, of course. The eldest."

Elizabeth arched a brow.

"Leighton?"

"His title," Darcy clarified. "Francis Reginald Fitzwilliam, Lord Leighton."

"Oh…"

The turn of her countenance suggested surprise, but there was something else there; something he could not read, and it troubled him. There was every chance that she might not be ready to disclose precisely what she was thinking, but that did not stop him from asking, "Is anything the matter?"

Elizabeth shook her head.

"Nothing in particular," she said with a little flourish of her hand. "I am simply digesting the new information: that you have titled connections and your Christian name and your mother's maiden name are one and the same."

She seemed about to add something further, but the discreet knock on the door gave her pause, and Darcy could barely suppress a grimace. He had not taken into account the comings and goings of his people earlier, when he had rejoiced in the lack of interruptions.

"Come," he called, with as much evenness as he could muster, and armed himself with patience as Mr Howard and the footmen walked in to circle around the table, remove some serving plates and set down others, until the second cover was laid out with skill and care, the neat arrangement forming a pleasing pattern.

"I believe you were about to say something when they came in," Darcy prompted, once they were alone, and for a moment Elizabeth looked puzzled.

"Was I?" she mused, her brow furrowed as though she was seeking to remember. "Oh, yes. I think I was about to remark that there is so much that each of us does not know about the other."

"True," Darcy said and smiled. "We should remedy that as soon as may be."

"My thought entirely. So, are there any other cousins I should know of?"

"Four more on my father's side. Second and third cousins twice removed. No first cousins, though. My father was an only child," Darcy informed her. "But I shall not tax your patience with too many details about his side of the family. They live in Lincolnshire and rarely stir from home, so we are not likely to see them often. What of your own cousins?"

"Just my uncle Gardiner's children, the eldest but twelve. And on my father's side, the one with whom you are already acquainted," Elizabeth said rather tersely, putting a clear end to that particular topic.

That was a trifle disappointing, but as their conversation had been flowing with growing ease, Darcy had no difficulty in steering it towards a new subject.

"Speaking of new acquaintances, I am very glad that you already are on excellent terms with the Miss Lyles and their family. They are pleasing people, and good company, I think."

Elizabeth readily nodded in agreement, and he asked, "Did anyone else come to call?"

"Yes, in point of fact," she replied, a faint quirk in her lips. "Mrs Prescott and her daughter. Perhaps I should reserve judgement on such a short acquaintance, but they left me with the impression that they were not best pleased to see me in residence at Pemberley."

Darcy frowned, gripped by fresh guilt. He had not imagined that the call would be paid so soon, and perhaps he should have – for, after all, Miss Prescott had a vast deal in common with Miss Bingley, not least a firm determination to go where she was not wanted. But that was neither here nor there. The material point was that he *should* have been at home, to stand beside his wife and shield her from disagreeable encounters.

"I am distraught I was not here," he said with energy, then sighed. "Perhaps this is as good a time as any to observe that while the Lyles and many like them are welcoming and kind, some are of a different ilk – Mrs Prescott and her daughter among them. I hope neither one had the impertinence to say anything untoward," he added swiftly, and to his vague relief, Elizabeth shook her head.

"Oh, no, nothing of the sort. Just a certain something in their air, that is all. But it did make me wonder," she resumed, and the quirk in her lips grew wry. "Pray tell me, once we travel to town, need I prepare myself to brave an army of young ladies and their mammas, all disappointed and mightily resentful that I claimed the much-coveted prize?"

It might have been an uncomfortable question, were it not for her delightful archness. Darcy could not forbear a self-deprecating smile.

"I would not put it thus, myself," he said, then sobered as he privately owned that there *would* be a measure of ill will, and not just from strangers. He had yet to hear from his aunt Catherine, and it would be foolish to believe that the respite would last for very long. His lips tightened in a determined grimace. Be that as it may. Neither his outspoken aunt nor anyone else would be allowed to injure her.

Much as he had sought to maintain a guarded manner ever since she had joined him in the dining room, it was beyond him to keep his distance now, so he reached out and covered her small hand with his. She raised her eyes to his then – pools of dark amber sparkling in the candlelight – liquid eyes that robbed him of coherent thought. But this had to be said. It was of great import. So he rallied and spoke:

"That sort of malice will not touch you. Nor does it have any power over us. And I assure you that if there were any expectations of that nature, they were formed with no encouragement from me."

Elizabeth gave a rueful little chuckle.

"I think we can both agree that people will think what they will, with or without encouragement. But never mind that now. What I would dearly like to know is how I might sample Monsieur Gustave's appealing offerings when I find myself barely able to eat another morsel," she easily changed the subject with the cheerful delicacy and charm that she alone possessed, and her lips shaped themselves into a smile so engaging that it was a hardship to remain where he was and not lean forward to kiss her.

Darcy clasped her hand, then reluctantly released it, trailing his fingertips over her wrist in a lingering caress, and struggled with all his might to keep to the humorous note she had chosen for their conversation.

"I daresay he will not take it amiss if we tackle them as best we can. What surprises *me* is that Howard and the footmen did not arrive with Rufus on their heels. I have been expecting the patter of paws and some loud barks for a fair while. His restraint is admirable. Staggering, even. And if he went upstairs with you earlier to keep you company while you were readying for dinner, he must have been on his best behaviour. Or just very quiet," he finished with a quirk in his lips, choosing to archly qualify the praise that bordered on the excessive.

Elizabeth gave a little gesture of negation.

"Oh, no, it would not do for him to form bad habits. He is only brought in here on occasion, and never allowed in my bedchamber."

"Ah. I am very glad to hear it," Darcy quipped without thinking – only to see colour flaring in her cheeks. So he looked away and roundly cursed himself for drawing quite so much attention to the question that lurked around the edges of the cosy room and in the minds of both: were they to retire upstairs together at the end of the evening?

"If you would try anything, I recommend the praline fancies or the apple tart. They are Monsieur Gustave's specialities," he said to fill the silence, before it grew even more charged than it already was. "Or the redcurrant jelly. 'Tis light and refreshing," he added, and felt beyond ridiculous as soon as the words passed his lips. Good grief! He was well on his way to sounding just like Mrs Bennet pressing her guests to sample the refreshments!

Elizabeth helped herself to a sliver of apple tart, but Darcy rather suspected she only sought to give herself some employment, for she merely picked at it. He would not disconcert her all the more by fixing his eyes on her, but even with her hands at the periphery of his field of vision, he could not fail to register their every move. Graceful hands, adorned just with the ring he had placed on her finger on their wedding day, and a thin bracelet around her wrist.

The unpretentious ornament reminded him that the family heirlooms should be entrusted to her keeping. That matter should be addressed, and soon. It would be a great joy to see her wear the pieces that had been passed down from one Mrs Darcy to the next. Still, he could not but own that the filigree bracelet somehow suited her delicate wrist better.

With some determination, he redirected his attention to his plate and endeavoured not to dwell overmuch on the accursed folly of having blurted out the ill-judged comment that had caused the return to uneasy silence – for, much like at the start of dinner, nothing could be heard in the quiet room but the crackle of the fire and the clink of cutlery against their plates.

And then, with one last clink, Elizabeth set her fork and spoon alongside her unfinished slice of apple tart. Instinctively, Darcy looked up, and their eyes met over her napkin as she dabbed her lips, before she glanced away and set the napkin down as well. His interest in the contents of his plate long gone, Darcy followed suit – set down his own cutlery – made use of his napkin – left it on the table. And waited in silence, utterly at a loss as to how he should proceed.

It was plain to see that she was not faring any better. She parted her lips to speak, but must have changed her mind, for she said nothing. She darted her eyes over the barely touched array of dishes, then dropped her gaze to her right hand that was still worrying at a corner of her napkin.

A surge of tenderness flooded Darcy's heart at her patent and most affecting nervousness, and he wished he were skilled with words, so that he might find the best way to tell her that she need not fret. That he loved her, and would not rush her into anything.

Failing that, he would have wanted to at least try to reassure her without words, but before he could decide whether to reach out and stroke her hand or hold back, lest the gesture be perceived as an overture rather than mere reassurance, that choice was no longer his to make. She drew her hand away, to rest it on her lap.

Remaining thus, frozen in awkward inaction, was the worst option of all, so it was instantly discarded.

"Shall we sit by the fire?" Darcy asked, his voice lowered to a near-whisper.

She glanced up at that, her colour high. But her lips curled up into a faint smile.

"Yes, that would be... lovely," she tentatively said, so he stood to assist her.

He pulled her chair back and she rose to her feet, lifting the trailing end of her shawl and draping it over her shoulder with the unstudied grace of a vestal virgin donning her snow-white peplum.

Darcy's gaze remained fixed on her slender form as she went to take a seat in one of the wingchairs set before the fireplace. Her every move was both virginally graceful and artlessly seductive, a combination that inflamed the senses, and he drew an uneven breath, his senses already aflame. It would not be easy to tread slowly – at *her* pace, not his – when their courtship dance, this measured tiptoeing towards marital intimacy, was so wildly arousing. Far more than he could have imagined. So he drew another breath – a deep, steadying one this time – and followed in her footsteps to claim the other seat, all the while wishing he had had the foresight to commission his footmen to replace the pair of wingchairs with a sofa for two.

As matters stood, he found that he could not force himself to sit still for longer than five minutes – not if he had to sit across from her.

"Madeira?" he asked softly, and rose to his feet as soon as she nodded with a hesitant, "I… Yes, I thank you."

Darcy ambled towards the sideboard and poured her drink, then his, and carried the glasses to the fireplace. He handed her the thimbleful of sweet wine and did not resume his seat. He did not sip his drink either, but left it on the mantelpiece and crouched down to add more wood to the fire. Not that it was needed. Yet he did so nonetheless, and prodded the logs with the poker for good measure, sending sparks flying, until the pile of wood settled with a quiet thud and a small cloud of ash and smoke.

Heat smouldering within, over and above the heat of the fire, Darcy set the poker back in its place and turned around – only to encounter flying sparks of a different sort when he found her gaze fixed on him. Burning him. And when their eyes met with a jolt, she did not look away.

As far as Darcy was concerned, that served to decide the matter.

He retrieved his glass and went to sit beside her chair, on the floor.

His choice was not questioned – not that he imagined it would be. But this time she did lower her gaze, and her colour deepened.

Inwardly cursing the small screen of upholstery between them, Darcy rested his elbow on his bent knee and sipped his brandy, his unblinking stare fixed on the leaping flames. The sight might have been comforting in different circumstances. Might have been calming, too. Now it was neither. In fact, the ceaseless play of light and shadow was the very opposite of calming. And no amount of staring at burning logs or thinking around in circles could tell him where they were to go from here.

Only Elizabeth would. Not in so many words, perhaps. There was every chance that she did not have all the answers either. So the missing ones must be sought. They would have to find them – together.

Leaning sideways, Darcy set his glass down, then turned towards her and, slowly and deliberately, draped his arm over her armrest and reached out to hold her hand.

Her fingers twitched, once, then remained still, willingly left in his keeping. Their restless play had caught his eye all evening as she had toyed with her knife and fork, her napkin, had run her fingertips along the stem of her glass – and had thoroughly distracted him with the notion that they might glide over his bare skin before the night was out.

Now their nervous flutter had come to an end. It was just his thumb that moved and brushed her forefinger, traced a circle around the short-clipped nail and stroked its way to her knuckles as he carried her hand to his lips.

Her quiet gasp and tiny bumps of gooseflesh rising on her arm had him darting a searching look at her, and the instinctive glance turned into intense scrutiny as he lowered their joined hands. But, to his infinite relief, he could find no chilling shadows in her countenance, no telltale signs of misgivings or reluctance. A warm light shimmered in her eyes; shimmered undimmed even when her eyes grew very dark, and then darker still, gold-specked irises narrowing into haloes around jet-black pupils.

Lips parted, she held his gaze as he stroked her hand and kept searching her countenance in earnest, seeking clues in her mien and manner and hoping beyond hope that he could read them rightly. The rosy tint stealing upon her cheeks and sending them aglow. Her shallow breaths, rapid and uneven, each of them emphasised with profoundly stirring clarity by the rise and fall of her garnet cross that stood out, dark-red and eye-catching, against the creamy whiteness of her bosom. The faint but noticeable tremor of her other hand when she looked away and raised her small glass to take a sip of her Madeira – and rendered her mouth all the more luscious with the sheen of sweet wine glistening on her upper lip.

Darcy swallowed hard and dropped his gaze. He hooked his thumb around hers, turned her hand over and bent his head to press his lips to the warm softness of her palm.

Another quiet gasp was his reward – another clue? – so he did not draw back, but slowly trailed lingering kisses along the palm of her hand, in unhurried progression towards her dainty wrist.

Out of the corner of his eye, he saw the Madeira slosh dangerously in her glass and briefly considered reaching out and sparing her the effort of keeping it from spilling. But every notion of the kind completely slipped his mind when his lips found the spot beneath which her pulse was beating fast and strong – a forceful rush. Quite as forceful as the wild blood-rush of arousal racing through his veins.

His lips still caressing her skin, Darcy closed his eyes and suppressed a groan, aching to believe that she felt the same. That this was the beginning of her own awakening to desire. Heaven forbid that her heart should be pounding so because of nervousness!

He made to raise his head and anxiously search her eyes once more when, with a sharp intake of breath, she drew her hand from his clasp to weave her fingers through his hair. The light touch of her fingertips against his nape set him on fire – and a fraction of a second later, exhilarating hope exploded in his chest. He might have just had his answer: this was not remotely like nervousness – was it?

He did not raise his eyes to hers. Instead, he withdrew his hand and laid his head on her lap, abandoning himself to her caress. Her fingers froze into momentary stillness, but once a few exquisitely charged seconds had ticked away, she resumed stroking his hair, sending his scalp tingling.

His own breath growing fast and shallow, Darcy remained precisely where he was, revelling in her newfound daring and no less in the feel of her sensuous warmth beneath his cheek as he resisted the temptation to close his hand around her ankle, stroke and knead and return full circle to the fateful encounter that had brought them to where they were today.

Perhaps it was too much to hope that she had already come to regard that episode with as little regret as he – that is to say, with no regret at all – so he did not stir. Not until he felt her shiver. He raised his head then, and had no need to ask whether she was warm enough or not. The look in her eyes left him in no doubt that her shiver had naught to do with cold. Yet when she brought her glass to her lips for another sip, he reached for the fallen edge of her shawl, draped it over her shoulder, and tentatively trailed his thumb along her collarbone.

He might have chosen his timing better.

Elizabeth gave a violent start, and whatever was left of her Madeira sloshed out of the glass. For an impossibly long moment, her hand and the empty glass remained suspended in the air, and time itself stood still as Darcy assessed the damage. Translucent droplets beading her skin, just above the neckline. A splash of dark copper on the shimmering silk covering her bosom. A broken streak indelibly marking a path down her dress, all the way to the minute pool of tawny liquid in her lap, fast seeping into the fabric.

Darcy's throat went dry as wild imaginings took flight. His lips on her skin, seeking each sweet, sticky droplet... exploring every contour and tasting her exquisite flavour... then tracing the tantalising path of copper-coloured marks as he gathered her up to carry her to her bedchamber. Her stained dress undone... discarded. Gossamer undergarments discarded too. His lips on her bare skin. Her lips swollen with his kisses. Her cheeks flushed and her eyelids heavy with passion as they became one – in truth, not just in name. Now. Tonight. His at long last.

Her strangled, "Oh, my goodness!" jolted him back to reality, but sanity was still very far from his grasp. So, when Elizabeth made to scramble to her feet, he clasped her wrist and rasped, "Don't go!"

"I must," she said, her blush deepening. "This is... It will stain," she faltered as she drew her hand away to indicate the spillage with a jerky gesture.

Damn the dress! he very nearly choked out. Goodness knows that it was in his power to have a dozen new ones brought to Pemberley by the week's end. But by now sanity was gaining ground by inches, so he bit back the words and made no further protest. Instead, he moved sideways and made room for her to stand.

Elizabeth did so in a flash and went to retrieve her napkin from the table and dab at her dress, while he ran his hands over his face and rose to his feet as well, but with none of her haste and energy.

She kept dabbing, her back turned, then shook her head in exasperation.

"This will not do," she sighed. "Perhaps with cold water... But even then..."

Her voice trailed off, and she dropped the napkin on the table without finishing her sentence, while Darcy found it utterly beyond him to hold his peace.

"Leave it," he whispered hoarsely, and could not keep his distance either, but stepped closer and laid his hands on her shoulders, only to find that, to his unspeakable relief, this time she did not start. Nor did she jerk away. Instead, she gave a self-conscious chuckle.

"That was very foolish of me, and I apologise. I am not so clumsy as a rule. Nor so skittish," Elizabeth whispered as she leaned back into him, which was more than enough encouragement for Darcy to knead her shoulders with no care whatever for the silk of her puffed sleeves, now crushed under his palms as he leaned forward to press his lips just beneath the wisp of hair that formed a winsome curl behind her earlobe.

"No, *I* should beg forgiveness for ruining your dress," he breathed against her skin even as he incorrigibly trailed light kisses along her nape, then the side of her neck, and mightily fought against the temptation to slide his hands down and cup the soft swell of her breasts.

"No matter," Elizabeth murmured, her breath warming his cheek and his blood when she turned her head to cast him a little smile. "Give me half an hour – no, twenty minutes," she said, her low, throaty whisper full of delicious promise, which made it that much more difficult for him to release her.

"Very well," Darcy said at last, his fingertips trailing all the way down to her wrists, before he let his hands drop – and let her have her way.

With commendable restraint, even if he said so himself, he clung to the last shreds of patience and did not wrap his arms around her when she chose to briefly rest her temple on his shoulder, giving him a full and unimpeded view of the column of her throat and the wildly enticing hollow between her perfect breasts. Gentlemanly to the last, he did not claim the privilege to walk up with her and assist her in removing the ruined dress and every single layer of thin muslin that covered her alluring form. He watched her step away – watched the door closing noiselessly behind her, then heaved a deep breath, every fibre of his being vibrantly alive with anticipation, as though he, not she, were the one quivering through the last twenty minutes of carnal inexperience.

He started, brought up short by the sobering thought.

For God's sake, he was not some lust-crazed, untouched boy, and he had better keep that in mind and not act like one. He ached for her with all-consuming, almost terrifying passion, but he *could not* lose his head. Not tonight. For her sake and no less his own, seeing as he wished – needed – to be welcomed in her bed and not, God forbid, met with apprehension and reluctance. So he had better not take her like a savage. On this, their first night together, he *must* keep himself in check throughout. A daunting challenge, that, and very likely more than he could handle, Darcy thought and flinched, hating the onset of self-doubt. It would not help. Tonight he was supposed to be suave, skilled and reassuring, not a nervous weakling. But this was uncharted territory for him too. It was the first time that he bedded a maiden. And not just any maiden, but Elizabeth. His wife. Whom he loved beyond bounds and reason.

He raked his fingers through his hair and cast a glance at the clock on the mantelpiece, to find that only three minutes had elapsed from the twenty that she had requested. No, let it be thirty. He *should* allow her at least half an hour to make herself ready. Or perhaps a little longer.

He strode towards the fireplace, stooped to retrieve his abandoned glass and drained it in one draught, then left it on the table and took himself upstairs, for it really served no purpose to stand about fretting like a dolt. A self-deprecating grin flashed across his countenance at the thought that he might as well fret like a dolt in his own chambers while he disrobed and waited. Yet, the fleeting jollity aside, Darcy knew full well that however many minutes he would eventually allow, they would be the longest and most tormenting of his life.

Chapter 20

He was proven spectacularly wrong. The worst torment had come *after* the allotted half an hour. Although he could not honestly say which part had been the most difficult to bear. The span of time – he could not tell how long – in which, heart pounding in his chest, he had waited for a response to his first knock and strained to listen for a nervous whisper asking him within, only to hear nothing of the sort? The next stretch, when he had cursed himself for knocking too quietly or much too soon, and had struggled to decide when he should knock again? The moment when suspicion had settled in his gut, slick and ice-cold, and it had occurred to him that all her misgivings might have regained the upper hand? The wretched uncertainty over the best course of action while he had imagined her cowering under the bedcovers and staring wide-eyed at the door in fear of yet another knock or, worse still, his entrance? The moment when he had been forced to conclude that he would not even receive an answer to his quiet entreaty?

Come to think of it, what in heaven's name could he have done to reassure her other than say, "Elizabeth, I will not come in. I only wish to talk…"? Push a note under the door? Nonsense! The very notion was childish and absurd. As was she – and not in an endearing way – for refusing to even talk about it. Which had led to the agonising second when he could not bear it any longer and had tried the door – and found it locked. And then the rest of it – the span of time when he had endeavoured to determine if he should be consumed by tenderness and pity for her silent wretchedness behind the locked door – or give full rein to bitterness because she trusted him so little. Because she would not trust him at all. Would not even give him the courtesy of an answer. Even through the confounded door, if it must be so!

Naturally, he would not give himself the trouble to trade his robe for daytime apparel and return downstairs. To do what? Roam restlessly through the house? Drink himself into a stupor? Add fresh grist to the rumour mill that must be already grinding in the servants' hall?

An hour or so later, sleep had finally claimed him, but it had been fitful and had brought precious little rest. Nor had it improved his mood. What now? Go down and exchange civilities with her over breakfast as though nothing had happened? Bury his fears for the future of their marriage, smother his resentment at her complete silence and start pushing the accursed boulder up the hill once more, like Sisyphus?

With a muted, "Aye, blast it!" Darcy cast the counterpane aside. He *would* go back to push the loathsome boulder. There was nothing else to be done.

So he summoned his valet and submitted to the man's conspicuously blank-faced ministrations. Then, once Weston deemed him fit to face another day, outwardly at least, Darcy made his way downstairs to find the small dining room empty and, jaw set, he retired to his study to feign interest in his long-neglected papers.

He was only able to give them fifteen minutes of his time before he was interrupted by a quiet yet determined knock.

"Come," he called, only to discover that it was not his wife, but his housekeeper. "Mrs Reynolds," he said, rather tersely, unwilling to betray either his disappointment or his surprise at the unfamiliar occurrence. If memory served, she had never sought him in his study, but awaited his pleasure whenever he had wished to speak to her. "Yes? Do come in. What can I do for you?" he evenly enquired.

"I… Well… I thought I should come and ask if you wish me to send up an early breakfast. Or are you willing to wait for Mrs Darcy's return?"

Darcy arched a brow. There were at least two oddities in the elderly woman's words. First, the task to enquire about the preferred timing of daily repasts belonged with the footmen, and occasionally the butler. Second, this would not be an early breakfast. He had broken his fast a great deal earlier on many an occasion. Moreover, the housekeeper's countenance spoke volumes. But it seemed to speak in a foreign tongue.

Even so, he did not address the oddities, nor did he request clarifications. He only asked, "Mrs Darcy has gone out already?" and then cursed himself for speaking out of turn. Although dear old Reynolds had known him since he was a boy, it still would not do to speak too freely, not even with one of his most faithful retainers, and carelessly reveal that he had been married for mere days, yet had no notion as to where his wife was.

His housekeeper's countenance remained duly impassive.

"Aye, sir. She went out at her usual time. Mrs Darcy has formed the habit of taking her little friend for a walk at around half past seven, and then sits down for breakfast. By the bye, sir, I hope you are not put out that I brought Rufus to the house as a companion for her. I fancied she needed one, especially at this time of year. Even if it should be a four-legged companion who can listen, but cannot talk."

Darcy eyed her with a measure of suspicion.

Was his old housekeeper subtly taking him to task for leaving his wife alone so soon after their wedding, and with Christmas approaching?

He pressed his lips together into a tight line. If that were the case, he bore her no ill will for presuming to do so. For one thing, she was in the right. Besides, after more than two decades of loyal service to this house, Mrs Reynolds had earned the right to take some liberties.

So he looked up and said, "No, of course not. In fact, I appreciate your kindness in bringing Rufus here. I do not doubt that he gives her pleasure with his antics."

"I expect he does, sir. He was very boisterous this morning. But then, he always is. If anything, it was the Mistress who surprised me. I did not imagine she would come down as early as ever. She stayed up quite late last night."

With some effort, Darcy sought to smooth his countenance into blankness.

"Did she?"

"Aye, sir. She came down once you had retired and stayed in the small dining room for a while, then went into the library and sat there reading for above an hour. Quite forlorn she seemed, when I brought her a cup of chocolate and Mrs Darcy asked me to keep her company," the elderly woman said, the look in her eyes stating as plainly as could be stated without words that, to her way of thinking, *he* should have been the one keeping his new wife company. And then, once she had said her piece, Mrs Reynolds shuffled uncomfortably on her feet, as though thinking herself deserving of a rebuke for her aberrant forthrightness.

Yet rebuking her could not be further from her master's mind as relief flooded him and the proverbial boulder of Sisyphus was lifted from his heart, leaving it lighter than a feather.

A misunderstanding, nothing more! A foolish misunderstanding that might have been almost laughable, had it not caused him so much pain. He had taken her words to mean, "Give me twenty minutes and come up," whereas she had intended to change out of her ruined dress and return to him. Which was what she had done: she had returned, ready to pick up from where they had left off – only to find that he had vanished! Still, she had waited for him in the small dining room, and then the library. For over an hour. To no avail.

The rush of tenderness he had kept at bay in the darkness of the night rose and overwhelmed him. What had she made of his desertion? She must have been surprised at first – then disappointed – injured. Forlorn, Mrs Reynolds said. On account of what could only appear to her as another rejection, hard on the heels of the previous ones: his coldness on the way to Pemberley; his choice to abandon her without a word. Of course she was injured. And of course she would not send for him, nor seek him in his chambers and willingly risk being spurned again.

His heart twisted in his chest and took to beating a fast, aching rhythm at the thought of her waiting... then wondering, questioning, yet still waiting... and retiring to her chambers in low spirits. He tightened his grip around the armrests. What a senseless waste of a perfect evening! Her despondency. His. Needless heartache over a misunderstanding that was too foolish for words.

"It was very good of you to let me know, Mrs Reynolds," Darcy said at last, once he had found his voice and remembered the world around him. "Yes, I should be very glad to wait for Mrs Darcy and breakfast with her when she returns. I thank you," he offered with a warmth that had gradually faded from their interactions from around the time when he had taken up the mantle of Pemberley's master.

Her smile maternal, much like in the old days, his housekeeper nodded.

"Not at all, sir. Not at all."

◦◦◦

If patience was a virtue, then the lack of it ought to class amongst his natural flaws. It could even be said that, of all his shortcomings, this was the greatest, Darcy was compelled to own as he pushed aside the stack of papers with which he had endeavoured to while away the time until Elizabeth's return. Yet he could scarce pay heed, so he had made no progress. On the contrary. He had merely shuffled his papers around, and in all likelihood left them in a worse state than he had found them. But he could not care less as he stood from his desk, reaching for his pocket watch, although there was a perfectly serviceable clock on the mantelpiece before him. And no, it was not slow. Neither timepiece was. He had compared them many a time already. Yet that did not keep him from doing so again as he ambled towards the tall windows that afforded him a reasonably good view of three of the paths leading to the house.

There was still no sign of her.

Darcy grimaced as he pondered on the one perceivable disadvantage that came with extensive grounds and a large house. Had they been staying together at the hunting lodge, for instance, there could have been no misapprehensions as to the whereabouts of each last night. Likewise, it would have been a great deal easier to find her in the small garden, or spot her in the distance, on the moors.

He clasped his hands behind his back, his impatience by now mingled with concern. Where *was* she? It was cold. It was drizzling. And how was it possible that no one knew which way she went? He frowned. That was an unpardonable oversight. He should have instructed his butler yesterday to always ask her for some indication of her proposed walk, if she was so averse to having one of the footmen for an escort. Not that he was comfortable with the notion of her walking by herself, unless she was aiming to go for a stroll in the ornamental gardens. It did not bear thinking that something should befall her while she was goodness knows where, at a distance from the house and quite alone, with no one but a yapping little dog for company and protection. Darcy heaved a deep, uneasy breath, all too aware that he should have pressed his point. Yet he had not, deeming it irrelevant, for now he was at home and would henceforth escort her on her ambles through the grounds. He had not made allowances for misunderstandings.

He checked the time – again. Should she not have returned by now? Or did she always go on such long walks? After all, she had thought nothing of a distance of three miles when she had arrived on foot at Netherfield a month ago to enquire after her ailing sister. Unless she had purposely changed her routine this morning, so that she would stay away from the house for as long as possible. Away from him, Darcy thought and flinched, then turned on his heel and headed for the door.

᭡ᦂ ᦂ᭡

Walking from room to room all the way around the *piano nobile* – thrice – to investigate every approach to the house gained him nothing. Nor was he rewarded with a glimpse of her out of the glass panes of the orangery, when he went in search of a particular floral offering. He only had the minor satisfaction of finding just the sort of bloom that he was looking for.

The camellia was rose-shaped and rose-coloured, with velvety petals of an uncommonly dark pink, thinly veined in a shade that was even darker. A good match for the one that had been left on Elizabeth's pillow at the *Swan* in Bedford. Yet he could claim no credit for that thoughtful gesture. While in town, he had merely asked Mr Howard to ensure that there would be flowers in her chamber. The added touch – a perfect bloom placed on her pillow – had been his butler's. Even so, it had been beyond him to say as much when Elizabeth had thanked him for the offering, and insult her with the careless admission that it had had naught to do with him. Now he could only hope that once she had noted the similarity, Elizabeth would read the right message into it: *'I love you. Let us start again.'*

His penknife was sharp enough to do its office and, flower in hand, Darcy made his way back to the house, then up the family staircase towards Elizabeth's apartments, only to stop short on her doorstep as a sudden notion gave him pause. Would she be displeased to learn that he had wandered into her bedchamber in her absence – that he had intruded into the one part of the house where she could be assured of privacy?

Yet privacy was what he was hoping for as well. This was meant to be a deeply personal message from him to her. Not conveyed through the servants. Nor placed on the breakfast table by the side of her plate.

A moment more, and his mind was made up.

She was remarkably keen-witted. She *would* grasp his meaning. Hopefully. Aye, there was more than enough reason to hope that she would understand.

Under his firm hand, the door noiselessly swung open and the room that, for all the wrong reasons, had been out of bounds to him of late was now revealed.

It was entirely familiar, of course. The furnishings were unchanged – there had been no time for that, given their rushed marriage. Even so, it seemed heart-warmingly different. It had ceased to be the empty suite that had once belonged to his departed mother. It was Elizabeth's bedchamber now, although he could see precious little indication that she was in residence. Just a book on the bedside table – what was she reading? – and a small assortment of personal possessions on the rosewood dressing table that had long stood unused.

It was in use now, and the sight was unexpectedly moving. Elizabeth's hairbrushes. Her combs and ribbons. A small japanned box. A couple of scent bottles. Everyday objects that her hands often touched.

Yet Darcy did not step closer to examine them. That *would* have felt like an intrusion. His gaze drifted back towards the bed instead, only to find himself defenceless before a fresh surge of desire, simply because it was her bed – her set of pillows – the counterpane that kept her warm, and would now be permeated with her fragrance.

He grimaced as his sensible side, whatever was left of it, berated him for a lovelorn mooncalf, then snapped, *'Just leave the blessed thing on her pillow and be done with it!'*

The mental prod spurred him into action.

'And about time, too,' Darcy scoffed and made to cross the room, his strides long and purposeful, his footsteps quiet over the thick carpet.

The telltale splash reached him all too late, when he had already taken the last fateful step and had come to stand before the dressing room doorway, thunderstruck and spellbound, his gaze fixed on Elizabeth's perfect form. Her exquisitely perfect unclothed form, rising from her bath and regaling him with the vision of a wood nymph emerging from an enchanted pool.

Wide and hungry, his eyes swept over her, then lingered, beyond the reach of reason — not that he could lay claim to any capacity for rational thought as his rapt gaze glided ever so slowly over her, as though intent on keeping pace with the rivulets that trickled down her skin. Her flawless, glistening skin, overspread with a rosy glow on account of the hot water.

The rivulets were bound by the laws of gravity — but his gaze was not. So it glided back up along her graceful legs… her shapely *derrière* and the voluptuous curve of her hips… her slender waist, a delectable contrast… her back, all but concealed beneath the dark, wet canopy of her long tresses… until she raised her arms and gathered up her hair to squeeze out the water… and the sheer loveliness of her weakened his knees and took his breath away.

He had no hope whatever of telling whether he had betrayed his presence in some manner, or if something else entirely had alerted her to it. But she suddenly turned halfway, giving him the briefest glimpse of small breasts crowned by dusky-pink areolae, before she folded her arms over her chest and sank back into the tub with a loud splash.

"Sarah, the door!" she pleaded, her voice thin and high — and at that, her Longbourn maid scurried into view to do her bidding.

Lips twisted into an apologetic grimace, the girl bobbed an awkward curtsy and swiftly closed the door.

❧ ❧

Through the crimson haze of burning desire, he could see the scene played out in lifelike detail. The door pushed open. The maidservant ordered in no uncertain terms to leave them, and make haste about it. His hands on Elizabeth's glistening form — lifting her out of the water — gathering her to his chest — carrying her to her bed. Her exquisite body supine beneath him, warm and damp against his lips, responding to his touch, responding to his kisses. Blood singing in their veins and doing away with every unnatural restraint — every misconception — every nonsensical hindrance. All doubts vanquished. All barriers gone. The ultimate union. And long-craved peace settling over the pair of them at last.

What brought him back from the brink and sent him staggering away from the door was the chilling recollection of the look in her eyes. The stricken, mortified look when she had found him standing there, watching her.

The all-too-vivid recollection suddenly began to scream at him – to loudly clamour that there was no peace to be had. That their joining would *not* have been the ultimate union, but a thoughtless act of possession that would have tainted everything. And would have given substance to all her misgivings.

'If he should rue the day, he only has himself to blame...'

Branded in his memory and still festering, the overhearings discharged yet another gush of poison, and a shudder racked him at the thought of drawing back from her to find regret or resignation in her eyes, and not the sultry glow of fulfilled passion, when his own passion was spent.

The conjured picture was far too oppressive for him to give thanks that he had not lost his mind to the point of pushing forth – of dismissing the closed door as a mere sign of natural embarrassment, and counting her responses to a hillside kiss and to those few minutes by the fire as sufficient proof that her desire was well on its way to matching his.

It was only later – once he had gained his chambers in a dark trance without any recollection of having walked there, and found himself leaning against his closed door, his head tilted back, one hand splayed across his eyes, pressing them shut – that the thought crossed his mind: the only mercy was that he had kept *some* tenuous grip on reason and had walked away before it was too late.

Yet the errant notion was instantly rejected with a bitter scoff. Was *that* his consolation and his claim to glory: that he had not acted like a selfish beast? What the deuce did he expect now? Hearty huzzahs? Public acclaim? Decency was not some prodigious accomplishment. It was *the norm*, for goodness' sake! Or at least it should be. It had been the norm for him for eight-and-twenty years. Not once had he imagined that he would depart from it!

He choked out a singularly earthy oath as he let his hand drop and opened his eyes to stare blankly into space – only to dart them towards the interconnecting door when a faint sound of voices and the patter of footsteps could just about be heard from Elizabeth's bedchamber.

What was she doing? He flinched. He should not be surprised if she chose not to come out for the rest of the day. Or have Rufus brought up to her apartments to guard her from intruders.

Red-hot anger surged, overshadowing his guilt and mortification. He must have taken leave of his senses! What self-destructive madness had possessed him? As if their situation were not fraught enough already, he *had* to go into her bedchamber unbidden and make everything worse! A thousand times worse! Why the devil had he not knocked, at least? Even if he had imagined the room to be empty! All this for the sake of a greenhouse flower and an idiotic scheme!

He reached for the blameless camellia discarded on the small table at his elbow and raised it for a closer look, half expecting to find it as crushed and bruised as he felt. Yet the bloom looked no different: a vibrant splash of colour, with nary a blemish.

A bitter quirk tugged at a corner of his mouth. He might as well cast the wretched thing into the flames, for all the good it did him. Yet he heaved a deep breath, and did not walk towards the fireplace. For what it was worth, Elizabeth should have it, he tiredly resolved. Even if the bloom could not possibly serve its intended purpose now, at least it would provide an explanation. An insufficient one, and a feeble excuse for his ill-judged – nay, his disastrous intrusion. But it was the sole excuse he had.

Chapter 21

Set next to Elizabeth's unused plate, the camellia looked precisely as it should: like the colourful token of love that it was. Lips tightened, Darcy repositioned it slightly, then turned away, determined not to dwell on the course the day might have taken, had he brought the offering to the small dining room in the first place. Just as he endeavoured not to brood on the stark differences from the previous night when, for a few short hours, the selfsame room had been a private haven, full of promise. When most things had seemed about to veer onto the right course at last. Yet brood he did – which could not surprise him – as he walked towards the window and stood staring blankly over the wintry landscape still shrouded in mist.

He was but briefly interrupted from that unprofitable pastime when Thomas came to ask if he wished to break his fast.

"Perhaps later," Darcy said, even though his insides heaved at the mere thought of food. "You may leave me now," he told the younger man. "I will ring if I need you."

"Very well, sir," the other replied blandly, then made himself scarce with a bow.

For his part, Darcy remained just where he was, grimly resolved to wait for whatever was coming and bear the consequences of his actions, rather than skulk in his study like a coward. The only thing that remained a matter of conjecture was how he would bear it if she did not come down for the rest of the day.

A quiet, "Good morning," put that question to rest sooner than he had expected, and Darcy spun round, only to find that his relief was woefully premature.

Never, in the whole course of their acquaintance, had he seen her swathed in quite so much muslin. A veritable cuirass of it, covering her from her chin to the tips of her slippers. Almost to her fingertips too – the long sleeves went at least an inch beyond her knuckles. And there was more muslin covering her beautiful hair. Not the extravagant concoction she had donned on the previous morning to make her playful, teasing point, but some nondescript thing resembling a set of folded pancakes trimmed with a thin border of lace – the dullest complement to her austere choice of apparel. Gone were her habitual garments, light and pleasing, leaving her ample freedom of movement. Even the dress she had worn as recently as last night, with the low neckline of a ball gown and short puffed sleeves that left the arms bare, had been forcefully relegated amongst memories. There could not have been a greater contrast between that creation of lustrous silk shimmering in all the colours of the sunset and this dreary and ever so conspicuous cocoon. And the most harrowing thing of all was that *he*, and he alone, was to blame for the transformation. For the dismally unnatural transition from butterfly to chrysalis.

Darcy's heart twisted painfully in his chest as an overpowering wave of tenderness rocked him to his core. It was heartbreaking to imagine what agonising notions might have crossed her mind to make her think that this… *this*… was necessary. It was all the more heartbreaking to find himself at a loss for well-chosen, thoughtful things to say in order to persuade her that it most certainly *was not*. That she need not be wary of anything in this house – in this new life. Least of all him.

The worst curse was that now he did not even dare touch her. Yet he wanted nothing more than to be allowed to hold her. Just that. Hold her. Comfort her. Make her feel safe. Make her happy. And make this wretched nightmare go away.

How horribly ironic that mere hours ago, when he had woken up, he had been downcast at the thought of having to resume the uphill struggle – and then had blundered into the darkest pit. Picking his way out was utterly nerve-racking. Danger loomed at every step. He could only pray he would not falter.

"Good morning," Darcy said with a deep, deliberately honouring bow, and thought better of thanking her for choosing to join him. "Would you care to sit?" he tentatively asked instead.

Elizabeth nodded, and he took a couple of slow, measured steps, then paused at a fair distance to gesture towards her chair.

"May I?"

How painfully conspicuous. When was the last time he had felt the need to request permission to come close enough to pull a chair for her?

She nodded yet again, and the chair was pulled, and she was seated.

"Shall I ring for tea?" he offered as he stepped back.

"If you would…"

The bell was duly rung, and Darcy went to take his own seat and drape his napkin over his lap, although partaking of breakfast was the last thing on his mind.

It did not seem to be on her mind either. Elizabeth paid no heed to the bread rolls or the small lidded dishes filled with preserves. She reached to pick up the bloom that lay beside her plate.

"Another beautiful camellia," she quietly observed, stroking the deep-rose petals with her fingertips. "It looks very much like the one at the inn," she added, demonstrating that his confidence in her powers of perception was fully justified.

"Yes," he said simply, then leaned forward, compelled to elaborate. "I wanted to apologise for—"

"Don't! Pray don't," she cut him off in a breathless, strangled murmur. "The least said, the better."

"I was not about to speak of this morning," Darcy sought to explain, only to curse himself for his bluntness when he saw her lowering her face as if to inhale the flower's scent. Under his very eyes, her countenance grew uncannily close in hue to the dark-rose camellia and, judging by the sharp surge of heat in his own cheeks, Darcy could only assume that he was blushing too. An extraordinary experience in itself. He could not remember any such occurrence in upwards of ten years. But be that as it may. Much as he detested mortifying her further, he could not help adding, "I am utterly distraught about my intrusion and its wretched timing, but if you would rather I did not say anything else, then… I shall not. Only that I came to leave this in your chambers," he offered by way of justification, with a faint gesture towards the bright-coloured bloom. "As an apology for last night's misunderstanding."

"Oh?"

The footmen's entrance was irksomely ill timed.

Thomas came in with hot water for the tea urn, and Peter followed, along with Mr Howard, each carrying a tray laden with breakfast delicacies that no one had requested – and, in all likelihood, no one would consume.

Lips tightened in profound impatience, Darcy was hard-pressed to hold his peace until the finely choreographed routine came to an end, the serving dishes were arrayed, the tea was poured, and the pair of them were left alone once more.

By the looks of it, Elizabeth was scarcely less impatient. No sooner had the door closed behind the obliging Mr Howard than she quietly prompted, "You mentioned a misunderstanding. And that was…?"

Darcy cast her a small, conscious smile.

"I thought you meant I should come up and find you in twenty minutes to half an hour. So I believe we each finished by seeking the other in a different part of the house."

A look of unconcealed amusement flashed across Elizabeth's countenance, brightening it like a ray of sunshine. It was the most welcome sign, and greatly reassuring.

"Ah. The price that comes with living in an exceedingly large house. It would not have been anywhere as easy to miss each other in a smaller one," she airily remarked, her light tone and her diverted little chuckle making her sound like her usual self, and thus greatly reassuring too. As was the fact that what she had just said matched the thought with which he had greeted Mrs Reynolds' revelations that morning.

Darcy did not reach for her hand, much as he wished to. Instead, he placed his own on the table, palm up – a silent invitation. And the nauseating ache in the pit of his stomach lessened by a fraction when, after only a moment's hesitation, her hand came to rest in his.

He stroked it lightly, or rather the little that was left uncovered by the excessively long sleeve, then his thumb slid beneath the confounded muslin to brush her knuckles, one by one.

"I have an apology to make as well," Elizabeth suddenly said in a hesitant whisper, which had him darting his eyes away from their tentatively joined hands to search her countenance.

He found it still flushed. Becomingly so. Her rosy hue *was* exceedingly becoming. But, for goodness' sake, how long until she would no longer flush crimson in his presence?

"For?" he gently prompted, only to see her lips pursing into a self-conscious grimace.

"The locked door between our chambers," she said with manifest difficulty, yet raised her eyes at last and met his squarely, filling his heart with a poignant mixture of tenderness and admiration for her brave endeavour to conquer her discomfort. Plainly, her discomfort was great indeed – the turn of her countenance left him in no misapprehension on that score. And, yet again, Darcy ached to hold her.

"No matter. Pray, do not distress yourself," he said swiftly, but she shook her head.

"It does matter. And I would like to explain."

He held his peace then, and she resumed with endearing determination:

"I locked it while you were away. Then… after our walk, I forgot all about it as I readied myself for dinner. And afterwards, I…" She bit her lip and darted her eyes downwards, dropping her voice to a barely audible murmur. "After dinner, I did not think you would wish…"

There was no way under heaven for him to remain silent after that.

"Oh, I do!" Darcy rasped, his whisper rife with feeling, his thumb slipping beneath her fingers, into the palm of her hand, to knead the soft, warm skin with insistent pressure.

Elizabeth did not look up, but filtered a long glance towards him through lowered lashes.

"The door has been unlocked. And so it will stay," she breathed.

It was more than he had hoped to hear.

Likewise, in all his adult years, he had not found anything more seductive than his beloved bride shyly avowing that she would welcome him in her bed.

"Thank you," Darcy whispered, rather too dizzy with the swirl of long-supressed desire to coin a better response – a longer one – more cogent.

And then she clasped his hand, scattering his senses further.

"I never meant to keep you out," she said with energy. "Nor… chase you away this morning. That was… a surprise," she faltered – a far milder word than he would have chosen.

He readily gave a more fitting description:

"It was a thoughtless intrusion. Well-meaning, but…"

"Let us focus on *well-meaning.*' And agree to call the whole episode surprising," she said, generously choosing to make light of it, then gave a conscious little chuckle. "Just… give me a little warning next time. That is all."

"Should we also agree on what sort of warning I should give?" he teased softly, and was heartened to discover that his attempt to set her at ease was fairly successful.

Her air grew almost flirtatious when she retorted, "Oh, I believe I can safely leave it to you to think of something suitable." She sobered a little, her colour still high, when she added, "I thought we ought to speak of… all this because I wanted you to know that you can come to me at any time. Precisely because I was so startled earlier, I did not wish you to read the wrong message into it. Only… surprise. Certainly not reluctance to… assume my marital duties."

His hand froze under hers and the warm, heady swirl of desire congealed into ice.

"Your marital duties?"

He drew his hand away.

Her duty. She still saw it as her *duty!*

The small part of him that, as a rule, could be trusted to think clearly – with just a few notable exceptions – furiously worked to ascertain why this was so much worse than the poisonous overhearings at Longbourn.

The answer was self-evident and prompt. Her brief outpourings to her sister had come at a vulnerable time, a fraught time, when she had just tied the knot in haste and was deeply unnerved by having to quit everything familiar to follow him – to all intents and purposes a stranger who had incautiously placed her in a compromising situation and had not so much as courted her. Whereas now, in the middle of a tender moment, unmistakably tender, and after the promising evening that they had just had, she matter-of-factly said that she would give herself to him out of duty. As though it were natural, and just as she expected. As though she expected *him* to be satisfied with that: access to her bed, and her dutiful compliance.

Darcy flinched. So much for thinking he had seen exhilarating changes in her when he had kissed her, and last night by the fire. A new warmth. Interest. Attraction. Stirrings of desire.

His lips twisted into a bitter grimace.

More fool him for seeing what he had wished to see.

"I beg your pardon, perhaps I ought to have explained myself more clearly. Pray let me do so now," he said in a clipped tone. "You may be assured that I have never forced myself upon a woman. And I am not minded to begin with *you.*"

"Of course not! I did not wish to imply... to offend you. It was not intended as a reflection on you," she said, her colour deepening into scarlet. "I am only saying that I am aware of what is meant to... happen. To have happened, rather, were it not for our misunderstanding. We should not continue in that vein. Through a perverse set of circumstances, we are to make a life together, and I would wish it were for better, not for worse. So I am prepared to play my part. And not evade my... any of my duties."

Darcy's eyes widened. Perverse set of circumstances? *Play her part?* He took a deep breath, perilously close to the frayed edges of his temper. How in heaven's name did she imagine that she was making the detestable situation any better?

"I see. That is a great comfort," he retorted, and grudgingly allowed that sarcasm was beneath him. But by now he was past caring. He pushed his chair back and stood. "You will excuse me. I have my own duties to attend to."

And, with a rigid bow, he dropped his napkin on the table and strode out of the room.

∽৹৹ ৹৹৵

The long ride in the rain – ostensibly to inspect the drainage of the meadows on the eastern boundary of the estate – brought him no closer to equanimity, and Darcy seriously doubted that anything would, anytime soon. But since the weary beast beneath him had suffered on his account for long enough, he allowed his mount to draw to a halt and seek shelter under the couple of wind-whipped evergreens by the side of the road.

He was beyond weary too. Not from the ride. That was nothing. The weariness came from turning the dismal state of his marriage on every facet, just as he had done during his self-imposed seclusion at the hunting lodge. The thought of that interlude was met with a derisive snort. So much for those deliberations and their hopeful conclusions! Seemingly, what lay in store for him was a marriage of convenience and a practical wife. The very things he had endeavoured to avoid from his earliest days on the marriage mart.

Darcy scowled. He would have been better served had he wedded the first practical miss that had been introduced to him as a suitable partner in life. Not necessarily because Miss Lavinia Hatherley, now Lady Brentford, would have brought impeccable connections and a substantial dowry. But had he married her – or any of the others, for that matter – it would have been a practical marriage of convenience on both sides, instead of finding himself pining like a fool over his cool-headed wife.

The rattling of an approaching carriage drew him from his stormy musings with a start. His mood did not improve when he was hallooed by old Mr Kettering, his neighbour on the southern side of the river.

The old gentleman pulled the strap to lower the window, then leaned out.

"Darcy! I thought it was you. Good to know that these old eyes are not about to fail me yet. So, what brings you on my doorstep, m'boy? Have you come to call upon me? Good, good. As you can see, you are in luck."

On his doorstep? What was the man talking about?

Yet once he had looked around in earnest, Darcy owned that Mr Kettering should have been trusted to know where his own doorstep was. Clifton House, the old gentleman's Jacobean residence, stood but a few hundred yards ahead, in the lee of the hill. It was he who had lost his bearings.

"Well, then, m'boy, what are you waiting for? Turn about and come along," his neighbour urged him. "You will be pleased to hear that you have not had a wasted journey in more ways than one. A purveyor of mine has called upon me but three days ago with a certain consignment that has come a long way, if you get my meaning. I have already undertaken the onerous task of sampling it," the old gentleman added with a wink, "and I am happy to say that it did not disappoint. But I shall be glad of your opinion. A tot or two will stand you in good stead on the ride back. Just the ticket, to ward off the chill. And I hope I can persuade you to stay for dinner."

Darcy opened his lips to make his excuses, but a moment later he chose to hold his peace.

Why the deuce not? A glass of his neighbour's smuggled brandy and dinner at Clifton seemed rather more tempting than the sort of evening he had steeled himself for. And the dear old gentleman would be a comfortable companion. Mr Kettering was his departed father's closest friend and the pair of them had been inseparable, so it was no surprise that he often felt something of his father's presence whenever he was in Mr Kettering's society.

Moreover, no effort would be required of him. The old gentleman made singularly undemanding conversation. Mr Kettering was happy to talk without interruption and, after the manner of those who lived alone, had always had the habit of answering his own questions.

He was being disingenuous, of course. His main reason for accepting his neighbour's hospitality had naught to do with the old man's conversation. So it would be fair to say that he was not only disingenuous, but also cowardly. Even so, Darcy shrugged and turned his horse about. After a day such as he had had, anything was preferable to dinner at home and Elizabeth calmly offering herself alongside the sweetmeats.

There was only so much that a man could endure.

Chapter 22

Blood! So much blood! Down the flanks of the rearing horse… pooling around the motionless horseman… Thrown off. Injured. Why does he not move? He will catch a cold. 'Tis raining. So much rain streaming down her face– or blood – or both. And no one here to help her. Someone! Anyone! Yet no one is answering her frantic calls. No one can hear them. Not loud enough. Mere mumbles. Mumbling – thrashing – in the pouring blood – the pouring rain…

♠♣ ♣♠

It seemed like an age – an age of terror – until Elizabeth could shake off her nightmare and recognise it for what it was. A nightmare. Nothing more. No blood on her face. Just a flood of hot tears. He was not injured – did not lie dying.

'Hopefully!' she thought with a fresh jolt of terror, because he had not returned by the time she had taken herself up to her apartments.

Was he home now? Had he returned while she had slept her short and fitful sleep plagued by nightmares? At least she thought that it must have been a short sleep, but she could not tell. All she knew was that she had paced for an age in her chambers, then had tossed and turned in her bed, fretting over her headstrong and nonsensical husband. Her husband in name only, which seemed to be central to the entire baffling *contretemps*.

She could make no sense of it – nor of him. But that maddening conundrum was not her prime concern just now. She had to know, was he home safe or not?

Elizabeth sat up. She could not see the clock on the mantelpiece, but could sense the lateness of the hour. Too late to summon Sarah or one of the maids and ask if he had returned.

She pursed her lips and flung the counterpane aside.

Very well, then. She would have to see for herself.

She crossed the room with sure footsteps, not in the least hampered by the absence of light. Of course she knew precisely where *that door* was. She had stared at it for long enough. She could find it with her eyes closed. Which was scarcely any different from what she was doing now, Elizabeth thought with a nervous chuckle. But by the time the door was tentatively and ever so quietly opened, the hilarity was gone and she stood there, peering into the darkness on *the other side*. Entirely unfamiliar darkness. In more ways than one, it would be like stepping into a strange new world.

She did. She took one step, then another and another on naked floorboards, cold under her bare feet. Then the floorboards gave way to smooth carpet, and Elizabeth walked on, feeling her way with one hand as though blind, lest she stumble into some piece of furniture. When she could detect the bulky shape of the canopied bed she stopped, poised to listen for the sound of slow, even breaths, and fancied she could hear just that. Even so, she walked on until she could almost touch the bed, just to be certain.

And she finally was. The slow sound of breathing was perfectly audible now. In. Out. Even and quiet. No snoring. She smiled. Of course not. He was not old enough for that.

She could make out the contour of his head against the pale background of the furthermost pillow, but nothing more – could not even tell which way he was facing, let alone distinguish his features. But seeing as neither his valet nor any of the other servants would dare seek their rest in their master's bed, chances were that the sleeping form before her was Mr Darcy's.

Elizabeth shuffled on her feet and wrapped her arms around herself, rather wishing she could see his face, much as she should not spy upon him while he was sleeping. Yet, unfair as that might have been, and decidedly wrong, she frankly would if she could. Then perhaps she would have some answers to the riddle that he was.

Why the sullen temper on the journey north – so very different from the promising warmth in Hertfordshire? For that matter, what had done away with the peevishness? As for the… tension over dinner the other night – she had no better name for it – she fancied she could understand it. Likewise, the tentative and delectable advances that had followed, until she had spilt her Madeira like a ninny, just because he had stroked her collarbone. Now she knew why she could not find him downstairs upon her return, much as his choice to retire so abruptly had injured and perplexed her. A misunderstanding, nothing more. Another one of many. And she had had her fill of them. Which was why she had forced herself to come down for breakfast and speak to him, even though she had cringed at even facing him, given that he had seen so much of her already – in the most literal sense of the word.

A blaze erupted in her cheeks at the mere recollection. Of course she had expected that he would eventually see her in a state of undress. But *partial* undress, for goodness' sake! In a darkened bedchamber. Most of her person concealed by her nightgown and the counterpane. Not… *thus!* Fully disrobed. In broad daylight! And since he had not sought her out the night before, the shock of his presence when she had stood from her bath had been that much greater.

Elizabeth shrugged and scoffed. Well, what of it? She had survived the experience, had she not? And moreover had gone down – admittedly swathed in muslin to the tip of her nose. A ludicrously conspicuous dress. It was years and years since she had worn anything so prudish. Yet she could not help the choice of apparel. She had been convinced that any square inch of skin left exposed would blaze scarlet with mortification.

Even so, she could not help seeking him out. She had to speak her mind. She always did. And although so much of her new life was decidedly unnerving, the cat had not got her tongue yet. Nor would Mr Darcy, and he might as well know it. Just as he had to know everything else: that the morning's incident had been a shock, and nothing more; and that she fully aimed to play her part in this marriage and make it a tolerable union – for both of them.

Whatever possessed him to take offence at that?

What was so objectionable about it?

Elizabeth almost wished to wake him and ask him that, then smothered a giggle in her fist as she imagined his reaction. But the wicked little sprite that had put the notion in her head and made her giggle was not the only insubstantial creature keeping her company tonight. There was at least one other: a venturesome adviser that nudged her hand forward, towards the corner of the counterpane. And, slowly but steadily, her hand obeyed.

Her first thought was that the bed was delectably warm. Her toes certainly appreciated the sensation. She had not noticed at the time how cold her feet had grown while she had stood about on icy floorboards. So Elizabeth stretched her legs under the counterpane and allowed her toes to luxuriate in the newfound cosiness.

The rest of her was not quite so comfortable with the experience. In fact, now that she thought about it and paused to take note, every fibre of her being – except her grateful toes – was as taut as a bowstring at her unimaginable daring. She had tiptoed in the middle of the night into a gentleman's bedchamber, and was now lying beside him in his bed!

Her husband's bed, Elizabeth pointedly reminded herself, and took a deep breath. Needs must, and so forth. If he would not come to her, something *had* to be done about it.

She took another deep breath, then another, and it eventually occurred to her to time her breathing by his. It was slow – measured – calming. Very calming. So much so that the rest of her began to find wisdom in following her toes' example, relax and stretch and delight in the warmth, rather than give too much thought to its source. *That* would only serve to bring back the tension.

It would be a fine to-do if she were to fall asleep, Elizabeth thought when the tension ebbed and the warmth began to do its office. His response to finding her there in the morning made for yet another diverting speculation. Well, she could always claim she was given to sleepwalking.

The nervous little quip left her mind almost as soon as it came, for it was just that: a quip in response to agitation. She was not of a mind to fall asleep in his bed and brave whatever the morning was to bring. She would much rather brave her future now. If not, she would lose whatever was left of her proverbial courage.

She turned towards him, and another deep breath acquainted her with the pleasant scent of the pillow. Starch, lavender and… something else she could not name. Familiar, yet not, and decidedly pleasant. It brought a delectable sense of anticipation, and also a flutter deep in the pit of her stomach, neither of which Elizabeth could account for, not at first. Then it came to her: the vaguely familiar scent was his – as she had discovered the other day, on their walk, when he had kissed her.

The agreeable recollection made her bold – or at least a trifle bolder. So she tentatively reached out into the darkness, until her fingertips encountered his shoulder. Warm and unmistakably bare, Elizabeth found, and her hand shot back of its own volition. Then she rolled her eyes at her preconceptions. Why ever had she imagined that he would sleep in a nightshirt? Why not a nightcap too? How positively ludicrous!

Her hand regained its earlier boldness and unerringly returned to the same point of contact. Once her fingertips brushed his shoulder, she trailed them in a light caress along his arm and blindly traced the contour of well-defined muscles, then changed course to find the plane of his chest. The wiry texture of hair – a fair amount of it – was a surprise, but it was the throb of heartbeats under her fingertips that stopped her in her explorations, or rather light caresses which she had hoped would wake him, but so far had not. She spread out her hand over the spot where she had first sensed his heartbeats and lay perfectly still as she felt the steady rhythm beating against her skin. His heart thudding softly into the palm of her hand. It was an overpowering sensation. She could not imagine anything more moving. Nor more intimate.

The light caress that retraced the path to his shoulder did not wake him either, so Elizabeth drew her hand away and tucked her other arm under her head – until a new resolve had her instantly acting on impulse, lest she see sense and change her mind.

She reached down and tugged at her chemise with steadiness of purpose. The deed presented its own difficulties – it was not the easiest thing in the world to remove one's chemise while lying down – and the requisite wriggles brought enough of the awkward and the absurd as to amuse her briefly and distract her from the momentousness of her decision. But once she had managed to draw it all the way up, over her head and along her arms, and the garment was in her grasp, squeezed into a soft ball of fabric, Elizabeth was no longer disposed towards light merriment. She held on to the crumpled chemise for a few moments longer, hand poised above her head, then threw it into the darkness. Let the die be cast. After all, this was the natural conclusion of their latest encounters – the shocking one in her dressing room, and its baffling sequel over their unfinished breakfast.

She turned towards him yet again and inched closer, growing more and more aware of his radiating warmth. Intensely aware — unnervingly so.

She would have thought she would be all the more unnerved when a voice inside her head awoke to hiss, *'Have you completely lost your mind?'*

But Elizabeth silenced it and gave herself over to the recollection of the intoxicating heat that had seeped into her down to her very bones the other night, after dinner, when she had sat sipping sweet wine, warmed by the fire, his burning gaze and the electrifying thrill of his lips against her palm.

She leaned forward with nothing to guide her in the darkness but the feel of his breath on her face. It was a reliable guide though, and Elizabeth followed it, inhaling its appealing scent. Exceedingly appealing. And very masculine, she thought, only to chastise herself for the reflection. What did she know of masculine breaths?

Yet she did know that his was delightfully familiar. The kiss on their walk accounted for that too. So Elizabeth raised her chin and stretched a little further, until her lips brushed against something other than thin air and alighted on what seemed to be the tip of his nose.

And then she found his lips — softer than she remembered, warm and very still. But not still for long. They twitched under hers when she kissed him again, her mouth lingering on his with gentle pressure — another lesson learnt on their walk, the other day. Her experience was woefully limited in that regard, but she had always prided herself on being a quick learner and not averse to inquisitive exploration, Elizabeth impishly thought as she set about to diligently explore the contours of his lips.

The sweet response she had hoped to elicit was not long in coming. With a sleepy murmur, his lips moulded themselves to hers and he kissed her back — still half asleep, Elizabeth was prepared to wager. His growing eagerness was more than enough reason to hope that the surprise would be far from unpleasant, so she deepened the kiss with slow deliberation — and all of a sudden she was granted more than she had bargained for. His arm encircled her waist, drawing her close, his hand stroking her bare back, clasping her, fingers digging into her flesh, and his lips parted under hers with a groan. His tongue brushed lightly over her tingling lips, then plunged deep into her mouth – a startling but heady sensation. Instinctively, she met its play with hers, and he groaned again as the kiss they shared grew nothing short of ravenous.

Elizabeth could easily tell the exact moment when he became fully awake. His arm went rigid and, with a sharp intake of breath, his lips froze into perfect stillness under hers. His whole frame froze too, still as a statue. A very warm statue that sprang back into life a fraction of a second later. His arm slipped from around her, and he drew back as he choked out a shocked, "Elizabeth?"

A nervous little chuckle escaped her, and then she whispered, "Yes. Who else were you expecting?"

For a long moment, there was silence, and she could sense nothing but his fast and shallow breaths on her face, which could not fail to make her intensely aware that he was very close – inches away. But still motionless. Not reaching. Not touching.

"I was not expecting *you*," Darcy said at last, stating the obvious, and she could not determine what was the best answer she could make.

Out of necessity, she settled on archness.

"Perhaps I should have warned you of my worst tendency: I take perverse pleasure in confounding people by acting contrary to their expectations."

"Don't jest," he shot back, his voice low and almost pleading.

Silence fell again – the sort of silence that threatened to stretch into eternity – and Elizabeth pondered on what she might say to break it, her mind working more frantically than ever. Frantically, but most ineffectually, for it kept stumbling at every turn over any number of unnerving notions.

The distance he had put between them was deeply unnerving too – a chasm Elizabeth dared not bridge, now that he was awake. A formidable chasm, however narrow, and severely daunting because it endured, even though he must have known as well as she that there was nothing but thin air – charged air, warm, vibrant, and not much of it – between their motionless bodies. Yet he remained as still as a living, breathing statue, and eventually asked in a gravelly whisper, "Why did you come?"

"I rather thought it was self-explanatory," Elizabeth resorted to archness yet again.

But she did not wait for a second entreaty to resist the ill-timed urge to jest, and in the same breath murmured, "Forgive me. One of my other tendencies is to be flippant when I am nervous."

"I know," Darcy said softly, and did not leave as long an interval of silence before he spoke again. "I do not wish you to be nervous. Nor feel coerced into anything."

"Some nervousness is only natural, I think," she sensibly replied. "As for the other, I *would* point out that I am here of my own free will. Impetuous of me, I grant you, and excessively forward," Elizabeth added with a conscious chuckle, but sobered when she concluded, "Even so, I find it no less needful."

"Needful!" he echoed harshly, and she felt the mattress move with energy when he rolled away from her, flinging himself onto his back. "No more talk of your *duties*, I beg you," Darcy snapped – a demand, not a request. "This is not to be borne! I cannot— Will not— Elizabeth, you *will not* give yourself to me out of duty!"

The last word was spat out as if it were poison, which sparked the notion that he saw it thus – and gave her an increasingly clearer understanding of the root of their difficulties. The most recent one, at least.

"That was not my meaning," Elizabeth said swiftly, with a forceful shake of her head, forgetting that he stood no chance of seeing that in the pitch-black room. "Not needful in the sense of an obligation. In the sense that something needed to be done," she went on to explain, words flowing with greater ease once she had begun to grasp the reason for his withdrawal, and had ceased to see it as yet another dispiriting rejection. "To my way of thinking, we have laboured for long enough under the misconception that each wanted to have as little as possible to do with the other. So, since you would not come to me, it stood to reason that I needed to cross into your territory and put an end to our latest *contretemps*. Which, as I see it now, stemmed from awkwardness and… a euphemism."

"A euphemism," he repeated.

It was not worded as a question, but Elizabeth did not doubt that it was meant as such, so she elaborated, "I am yet to learn the language of marriage and acquire some ease in using it. On reflection, '*marital duties*' was a poor choice of words. I should have found another way of saying that I had not entered into this union with the wish to be married in name only. Nor, I daresay, did you."

"No," he breathed, and judging by the direction of his voice, she could tell that he had at least turned his head towards her. "But I will not make any demands of you until you are ready. Elizabeth, if you would rather wait—"

In a flash, she reached out into the darkness to press her fingers to his lips. She found that she could take some pride in the accuracy of her aim this time, yet lost all interest in congratulating herself on that particular achievement when a puff of air brushed her skin and sent her fingertips tingling. She trailed them over his cheek, and found it a little rough with late-night stubble, which sent them tingling too as she whispered, "I never thought that I should need to tell *you* this, but you do talk far too much sometimes."

A strangled, throaty chuckle escaped him.

Then he quietly observed, "First time I was accused of *that*."

Her hand slid further in slow, caressing exploration, and she felt the jerky bob of his Adam's apple when she airily replied, "Yes, well, there is a first time for everything."

❧ ❧

And then there were no more words. Just the warm darkness, and anticipation shimmering like a muted bell in the perfect silence as his hands and his lips discovered her, inch by flushed, quivering inch. Gentle hands, unspeakably tender. Soft lips sending wave after wave of heat rippling over her. Heat building within as, with fluttering and increasingly bolder fingertips, she discovered him too. Soft lips on hers, and long, lingering kisses, light and tame, with none of the flaring passion of that one time, when she had caught him unawares, his guard decidedly down. Too tame kisses, Elizabeth thought after a while, when longing rose and peaked, then rose again. So she brushed his lips with the tip of her tongue and tentatively probed – and a sharp thrill coursed through her when he groaned, a deep, delectably rumbling sound, and the kiss grew as far from tame as she could wish it.

Yet soon – too soon; maddeningly soon – he tore his lips from hers and buried his face in the all-too-sensitive curve of her neck to trail a path of fire over her already burning skin and render her breathless and light-headed… floating… floating… Floating rudderless on waves of achingly sweet longing that rushed towards her from all sides.

The longing was positively senseless. Inexplicable. For she no longer was curled up all alone in her absurdly large new bed, wary of the unpredictable course of her married life and in turns mystified, unsettled and a little wounded – in her pride, if nothing else – by the fact that, night after night, she remained conspicuously alone.

Not alone now. He was beside her, filling the darkness. As though darkness itself was caressing her skin with feather-light touches – tantalising – sending shivers from her scalp to her toes with each new sensation that the caresses sparked. Scintillating sparks, each igniting a wildfire. Exquisite, bewildering wildfires, all new to her inexperienced senses – yet each of them recognised at once as yet another blaze she had been unknowingly yearning for.

She might have blushed at the dizzying new intimacy. Perhaps she *was* blushing, Elizabeth could not tell. Every inch of her skin was aflame already. Perhaps she would have met his eyes with more than a touch of self-consciousness, if she could see him clearly. But every degree of self-consciousness melted away in the electrifying darkness. And he was the whole darkness, the whole world, as his hands and his lips were slowly melting her into a swirling pool of sensation. Melting her into him.

Was it hers, the strangled cry of pure pleasure? It must have been. Who else was there, except for her – and him? Just the pair of them, caught in a maelstrom that whirled with unfathomable force, faster and faster, until she suddenly found herself in the eye of it – not alone – not alone – shaking like a leaf, soft whimpers of abandon on her lips.

He matched them with a throaty, "Oh, Lord… Elizabeth… my love…" and she could barely hear him through the rush of blood pounding in her ears – singing in her veins.

The sharp pain that followed was short and soon forgotten in an overwhelming flood of feeling as she clung to him – the only certainty in the whirlwind that swept them away.

And when they finally stilled, joined as one – the ultimate union – and clinging to each other as they floated back down to earth, together, through the welcoming darkness, the glowing aura of belonging enveloped them, and blissful peace settled over them at last.

The blissful peace endured, and so did the delightful sense of belonging, even when he rolled away – a disappointment, somewhat mitigated by the fact that he still held her close, wrapped in his arms.

As for the cosy silence, he was the first to break it.

"You are… comfortable, I hope?" he softly asked, brushing a light kiss on her still flushed cheek.

"Very much so, thank you," Elizabeth replied, only to giggle into his shoulder at their bland choice of words. Nothing short of ludicrous, really. As though they were exchanging civilities over tea and refreshments.

When he ran his fingers through her hair and wished to know what had amused her, Elizabeth saw no reason why she should not tell him. She gave voice to her impish reflections, word for word, finishing with, "Now there is nothing left but for you to thank me for calling." She chuckled softly in the darkness, wondering by and by if it was the selfsame darkness that made it quite so easy for her to regain some of her playful spirits.

He cupped her cheek and caressed it with his thumb, then breathed against her lips, "Am I not allowed to?" before he kissed her.

The kiss itself pleased her no less than the hint of playfulness in his voice when he drew back and remarked, "That is most inconvenient." Yet she did not miss the playfulness when it suddenly vanished, to be replaced by unmistakably ardent undertones when he spoke again. "Because I am very grateful. More than I can say."

Elizabeth gave a faint shrug.

"I thought it was high time we overcame that particular hurdle."

Darcy choked out an immoderate chuckle.

"Hurdle, was it? Not quite the sentiment with which I was hoping you would approach the matter," he said, brushing her lips with his. "But, judging by your delightful response to the way in which we overcame said hurdle, I have some cause to hope that you are teasing."

"A little," she owned. "But not entirely. I have no patience with Gordian knots, you see. Nor with making an elephant of a fly, and a mountain of a molehill."

This time the kiss was long and lingering, before he remarked, "You are quite the collection of adages tonight."

She gave a conscious little laugh.

"Am I? Presumably because, apart from being flippant, I occasionally babble when I am ill at ease."

His hand took to stroking her back in slow, soothing motions.

"Ill at ease? *Now?* After all this?"

"Oh, absolutely, and for good reason. Earlier I was most delectably distracted," she chose to inform him with stark honesty. "And now… I am not."

"I see," he whispered, nuzzling her neck. "That could be remedied, you know…"

But she could hear the smile in his voice, which gave sufficient indication that he was merely teasing too. And then he clarified the matter by reaching for the counterpane to draw it over them and tuck it around her, fashioning a cosy cocoon.

"Are you warm enough?" he asked as he cradled her in his arms and dropped a kiss on her temple.

"Oh, yes," Elizabeth whispered back, nestling into the exquisite warmth of his embrace, her fluid limbs sinking into the soft mattress. And although she knew full well that most married couples did not share quarters, for now she chose to remain precisely where she was.

Chapter 23

Darcy awoke to an empty bed – and likewise to an empty, sinking feeling when, despite the poor light, it could not be denied that Elizabeth was no longer there.

Why?

The ugly question squirmed and twisted, and he cursed the return of the loathed uncertainty. Were it not for her haunting fragrance on his pillow and her scent on his skin, he might have thought that their night of passion had been nothing but a figment of his imagination. Then recollections flooded in and, body and soul, he responded to the onslaught of agonisingly perfect mental pictures. A deep groan tore from his chest, and he raised his head – only to find the most uplifting proof that the blissful hours of the night were not an impulse she had come to regret once she had awoken.

The door between their chambers had been left open. Open as wide as could be.

ᴥᴥ ᴥᴥ

Common decency required that he don a robe, so he did, before making his way towards the beckoning light. No, he was not given to coining metaphors in the early hours, Darcy thought, a smile tugging at the corner of his lips. The open door revealed that Elizabeth's bedchamber was bathed in a soft, flickering light. From the fire. Or a candle.

The light came from the candle on her bedside table, he found, once he reached the doorway and was treated to the delightful sight of his darling wife ensconced in her bed – attired in a chemise this time – and propped up against a stack of pillows, reading.

A creaking floorboard drew her notice, and Elizabeth looked up to cast him a heart-warming smile. She lowered her book and whispered, "Oh. You are awake, then. Almost time to say good morning."

He did not contest that, but mildly observed, "You did not stay," forbearing to enquire into her reasons.

She supplied them nonetheless:

"I did not wish to light a candle and disturb you." Then added with the faintest hesitation, "And I did not know if you wished me to stay."

He flashed a wide grin towards her.

"Oh, dear. There I was flattering myself that I had already given you sufficient proof of that," he teased, only to drop his voice to a low, earnest whisper. "You need not wonder on that score again. I will always wish you to stay."

Her eyes crinkled at the corners as she cast him a little smile.

"I shall remember that in future."

"Do," he urged, all levity abandoned. "May I join you?"

"I daresay you never need wonder on that score either," she airily replied and reached for the corner of the counterpane to turn it over – a clear invitation to her bed, not just her bedchamber.

Darcy lost no time in availing himself of it and crossed the room to slip into bed beside her and take her in his arms. A long kiss was his first greeting of the day – which, to his mind, was just as it should be. It was only later – the best part of an ardent minute later – that he whispered, "Good morning," his lips still a mere hair's breadth from hers. But even that small distance could not be suffered to endure for a moment longer than strictly necessary, so he claimed her lips again, the hunger barely held in check.

When she drew back and inched away from him, he was reassured to find that she was merely reaching for the douter to put out the candle.

He wrapped his fingers around hers.

"Leave it," Darcy whispered hoarsely into the exposed hollow above her collarbone. "If you would," he considerately amended, raising his head to meet her eyes.

He released her hand, now motionless atop the bedsheets, and trailed his fingertips along her arm... her half-bared shoulder... the side of her neck. When his palm was curved around her cheek, he could not forbear making his meaning clearer.

"This was the only thing I could have possibly wished for last night: to be able to see you." He brushed her lower lip with his thumb as he searched her eyes for an indication of her thoughts. When he could garner none, he cautiously asked, "Would you… mind?"

Elizabeth shook her head, ever so slowly, then raised her hand to cover his and drew it to her lips. Her lingering kiss on the tips of his fingers and the long look she fixed on him from beneath half-lidded eyes hit him full on – a red-hot cannonball setting him ablaze. In a flash, the layers of clothing became a detested nuisance, and were soon tugged out of the way. Patience and restraint might not have been quite as mandatory as on their first time together, yet he tried with all his might not to discard them wholly. A futile effort, as it turned out to be, and thoroughly undone by her readiness to welcome him – nay, her wildly arousing eagerness. Desire erupted, unconstrained. And Darcy was proven blissfully wrong: the most seductive sight in all his adult years was not his virgin bride shyly voicing a veiled invitation to her bed, but his beloved wife in his arms, flushed, breathless and more beautiful than ever as she joined him in the realms of passion.

ೞಲ ಲೞ

This time it was her voice that broke the silence of their languid rest in each other's arms.

"What will you do today?"

Darcy's fingertips skimmed over her cheek, then her jaw line, and he finally replied, "I think there is much to be said for the old dictum: begin as you mean to continue."

Elizabeth glanced his way and the smile she cast him was small and fleeting, almost perfunctory, so he dropped a light kiss on her cheek and assured her, "I was teasing."

"I know. But that dictum of yours had me thinking about something else," she said without any particular inflection and turned on one side to face him, countenance solemn, eyes alert.

By then, Darcy was fully alert as well.

"Yes?" he prompted, only to grow concerned when no answer was forthcoming. "What is it? Elizabeth? What troubles you?"

She caught the corner of her lip between her teeth, and eventually spoke:

"Will you tell me why our marriage began as it did? Why you left me here and vanished?"

And with that, the day's glow dimmed, overshadowed by the recollection of dark hours, and no less by her choice to claim no knowledge of their troubles. Disguise never served. Not even when it was owed to good intentions. He would have hoped that it was not her way to resort to dissembling. It certainly was not his. So Darcy gave her the unvarnished truth, however disagreeable:

"Because I learnt that you blamed me for trapping you into an unwanted union. And I could not bear it. Least of all to hear it within hours of our wedding and in a roundabout manner instead of an honest talk between us."

Her brows arched.

"What are you saying? I never blamed *you!*" Elizabeth countered, her show of astonishment more than a little disappointing. And both hurtful and alarming, truth be told. Had he not known better, he would have believed her without question. Which was as it should be. Absolute trust. But absolute trust placed one at a woeful disadvantage when faced with pretence that looked so much like candour.

Darcy's lips tightened.

"Elizabeth, I overheard," he said, reproach unavoidably seeping into his voice. "I am not proud of my eavesdropping, I assure you, but it was purely accidental. I was close by and I heard you tell your sister Jane that the blame lay with me and my brazen presumption. That your simple *'No'* should have been enough to send me on my way. And that the very recollection of that day was distasteful to you. I believe the word you used was *'sickening',*" he concluded, his voice tainted with all the gall of the poisoned chalice which he could no longer push from him.

Her eyes grew impossibly wide. And then she drew back and spluttered, "I was not speaking of *you!*"

Darcy frowned in a mixture of disbelief and incomprehension.

"You were not?"

"Of course not!" she heatedly retorted, then heaved a long sigh that sounded like exasperation, Darcy thought, his mind still reeling.

"Who, then?" he asked as soon as he could speak.

Her mouth tightened into a very small, flat circle, as though sealed with a patch of wax. She looked away and muttered, "Mr Collins, if you must know."

"Collins?" he exclaimed. "What did he do to vex you?"

"Vex me!" Elizabeth echoed, her voice brittle. "I daresay one might call it that."

He brushed a stray lock from her face and ran his thumb over her knitted brows.

"Tell me," he urged softly.

After a long moment, her lips shaped themselves out of their frozen grimace of distaste. She began to speak and, in a few terse words, did tell him precisely what had driven her out of her own home that morning, prey to sentiments a great deal stronger than vexation.

Concern and compassion swelled – and crashed into a solid wall of fury that had risen from the depths and stood rock-still and ominous, waiting to be found. The impact was savagely forceful, and so was the violent surge of his outrage. The lewd swine had had the impudence to impose himself upon her! Lay hands on her. A lecherous degenerate masquerading as a man of God!

It was beyond enraging that the very cloth that Collins had disgraced should be shielding him from the punishment the reprobate deserved, and Darcy clenched his teeth, wanting nothing more at that precise moment than to thrash the depraved fiend within an inch of his life.

He drew a deep breath, then another, as he struggled to remind himself that, today and every day, Elizabeth was his prime concern. But livid anger was still choking him, and was very slow in slackening its grip. He had always thought that *'shaking with rage'* was a mere figure of speech, meant to add visual detail to a narrative. Yet his hand was far from steady when he reached out and stroked Elizabeth's cheek, then opened his arms in a silent offer of comfort.

When she did nestle in his embrace, readily accepting whatever comfort it was in his power to give, Darcy pressed his lips to her temple and clasped her to his chest in a tight hold which, he hoped, was protective rather than possessive.

"I am so sorry… so sorry…" he breathed against her skin, making her wispy ringlets flutter.

Elizabeth gave a startled gasp of protest.

"You are not to apologise for my cousin's sins!"

"No. Not his. Mine," Darcy whispered, his voice laden with contrition.

Deep and overwhelming, remorse washed over him, for all manner of oppressively valid reasons. His own ill-judged conduct upon their encounter later that day. The frosty and inauspicious beginnings of their marriage. All the unease and disharmony he had caused between them by leaping to the worst possible conclusions. And above all for storming away in a fit of pique and leaving her to come to grips with her new life – alone.

"Ah, yes. Your sins," she ruefully said, a clear indication that she was in agreement with him on that score, and drew back a little, so that she could catch his eye. "I did not blame you for trapping me into marriage, as you called it. Ultimately, our reputations suffered at the hands of repulsive scandalmongers. If anything, I was grateful for your offer to take me away from their malice and the whole hideous business." But, just as blessed relief began to trickle in and soothe Darcy's spirits, filling him with thankful wonder at her lenience, Elizabeth spoke again and qualified it. "That aside, I *will* say that I was less than grateful for having to spend a se'nnight or so fretting that I was wedded to an ogre intent on keeping me hostage in his lair in the north."

"A foul-tempered ogre," Darcy concurred, repentantly conceding her the point, as he loosened his hold around her lithe form to run his fingers through her hair.

She gave a little shrug.

"Naturally. Ogres are foul-tempered by definition," she teased – another awe-inspiring sign that he might soon be forgiven, little as he deserved it. "Now, in all fairness, your lair is delightful, and your people exceedingly kind. They made me think I had walked right into a children's tale—"

"Madame de Villeneuve's *Beauty and the Beast*, perchance?"

Elizabeth cast him an impish grin.

"The very one." And then she cupped his cheek, and her gaze grew very solemn. "That wretched misunderstanding was blown out of all proportion," she said, her mild voice in stark contrast with her gravity of manner. "And yet it could have been cleared in no time at all, had you but told me what it was that you were thinking. Then this – all this – would have been resolved within minutes of our quitting Longbourn. And we would have been spared so many days of doubt and needless misery."

Darcy nodded slowly as he reached up to cover her hand with his and bring it to his lips.

"I cannot tell you how much I regret the doubt and misery I caused," he earnestly said, little as he was in the habit of apologising – which was no wonder for, to date, he had never been so abysmally in the wrong. He frowned as he unreservedly continued, "It was unpardonably foolish of me – hot-headed – cowardly—"

Several other fitting epithets sprang to mind, but Elizabeth did not let him finish.

"I would not go as far as to deem you a foolish coward, but I do wish you would temper your hot-headedness with a little of my philosophy – which, come to think of it, might also work wonders on your patent inclination to stubbornly trust your own views above all else."

Darcy could not forbear a smile.

"You read me rightly. And your philosophy is…?"

To his delight, her impish grin made an eye-catching reappearance.

"Let me begin by saying that I am not about to censure you for your vast confidence in your own opinions. It would be unfair of me – nay, it would be nothing short of hypocritical – seeing as I bear that noble burden too. You will discover soon enough that my opinions are many and liberally bestowed. Now, as to our original subject, my philosophy is this: however bad a set of circumstances might be, open discussion can only bring improvement. Reticence should be reserved for strangers. And on that note, I give you my word that you will always hear the full truth from me. Even when you will dearly wish for some civil and compliant falsehood for the sake of harmony. Still, I daresay we shall reap the questionable rewards of my frankness in due course," Elizabeth quipped, then sobered. "For now, I shall only add that, in my opinion, silence never serves. It only makes a bad situation worse. So pray do not build a wall of silence between us ever again, Fitzwilliam," she solemnly entreated, reaching up to hold his face between her palms.

Warmth flooded Darcy's heart. Unless he was much mistaken, this was the first time that she had addressed him by his Christian name. And her plea was all the more affecting for it.

"I will not. Never again!" he said with fervour – a heartfelt vow – readily giving her what she asked for, and not just because he could not have denied her anything on this blissful day. Her request was perfectly in tune with his best hopes, and he lost no time in saying so. "I do not hold with reticence and silence between us either. I wish for the very opposite. Openness. Trust. A shared life in every sense of the word. And I am overjoyed to find you in agreement."

Her countenance brightened into a smile.

"Of course," Elizabeth declared with emphasis. "I have always known that this is how it ought to be. But... it does not follow that I am not astonished," she added softly, puzzling him anew. A joy-filled puzzle, though. Just as life with her promised to be.

"Astonished?" Darcy prompted, and she gave a pensive little nod.

"Oh, yes. Very much so."

"At?" he gently queried.

Elizabeth raised her hand to trace a small circle in the air.

"This. You. The fair number of delectable surprises," she replied, which failed to make her meaning any clearer. But the smile she cast him was the warmest yet. Then she elaborated: "What I am trying to say – not very coherently, it seems," she ruefully chuckled, "is that our ever-so-short betrothal led me to hope that we would build our marriage on some sort of... cautious friendliness. I did not imagine that we would have so much more in mere days."

"Such as?" Darcy asked, his eyes crinkling at the corners.

Elizabeth gave a little shrug and her smile grew bashful.

"You must know what I mean. I was not expecting openness, not for a while yet. Nor quite so much harmony... affinity... affection..."

"Oh, nothing so tame as affection. Love," Darcy countered softly as he twirled a lock of her hair around his finger.

"Love?" she whispered back, her eyes alight with wonder.

He nodded.

"Ardent love. It has been thus for me for quite some time."

Her brows arched into a pair of crescents above her sparkling eyes.

"It has? Since when?"

"The earliest days of our acquaintance, I believe. And it would be fair to say it was inevitable."

"Why?" she whispered barely audibly – just that and nothing more, lost for words for the first time in her all-but-one-and-twenty years.

Darcy gave the faintest shrug.

"Does anyone catalogue the reasons behind unconquerable attraction? I know I have not. But, had I paused to think of that, I would have found a host of them," he said, his gaze growing even warmer, something which a moment earlier Elizabeth would have said was not remotely possible. "This, for instance: the way your eyes light up when you are surprised… and your lips curl just so. And when you are deeply moved or excessively diverted, a dimple forms… right here," he continued, trailing his fingertip to a precise spot on her left cheek. "Ah, there it is. Just as I said," he smilingly observed, tracing a small circle on her skin – around the dimple in question, Elizabeth supposed, only to forget about it altogether when his voice lost every hint of teasing and was lowered to a near-whisper, caressing and unspeakably intense. "And because of what you do to me with a mere glance or an arch smile. Because I learnt to pick out your voice in a crowded room, and the sound of it alone was enough to drive me to distraction – to say nothing of the times when we were close enough for conversation or, heaven help me, the four nights we spent under the same roof at Netherfield. And the daytime hours too, when I had to keep my wits about me if I was to have a hope of matching yours. A challenge in itself, that," he said with a rueful smile as he ran his fingers through her hair. "When it comes to you, my wits invariably fail me. Because you are everything I have ever wanted. Heartbreakingly charming. Bright. Beautiful. Artless. The soul of kindness. Fiercely loyal. And utterly devoted to those you love. I expect I had not known you a fortnight before I began to covet that."

Unbeknownst to her, the look of wonder in her eyes turned incandescent.

"But… you gave no sign of it!" Elizabeth faltered – an awestruck murmur. "I thought you married me because of your scrupulous sense of honour. Why did you not say a word of this when you came to Longbourn to make your offer?"

"I could claim that having your father pacing just outside the door was not conducive to heartfelt declarations," Darcy chuckled softly. "But, as we are aiming for full and uncompromising honesty, I will own that I was enough of a dunce not to know it myself. Not then." He gave a mirthless laugh. "What will you think of my slow wits now? I did not see how much you meant to me until all hope seemed lost. It was only then that I knew I could not be happy until I earned your devotion for myself. And that it was no wonder that you did not love me, when our wedding was such a rushed and fraught affair – when I had not even courted you as you deserve to be courted." His hand lingered on her cheek, his thumb moving back and forth in a slow caress. "I came back to do that: court you, and hope for the best. But I did not dare hope for quite so much either. Nor did I have an inkling of the joy I was missing, once I had taken it into my head to go wandering in the wilderness," he whispered, sending her heart brimming.

Elizabeth weaved her fingers through his hair.

"You never told me where you went. *'Wandering in the wilderness'* paints an awfully bleak picture."

"The wilderness was metaphorical," Darcy assured her. "I thank you for your sweet concern, but it is ill-deserved. The bleakness was of my own making. Besides, I did have physical shelter."

"Where?"

"The hunting lodge on the northern boundary of the estate."

"Oh," Elizabeth whispered, her mind's eye conjuring up the image of a chalet lost in a dark, forbidding woodland.

Tenderness surged, as did compassion. It was deeply distressing that her words should have been so horribly misconstrued, and her heart lurched at the thought of what he must have suffered. Needlessly. For days on end! And goodness knows for how much longer they might have had to live with the effects of that misapprehension, had it been allowed to linger and spread like an insidious poison, tainting everything.

Frustration at his silence, at his absence, might have swelled again, just as it had so many times during her first se'nnight at Pemberley – alone – had it not occurred to her to ask herself what *she* would have done, had she thought she had heard him say that he resented her, and had only married her because he had no other option.

Elizabeth bit her lip. She *would* have brought it up, of course. But not on the day – nor for a fair while. Not until she was assured that she would not succumb to anger or, worse still, to tears of humiliation. She would not have said a word until she had brought herself under good regulation, so that she could speak with a semblance of composure about what was to be done.

Seemingly, they were not so different after all. As prideful as each other, and just as reluctant to show weakness and speak of injured feelings.

Elizabeth gave a small sigh of exasperation.

More fools them, then. Both of them.

She reached up to brush a stray lock from his brow, then caressingly trailed her fingers to the back of his head to draw him closer, and pressed her lips to his. "Do not go into the wilderness again. Metaphorical or otherwise. Talk to me instead," she pleaded softly between light, consoling kisses. "Or at least talk to me sooner, before matters get well and truly out of hand. And I promise I will do the same. I never wish to have another misconception festering between us. We had much better air our differences – any differences – rather than make assumptions on what the other might be thinking, just because injured pride or injured feelings got in the way. Or because either one of us was driven to put two and two together and make five. Or five hundred."

Darcy chuckled.

"Five hundred? Not very likely, I am relieved to say." He stroked her cheek with the back of his fingers. "You are too sensible for such absurd misjudgements. As for myself, you may call me boastful, but my sums generally are in perfect order, this blundering exception notwithstanding. And I learn from my errors. This will not happen again," he concluded with quiet yet firm conviction and sought her lips, sealing that promise with a kiss.

"Oh, I believe it will," Elizabeth evenly countered as soon as he drew back, and Darcy arched a brow at her untroubled intimation that she expected other storms to come.

"You do?"

"Naturally," she replied with perfect nonchalance. "No marriage is a bed of roses. Wise people say that there will always be misunderstandings, disagreements and any number of vexations—"

"Wise, you call them?" he protested. "I would say cynical."

'*Or mismatched and disillusioned,*' Elizabeth thought, her parents' marriage the nearest example, and the starkest. Yet she would not dwell upon that now. So she gave a little shrug and airily resumed, "Be that as it may, I do not doubt that we shall find ourselves at loggerheads many a time. More often than most couples, I am prepared to wager, since we are both so wilful. The salient point is that our marital differences will not cause quite so much mischief if we agree to always talk without reserve about them. As for mistakes, I hope we do learn from them, but I will not put it past us to keep making new ones."

"Oh, ye of little faith," Darcy chuckled and claimed her lips again. "Very well," he said at length as he dropped his head beside hers on the pillow and gathered her to his chest. "As and when we find fresh mistakes to make, you have my word that we shall discuss them freely. Still, it would be prudent to secure your indulgence in advance for predictable lapses," he said, his air mildly apologetic, before it veered towards playfulness again. "Because, contrary to some opinions, I am not yet in the habit of saying all that much."

Elizabeth laughed.

"That is an extraordinary claim from one who had just made the most beautiful declaration of love that I could have possibly imagined. Not to mention that, within the space of mere hours, you have said a vast deal more than in all the time you spent in Hertfordshire. But if you are contemplating a return to old patterns, I hope you will reconsider. I dearly like to talk. And there is much that I would wish to learn of you."

Darcy sought her hand and held it, palm on palm, fingers interlaced.

"Ask me anything," he whispered and turned his head to press his lips to her temple. "What should you wish to know?"

"Oh, everything. What were you like as a boy? How is it that you had not been tempted into matrimony long before you came into Hertfordshire? Why have you chosen to befriend Mr Bingley, whose disposition could not offer a greater contrast to your own? Do you spend more time in town or in the country? Where have you travelled? What books have you read? What music do you favour? What delights you, and what sets your teeth on edge? Why do you dislike dancing quite so much – and are you likely to change your mind about it, seeing as I love to dance almost as much as I love to talk, and as a newly married woman, it really would not do to stand up with other gentlemen more often than with my own husband."

"Is that all?" he smiled.

"No, not by a fair margin. And once we have covered the intriguing subject of your good self, I should like to learn what is expected of your wife, at Pemberley and elsewhere. Would it drive you to despair to find me traipsing over the countryside or curled up with a book rather than poring over household ledgers? What if Papa should make a habit of calling when least expected and pretend he had not come to assure himself of my happiness, but to devour the contents of your extensive library?"

Darcy released her hand to weave his fingers through her tresses.

"He will always be welcome," he said simply. "It seems to me that your father and I have much in common. Not least the wish to see you happy. So your second set of questions has but one answer: you should do whatever gives you pleasure. No demands. No expectations. If you are happy, so am I."

Elizabeth stroked his cheek and shook her head in bemusement and tender disagreement.

"Surely I can do better than please myself. From what I understand, the master of Pemberley is not self-indulgent. So why should its mistress spend her days in pursuit of selfish diversions?"

Darcy cast her a wide smile and countered, "There is no trace of selfishness in you." He pressed his lips to her cheek, then spoke with quite as much conviction as affection. "Your kindness and common sense will guide you, and you will soon find the best ways to make your mark. But no one is expecting you to pore over household ledgers. Mrs Reynolds has been in her post for above two decades, and is exceedingly efficient. You can safely leave the running of the house to her. Fear not, I am not suggesting that the dear old domestic general would object to relinquishing command," he chuckled. "I only meant to say that she would be content to carry on as she had always had until you tell her otherwise. She will gladly explain everything there is to know, and answer all your questions. And so shall I, and every member of the household. If there is anything you wish for – information, assistance, guidance – you only need ask, my love. Do remember that," he urged, cupping her cheek and shifting sideways by a fraction, so as to lock his gaze with hers.

Elizabeth nodded, and her lips parted to dreamily murmur, "You called me that last night: *'my love.'* I wondered at it for a second. But then I was…"

"Distracted?" Darcy supplied when her voice trailed off, and she gave a little chuckle as she choked out, "Just so."

Heat flared in her cheeks – a response she deemed ludicrously missish, given the intimacies they had already shared. But the heat did not subside, quite the opposite, when his thumb brushed against her glowing skin.

"Until this morning, I would have said you look at your most entrancing when you are blushing. Of course, now I know better," he added, his voice lowered to a husky whisper. "I *should* beg your pardon for making you blush. But in truth, I am shockingly unrepentant," Darcy owned, raising his head from the pillow to skim her jaw line with his nose and drop a kiss in the hollow underneath her ear. "And on that note, dare I hope that passion and sensual gratification feature somewhere among the delectable surprises you spoke of?" he asked, just before he began to devote himself to a thorough exploration of her neck.

With a breathless giggle, Elizabeth drew back and tucked her chin into her chest.

"That was ticklish. As for your question, it smacks of pride. Nay, of intolerable smugness," she playfully admonished, her cheeks still tingling but her missish blush entirely forgotten as, with wicked intent, she slipped her hand underneath his robe in search of a certain spot along his lower ribs which experience had already taught her that it could be as ticklish as her neck in the right circumstances.

The endeavour met with utter success. He jumped, then swooped down to take full possession of her lips as he imprisoned her roguish hand in his.

"Vixen," he growled, then rolled back and drew her with him, secure in the crook of his arm, her hair falling in a soft canopy over their faces. He brushed it over her shoulder as he airily observed, "I will have you know that pride and smugness have already been imputed to me too many times to count. But in this case, for the life of me I cannot see what is objectionable about taking honest pride in one's achievements."

He might have expected a mildly scandalised blush, but instead her eyes grew very soft as she reached up and cupped his cheek, her fingertips stroking his temple.

"Oh, that reminds me. Two more entries on my list: the ogre is unexpectedly adept at flirting. And he has a pleasing sense of humour. Although that is not entirely surprising. He had previously responded well to occasional teasing."

"Occasional, you call it? You live to tease me. In fact, I would wager that you were born for that very purpose," Darcy rasped between ardent kisses. His hands slipped beneath her wavy cloak of lustrous chestnut-coloured hair to sweep caressingly over her back. "And I say thank goodness," he breathed against her lips. "I would not have it any other way."

Chapter 24

Daylight filtered into the room through the narrow gap between the curtains, heralding the start of a new day, but neither one saw fit to sit up and extinguish the low-burning candle.

"Would you like me to draw the curtains?" Darcy asked, but Elizabeth shook her head.

"No. Stay," she sleepily murmured, and he was all too glad to remain blissfully still under his wife's counterpane, with her limbs wrapped languidly around him, her naked form in his arms – at the last flare of passion, they had jointly decided that they were overdressed. And while Elizabeth had not explicitly added passion to her list of welcome surprises, they had no reason to doubt that their marriage was generously blessed with it.

"So, what shall we do today?" Elizabeth asked a little later, proving him wrong in thinking that she had drifted off to sleep.

Darcy pressed his lips to the top of her head.

"In case I have not made it plain enough already, the ogre you married would like nothing better than to lock himself with you in your bedchamber for the rest of the day – nay, make that the foreseeable future. Still, I imagine you would appreciate some variety. A walk, perhaps, if the rain abates?"

"Perhaps," she lazily replied. "I will own that I have grown quite fond of my early morning rambles through your grounds—"

"Our grounds," he corrected her and, lips curled up at the corners, Elizabeth amended:

"Our grounds. Rufus will miss the old routine, but I daresay he will have to brook some alterations."

"And preferably learn not to attack me when he finds that I cannot keep my hands off you."

"That, too," Elizabeth agreed with a giggle and raised her head off his chest to kiss him.

And that was when, almost without warning except a brief, perfunctory knock, the door that led into the corridor opened to reveal a cheerfully matter-of-fact Sarah who wandered in, laden tray in hand and prattling all the way.

"Good morning, Miss Lizzy. Hope I haven't kept you waiting long. Molly said she saw light under your door well-nigh an hour gone, when she came up to sweep the carpets and whatnot. Still, she didn't think to come and tell me sooner, the silly goose." And then she must have caught sight of the chemise and the burgundy-coloured robe abandoned in a heap upon the floor, for her glance darted to the bed, only to be averted in a flash as she recoiled, the tray in her hands jolted by her violent start. "Oh, my days! Dear me! Beg pardon, Miss Lizzy – Mr Darcy!" she stuttered and, in the heat of her acute mortification, she forgot herself and blurted out, "I didn't think you'd be here too, sir."

Darcy's lips twitched, but he replied blandly, "Well, you will have to grow accustomed to that notion."

"Aye, sir. Will do. Sure will. I beg you'd pardon the intrusion. And this, too," Sarah stammered with a jerky tilt of her chin towards the tray, from which some liquid had just begun to fall in steady drips. She balanced the tray on one hand to redress the overturned receptacle, then hastily offered, "Let me find something to mop up the spills and I'll be out of here in a trice."

"No matter, Sarah. And do not trouble yourself with the spillage either. Just set the tray down in my dressing room. You can leave it on the washstand, or even in the tub. If it should still be dripping, it will cause no damage there. That will be all, I thank you. I will ring for you later," Elizabeth said, and Darcy was inclined to hope that she was seeking to hasten the maid's departure in order to alleviate the girl's discomfort, and not his. With any luck, the wry glance they had exchanged had already told her that his own unease was non-existent. In fact, he was cheerfully unconcerned about the entire business and, if anything, diverted by the sheer absurdity of it.

Once the flustered maidservant did as bid, her eyes studiously averted, and darted out with a curtsy and a conspicuous, "I'll be ready when you need me, Miss Li— That is to say, Mrs Darcy," Elizabeth gave full rein to her own amusement. But, lest she be heard from the corridor, she buried her face into his chest, her giggles muffled in her hands, her shoulders shaking with quiet laughter.

"Poor Sarah," she choked out at last. "Much like Rufus and the rest of us, she, too, will have to grow accustomed to some changes in the usual routine. Such as following your man's sterling example and not coming up without a summons. And form the habit of addressing me as Mrs Darcy." She gave a rueful little chuckle. "That will take some time, after nearly six years of *'Miss Lizzy.'* She came to Longbourn when I was fifteen."

Darcy smiled.

"So… the fifteen-year-old Miss Lizzy Bennet – what was she like?" he softly asked.

"Not that much different from the new Mrs Darcy," Elizabeth replied with an airy wave of her hand. "Coltish, perhaps, but just as wilful. And generally the bane of her mother's existence."

His smile grew wider.

"Is that so?"

"Oh, definitely. Hoydenish. Wild. Forever out of doors. Often setting a bad example to my sisters and encouraging them daily into mischief. Not Jane, of course. She always was well-mannered and angelic. As for Mary, she would never leave the house if she could help it. But Mamma claims – I daresay with ample reason – that it was entirely my doing if the rest of us should be wandering about the place with our skirts twelve inches deep in mud, as though we were raised by gypsies. And even at fifteen I was more likely to climb trees than apply myself to acquiring ladylike accomplishments."

Lips twitching, Darcy shook his head, then leaned to drop a kiss on her bare shoulder.

"*You* climbed trees," he smilingly observed. "Now, why does that not surprise me?"

Elizabeth laughed.

"Just one, to be fair. An accommodating chestnut at the furthest end of our wilderness. It had a short trunk, a couple of convenient bulges for footholds and a low branch forked just so. Ideal for curling up with a book – or rather perching with it. Especially in the summer."

"Because a seat in the parlour simply would not do," he teased.

"Precisely," she grinned back and shrugged. "When you grow up with four sisters, you take your peace and quiet wherever you find them. Now, if you would be so kind as to reach for my dressing gown," she gestured towards the foot of the bed, "I will fetch the tea before it grows cold."

Darcy obliged and retrieved the garment from where it lay draped atop the counterpane, then held it for her and valiantly bore the disappointment of seeing her covering herself – only to discover that, all in all, he could not find fault with sheer muslin.

Once Elizabeth had left the bedchamber, Darcy leaned back against the pillows and remained thus, arms crossed under his head, listening to the quiet clink of china as she pottered about in the other room. Familiar sounds, yet utterly novel in that setting. Heart-warming sounds, adorably domestic. And unspeakably comforting too. He drew a deep breath, savouring the comfort and the exquisite joy of her presence. The infinite joy of sharing his life with her.

Elizabeth returned in no time at all, cup and saucer in one hand, a small plate in the other.

"There is just one cup, so we shall have to make do. Not much milk in the tea, either. But at least the almond biscuits have escaped the deluge."

As soon as Darcy had propped himself up on one elbow, she handed him the cup, then clambered into bed and sat, leaning against the headboard. She brushed the hair from her face and carelessly tucked a few stray locks behind her ear – a simple, casual gesture, yet touching all the same. Because it belonged here, in the delightful privacy of the bedchamber, not in the outer world, where her chestnut tresses had to be pinned up and tamed. And because it was a small, inconsequential gesture he had never witnessed, yet henceforth would see every morning – a tiny part of the glorious notion that he would wake up beside her every day, for the rest of his life.

Darcy's lips curled up into a smile at finding himself caught up in besotted musings. Then his smile widened. Praise be, that would become a natural part of his life as well.

"It suits you, that smile," Elizabeth remarked. "You should use it often."

His eyes crinkled at the corners.

"Thank you. I believe I shall. Tea?" he asked, offering her the cup, but she shook her head.

"You first. And this. It will sustain you through your ordeal," she added, breaking an almond biscuit in two and popping one half into his mouth.

Crumbs flew as Darcy succumbed to laughter.

"Ordeal?" he asked as soon as he could speak.

Elizabeth nodded sagely.

"My five thousand questions, remember? And recounting your life story."

Darcy took a sip of tea and, brow raised, he eyed her over the rim of the cup.

"So, you were not teasing?"

"Not at all. Except as to the overall number, perhaps. I might content myself with less than five thousand. But you should not count on it."

"I see. Well, if we make haste about it, I expect we might cover your however-many questions before dinner. Ask away," he smiled, offering her the cup again.

This time she took it, but did not drink. Instead, she cast him an arch glance.

"I was not suggesting we closet ourselves here until dinner."

"Were you not? A pity," Darcy grinned back, then raised his hand. "Shh. Listen."

"What?"

Nothing could be heard but the hammering of the rain against the glass panes.

"The rain?" she asked at last.

"Aye. And the howling wind. By the sound of it, the weather is dismal. So I ask you, what else are we to do on a wet and windy day such as this?"

"What, indeed?" Elizabeth chuckled, and took great care not to overset the cup as she leaned closer and pressed her lips to his.

৵৹৻৻ড়৹৶

They were both jesting, as it happened.

Elizabeth did not pepper him with five thousand questions, nor did she insist on hearing his life story, just welcomed the details that he saw fit to share. For his part, Darcy did not stick to his guns as regards closeting themselves in her bedchamber until dinner. So, in due course, they summoned their attendants to ready them for the day and came down for breakfast – a great deal later than expected, but did come down nevertheless.

Neither one had cause to regret it. The cosy room easily became their private haven yet again, but without any of the reticence that had hampered them the other night, over dinner. Nothing left to question. No room for doubt. No more treading on eggshells. As for the wretchedness of the previous morning, it had been laid to rest and could be entirely forgotten now.

They sat together and served each other, talking, laughing, their hands touching without the slightest need to think of an excuse. Nor did they see why they should hold back from the temptation to lean in and exchange a kiss – or several – over the corner of the table. So they gave in to that sweet compulsion eagerly and often – until, as they might have expected, the door opened and Peter came in with a plate of fresh scones at a decidedly inconvenient time.

Unlike Sarah, Peter did not start, so there was no domestic mishap. But the young man turned beet-red, gave a clumsy bow and set the plate on the sideboard by the door with the utmost haste, as though it had suddenly grown flame-hot and burned his fingers through the pristine gloves. Then the footman backed out of the room, firmly closed the door behind him and, unbeknownst to his master and new mistress, remained rooted to the spot for a few brief moments as he silently but roundly cursed himself for his stupidity.

He damned well should have knocked instead of walking right in with the serving plate, as was the old custom, Peter thought, sorely tempted to smack his forehead for good measure. Customs were a-changing. Of course. They always did when a man took a wife. And only a blockhead would blunder in and trespass upon the privacy of a newly wedded couple without knocking.

"Numbskull," Peter muttered and took himself away, clinging tooth and nail to the hope that happy men were not quick to take offence. As far as he could tell, his doltish blunder had met with nary a frown. In fact, he could almost swear that he had heard his master's chuckle mingled with Mrs Darcy's giggle, once the door was closed. So, fingers crossed, he had not landed himself into a spot of bother. Nor had Mr Howard been around, thank goodness, to note his error or, worse still, see him loitering about and looking as if he were listening at doors.

Then there would've been hell to pay an' all!' Peter thought and flinched, for the lash of Mr Howard's tongue had always been more daunting than the master's even temper.

The flustered footman would have been vastly reassured, had he been listening at doors in earnest, for he would have detected precious little censure for his *faux pas* in the exchange between his master and new mistress.

Elizabeth's quiet giggle was followed by a rueful, "Oh, dear. First Sarah, and now Peter. How many of them do you imagine we might discompose before the day is out?"

Darcy matched her sheepish smile with a wide grin of his own.

"There is no telling, is there? Hopefully, word will start to spread that they had better learn to knock. Perhaps I should ask Howard and Mrs Reynolds to give express instructions."

She laughed.

"For shame, Fitzwilliam! You would not!"

Darcy shrugged and kept to banter.

"Frankly, I am astonished that they have not thought of it already. The other night, at dinner, Howard did see wisdom in knocking, so he might have impressed that notion upon the footmen too." He brought her hand to his lips and shamelessly opted for teasing with intent. "The concept will take hold, no doubt. But until then, I believe it would be an act of kindness for us to keep out of their way."

"That is very thoughtful," Elizabeth said, her eyes twinkling with mischief. "Have you any suggestions?"

"Oh, I expect we can think of something if we put our minds to it," Darcy murmured as he caressed the back of her fingers with his lips.

And thus, the last days of the old year drifted by, seamlessly blending into a time of blissful harmony. And, day by day, the household found its way towards new patterns. Joyful patterns they turned out to be, as the happiness of the newly wedded couple subtly spoke to everyone who dwelt at Pemberley. It spoke of hope and a new dawn, heralding peaceful years ahead when, slowly but surely, the ancient house would become a home once more, and there would be stability and comfort in the service of a contented master and a fair and undemanding mistress. Their people could not wish for anything better.

As for the master and new mistress, they basked in their good fortune, and in each other. Eventually, they grew accustomed to spending *some* of their time fully attired and out of their apartments, once the household had become attuned to a new fact of life: namely, that in order to avoid the ultimate discomfort of interrupting Mr and Mrs Darcy's private moments, one must tread with care and always, *always* knock.

The weather remained dismal, leaving but rare opportunities for walks — it was December after all. So Elizabeth and Darcy retired to the library instead, or her book-room, or the music room, and occasionally strolled in the long gallery, for Rufus to scamper about in lieu of his daily constitutional and Elizabeth to learn more about family portraits and her husband's ancestry.

His parents' likenesses were already known to her, and so was his sister's. Mrs Reynolds had pointed them out during the tour of the house. In time, Darcy acquainted her with the rest: renditions of his grandparents, great-grandparents and many others of the line that stretched unbroken to the Norman Conquest, along with sundry offshoots, and great-aunts, and all manner of cousins.

It came as no surprise to Elizabeth that Colonel Fitzwilliam's likeness was vouchsafed a very early mention. On the morning when she and her husband had shared old stories, almond biscuits and one cup of tea, she had learnt that there was a strong bond between Darcy and his dearest cousin. The gentleman's portrait only served to augment her favourable impression. It depicted a friendly visage — not handsome, strictly speaking, not by common standards — yet amiable and cheerful, which made her look forward to meeting that member of the family.

Lord and Lady Malvern, the colonel's parents, were cast in a different mould, Darcy told her, and when Elizabeth enquired into his meaning, he revealed with manifest displeasure that he expected his aunt and uncle to respond less than enthusiastically to his marriage.

"It matters not, my love," he tenderly assured her. "Their station in life colours their views, but so be it. Our life together is our own, and their sanction or lack thereof has no bearing. I require neither their consent, nor their blessing. My uncle and his wife can only lay claim to the natural affection I owe my mother's brother and her sister by marriage. That is all. As for my mother's sister, 'tis a hopeless business."

That would be Lady Catherine, Mr Collins' patroness, Elizabeth knew full well. But her revolting cousin had no place in this discussion, so she did not mention him. She merely asked, "How so?"

Darcy gave an irritable shrug.

"My aunt Catherine had always treasured the notion that my cousin Anne and I would become united. She often claimed that it had been my mother's dearest wish ever since Anne and I were in our cradles. For all I know, that scheme might have appealed to my mother at one time, but she said nothing of the sort to me, nor mentioned it in the letter she left for me to open when I came of age. This gives me every reason to believe that, were she still with us, she would not have supported her sister in that particular crusade. Yet logic does not speak to Lady Catherine – not if it argues against her own wishes. So it was no surprise that she and I came to a parting of ways, once I had written to inform her of our marriage."

"Surely there is no cause for that!" Elizabeth exclaimed – and it was only then that Darcy reluctantly imparted that Lady Catherine's reply had arrived six days prior, and had been expressed in a language so offensive that he had no wish to receive further communications from her ladyship until such time that she penned a full and formal letter of apology.

"I have conveyed as much to my aunt and, in truth, I expect no answer. Lady Catherine has no equal in both pride and obstinacy. Still, Anne has written to give us joy, which is a comfort. I never wanted a rupture with my cousin. Even so, keeping up a correspondence with her under my aunt's wrathful nose requires more subterfuge than I should wish for."

Elizabeth stroked his hand.

"And there was I thinking that our troublesome relations were strictly on my side," she ruefully observed, only to follow it with an earnest, "I am so sorry."

"This is not your doing, my love, and certainly not your fault," Darcy declared, then promptly changed the subject. "I believe the rain is down to a mere drizzle now. Would you care for a walk?"

They did go for a walk, and Rufus escorted them, as boisterous as ever, but thankfully by then his relationship with Darcy had undergone a substantial improvement.

"Because you are much better at throwing sticks than me," Elizabeth speculated.

"That, or Mrs Reynolds' biscuits," Darcy countered, for it could not be denied that their truce had changed course towards a cautious friendship around the time when he had formed the habit of rewarding the terrier's good behaviour with bran and bone-marrow rusks.

For whatever reason, Rufus finished by submitting with good grace to all the changes he had previously resisted – so much so that, when she came down for breakfast, Elizabeth no longer found him scampering in the great hall under Mr Howard's eagle eye, nor whining at the foot of the great staircase. These days, he was perfectly content with being allowed to curl up next to Darcy on the sofa that had replaced the pair of armchairs in the small dining room, and he often dozed, his head on Darcy's knee, as his companion scratched his back and whiled away the time with a book or the latest papers.

Overall, Rufus remained deficient in only one regard: unlike the human members of the household, he had yet to learn discretion. So he still bounded, marking their attire with muddy paws, and barked with energy, as though at a diverting game, whenever Elizabeth and Darcy paused on their walks to share a kiss under the evergreens.

Thus – predictably – the uncomprehending little bundle of russet fur was left in the servants' care in the evenings, and not suffered to disrupt the couple's privacy at dinner, nor their cosy hours by the fire, on the sofa for two.

Yet it was not just Rufus who would have blithely made inroads on their precious time together, if given leave to do so. With Christmas approaching, invitations to seasonal gaieties were coming thick and fast – but, with Elizabeth's comfort in mind and no less his own, Darcy advocated accepting the ones born from goodwill, and deferring those extended out of mere curiosity. January would be soon enough – too soon – for dining with the Mrs Prescotts of the parish. Likewise, they both agreed that January would be soon enough for reciprocating with a grand affair that would please the friendly and appease the curious. For now, they were supremely disinclined to put the stately dining room to use and fill their house with company.

There was a sole exception to that rule: they had no reservations about asking Mr Lyle and his family to dine at Pemberley one evening along with Mr Kettering, and the first engagement they hosted as husband and wife was as pleasant as anticipated – even though Mr Kettering did not scruple to ask Darcy why he had not breathed a word about his marriage upon their previous encounter.

"More to the point," the old man added, "whatever possessed you to agree to dine at Clifton in the first place, while this delightful creature here was waiting for you at home?"

As was his wont, Mr Kettering launched into a different topic without waiting for an answer, which was just as well, for none was forthcoming. Darcy was not of a mind to seek some convenient excuse. He was too busily engaged in searching Elizabeth's countenance, only to rejoice in finding that his neighbour's question had brought no shadows to his darling wife's visage. Elizabeth merely smiled as though at a private jest as she filtered an arch glance towards him.

And later, as he was bidding his adieus, Mr Kettering could not fail to endear himself to both when he patted Elizabeth's hand and said, his voice thick with emotion, "Bless you, child. 'Tis a vast relief to see the lad so happy. A pity that his father did not live long enough to meet you. Dear old George, God rest his soul, would have adored you."

The heartfelt remark brought a lump to Darcy's throat. He had thought the same for quite some time. Even so, it was deeply affecting to hear his sire's oldest friend confirm it.

For a great many reasons, Christmas was deeply affecting too. They spent it just as they both wished: at home, with their very private joy – then saw the New Year in likewise. And the revelries that were the most likely to capture Elizabeth's interest and the hearts of both were the ones held in their own household – age-old traditions observed more gleefully than ever above-stairs and in the servants' hall.

The Twelfth Night ball, however, was a time for conviviality. It mattered not to Darcy that they would mingle with kindly souls as well as prying busybodies. Elizabeth was eagerly anticipating the occasion, and as for himself, he was ready to acquaint the world with his good fortune.

If anything, it was the best place to start: not in the grand salons thronged with the fashionable set puffed up with their own importance, but here, close to home, among people he had known all his life, many of whom he held in his affection and esteem.

As he glanced around Mr and Mrs Lyle's ballroom, Darcy could readily conclude that most of his friends and acquaintances in a fifteen-mile radius were already gathered there – the fixed number of families that would form the backdrop of his married life – and, for once, he felt nothing of the *blasé* indifference with which he had greeted social events for above a decade.

It was pure delight to join the merry crowd with Elizabeth on his arm, cheeks aglow and eyes sparkling, clearly enjoying the evening, and his heart was brimming with happiness and pride at introducing her as Mrs Darcy – seeing her take her rightful place among his peers and effortlessly finding just the right thing to say to each of them, with perfect poise and her very own inimitable charm.

Last but not least, he was entirely at leisure to enjoy the occasion too. The old constraints had vanished, along with the expectations placed upon him, and that was nothing short of liberating. Matchmaking schemes were no longer a concern. Henceforth, he need not look for ways of foiling them without giving offence to neighbours who had known him from his boyhood. Thus, once he had done his duty and stood up with the daughters of the house, he was allowed the novel and exquisite enjoyment of surprising his darling wife with his newfound interest in dancing.

Her light-hearted teasing on the subject was not meant to dissuade him – quite the opposite, in fact – so it did not. He asked her to stand up with him for most of the dances, delighting in her every move and the smiles she had for him alone. And could not spare a thought for the stir he inevitably caused with such a blatant departure from the norm – much less for Miss Prescott, who was sourly assessing them from across the ballroom, then raised her fan to share her venomous frustrations with her mother:

"Humph! Charming, that is. Darcy's little nobody hardly has a good feature in her face, smiles too much and is shockingly provincial in her choice of apparel – and yet he is gawping at her as if she were the greatest prize of all. I can scarce credit it, Mamma, but there we have it: I do believe that the foolish man married her for love!"

Chapter 25

January and most of February passed in a happy blur, and Mr and Mrs Darcy's delightful privacy was hardly ever interrupted. With the exception of the one grand dinner they had hosted as intended, their engagements had decreased after the Twelfth Night ball, which had not failed to please them. What came as a disappointment was Georgiana's change of heart about travelling to Pemberley. She had written to request Darcy's permission to extend her stay in Berkeley Square, and he had bowed to her wishes. But it was not long until his brotherly concern had prevailed and urged him to suggest they join his sister in London for a while.

Elizabeth readily agreed. She longed to see her family and be reassured that Jane's heart was mending. The letters that her dearest sister had sent in the intervening months serenely dealt with commonplaces, but Elizabeth could not be persuaded that they portrayed a true lightness of spirit. A couple of days at Longbourn and the chance to speak with Jane face to face would be more revealing. Besides, she was eager to meet her new sister, of whom Darcy had spoken often and with deep affection, and the prospect of spending some time in town was exceedingly appealing too.

Thus, arrangements were made, and on a crisp and cold morning towards the end of February, they finally set off.

The journey south was everything that the ill-starred wedding tour should have been, and had not. They travelled alone – that is to say, without any intrusive company in the carriage. Of all the members of the household who were meant to attend them in town, it was only Thomas, the first footman, who escorted them – and the coachman of course. The others – Mr Howard, Weston, Simon, Peter, Sarah and two other maids – were to follow them to town by stagecoach. But not yet. Their people could take their time, for Darcy and Elizabeth had every intention of doing likewise.

And that was precisely what they did.

They travelled slowly, scarce covering thirty miles each day, and their chosen route was the very one that had been so precipitously abandoned two and a half months prior. They stopped often to admire the sights, or explore an old ruin, or partake of luncheon at some coaching inn that seemed especially pleasing, or for no reason in particular. Each day of travel was brought to a close long before dusk, so as to leave ample time for casual strolls and leisurely dinners. They fortunately had no difficulty in engaging private parlours, so their dinners were deliciously tranquil. And all of them were followed by nights of passion and exquisite intimacy.

Their time in Bedford was the best of all. They stopped at the *Swan* – there was no better choice in the vicinity. When they were offered the same suite as last December, Darcy hesitantly asked, "Do you... mind?" only to receive a warm smile in response.

"Not at all," Elizabeth assured him. "In fact, I would call it pure serendipity."

The bedchamber that had been hers for that one night was bright and welcoming, bathed in the reddish glow of the setting sun, and they went on to make excellent use of it, and replace all the bleak recollections with blissfully happy ones. They stayed for three days, not just one, and somehow found the time to stroll along the more fashionable streets of Bedford. Even the river and the looming bridge were redeemed when they spent several joyful hours on the Ouse, boating in the wintry sunshine.

They made no effort whatsoever to rise early on their last morning at the *Swan*. Although eager to be reunited with her family, Elizabeth could not bring herself to curtail the precious privacy, knowing full well that it would be hard to come by in Hertfordshire.

They were to stay at Longbourn, naturally. The *Red Lion* was not an option, and neither was Netherfield. Although clearly tempted, Darcy had not approached his friend with any request of the kind.

"'Tis but a short visit, and you will want to spend as much time as possible with your relations," he had considerately observed. "Besides, I would rather not ask Bingley for another favour quite so soon. I do not doubt that he would oblige me, but I should not trespass on his kindness."

For her part, Elizabeth had different views about Mr Bingley's kindness, and no wish to be indebted to him for his hospitality – which inevitably served to remind her that she would have to find a way to be civil towards her husband's friend, even though he had jilted her sister. But that challenge was for another day. So, when Darcy sought her lips, she weaved her fingers through his hair to draw him closer, and kissed him back with ever-growing fervour.

❦

The return to Longbourn was unadulterated joy. There were no shadows, not even in Jane's countenance. To Elizabeth's immense relief, her sister's gentle visage seemed to have regained most of its old serenity, so she gave silent thanks for time's healing powers and could scarce wait for a chance to speak at length with Jane and learn everything that her dear sister might have omitted to put in her letters. But for now, she sat back to rejoice in an exceedingly pleasant evening.

Truth be told, she had not expected her dear husband to rise quite so much to the occasion. She could not go so far as to call him loquacious, but he did not hesitate to have his share in the conversation, and met silliness with equanimity.

That was another source of relief to Elizabeth, for she knew not how she would have borne seeing him treat her mother and her younger sisters with the old indifference bordering on disdain. So she did not miss the chance to squeeze his hand under the table by way of thanks for his forbearance – only to raise her eyes and find her father studying her with rapt attention, a quirk in his brow and another in his lips, which made her blush, her own lips twitching sheepishly.

Elizabeth was thrilled to see that her dear papa was in excellent form, more willing than ever to engage in banter and casual chatter. Moreover, it was deeply touching to find him constantly on guard, intent upon ensuring her comfort. He never failed to intervene and redirect the conversation whenever it showed signs of heading the wrong way.

As did Jane. The pair of them were sure to speak up and introduce another topic whenever Mrs Bennet's queries about Pemberley hinted on the mercenary, or when Lydia and Kitty started to spout nonsense about bonnets, finery and officers.

Likewise, her father and her dearest sister steered the exchanges away from talk of the neighbourhood, which pleased Elizabeth quite as much as their other interventions. She dearly wished to learn if her relations had met with any more malice, but the spiteful matrons of Meryton had no place in this happy moment. She would enquire on the morrow, preferably in private, and spare her husband the full extent of that distasteful conversation. A summary should suffice.

But, as ever, her mother had other thoughts on the matter.

"It will cause a stir, your visit, but 'tis just as it should be," she said smugly. "Just as I thought, all the decent folk wish to come and rejoice with you, but they shall have to wait until the morrow. Your father and I wanted to have you all to ourselves tonight. The others will dine with us tomorrow evening. The good eggs, you know. Much the same merry gathering that was here for your wedding breakfast, and one notable addition. Oh, Lizzy, what a surprise that was! Everything that is charming! Wait till you hear. You shall scarce credit it," Mrs Bennet beamed, and Elizabeth endeavoured to suppress a grimace.

Judging from her mother's countenance, she was inclined to think that she did not wish to know. That supposition received fresh confirmation when her father spoke:

"My dear madam, I believe we have agreed to leave surprises for the morrow, charming or otherwise," he said, his tone of voice admitting no protest, then turned towards her. "So, Lizzy, a pup, eh? I expect you are pleased. You have always wanted one. But I am in two minds between congratulations and commiserations. Terriers are an excitable breed. Frolicsome and friendly, I grant you, but apt to cause a great deal of fuss when bored."

"Too true. As we have already discovered," Elizabeth laughed, exchanging a diverted glance with Darcy. "That is why we decided that he would be happier at Pemberley, where he can scamper to his heart's content. Confinement to the townhouse would have driven him to distraction."

Besides, their leisurely travel towards town was meant to make up for the wedding tour that never was, and not many people brought a roistering pup on their wedding journey. But Elizabeth was not about to speak of that. Instead, she chose to prove her father's point by entertaining her relations with an account of Rufus and his spirited antics.

Yet no sooner had she made a beginning than Lydia cut in with antics of her own:

"That is ever so unfair!" she pouted. "Lizzy always finishes by having everything she wants. Why can I not have a dog of my own, Papa? I have been asking for a pug for ten years together!"

A low huff of vexation gave Elizabeth ample indication of her husband's feelings on the matter, so she rested a soothing hand on his knee. He covered it with his, and held his peace. Not that there was any need for him to have his say. Mr Bennet's quelling stare was already fixed on his unruliest offspring, and he muttered by way of warning, "There is a fine old saying, child, which will serve you well: keep your breath to cool your porridge."

But the most vocal reprimand came from Mrs Bennet:

"A pug? The very notion! That is the last thing we need. And have I not told you to guard your tongue and show your brother every courtesy? How is that in keeping with what I said? Well! Ahem. Pray do not take offence, Mr Darcy. I assure you, it shall not happen again," she enunciated glowering at Lydia, who gaped in shock and outrage at meeting with censure from that quarter. "Now, girls, shall we retire and leave your father and Mr Darcy to their port? But pray do not tarry long, Mr Bennet, so that we can all sit and chat for a little longer before bedtime. I should not be surprised if Lizzy and Mr Darcy will wish to retire early, after all that exhausting travel. By the bye, Lizzy, I was going to have Hill prepare the guest chamber for you and Mr Darcy, but Jane was adamant that you will prefer to stay in your old room," she said, and Elizabeth cast her sister a warm look of appreciation.

Of course she would not even consider the guest chamber!

The last guest had been Mr Collins.

"Oh, dear," Mrs Bennet exclaimed, recapturing Elizabeth's attention. "I suppose I should have asked, but since you are so recently married, I thought... Ahem! The pair of you won't mind sharing quarters, will you?"

"No, Mamma," Elizabeth replied, blushing to the hairline.

Retiring to her old bedchamber with Darcy was… extraordinary. Disrobing for the night with each other's help, in the absence of their habitual attendants, was barely less so. It felt strange in those surroundings. It also felt deliciously forbidden. As did the passionate interlude that followed. Exquisitely forbidden. And exhilarating, too.

Afterwards, as she lay ensconced in her husband's embrace, her fingertips lazily gliding back and forth over his nape, Elizabeth glanced at the narrow canopy above them, and a diverted little smile fluttered on her lips.

"I do believe your bed is more than twice the size of this. And so is mine."

"Probably," he murmured, nuzzling her neck. "What an absurd extravagance."

Elizabeth chuckled.

"Quite."

It was absurd indeed, having so much unnecessary space when as little as a third would have sufficed. Even in their sleep, they always sought each other.

Darcy raised his hand and cupped her cheek.

"Happy?"

"Very happy."

"Good," he breathed against her lips. "I love you."

"And I you," she whispered back, unaccountably close to tears. "I love you, Fitzwilliam. More than I can say."

It might have been the first time that she had put it into so many words, Elizabeth idly mused. If so, that was unaccountable as well. She felt as though she had grown to love him a long time ago.

He reached out and extinguished the candle, then wrapped his arm around her yet again. With a sigh of absolute contentment, Elizabeth nestled her head against his shoulder and closed her eyes, relishing the feel of his fingertips stroking her hair, until she drifted off to sleep, and the light caresses made their way into her dreams.

❦

Elizabeth stirred and stretched, dimly aware that he was no longer beside her. She reached out, searching blindly, but to no avail, so she forced her eyes to open. She found that greyish daylight was seeping through the curtains, and that Darcy was up, already half dressed.

"What time is it?" she murmured, making him start.

"Twenty past seven. I am sorry I woke you. Go back to sleep," he urged, but she propped herself up on one elbow and gave a little tut.

"This is foolish, you know."

"What is?"

"Making your way downstairs so early in the morning. If it was self-consciousness that drove you out of bed, 'tis needless, I assure you. There is nothing shocking about going down for breakfast at a reasonable hour. And if my relations prove me wrong, then they will recover from their shock as soon as they remind themselves that we are but recently married, as Mamma had so bluntly put it. So leave that neckcloth be and come back to bed."

In part at least, Darcy complied, and came to sit on the edge of the bed and render her breathless with a long and ardent kiss. And then he drew back and teasingly whispered, "Nothing would please me better, as you may imagine. I hope I shall never have cause to refuse you again, but this time I must. I am to go shooting with your father this morning, if you remember."

"Oh," Elizabeth pouted. She had completely forgotten about that.

It was good of her father to give himself the trouble, but it would have been a great deal better if they had not made plans to set out so early. She was not vouchsafed sufficient time to come to terms with the notion. Darcy groaned and claimed her lips again.

"Elizabeth, have mercy," he rasped between hungry kisses. "How am I to leave you… when you look at me this way?"

"What way is that?"

"As if you wished I were not leaving."

She gave a rueful little chuckle.

"I do wish you were not. But needs must, I suppose," Elizabeth shrugged with manifest reluctance, then resorted to archness. "So I shall not look at you in any particular manner, and let you carry on. Would you like me to hide my face under the counterpane for good measure?"

"Pray don't. I am rather partial to it, as it happens," Darcy retorted and stroked her cheek as he dropped a playful kiss on the tip of her nose.

When he half-heartedly stood and resumed dressing, Elizabeth tucked her arm under her pillow and settled down to watch him do so.

This was extraordinary too, and more than a little endearing, seeing him tie his neckcloth before the looking glass on her old dressing table, then donning his waistcoat and reaching for the tight-fitting coat.

"Do you need help?" she offered.

Darcy shook his head.

"I thank you, no. I daresay I can manage. Stay in bed. The room has grown quite cold. I hope you will go back to sleep once I am gone."

Elizabeth stretched lazily under the counterpane, inwardly conceding that she might as well. She knew from long experience that her mother and sisters would not leave their rooms for another couple of hours. She briefly toyed with the notion of joining her husband and her father for breakfast, but then decided against it. She would delay them. She would require at least half an hour to ready herself for the day – don her apparel, brush her hair, pin it up and everything. Besides, it would be good to let them strengthen their connection without her mediation. She had already had the chance to let her dear papa know that she was exceedingly happy – that her married life was more joyful than any of them could have anticipated. She had briefly seen him in private on the previous evening, and Jane likewise, and they would find the opportunity to speak again before her departure.

So she remained abed, her gaze resting on her beloved husband – his handsome countenance; his broad shoulders; his tall frame; the impeccable fall of his coat, once he had donned and buttoned it.

"Enjoy your morning," she said when he was quite finished. "And pray do not take it amiss if Papa should choose to be uncommunicative or… eccentric."

"Or downright cross with me for spiriting you halfway across the country," Darcy smiled. "Fear not, my love. If that be the case, I shall remember that your father has a point, so I shall bear his ill humour with all the grace that I can muster."

The parting kiss was long and tantalising. Then Darcy tucked the counterpane around her, and most reluctantly rose to his feet.

"Sleep well," he whispered. "I shall see you later."

"Ah, Lizzy, there you are!" Mrs Bennet exclaimed with satisfaction when Elizabeth finally joined her mother and sisters in the breakfast parlour.

She *had* slept well, far better and for a great deal longer than she had imagined, and her mamma was quick to remark upon it.

"I thought you might have gone on one of your rambles for old times' sake, but then I was told you were still abed. Not that I mind, of course," Mrs Bennet swiftly added. "It was no trouble to keep the dishes warm. 'Tis just that this is most unlike you. Are you well, Lizzy?"

"Yes, Mamma. Never better," Elizabeth assured her, colour rising in her cheeks.

"Splendid! Then do you think you might be— Ahem. Kitty, Lydia, are you quite done? And you, Mary? Very good. Then run along now, all three of you, if you have finished your breakfast. I wish to speak to Lizzy in peace. You can stay, Jane, if you like. You can very well hear what I have to say, for you *are* the eldest, after all," Mrs Bennet said with energy, while Jane placidly sipped her tea, already giving sufficient indication that the express permission had little bearing, for she had no intention of going anywhere.

As for Elizabeth, she had found sufficient clues in their mother's monologue to guess where the conversation was headed. She helped herself to a toasted muffin and suppressed a sigh.

A few moments later, once Mary had followed Lydia and Kitty out of the room and closed the door behind her, Elizabeth learnt that she had guessed aright.

"There. Now we can speak at leisure," her mother announced, then leaned towards her, beaming in anticipation. "So, dear girl, this is what I wished to ask: are you with child?"

"No, I— I think not," Elizabeth stammered, her unease hard to conquer, even though she had expected that very question.

Her reply knocked the wind out of Mrs Bennet's sails.

"Oh... I thought that was why you slept so late. I could scarce keep myself awake whenever I was in the family way, and I should not wonder if all of you girls take after me. Well... A pity that you have no such tidings yet. I was hoping you would. By the time I had been married for two months or so, I already knew that a babe was on its way. Still, early days, I suppose, so let us not fret. All will be well. That is, I *am* assuming that everything is as it should be in that regard, Lizzy... is it? Does he come to you often enough?"

"Yes," Elizabeth muttered, her cheeks intolerably hot.

Mrs Bennet patted her hand and chuckled.

"Dear me, just look at you blushing like I know not what! There is no need to be embarrassed. 'Tis only natural for mothers and daughters to speak of such things. How else are you to learn about the facts of life?"

Her thoughts flying to her loving husband and her decorous aunt, Elizabeth lowered her gaze to her plate, detesting the sense of guilt that invariably came over her whenever she was compelled to own that there was precious little she had ever wished to learn from her mother.

Never one to look for undercurrents, Mrs Bennet remained blissfully oblivious. Smiling broadly, she kept her sights on practical matters and basic necessities:

"Well then, if all is as it should be, then we shall have to wait for nature to take its course. Help yourself to bacon, Lizzy, and sausages or black pudding. A hearty breakfast will do you good in any case."

"Thank you," Elizabeth said, not in the least tempted, and hastened to ask, "How is everything here? Is anyone in Meryton still causing trouble?"

"Oh, no, there is no more of that," her mother replied with a dismissive gesture. "They all quit their caterwauling, once reports of your marriage had begun to spread. Mrs Purvis and Mrs Robinson even had the gall to call upon me and offer their good wishes. Not Dorothea Goulding, naturally. She still holds court at Haye and pretends that nothing ever happened, which is precisely what I expected of her," Mrs Bennet sniffed.

"And what of Mr Wickham? Has he left the regiment?" Elizabeth asked, however distasteful the topic. Thankfully, she had seen neither hide nor hair of him between her betrothal and her wedding, and could not fail to wonder if he had made himself scarce in fear of retribution.

"No. He is still around," Mrs Bennet frowned, "but he gives us a wide berth. And so he should, if he knows what's good for him. He made eyes at Mary King for a while, or rather at her ten thousand pounds, until the girl went away to Liverpool to stay with Mrs King's brother, at a safe distance from Wickham. But never mind the rogue! You had much better tell me, Lizzy, is Pemberley entailed?"

This intrusive question was one which Elizabeth could easily excuse, so there was no edge to her voice when she replied, "No, Mamma. Rest easy, it is not."

"That *is* a relief! At least you and your daughters shan't have to fret about being cast out of your home by some man whom no one cares about. And those of us who must come to live with you if the worst should happen shan't have to worry about being turned out either. I could not bear that sort of terror again, Lizzy! Now that your marriage has freed us from the dread of having no roof over our heads, I could not bear it again!"

Elizabeth stared, her goodwill blasted by the selfishness of the remark – by its sheer callousness. That her mother should speak so blithely of surviving Darcy, that she should even mention the possibility of his demise and consider that devastating tragedy from a self-absorbed perspective, left her speechless. But it was not merely outrage that robbed her of words. The chill that stole upon her heart was even more numbing – to think, however unlikely, that he might be taken from her in his prime.

What brought her from the horrific trance was Jane's reproachful, "Mother!" – so, as she endeavoured to free herself from harrowing thoughts, Elizabeth exchanged a long glance with her sister as if to say, as oftentimes before, *'That is Mamma…'*

And, as oftentimes before, the reproach fell on uncomprehending ears.

"Yes, Jane? What is it?" Mrs Bennet innocently asked, and at that even Jane – sweet-tempered and ever-patient Jane – rolled her eyes and huffed in exasperation.

"How can you say such a thing?" she chided.

Mrs Bennet shrugged.

"Why ever not? 'Tis true, I assure you." And then her eyes widened. "Oh, I see your meaning. Yes, indeed, my dear, there is fresh hope at Netherfield, but nothing is certain, is it?"

"Netherfield?" Elizabeth echoed, buoyed by this promise of a happy outcome for her sister. "Has Mr Bingley returned, then?"

Jane's quiet, "No," could barely be heard before Mrs Bennet rushed to speak over her.

"No, he has not. He is never coming back. He has given up the lease and—"

"He has?" Elizabeth gasped. "When?"

"Just before Christmas," Jane supplied, and Elizabeth's brows rose in stunned disbelief.

"Christmas? And not a word of it in your letters! Why did you not tell me?"

Jane gave a vaguely apologetic gesture.

"You had enough on your mind. I did not wish you to be distressed on my account."

"You should have told me!" Elizabeth whispered with the deepest compassion, and left her seat to take the empty one next to Jane. "You should have told me," she repeated, clasping her sister's hand in both of hers.

Jane shook her head and said with determination, "It would have served no purpose, would it?"

Yet again, Mrs Bennet hastened to have her say:

"No, indeed. He has made his choice, and much good may it do him! I say good riddance. There is a new tenant at Netherfield now: a Mr Vincent. Colonel Vincent, rather. Although he does not make use of his rank in introductions."

"A new tenant? Already?"

"Yes, Lizzy, just so," Mrs Bennet excitedly resumed. "I wished to tell you all about him yesterday, but Jane insisted that nothing should intrude upon the joy of your first day at home, and as you would imagine, your father was in agreement. But now you must have the full story. So, Mr Vincent— Nay, in fact I would much rather say *Colonel* Vincent, it has such a ring to it! Colonel Vincent took possession promptly, and by Epiphany he was installed at Netherfield. But it took me a great deal longer to learn more about him, for he is as tight-lipped as may be. Quite as tight-lipped as your Mr Darcy. Still, we applied ourselves to the task, your aunt Phillips and I. Mrs Long lent a hand, as did Mrs King, Mrs Watson and their servants. Thankfully, reserved as the colonel might be, his people *could* be worked upon with a little flattery and probing, so in due course we managed to piece several titbits together. He hails from the West Country. The family seat is in Devon, somewhere near Torquay, and his elder brother is a viscount. We have also learnt of a link to the East India Company. We do not have all the particulars, but I understand that the colonel was able to quit the army because a relation of his, an East India nabob, had left him a considerable fortune. Seven thousand a year, Lizzy! Well, to be fair, some say he is only worth six, but no matter. That is a respectable fortune, too. What a fine thing for us, eh?"

The conversation – or rather monologue – had already grown vexingly familiar, so Elizabeth frowned.

"Is it?"

"Of course it is! Oh, Lizzy, surely you must see that I am hoping he will take a fancy to Jane! And why should he not? She is by far the most handsome girl in the vicinity. I hope you are not put out by my saying so, dear, but we have long established that Jane is more handsome than you. And anyway, it makes no difference, since you are already married. Now, I am inclined to think that the signs are hopeful. What say you, Jane?"

For once, Elizabeth followed her mother's example and trained her searching gaze on her sister's countenance, only to find it overspread with a look of weary forbearance.

"I do wish you would not indulge such notions, Mamma," Jane urged, but to no avail.

"Well, *I* say that the signs are hopeful, and I am not alone in this. Mrs Long also noticed that the colonel often seeks you out at dinners and whatnot. I told you what she said to me the other day, when we were all gathered together at your aunt Phillips'. But *you* won't know, Lizzy, so here it is: she said to me – Mrs Long, that is – she said: 'Ah, Mrs Bennet, if there is any justice in the world, we shall see her at Netherfield after all.' She did indeed! I do think Mrs Long is as good a creature as ever lived – and her nieces are well-mannered girls, and not at all handsome. I like them prodigiously. So I *shall* maintain that the signs are hopeful. Aye, hopeful enough, under the circumstances. Many a widower is known to take his time before he weds again."

Elizabeth gaped at her mother in shock mingled with horror. Her mamma would foist a widower upon Jane, for the sake of Netherfield and the man's fortune? Good gracious! Had she been so deeply scarred by the decades spent under the threat of the entail that *one* rich son-in-law was not deemed a sufficient safeguard?

"How old is he?" she asked, lips taut.

Mrs Bennet shrugged.

"How am I to know? Older than your husband, but—"

"Mamma!" Elizabeth spluttered. Yet a fraction of a second later she was astounded to hear her sister chuckling softly.

"By a few years, Lizzy," Jane imparted, a mildly diverted smile still playing on her lips. "Mr Vincent is in his thirties."

"Oh…" Elizabeth murmured, and Mrs Bennet nodded with vigour.

"Aye, by the looks of him, that would be my guess too. Besides, his daughter is only seven, so—"

"He has a daughter," Elizabeth said – a flat-toned observation, not a question.

"Why, yes. Did I not say?" Mrs Bennet mused, a puzzled furrow in her brow.

Elizabeth shook her head. No, her mother had most certainly *not* mentioned that particular detail.

"Well, he does have a daughter, Eleanor. He calls her Ella. And she is such an angel, the poor motherless mite! The colonel often brings her along when he calls upon us, and sometimes they stay for dinner. She has grown quite fond of Kitty and Lydia, who have indulged her with parlour games and whatnot, but what she likes best is to have Jane read for her. She sits and listens with rapt attention for as long as may be. From what I understand, that was something she used to do with her mamma, and it gives her comfort. So much the better, to my way of thinking. They say that the way to a man's heart is through his stomach, and that holds true for bachelors, I'm sure. But if we are speaking of a widower who happens to be a devoted father, I reckon that gaining his child's affections is the surest way to secure him."

The turn of Jane's countenance showed that she was at pains to hold back more words of censure. She succeeded. As she rose to her feet, she only said, "Excuse me, Mamma. I should like to go for a walk. Lizzy, will you join me?"

Elizabeth agreed with alacrity, wishing she had thought of that herself and suggested it sooner. She could only sigh and nod with the familiar mixture of filial love and exasperation when Jane left them to fetch a shawl and her mother used that opportunity to urge her in a whisper, "See if you can make out what she really thinks about this business with the colonel, Lizzy, will you, dear? There's a good girl. I do despair sometimes, for no one ever tells me anything!"

Chapter 26

The day was overcast but dry, and the amble along the familiar paths filled Elizabeth's heart to overflowing – as did the chance to have Jane all to herself, and finally speak as freely as they always had.

"You know, I genuinely thought that Mamma would find sufficient comfort in my marriage, and would no longer be so…"

Her voice trailed off, and Jane pressed her hand with a wan smile.

"I am guessing that what you are thinking, but would not say, is *'mercenary.'* Poor Mamma… Her heart is in the right place, and she is not grasping, Lizzy. You know she is not. But the sole purpose of her life – verily, her badge of honour – is to ensure that we marry well." She sighed. "I only wish she were more tactful in the way she goes about it."

It was exceedingly like Jane to generously make excuses for anyone and anything, yet Elizabeth could not but concede her the point.

"Yes, well… I daresay tact had never been Mamma's forte. And I should have made my peace with that by now."

Jane chuckled mildly.

"Perhaps you should have."

"That aside, though," Elizabeth set forth to address her main concern with determination, "pray tell me that you will not be coaxed into marriage just to please our mother!"

"Lizzy! What sort of a weak-willed milksop do you think me?" Jane ruefully chided. "No, dearest, there is no risk of that."

"Is there not? So, all those hopeful signs that Mamma spoke of, are they merely the product of her fertile imagination?"

"Just so," Jane said with a weary little smile. "Much as Mamma chooses to think otherwise, I know better than to call this a courtship."

"What would you call it, then?"

"A quest for solace. Which brings me solace, too. Each of us has an understanding of heartache. Not to the same degree, of course.

I should never presume to compare the tragedy that befell him with my disappointed hopes. But there is much to be said for lending assistance to a fellow soul."

"Oh, Jane!" Elizabeth murmured, stroking her sister's hand. "Why did you not write a single word about him? And neither did Mamma," she suddenly realised, and cast her sister a suspicious glance. "What did you do, censor her letters?"

Jane gave another rueful chuckle.

"I must confess I did."

"*Why?*"

"I did not wish you to form the wrong impression. He has no designs on me, Lizzy, and certainly no romantic inclination. If he should ever consider remarrying, it will be so that his little girl does not grow up without a mother. But speaking of censored letters, I might as well ask, why did you not write that you had fallen madly in love with Mr Darcy?"

"Madly in love?" Elizabeth echoed, the abrupt change of topic giving rise to a strange mixture of self-consciousness, discomfort and elation.

"Come now, do not deny it! 'Tis there for all to see."

Elizabeth bit her lip.

"I have no wish to deny it. I… Very well," she conceded, opting for honesty. "I did not confide in you because I did not wish to flaunt my happiness, when I left you so unhappy."

Jane tutted.

"Foolish girl! Such tidings would have given me the greatest joy."

Pausing on their walk, Elizabeth wrapped her arms around her sister. For a long moment, they held each other in silence.

"Forgive me," Elizabeth said at last. "Perhaps I should have seen that."

"Indeed you should have!" Jane said with energy. "Come now – tell me everything!"

"Oh, no, no!" Elizabeth protested. "You shall not distract me. First, tell me all there is to know of Colonel Vincent."

"*Mr* Vincent," Jane corrected, then released her from the embrace, and they resumed walking. "He does not wish to be reminded of his time in the army. So I shall have to find a way of persuading Mamma to set aside her fondness for redcoats and cease addressing him as '*Colonel*'."

"Why does he not wish to be reminded of his military career?" Elizabeth felt compelled to ask.

"Because it had kept him away from his wife and deprived them both of much of the joyous time they might have had together."

"Oh… How long had they been married?"

"Eight years. She passed away the April before last. Childbirth," Jane supplied – a full complement of concise answers offered in quick succession, without prompting, and neatly addressing all the questions that Elizabeth had thought to ask.

"How terrible…" she murmured. "Poor woman. And poor Mr Vincent…"

"Yes… It was a dreadful blow. He was… He said that he came to live in Hertfordshire because he could no longer bear the house in which they had been so happy. At first, he had endeavoured to continue there for his daughter's sake, but he could not bear it. The pair of them travelled for a while, and then his agent brought Netherfield to his attention, so he relinquished his home in Hammersmith and came here – a fresh start for him and Ella." She fell silent for a moment, then pensively added, "Mamma put it very badly, but a child does make all the difference. The first thing I noticed and admired is that he is a deeply devoted father."

That *was* admirable, Elizabeth mused, and could not help pressing her sister for details:

"What else? What sort of a man is he, I mean?"

Without warning, Jane's air veered towards amusement.

"To begin with, you ought to know that he may confound your expectations," she teased, then tenderly exclaimed, "Dearest Lizzy! You should have seen your face when Mamma said she thinks him older than Mr Darcy. What were you picturing? A bald and portly gentleman in his middle age?"

"Frankly, yes," Elizabeth owned with a wide grin, which Jane mirrored.

"I thought as much. Well, do not discard that image altogether. This way, you will be pleasantly surprised when you make his acquaintance this evening at dinner."

"This evening? Oh, so *he* is the notable addition of which Mamma spoke yesterday?"

"Indeed."

"Very well. Until this evening, I shall see him as a marginally younger version of Mr Goulding: rotund, clumsy and broad-faced. There, will that do?"

"Perfectly, I thank you."

"Anything to please you. And now, give me leave to say that you have begun to sound very much like Papa," Elizabeth teased her back. "Have you perchance spent a vast amount of time with him of late?"

"Yes, I have, in fact," Jane confirmed, her jesting tone of voice abandoned. "He misses you a great deal, Lizzy. He often seeks me out for comfort."

Elizabeth winced.

"And you? Where do you—?" She bit her lip, and did not finish her question, but said instead, "I only wish we did not live so far apart…"

Astute as ever, and knowing her all too well, Jane guessed her thoughts with no difficulty.

"You were about to ask where *I* go for comfort," she said matter-of-factly, then quietly added, "In case you have not gathered that already, Mr Vincent and I do talk at length and often."

"You told him about Mr Bingley?"

"Yes, of course. I told him everything."

"Oh…" Elizabeth whispered, only to inwardly chastise herself for her surprise at the intelligence. She should have read between the lines and ascertained the full extent of the openness between them. Their mother had painted Mr Vincent as a deeply reserved man – and yet he had revealed much about himself to Jane. Perhaps it was to be expected that she had reciprocated.

"In truth, sometimes it seems to me that he is the only one who understands," Jane resumed, making Elizabeth feel supplanted and bereft, then heartily ashamed of her self-centred thoughts. She should be relieved that her dearest sister had found succour! Of course *she* could not enter into Jane's feelings as fully as one who had experienced the pain of loss.

Jane drew a deep breath, then forced the faintest smile.

"But, as I said, there is no comparison. At least I know that Mr Bingley is alive and well…" she said, and since Elizabeth made no answer, Jane pressed the point: "Is he well, Lizzy? Have you heard anything about him?"

Elizabeth shook her head.

"No. Nothing at all. In fact, I am astounded that he had not even written to my husband about his intention to give up the lease on Netherfield."

"So Mr Darcy did not know either?" Jane asked, patently astonished, then added in the same breath, before Elizabeth had the chance to answer, "How foolish of me! No, he could not have, else you would have heard about it too. Perhaps Mr Bingley had no time to write to Mr Darcy of his plans. Christmas was the nearest quarter day, so a quick decision must have been in order, if he did not wish to be lumbered until Lady Day with a house in which he would no longer reside." She sighed. "For your husband's sake and Mr Bingley's, I hope that their friendship will not suffer. You have not said anything to Mr Darcy — have you, Lizzy? About me, I mean, and my foolish infatuation with his friend…?"

"No, of course not! You have urged me not to — so I have not. But you should not call it that!" Elizabeth firmly argued against Jane's endeavour to make her sentiments seem trifling and shallow. "We both know it is not a foolish infatuation. Which is why I need to ask again: will you not change your mind and let my husband have a word with Mr Bingley?"

"Lizzy, no! Leave be!" Jane exclaimed and spun round to clasp her hands. "I thank you, truly, but leave be," she repeated in a lowered voice, yet with as much urgency. "I told you before: I cannot bear to see him offer for me simply because he has to. Not even if Mr Darcy had brought him back last December. Least of all now. Do you not see? He has relinquished Netherfield. Has severed all his ties to Hertfordshire — to me. If this does not show plainly enough that he has no wish to be here, I know not what would. So he must be left in peace — and I must regain my senses. And I shall! I promise. You need not fret on my account. I will be well. I will be content. In truth, I am halfway there already — more than halfway."

"Are you?" Elizabeth insisted when Jane's rush of words came to a halt — a torrent of assurances that did little to set her mind at rest, and only left her with the impression that her dearest sister did protest too much.

Jane squeezed her hands once more, and then released them.

"Yes. Truly," she said with determination and, glancing over Elizabeth's shoulder, she cast her a knowing little smile. "But enough of this. It seems to me that you are needed."

Elizabeth turned around, and her countenance brightened at the sight of Darcy advancing towards them in long, endearingly impatient strides.

"You are very fortunate, you know. You have peppered me with questions – and now you are rescued, just when I was about to do the same," Jane teased with great affection, yet her words struck a very different chord.

Fortunate? Yes. Yes, she was! Her gaze still fixed on her beloved husband, Elizabeth knew beyond a doubt that she was very fortunate indeed.

No sooner had Jane left them, considerate as always, and rounded the corner of the house, than Elizabeth reached up to draw him to her and kissed him almost savagely, with no concern whatever about who might be watching from the two windows that overlooked that corner of the garden.

"How long have I been away?" Darcy chuckled softly, as soon as he caught his breath.

"Long enough," Elizabeth whispered, nestling into his chest, only to find him drawing back a little, so that he could search her eyes.

"Is anything the matter?"

Hoping it was not a sophistry to claim that the promise she had made him – that he would always hear the full truth from her – applied to the pair of them, and not her sister's secrets, Elizabeth answered his question with another:

"Why do you ask?"

"Just wondering to what I owe this delightful welcome."

Elizabeth shrugged.

"Jane said I was very fortunate. It reminded me that I happen to agree."

"We will not quarrel for the greater share of good fortune—" Darcy began, before she silenced him most effectively with another kiss.

"How was your morning?" Elizabeth asked after a while, once they had brought themselves to behave with some decorum, leave the secluded spot and stroll about the garden.

"Most enjoyable. Exceedingly so, in fact. Your father was a remarkably agreeable companion. You will be pleased to hear that he was not at all eccentric, as you put it, and that he poked fun at me no more than thrice."

Elizabeth flashed a wide grin towards him.

"You should take that as the greatest compliment."

"You think so? Then I shall bow to your superior judgement. But I must confess, I was far more flattered to find him disposed to regale me with a few choice tales."

"About?"

"You."

She gave a sheepish chuckle.

"Heavens! What did he tell you?"

The look that enveloped her was a heart-warming complement to his light teasing:

"Suffice it to say that now I have a better understanding as to why you said you were the bane of your mother's existence – and, might I add, the apple of your father's eye. If you kindly show me the tree you used to climb, I daresay my education into the finer points of Miss Lizzy Bennet's girlhood will be complete."

It was delectably astounding how a short walk in her father's garden should feel so much like courtship, even though they had been married for nigh on three months. But by now it was not in the least surprising that he could still give her fresh reasons to love him.

"Very well," Elizabeth beamed. "But let me give fair warning, if you are hoping for a demonstration, you will be disappointed. The footholds will be wet and slippery, and I would much rather not hobble on a sprained ankle tonight at dinner, nor be forced to explain to all and sundry just how I came by it."

※ ※

Reluctant as she was to alter the tone of their time in the garden, Elizabeth was nonetheless compelled to mention that a new tenant was now in residence at Netherfield, and that Mr Vincent would be among those who would dine with them that evening.

Thus, she discovered that her husband had already learnt as much from her father while they were out shooting, and that Darcy had not expected Mr Bingley to act so swiftly and decisively either.

By the time the guests had arrived, Elizabeth had long lost interest in the whys and wherefores of Mr Bingley's choices.

She was very pleased to see so many friendly faces – largely the same who had gathered at Longbourn for the wedding breakfast – although she still wondered how such a large party might be accommodated in the dining room in any degree of comfort. The wedding breakfast had not posed a similar challenge, for on that occasion their relations and friends had been at liberty to wander around with small plates in hand and sit wherever fancy took them. But this was the first time in many years that two dozen guests had been asked to dine at Longbourn.

To Elizabeth's delight, her friend Charlotte was among them. She was also glad to note that some bridges seemed to have been mended. This time, Charlotte had not come alone. Sir William had accompanied her, as had Lady Lucas and Maria, which was very good to see.

Three months ago, Mrs Bennet had not taken kindly to their nearest neighbours' withdrawal from the battlefield – something which Elizabeth's mother had often called *'the Lucases' betrayal'* – and that state of affairs had inevitably put a strain on Kitty's friendship with Maria. The enduring bitterness could not have done Mrs Bennet any favours either. Thus, it was encouraging to find that Mrs Bennet had relinquished it, and that the younger girls were no longer caught in the crossfire of their mothers' squabbles – even though Elizabeth could not but think the joy dearly bought when she saw Darcy exposed to Sir William's profuse civilities.

Keen to shield her husband from that gentleman's attentions, as well as from those of her aunt Phillips – and just as eager to civilly excuse themselves, so that they might steer a course towards Mr and Mrs Jones, with whom they could converse with gratitude and pleasure and, above all, without mortification – Elizabeth failed to register Mr Vincent's arrival. But once Jane had brought him to their side and performed the introductions, Elizabeth resolved to surreptitiously keep him in her sights for the rest of the evening.

From Jane's teasing earlier that day, she had come to expect that he would be at least moderately handsome, and he was. Other than that, there was not much that she could ascertain about him.

They had little opportunity to talk, beyond the first few minutes in the drawing room. Once the time came for everyone to congregate around the dinner table that had been extended to its full capacity, she found that they were not seated close enough for conversation. Likewise, when they eventually returned to the drawing room, there was too much chatter and too many people to permit any meaningful discourse.

Thus, Elizabeth had to content herself with observing him from a distance, all the while sensing that there was something quite familiar about him. Not in his countenance – not that. Mr Vincent did not look like anyone she knew. But in his air altogether there was something that she recognised, although she could not name it. Something that was both familiar and reassuring.

That elusive impression was perplexing, but Elizabeth would not allow herself to become engrossed by that particular conundrum. For now, it was enough to know that it had naught to do with Mr Bingley. Thankfully, nothing about the current occupant of Netherfield evoked his predecessor. Mr Vincent was as reserved as Mr Bingley had been garrulous, and at no time did he exhibit any resemblance to an excitable pup, which was no wonder, given his age and circumstances.

What did come as a mild surprise to Elizabeth was that he did not seem to single her eldest sister out. Her mother's high hopes, so liberally expressed, had led her to believe that she would find him gravitating towards Jane in the same fashion as Mr Bingley had. Yet he did not. All that Elizabeth could note, upon discreet investigation, was that Mr Vincent's gaze would often veer towards Jane's side of the room, although not necessarily with interest, nor with any telltale signs of partiality.

Her dearest sister Elizabeth also watched, and was relieved to find that Jane seemed at peace, her air greatly reminiscent of her former ease in company. Whether that was owed to time's healing powers, or the comfort she had found in the fellowship with another grieving soul, or perhaps a combination of the two, Elizabeth could not tell. But she knew enough of her sister's disposition to read her rightly, and the evening's careful observation served to persuade her that Jane's association with Mr Vincent was just as it had been presented: a fellowship of kindred souls, uncomplicated by romantic interest. Which was a pity, Elizabeth privately owned, for Jane needed a great deal more than that. She needed to form a new attachment – love and be loved – start afresh – find her life's purpose.

But, after the first stab of disappointment, Elizabeth worked to remind herself that there was much to be said for patience. If Jane's spirits had begun to recover, then perhaps she would be less daunted by the prospect of crossing paths with Mr Bingley, and might be persuaded to visit her in town, or at Pemberley in the summer.

Who could tell what the future might bring? Mr Geoffrey Lyle was exceedingly agreeable, and her husband held him in high esteem. There must be other worthy gentlemen in his circle, whom she would meet once they arrived in town. Was it too much to hope that one of them should be able to supplant Mr Bingley in Jane's tender heart and, in his turn, treasure her as she deserved?

The notion filled her with wistful impatience, yet a moment later it also sparked amusement. There she was, quite as eager as her mother to throw Jane in the path of eligible men. Seemingly, the only difference between them lay in their methods and their definition of a worthy gentleman.

As her gaze drifted towards Mr Vincent yet again, Elizabeth decided that, much as he stood to disappoint her matchmaking mamma, *she* had no quarrel with him. On the contrary, if he was instrumental in her sister's recovery, he was entitled to her gratitude. But if all he wanted was a mother for his daughter, then he should do everyone a favour and set his sights on her friend Charlotte.

Chapter 27

The music swelled, filling the vast auditorium, and Elizabeth leaned forward as the flowing harmonies washed over her, ebbed, then swelled again, reverberating in her soul. She drew a deep breath, relishing every moment of the sublime experience, and her eyes sought Darcy's when he stroked her gloved hand.

His warm gaze enveloped her, the half-smile she loved fluttering on his lips, and she returned it in full, her heart brimming. The soprano's voice soared, the aria came to a stirring close, and all the while Elizabeth could see out of the corner of her eye that her husband's steady gaze never veered from her. It easily accounted for her brimming heart skipping into a delicious flutter.

She relished that too, and thrilled to the exquisite joy of finding that he still made her feel every inch the bride. And then her glowing countenance brightened even further at the delightful notion that he might very well continue to do so for some considerable time.

Nevertheless, she clasped his hand and leaned closer to suggest in a low voice, meant for him alone:

"Should you not feign at least *some* interest in the happenings below? Now, lest you wonder, I say that for your sake rather than mine," she resumed as she gloried in finding him far from impervious to the feel of her breath brushing his cheek. "You may imagine that I am overjoyed and vastly flattered to see that, more than four months into our marriage, my countenance still holds greater fascination for you than whatever is taking place on the stage, but I expect your acquaintances watching us from the other boxes will deem it *outré* and decidedly unfashionable to be so taken with your wife."

"Let them," Darcy whispered back. "I have never held with fashion. Nor do I care one jot for their opinion, as long as my wife has no objections. And I hope she knows that I am not likely to lose interest in her bewitching countenance in four months, five, six or six hundred."

Elizabeth gave a breathless little chuckle.

"Oh, she cannot possibly object to that. In fact, I have it on good authority that she is elated."

"Then that is all that matters," he said softly. "And by the bye, no part of the performance is as appealing as the sight of you enjoying it."

"What a delightfully unfashionable thing to say! Pray remind me to thank you properly later."

"Very well. You may be assured I shall."

Eyes crinkled at the corners and a very private smile on her lips, Elizabeth pressed his hand and found fresh delight in being unfashionably besotted too, and thus absurdly eager for the end of a musical performance she enjoyed, so that she might return with him to the blissful intimacy of their apartments.

⚬◦⚬ ⚬◦⚬

The familiar sense of homecoming warmed Elizabeth's heart as she stepped into her bedchamber, where Sarah was waiting to ready her for the night. None of the rooms of the elegant townhouse were as dear to her, and for good reason: this was their private haven, and a beautiful token of love, done up for her at her husband's thoughtful and detailed request.

There had been no time to remodel her bedchamber at Pemberley prior to their arrival, and although the room evinced his mother's tastes, it was to remain unaltered because Elizabeth had learnt to treasure it. But during their stay in the north, Darcy had charged Mrs Blake, the housekeeper in town, to make all the necessary arrangements, and the efficient woman had carried out his instructions to the letter. Thus, when they arrived in Berkeley Square, Elizabeth was presented with a newly appointed suite that captured her own tastes to perfection, and could not fail to capture her heart and make her marvel yet again at how well her husband knew her. At times, he seemed to know her better than she knew herself.

"Did you have a pleasant evening, ma'am?" Sarah asked, misinterpreting her smile, and came closer to remove her wrap, then began unfastening her gown.

"Very pleasant, thank you," Elizabeth replied regardless, and Sarah beamed as she helped her out of the honey-coloured swathe of silk and went to carefully lay the dress on the bed.

She brought back the nightgown and the satin dressing gown, and lost little time in assisting her mistress to substitute undergarments for fetching night-time apparel. Then, once Elizabeth took a seat at her dressing table, Sarah removed her glittering headdress and, with the lightest touch, began to free her tresses from the elaborate *coiffure*.

No new lady's maid had been engaged, and no such change was necessary. Sarah had shown great aptitude and dedication for the role, so that position was now formally hers. A young girl, Jenny, had been brought in to assist her, and for a while Sarah had seemed as disconcerted by the novelty of having a subordinate as by being known as Parsons in the household, once she had joined the ranks of upper servants. But, true to form, she had been quick to rally, and had set about proving that Elizabeth's trust in her abilities was fully justified.

For her part, Elizabeth would not have exchanged her for half a dozen stiff and pompous ladies' maids that seemed to be the fashion. Much like her husband, she did not hold with fashion for fashion's sake, nor with Frenchified ladies' maids full of airs and graces. Sarah was a treasured link with her girlhood and her former home. Moreover, she was loyal, warm-hearted and eager to learn.

'And no less eager to put new knowledge into practice,' Elizabeth thought with an affectionate smile, remembering the day when a turn in the weather had ruined Darcy's plans of several leisurely hours spent strolling through the Royal Gardens at Kew, and they had returned early, for her to find Sarah practising an intricate hair arrangement on an awed and self-conscious Jenny, using *La Belle Assemblée* or some such publication as a source of inspiration. Poor Jenny had been mortified to be found thus, but the girl's meek patience and Sarah's diligence had borne very flattering results. Not for a moment had Elizabeth felt at a disadvantage before the grand ladies encountered at the musical *soirées*, elegant balls and fashionable dinners that she and Darcy had attended over the last month or so, since their arrival in town.

With a slight grimace, Elizabeth owned that their time in London would be a vast deal more enjoyable if they could avoid some of those social engagements.

She had always been one for going into company, but she found no pleasure in being examined as a curious and perturbing specimen. She could not honestly say what was more insulting: being examined and found wanting, or hearing herself pronounced with unbearable condescension as surprisingly well-informed and well-spoken.

What did they imagine, that no one of her station had ever read a book? Or that only those born with a silver spoon in their mouth could string two words together?

It was regrettable, but not at all astonishing, that many of the new acquaintances she had formed in the grand salons should be supercilious and cold. Moreover, superciliousness came uncomfortably close to home. Lord Malvern, Darcy's maternal uncle, seemed to count his nephew's marriage among the things which could not be cured, and therefore must be endured, and his lady had already given every sign that she shared his opinion.

Their response was predictable, and Elizabeth steadfastly refused to take it to heart, but sensibly told herself that it would have been nothing short of miraculous to be welcomed with open arms into an earl's family – she, a modest gentleman's daughter with no connections and no portion. In truth, their manner pained Darcy a great deal more than it did her, even though he had expected that sort of conduct – had even warned her about the possibility.

Likewise, he was more affronted than she to find that, by and large, his uncle and aunt's circle, their offspring included, toed a cautious line with regard to her acceptance in their midst. There were but few exceptions, of which the most notable were three: her husband's cousin, Colonel Fitzwilliam; Lady Amelia, the colonel's youngest sister, who adored him unconditionally and took his views in everything; and Lady Rosemary Sinclair, a close friend of the family.

That warm-hearted trio had uniformly been welcoming and kind, but of them all, Lady Rosemary had it in her power to offer the greatest share of assistance in society. As Elizabeth had eventually learnt, Lady Rosemary was a far from inconsequential presence in the grand salons. Her husband had passed away some six years prior and left her a considerable fortune, and her connections were impeccable. She was the Earl of Rosedale's only daughter and numbered dozens of the names listed in *Debrett's Peerage and Baronetage* among her kin, not least Lady Jersey, one of the patronesses of Almack's, and two of her cousins were ladies in waiting to Her Majesty the Queen.

Thus, it could certainly be said that her acquaintance counted for something, and her goodwill for a vast deal more.

To her surprise, Elizabeth found herself lavished with Lady Rosemary's goodwill. Almost from the day when Lady Malvern had rather uneasily introduced Elizabeth to her ladyship's acquaintance, Lady Rosemary had taken it upon herself to be to her everything that Lady Malvern was not: a helping hand, most willingly extended; a guide through the confounding and often irksome maze that was high society; and before long, to Elizabeth's growing pleasure, she had good cause to think that Lady Rosemary had become her friend. Perhaps her only real friend in town – outside the home, of course, for her first and best friend in this new world was, and would always be, her beloved husband.

Elizabeth was more than thankful for the other friendly faces – for Colonel Fitzwilliam and the chatty and endearingly candid Lady Amelia – but those two she already counted as dear relations, not just friends.

As for Darcy's sister, Elizabeth had found herself faced with an unexpected challenge. She had imagined that, once she and Georgiana came to live under the same roof and get to know each other better, they would soon establish an open and affectionate relationship. Sadly, several weeks later, it was plain to see that her wish would not be easily fulfilled.

A fair while ago, before Christmas, when her husband had told her a little of his family, he had not omitted to speak of Georgiana's shyness, but it was only after their arrival in town that Elizabeth could grasp the almost crippling severity of it. What was reserve in Darcy, in his sister it came to be augmented into an exceedingly private nature, so retiring that it bordered on reclusive. The dear girl would scarce say a word if she could help it, and every attempt at conversation soon turned into a stilted exchange, or rather into short monologues interspersed with monosyllables and awkward silence. Georgiana was unfailingly civil, yet her strained politeness was on the par with that of a young girl towards a stern and unforgiving governess, and neither open and heartfelt overtures nor blatant cajoling seemed to make the slightest shade of difference. Thus, despite her best efforts, Elizabeth was forced to own that she was still no closer to forging a bond with the younger girl.

Given half a chance, Georgiana would spend most of her time shut away in the music room practising long and difficult concertos, and Elizabeth had swiftly learnt that coming in to listen and compliment her on her astounding proficiency would only serve to discompose her and render her unable or unwilling to play another note.

Georgiana was not out, so she rarely joined them in the evenings, unless they dined at home of course, or at Lord and Lady Malvern's house. Moreover, despite her great passion for music, she seldom agreed to accompany them to operas and concerts, and even less frequently to plays. At Darcy's gentle but sedulous insistence, she would be persuaded on occasion to make a third on their walks in the park, or their trips of pleasure to Hampton Court and the Royal Gardens at Kew, or the odd visit to art galleries and the Aladdin's Cave that was Hatchard's. But it was plain to see that her heart was not in it, and more often than not she begged to be excused, preferring to stay behind with Mrs Annesley, her soft-spoken and affable companion.

The only pursuit she agreed to with alacrity was riding with her brother every other morning, and then she would vanish into the music room for many hours together, and do her utmost to devote as little time as possible to those tedious affairs – Lucifer's own invention – commonly known as morning calls.

In that final regard, Elizabeth shared her views entirely, and wished she were at liberty to make her own escape as well. Almost as a rule, they were as dreary as they were disingenuous, and the repetitiveness was not only wearying but vexing. She could not but find it so, especially when she received manifestly false attentions from ladies who had scarce deigned to offer more than bland civilities before it had become apparent that she basked in Lady Rosemary Sinclair's favour.

Sensible by nature and hardly ever vain, Elizabeth did wonder what might have induced that dear lady to bestow it, when she could have selected some high-born young woman from the fashionable circles as her particular friend.

Yet, much like Darcy, Lady Rosemary refused to be ruled by fashion, and found pleasure in companions who were not given to fawning.

"Either that, or she has made it her life's work to crusade against snobbery," Elizabeth had speculated one evening, once she and Darcy had returned to Berkeley Square after a pleasant evening spent at dinner with Lady Rosemary and a small set of agreeable people, of which Colonel Fitzwilliam was one. "For otherwise I can scarce fathom what she hopes to find in me."

"And I cannot fathom how it is that you cannot see yourself clearly. Any person of feeling and discernment could not fail to value you," Darcy had tenderly replied, and she had nestled into his arms and kissed him, knowing all too well that it was he who did not see her clearly. He saw her through a lover's eyes. But she was not likely to find fault with that.

As for Lady Rosemary's reasons, the fact that Elizabeth could not fully comprehend them made her no less grateful for the lady's kindness. Not merely because Lady Rosemary was of material assistance in easing her way into society. The warm friendship, offered openly and simply, without artifice, was something that Elizabeth treasured all the more. She did need genuine friends. She missed Jane, missed her grievously, and missed Charlotte a great deal too, and the society of a lively and intelligent woman, a like-minded woman who seemed to appreciate the same things as she, served to fill at least some of the void left by Jane's absence, and by Charlotte's.

In fact, Lady Rosemary did remind her a great deal of Charlotte. Not on account of her physical appearance, for Lady Rosemary was a statuesque woman of great beauty. But she was the same age as Elizabeth's lifelong friend, or perhaps a couple of years older, and had the same acerbic sense of humour mixed with a hefty dose of common sense. And, much like Charlotte, she did not suffer fools gladly, had no time for airs and graces, and readily saw through deviousness and artifice.

Thus, it was little wonder that Lady Rosemary could scarce abide Mrs Hurst and Miss Bingley – which would have been reason enough for Elizabeth to find herself in harmony with her.

Of all the morning callers whom Elizabeth despised, Mr Bingley's sisters were the most vexing. They called far more frequently than any visitors and stayed for a great deal longer, but Elizabeth was under no illusion that it was her society that they were seeking.

They were generally thwarted, for at that time of day her husband was at one of his clubs, or in his study with his man of business. Yet, as though keen to demonstrate that there was no limit to their impudent desire to ingratiate themselves with at least one resident who had been born a Darcy, they presumed upon Georgiana's patience, insistently sought to claim her attention, and thus made it very difficult indeed for her to escape from the drawing room.

Elizabeth had made a point of offering her a convenient excuse or another, and at one time had even gone as far as to plainly say, "If you wish to return to your music practice, Georgiana, I am quite sure that all of us will understand."

But, in deference to the relations of her brother's longstanding friend, the young girl had civilly declined, and the smug smile that had overspread Miss Bingley's countenance had done nothing to improve Elizabeth's opinion of her.

There was no improvement in Elizabeth's views on Mr Bingley either. She had not imagined that she would forgive him anytime soon for his callous want of attention to Jane's feelings, but finding him shockingly deficient in common courtesy had only served to antagonise her all the more.

Ever since their arrival in town, Mr Bingley had only called upon them twice, and on both occasions he seemed to have become a stranger to the basic requirements of civility. Gone was the affable manner that had garnered him so many friends in Hertfordshire. He had barely spoken – and when he had addressed her, it had been as though she were a distant and indifferent acquaintance. He had offered curt congratulations on the occasion of her marriage, then said, "I hope your family is in good health."

And that was all! Not even the vaguest, most oblique attempt to mention Jane! As though he had not deported himself with so little prudence as to make her hope he returned her affection! As though he had not singled her out at every opportunity for five weeks together, and thus given the whole of Meryton reason to talk about their imminent betrothal!

Seething, Elizabeth had merely supplied an equally curt, "I thank you, yes, they are," and made no comment on his sudden decision to quit Netherfield for ever.

Neither did he. As she eventually learnt, the topic was mentioned on his second visit, when Mr Bingley had spent some time with her husband in his study. And it had not been Mr Bingley who had brought it up.

Apparently, Darcy's query had met with another terse answer: "It had to be done."

And then Mr Bingley had changed the subject, leaving it at that: a short, dismissive sentence – a line drawn under a meaningless foray into the country, and not a care in the world for the damage done!

It had required a great deal of effort for Elizabeth to restrain herself and not abuse him to her husband – a generous forbearance that his fickle friend had done nothing to deserve. But her forbearance was for Jane's sake, and Darcy's. She dearly wished to let Mr Bingley know that he stood on thin ice, and warn him that her hard-won equanimity might fail her. She knew full well that her forced composure would be severely tested, and she *would* take all her frustrations to her husband, if she came across Mr Bingley gaily prancing in the glittering ballrooms of the *bon ton* with some young lady or another. So far, to his good fortune, she had not, but Elizabeth was loath to credit him with having the decency not to parade his most recent conquests before her. His absence from the Marquess of Lansdowne's ballroom, and Lord Malvern's, must have simply been a matter of pedigree, for the Hursts and Miss Bingley had not been in attendance either.

"There, ma'am. That should do, I think. But I'd gladly carry on if you wish," Sarah said, reawakening Elizabeth to her surroundings.

The obliging soul had loosened her hair and carefully brushed it, while she had been sitting there lost in musings and resentful thoughts.

Elizabeth smiled towards her maid's reflection in the looking glass.

"Oh, no, there is no need. I thank you," she said, and before long urged Sarah to go up and seek her rest.

It was very late, she noted as she chose to wait for Darcy on the small sofa by the fire, lest she fall asleep if she snuggled into bed. Her eyelids were growing heavier by the minute, and in the end it was a wonder that he did find her still awake, for he came in some twenty minutes later.

"I am sorry it took me so long," he said, little knowing that his tardiness was of no consequence from the moment she had seen him walking in. The sight of him in his shirtsleeves was a fair return for her patience.

"No matter," Elizabeth whispered back. And then it occurred to her to wonder why he had barely had sufficient time to remove his coat. "Is there anything amiss?" she asked, brow furrowed.

"No. Georgiana wanted a word, so I went to see her."

"Oh. I did not think she would be awake."

"She waited up to speak of the ride planned for the morrow. She would like to start earlier and go further afield. Would you mind?"

"No, of course not," Elizabeth promptly assured him. "Sometimes I think that the only pastimes that truly give her pleasure are her music practice and her morning rides with you."

"I— Yes, it may be so," Darcy sighed, then came to sit beside her and took her hand. "What will you do with yourself in the meanwhile? Call upon Mr and Mrs Gardiner, perhaps?"

Elizabeth smiled. The fact that her husband had grown fond of her uncle and aunt Gardiner was one of her greatest joys, and if she loved him less, she would have taken a measure of offence at the obvious surprise with which he had declared them to be very pleasant people of marked intelligence, good taste and genteel manners, for it suspiciously smacked of his aristocratic friends' astonishment at finding *her* cultured and genteel. But she did love him dearly, so she could make allowance for prejudices that must have been instilled in him from his boyhood. They were easily forgiven, seeing as he was so ready to relinquish them and welcome her aunt and uncle without condescension. In the end, the greatest surprise was hers, and the best one at that, when Mrs Gardiner's connection to Lambton came to light. Not even in her most hopeful moments had Elizabeth imagined that, within days of their acquaintance, her aunt and her husband would sit laughing and chatting as though they had known each other for a decade, while sharing tales of people and places that were so familiar to both.

"I would like that very much," she finally replied to his suggestion, "but I expect they are at Longbourn. They were planning to set off for Hertfordshire this morning."

"I see. A pity…" Darcy said as he twined his fingers around hers, then asked, "Would you wish to be there for the family gathering? 'Tis but half a day's journey, after all."

Elizabeth stroked his hand in recognition of his thoughtfulness.

"Tempting, but no. Not until we can bring ourselves to stay at the *Red Lion* or at my aunt Phillips'. Longbourn will be awfully crowded, and Mamma would go distracted at having to accommodate us too. Besides, we should not leave your sister when you have just been reunited," she said, instantly dismissing the notion that they might have asked her to join them.

They could not. So retiring a girl would be deeply uneasy at an overcrowded Longbourn.

Elizabeth gave a little sigh and added, "Come to think of it, we should have insisted she join us at Pemberley. She must have been very lonely here. I imagined she was spending her time with relations and friends but…"

"She did, to an extent. She stayed at Malvern House for a fortnight around Christmas, and afterwards Richard took her riding nearly every day—"

"Oh, surely there would have been greater scope for that at Pemberley," Elizabeth exclaimed, only to find that her husband's countenance clouded.

"I know," Darcy said, his voice low and weary. "And believe me, I did urge her to join us in January as planned. But she did not wish it. Pemberley is… It brings unhappy recollections."

Elizabeth very nearly asked why, and then silently chastised herself. It would have been a foolish question.

"Your father's passing," she said instead, pressing his hand, and his fingers twitched under hers into a vague gesture of agreement.

"That, too. But mostly a more recent—" He broke off and turned in his seat to face her. "There is something else you need to know," Darcy said with subdued determination. "But I wanted to meet her first – get to know her without preconceptions, lest you judge her for faults which are not her own."

He did not pause to wait for her answer. His account began innocently enough – a sojourn in Ramsgate, a different lady employed as a companion – but it soon twisted into a hideous tale of betrayal. Connivance. Monstrous greed. Wickham and the two-faced companion conspiring to prey upon Georgiana and persuade her to consent to an elopement, so that he may lay hands on her fortune of thirty thousand pounds.

By the time Darcy had finished speaking of his sister's frightfully narrow escape from a lifetime of misery and went on to make a brief, heartbreaking reference to the months that had followed once he had brought her to Pemberley – dark months of guilt and self-recrimination, and too much solitude and silence, and far too much time to think – Elizabeth was overcome with sorrow and her eyes were brimming.

She had held his hand throughout the harrowing narrative, held it fast, clasped between both of hers, and when silence fell she stroked it, then brought it to her lips.

"I am so sorry," she tearfully whispered. "For her... you... for—"

She released his hand and, curling her legs under her on the sofa, she put her arms around him and drew him close. She pressed her face to his, then raised her chin and brushed his temple with her lips.

"Forgive me..." she choked out, and at that he reached up and cupped her cheek.

"Forgive *you?* Whatever for?"

Tears spilled from her brimming eyes as she answered, sick with self-loathing:

"For giving him succour, and believing for a single moment that *you* had injured *him*. You had this weighing on you... had this... this... poison in your heart – and I added to it! I am so sorry," Elizabeth fervently repeated, for truly there was nothing else that she could say to mitigate her worst error of judgement. So she said it again: "Dreadfully sorry. For everything."

"Shhh," he tenderly whispered, clasping her to his chest. "It matters not, my love. After all this time... It matters not."

Elizabeth kissed him then, tears streaming down her cheeks, yet could not agree. It did matter. She had injured him with her mistrust, and with her misplaced confidence in her ability to judge people rightly. How she wished she had been more observant, more discerning! But he was right in one regard: after all this time, her self-reproaches were of no consequence – for she could change nothing.

So she ought not offer worthless apologies, but love him with all her heart. That, she already did. And she also could – and should – unconditionally love his sister too, and renew her efforts to make the dear girl believe once more that there *was* decency and goodness in the world.

Chapter 28

The strong wave of nausea assailed her with so little warning that Elizabeth barely had the time to scramble to her feet and dart from her dressing table to the washbowl in the adjoining room, before she was violently sick.

As always, Sarah was a treasure. Quick to follow her, the maid drew her loose tresses out of the way – the incident had occurred while Sarah was dressing her hair, and just one side had been pinned up – then dampened a cloth and offered it.

"Thank you," Elizabeth whispered, once she had wiped her mouth and set the cloth aside. "Goodness…" she added, not a little mortified. "My apologies. Something must have disagreed with me at dinner."

"It might have, ma'am, but I think not, if you don't mind me saying," Sarah countered softly, her smile almost maternal even though she was only a few years older. "I reckon, given your late courses and whatnot… Well… I'd say this might be a good time to have a word with your physician."

❧❦❧

So Dr Graham came. He was not *her* physician, strictly speaking. Not once had Elizabeth found herself in need of a medical man since her arrival in town. Dr Graham was the Darcys' physician – had been for many decades. But either way, he promptly arrived to attend her, and in short order confirmed Sarah's suspicions.

Once he had taken his leave and the first flush of delight had given way to calmer joy, Elizabeth could not but shake her head in bemused exasperation at how ludicrous it was that Sarah should have guessed how matters stood before *she* did. She had not counted the days – had lost track of them – lost track of many things besides, too engrossed in the novelties, both the attractive ones and the vexing, that life in town had brought. She had not paid much heed to her mother's words either, and had not made the connection between them and her newfound propensity to sleep late whenever the opportunity arose, blaming it on far too many social engagements.

None were planned for that day, which could not fail to please her, and Elizabeth was likewise glad that the morning's fuss in the dressing room, as well as Dr Graham's visit, had occurred in Darcy's absence. But now that she had such momentous intelligence to impart, she could scarce wait for his return.

She sought to temper her impatience in the library. Sarah's suggestion that she should rest abed was dismissed with incredulous amusement, for surely someone who had known her for upwards of six years should have grasped how contrary that was to her nature. Yet Sarah might have had the right of it again, Elizabeth was compelled to own when she stirred, blinked and noticed that she had dropped off to sleep curled up on one of the sofas in the library. And now she was covered with a quilt. Elizabeth made to push it away, but the scraping of a chair had her tilting her head back to instinctively seek the source of the unexpected noise.

"Oh. You have returned," she beamed at her husband when she saw him approaching.

He bent down on one knee beside her and brought the back of his fingers to her cheek.

"How are you feeling?" he whispered.

"Fine. I am perfectly fine," Elizabeth assured him, a joyous smile tugging at her lips, but Darcy's brow furrowed in impatience.

"Do not make light of it," he urged. "You have never fallen asleep in the library in the middle of the day. And your face is very warm."

"So would yours be, had you been smothered under a quilt," Elizabeth chuckled and reached up to weave her fingers into the soft tangle at his nape. She opted to tell him later that she might make a habit of dropping off to sleep in the middle of the day, if her mother should be proven right as to that predisposition, and said instead, "Rest easy, my love. I have not caught a fever. This has naught to do with—"

Yet, to his detriment, Darcy could not summon enough patience to wait for her to finish.

"I hear Graham was summoned. What did he have to say?" he asked, and at that Elizabeth's smile grew both appreciative and indulgent.

"Does anything ever happen in this house without your knowledge?"

"Not a vast deal, I should like to think." He brushed the ringlets from her face and quietly insisted, "Well?"

Elizabeth thought that she already had a set of perfectly good words at the ready – clever words; better words – to suit the wondrous tidings. Yet once the moment was upon her, she found herself simply saying, "I am with child."

If she needed further proof that they were two of a kind – which she did not – Elizabeth had it then, as she discovered him equally lost for words. Darcy swallowed hard, and made no answer beyond greeting the intelligence with a strangled, "You are?"

But all the answers she could wish for were glowing in his eyes. And then he wrapped his arms around her, and there was neither room nor need for words.

"Fitzwilliam, *go!*" Elizabeth entreated as she leaned over the bowl that had been brought to her dressing room for the purpose a few days ago, once she had decided that the blue-patterned washbowl was too pretty to deserve such ignominious treatment. Thankfully, it seemed to be a false alarm this time, but she was not prepared to take any chances. "I will not have you… see me thus… *again*," she gasped between shallow breaths, but the infuriating man would not heed her.

"Shh. Do not talk such nonsense," Darcy murmured, his warm hand tracing circles around her shoulder blade – which *was* quite soothing, Elizabeth grudgingly allowed. But then he dropped a light kiss on the back of her head – of all the times he might have chosen! – and urged, "Take deep breaths. It helped a little last time, did it not?"

Clutching the edges of the table, Elizabeth scowled at the plain white bowl, not daring to raise her head just yet to scowl at him. She needed no reminder of the mortifying episode the other morning, when he had followed her into the dressing room and just as stubbornly stayed to assist her – and, as rotten luck would have it, the attack of nausea had not been a false alarm. Still, he was not wrong about the deep breaths – they *had* helped then, and on a couple of other occasions too, so there was good reason to hope that they might do so again.

They did. The nausea *was* abating, so Elizabeth released her grip on the wooden table and straightened up.

"Better?" Darcy whispered, still stroking her back, and by then she was not in the least inclined to scowl.

She cast him a weary little smile instead.

"A little, yes, I think so."

"Are you ready to lie down?"

"Goodness knows," Elizabeth ruefully chuckled. "But I might as well try."

One arm around her waist, he escorted her into the bedchamber and settled her into bed, then returned to the dressing room and came back with the large white bowl and a plate of thin biscuits.

"No, *that* has no business here," Elizabeth protested, but he set the bowl on her bedside table nonetheless, and cast her a disarming little smile.

"It saves time," he argued, then rolled his eyes when she made to self-consciously press her point. "Elizabeth, nothing matters but your comfort. Do cease fussing, my love. There is no shame in what is natural."

Lips twitching, Elizabeth could not but own that it was a good translation of the Latin dictum, and moreover apt for the occasion, so she teasingly retorted, "A classical education seems to be of use at the strangest times."

"Indeed. Who would have thought?" Darcy grinned back, then offered her the plate. "Here, try these. Mrs Blake claims that dry biscuits work wonders. And ginger-flavoured ones, apparently."

Elizabeth cast him a suspicious glance.

"Now, why would she give you that sort of information?"

"Because I asked," Darcy shrugged, as though it were perfectly reasonable that he should do so. "And lest you wonder, no, I have not spoken with anyone else, not even Georgiana. So – no announcements yet, as we agreed. Still, I did think that Mrs Blake would be best-placed to give advice."

There was truth in that, which was why Elizabeth had already consulted the discreet and knowledgeable housekeeper.

That he should do so too was as extraordinary as it was thoughtful. But then, so was he: extraordinary, thoughtful, and a great many wonderful things besides, so Elizabeth beamed at him as she sat up and took the plate.

She selected a biscuit and cautiously nibbled at its edges. Time would tell if Mrs Blake's recommendation would be of material assistance, but for now Elizabeth was content to find the crisp and salty cracker entirely to her taste. She finished it and chose another. Then, once her husband joined her under the bedcovers, she wordlessly offered to share the small hoard.

She grinned when he shook his head.

"Your loss. They are delicious."

"I am very glad you think so."

A third palatable cracker had the same fate as the first two, and then Elizabeth set the plate on her bedside table and nestled into her husband's arms.

"I hope you will not tax yourself today," Darcy said after a while, breaking the cosy silence. "You should postpone your outing if you do not feel equal to a morning about town. And the same goes for our dinner engagement."

Elizabeth's lips quirked into a fleeting grimace as she made her answer without raising her head off his chest.

"I shall not claim that I am eager to dine with Lady Dalrymple and her guests, but it would not do to send our regrets at the last moment unless strictly necessary. Which will not be the case. I tend to be as right as rain in the evenings. As for this morning, 'tis but a visit to *Messrs Harding and Howell's*. Hardly taxing, by anyone's imagination," she added, tilting her chin upwards to cast him a smile. "Besides, I should not wish to disappoint Lady Rosemary and your sister."

"Oh. Georgiana is to join you?" Darcy asked, a hint of surprised pleasure in his voice, and Elizabeth nodded.

"Lady Rosemary was able to persuade her. She is very fond of Georgiana, and I believe the sentiment is mutual. At any rate, it seems to me that she is one of the few people whose society your sister genuinely enjoys."

"Aye. So she is. Especially of late," he concurred, and the last couple of words made Elizabeth raise her head to meet his eyes.

"Does she know? Of… Ramsgate, I mean?" she tentatively asked.

It was needless, that clarification. Of course he had already grasped her meaning. His answer came, prompt and firm, before she had even finished speaking:

"No. I have not disclosed that to any living soul except you and Richard. He *had* to know; he is Georgiana's other guardian. As for Lady Rosemary, I merely asked her to lend a hand, if she would. Assist her in company, encourage her a little. That is all."

"I see," Elizabeth said – and that held true in more than one regard. She could detect the clues in his air and his choice of words, and they were worth investigating. So she rolled towards him to rest her folded hands on his chest and her chin atop them, and enquired without preamble: "Did you by any chance ask Lady Rosemary to do the same for me?"

The turn of his countenance told its own story – the guarded look of unease, the sudden tightness in his lips. He was an open book to her by now, and all the signs were there, each plain to see. Thus, it was the work of a moment for her to conclude that, in good conscience, he could not make a secret of his involvement – and he knew it.

Contrition in his eyes, Darcy weaved his fingers through her hair.

"Elizabeth, this is not— There is something that I…" he began, the reluctance in his quiet tones giving her to think that his natural abhorrence of dissimulation was at war with the desire to spare her feelings.

"That you…?" she prompted when his voice trailed off, and her tender gaze grew a little arch as she quirked up a brow, daring him to choose openness over prevarication, however well-meaning.

It must have done its office, that arch look she fixed on him, for he searched her eyes for a long moment, then his tense countenance smoothed into resignation. He exhaled and brushed her cheek with the back of his fingers as he whispered, "I might have suggested something of that nature. Do you mind?"

Elizabeth gave a faint shrug.

"Not especially. But you could have said as much when I was puzzling over her reasons for befriending me," she affectionately chided.

"So that you would give me the credit?" He shook his head. "I think not, my love. No borrowed feathers. I only asked her to lend you some assistance in society. That she should have recognised your worth and sought your friendship had naught to do with me."

Elizabeth chuckled softly in response.

"I did say once that my good qualities are under your protection and you are to exaggerate them as much as possible, but that was before I knew your penchant for exaggeration. Now I think I should release you from our agreement, lest excessive praise make me insufferable."

"Thank you. But I shall take my chance all the same," he smiled, before he drew her very close and sought her lips.

෨෧෨ ෨෧෨

The morning at *Messrs Harding and Howell's* was shown to be even more enjoyable than Elizabeth had anticipated. Lady Rosemary was in high spirits as always, and her good cheer and amiable manner went a long way towards drawing Georgiana out of her shell.

The elegant wares likewise played a part, and as they wandered from one appealing display to another discussing the relative merits of silks and gossamer satins, jacquards and jaconets, vellum gauze and Venetian velvet, Elizabeth discovered that even a shy young girl who was not yet out could take pleasure in selecting fabrics and trimmings.

For her own part, she was eminently satisfied with her purchases of plum-coloured silk and frosted gauze. They would add a touch of townish sophistication to her wardrobe, with the aid of the skilled dressmaker whom Lady Rosemary had sent to Berkeley Square. It was another subtle attention, and yet another reason to be grateful. Elizabeth had already seen for herself from her first weeks in town that the dress-lengths acquired in St Albans, later turned into flattering gowns by the competent and obliging seamstress in Lambton, needed a dash of stylishness and flair in order to pass muster in the salons of London.

A scarf of silver tissue and a new pair of evening gloves would add to the effect, and since Georgiana also wished to look for pale blue ribbons and a new cashmere shawl, they made their way into the room devoted to such items. Yet a short while later Georgiana lost all interest in shawls and ribbons. With an uncommonly decisive, "Pray excuse me," she crossed the wide aisle to greet two ladies engrossed in the examination of several varieties of lace.

The pair – mother and daughter, judging by their ages and obvious resemblance – returned her greeting with something akin to wary pleasure, but wariness appeared to prevail as they glanced over Georgiana's shoulder, and the matron requested the pleasure of an introduction.

An introduction to *her*, that is to say, for Elizabeth soon learnt that they were already acquainted with Lady Rosemary. When the latter performed that civil office, she revealed that the ladies were indeed mother and daughter, and also that Miss Endicott had attended the same finishing school as Georgiana, during which time they had become close friends.

As to the closeness of that friendship, Elizabeth could only take Lady Rosemary at her word, for to her way of thinking the joy of the encounter seemed to be largely, if not wholly, on Georgiana's side. Once civilities were exchanged and the ladies offered their congratulations on the occasion of her marriage, Elizabeth did not fail to note Miss Endicott's very subdued responses to Georgiana's overtures. She gave but monosyllabic answers to a number of questions, and looked decidedly uneasy when obliged to acknowledge that she had returned to town some eight days prior, but had made no effort to be reunited with her friend. And lastly, Miss Endicott's vague discontent veered towards downright alarm when Georgiana warmly invited the young lady and her mother to come to Berkeley Square for a cup of tea and a long chat as soon as they had finished their shopping expedition.

"Do come, Beatrice! We have so much to speak of," the dear girl insisted when faced with the other's manifest reluctance, which only served to raise Elizabeth's concern for her new sister's feelings – and all the more so once Miss Endicott muttered a faltering refusal, just as Elizabeth had predicted.

"I think not… I mean… we are exceedingly obliged, but… another time, perhaps? It would not do to intrude and disrupt your plans…"

Under normal circumstances – that is, had she not suspected that the excuse was manufactured – Elizabeth would have spoken up to second Georgiana's invitation, but as matters stood, she forbore to compound the awkwardness of the situation. It was the young lady's mother who chose to step into the fray:

"What Beatrice means to say is that we were just leaving, and we would be loath to rush you. But, my dear Georgiana, if by any chance you are ready to depart as well, perhaps you could come with us, and then you girls can have your chat in Portman Square. Of course, we would be delighted if Lady Rosemary and Mrs Darcy would care to join us too. By all means, ladies, pray come, if you wish. You would be most welcome," Mrs Endicott added, and although her manner was courteous to a fault, Elizabeth vaguely sensed that the general invitation had only been extended for form's sake.

Lady Rosemary must have garnered that as well, for she was quick to offer thanks, then spoke in favour of the original suggestion. So did Georgiana – promptly and with fervour, leaving them in no doubt that she dearly wished to go – and since Lady Rosemary, who was acquainted with all parties, did not seem to find anything amiss in relinquishing their young charge into Mrs Endicott's care, Elizabeth voiced her own agreement. Thus, everything was settled, and very swiftly too. Mrs Endicott undertook to convey Georgiana home in a few hours, and the three made haste to depart, as though in fear that someone might change their mind and alter the arrangements.

"I expect you are wondering what that was all about," Lady Rosemary observed a little later when, left to their own devices, they resumed perusing gloves and blonde lace. "Perhaps the pair of us should have some tea and conversation too," she airily concluded, but before Elizabeth could offer more than a smiling nod, her friend's mildly conspiratorial air gave way to a grimace, and Lady Rosemary tutted. "And sooner rather than later, I should think," she muttered. "All the world and his wife are out to purchase finery today."

Following her glance, Elizabeth could instantly detect the reason for the turn of her companion's humour: Mrs Hurst and Miss Bingley had just made their way into the haberdashery hall and were ambling towards them.

"We have just encountered Georgiana leaving with Miss Endicott and her mother," Miss Bingley said, as soon as greetings were exchanged. "How commendable – is it not? – that she still finds time for old friends," she added, her habitually sneering tone laden with insinuation.

What precisely she was insinuating, Elizabeth could not tell, but she had long learnt to pay no heed to Miss Bingley and her paltry tactics, so her sole reply was a flat, "Indeed."

It was Lady Rosemary who chose to make a lengthier answer.

"Oh, yes, Georgiana's loyalty to old friends is most commendable, but I daresay 'tis high time for her to make new ones as well."

Miss Bingley pursed her lips.

"You think so, ma'am?" she asked quite crisply, and Lady Rosemary shrugged.

"But of course," she retorted with an air of perfect nonchalance. "Her coming out is drawing nearer, so she must make many friends, and likewise grow accustomed to moving in a variety of circles, in order to make a suitable marriage."

"Perhaps," Mrs Hurst sniffed. "Yet a young lady should be allowed *some* choice in the matter."

"Naturally," Lady Rosemary shot back. "And in order to choose, one must be presented with an array of eligible options. Well, it was a pleasure seeing you, as always, but we must take our leave. Unless you would care to choose one of these wreaths of silk roses, Elizabeth? They would look charming against your dark hair, and complement any blossom-coloured gown. A small ornament for Lady Melbourne's musical *soirée*, perhaps?"

"Oh, yes, such a perfect touch of rustic charm. A much more fitting embellishment than precious stones. Now, who would have thought, my dear Eliza, when you left us speechless with your appearance at Netherfield, skirts six inches deep in mud, that not half a year later you would be invited to the most exclusive gatherings in town?" Miss Bingley said, her smile thin and sour, presumably because, to the best of Elizabeth's knowledge, the lady and her kin had not been vouchsafed an invitation.

If Miss Bingley thought that she might injure her with double-edged compliments on her rustic charm and social achievements, she was sorely mistaken, Elizabeth thought. The spectacle was nothing but diverting. With considerable effort, she kept herself from smiling too widely as she remarked, "To own the truth, *I* most certainly did not. But then, I imagine that stranger things have happened."

"Quite," came Miss Bingley's terse reply, yet Lady Rosemary did not seem minded to let her barbs pass without comment.

"Oh, come, Miss Bingley," she said with a little laugh. "Pray have a care, or you will have us think that you would have gladly traipsed through mud yourself, in the hope of a similar outcome. But nay, let me not do you an injustice, for it cannot be so. As you are well aware, your talents lie elsewhere, and you would know better than to devote yourself to a lost cause. To each, her own, that is what I always say," she blithely declared as she enveloped the scowling sisters in a cheerful glance. "Enjoy your morning, Mrs Hurst – Miss Bingley, and farewell until we meet again," her ladyship intoned, and in short order she and Elizabeth made their way towards the vast glazed doors.

It was only when there was no risk of being overheard that she pressed Elizabeth's arm and chuckled.

"I must beg your pardon," Lady Rosemary murmured, the earlier false cheer giving way to genuine amusement, however rueful. "Some people have a knack for provoking me into outrageous behaviour."

Chapter 29

"I should not wish you to think that I am swayed by the prejudices of my class as regards Miss Bingley and her sister," Lady Rosemary returned to that subject without warning, once she and Elizabeth had spent the best part of an hour in her intimate yet very elegant sitting room, drinking tea and speaking of music, books and other innocuous matters. "If I think ill of them, 'tis not because their fortune was made in trade. What displeases me the most is that they seem to view everything from the perspective of their own advancement. And you may call me suspicious, but I do believe that they are showing excessive interest in Georgiana of late. Do they call often?"

Elizabeth's lips quirked into a little grimace before she acknowledged, "Aye, they do. More so than anyone."

"Hm," Lady Rosemary scoffed. "By themselves, or do they bring their brother along?"

"Oh," Elizabeth murmured, beginning to understand her. "Do you think they are hoping for a union between Georgiana and Mr Bingley?"

Lady Rosemary frowned.

"Indeed I do. A connection with the Darcys would open many of the doors that are currently closed to them, so I would not put it past them to pursue the remaining option, once they had lost all hope of the other. And what a foolish hope that was!" she exclaimed with a gesture of impatience. "I know him, so I know whereof I speak: there is no way under heaven that Darcy would have ever offered for Miss Bingley!"

Elizabeth had a warm smile for her thoughtful friend.

"I thank you. That was my impression too. As for Mr Bingley, come to think of it, his sisters do bring him up in conversation and praise him in Georgiana's hearing. But he has joined them on their calls no more than twice."

"I see. Then perhaps he is not party to their scheming. Frankly, I am relieved to hear it. Darcy has always been a good judge of character, and I should be sorry to think that he was wrong to hold Mr Bingley in high regard all these years. By the bye, it *has* perplexed me, their friendship, seeing as they have so little in common. But then, there is the old adage: opposites attract. And in truth, there is not much that is objectionable about the young man, except his presumptuous sisters. *He* is a pleasant enough fellow, although rather too excitable and flighty. If Georgiana should form a genuine *tendre* for him, and he for her, well…" She shrugged. "Darcy might sanction the attachment in order to make her happy. Of course, she can do a vast deal better," Lady Rosemary declared with emphasis – thus giving proof that, despite claims to the contrary, as the daughter of an earl, she was inevitably prejudiced against acquaintances who were just one or two generations removed from trade. "But I can think of nothing worse than knowing that such a difficult decision might never arise, were it not for that man's conniving sisters."

Elizabeth flinched – for she *could* think of something worse. And that would be Jane faced with the heartache of having Mr Bingley firmly established in her extended family as Georgiana's husband.

"I thank you for the warning," she said with quiet energy. "I shall keep a closer eye on their interactions."

"That would be best," Lady Rosemary nodded. "And perhaps put your husband on his guard as well. I wished to ask him if he had noticed something, but I lacked the opportunity. He might have – and then again might not, if the sly overtures were made in his absence."

Elizabeth's eyes widened.

"You see keenly," she said, quick to give credit where it was due. "More often than not, they did call in his absence."

She released a quiet snort. Foolishly, she had imagined Miss Bingley to be disappointed at hardly ever finding Darcy there to welcome them, and – with the unbecoming smugness of the victor – had privately smirked at that, never pausing to consider that the timing of the calls might have been chosen on purpose. Nor had she found reasons for concern in the fact that, while one sister was keeping her engaged in conversation, the other was fawning over Georgiana. And goodness knows what might have been said on the few occasions when the dear girl had been invited to walk with Mr Bingley's sisters, or have tea in Grosvenor Square.

Elizabeth tutted, then gave a self-deprecating grimace.

"Now I am vexed with myself for being so easily duped and outmanoeuvred," she confessed. "In cases such as these, anything approaching *naïveté* is unpardonable."

Lady Rosemary cast her a reassuring smile.

"Not at all. What you call *naïveté* is a sign of an honest heart and a clear conscience. Which is one of the reasons I have spoken. I should not wish to see you or Georgiana unprepared before scheming and malice, nor Darcy taken in by his fondness for Mr Bingley, which compels him to tolerate his friend's sisters. Still, judging by Mr Bingley's infrequent visits in Berkeley Square, it seems to me that their friendship is cooling, which may not be such a bad thing at the moment. Besides, I daresay it was to be expected. However close the bonds of fellowship between bachelors, some degree of distance invariably follows when one of them takes a wife."

Especially when the aforementioned wife was the sister of the lady whom the other had jilted, Elizabeth reflected, yet held her peace. She *would not* blame herself for the cooling of their friendship. Mr Bingley was the only one at fault. And no, he could not be trusted with Georgiana's young and already injured heart any more than he deserved Jane's. Excitable and flighty, Lady Rosemary had called him. Aye, so he was. Even if her friend did not find those traits objectionable, *she* did. For they led to a callous and selfish disregard for other people's feelings. So, to her way of thinking, he was the last man in the world whom either Jane or Georgiana should wish to marry.

But that was a matter to be addressed at home. For now, another question sprang to the forefront of her mind, so Elizabeth tentatively began, "Speaking of not leaving Georgiana unprepared in difficult situations, may I ask your opinion on a related subject?"

Lady Rosemary gave a warm smile and a small gesture of invitation.

"By all means. I shall be glad to assist you with anything, if I can."

"It is about Miss Endicott. Just how good a friend is she to Georgiana, do you know? For I could not help feeling that she had found little to no pleasure in the encounter at *Harding and Howell's*, and was patently unwilling to follow Georgiana's invitation and call in Berkeley Square."

"Ah. That," Lady Rosemary cryptically observed, setting her cup of tea on the table at her elbow. Hands folded together in her lap, she said nothing further for a long moment. Then, seemingly coming to a decision, she looked up. "This might be something you should hear from your husband or new sister, but I daresay it serves no purpose to leave you to fret over it until you arrive home."

"Longer than that. They are both out, and not due to return for several hours," Elizabeth said with a little smile. "But let me seek to overcome the nicety of your scruples. I believe I am gaining an inkling into the matter: was it perchance me whom she was avoiding, rather than Georgiana?"

"Just so," the other acknowledged.

"Oh," Elizabeth murmured. "A pity. And somewhat of a surprise, I have to own. Even on such a short acquaintance, I would not have placed her in Miss Bingley's camp."

"And with good reason," Lady Rosemary replied. "She is not the scheming sort. And, unlike Miss Bingley and those of her ilk, Beatrice Endicott had some chance of succeeding. But only on account of her excellent rapport with Darcy's sister," she added with another reassuring smile. "It was quite plain to everyone concerned that Georgiana had set her heart on her dearest friend marrying her brother, so there was good reason to believe that her brother would eventually oblige. Many of us thought it was simply a matter of time. Precisely because it would have made Georgiana happy, which easily singled out Beatrice Endicott from the crowd of eligible young ladies vying for his notice. There is little that he would not do to ensure his sister's happiness and comfort."

Elizabeth nodded with more good humour than she felt.

"He does have the habit of putting others before self."

"Too true," Lady Rosemary agreed, then added, "So I was very glad to see that, for once, he had made an exception and married to please himself – and you." She reached out to hold and press Elizabeth's hand, then resumed after the briefest pause. "I am happy for Darcy that he found you, my dear. A placid union for his sister's sake would have been a great deal less than he deserves. And he is too tender-hearted – or too old-fashioned in the best sense of the word, after the manner of the chivalrous knights of yore, if you will – to have fared tolerably well alongside the average jaded miss he might have found in the grand salons. You seem to be just what he needs: a fresh-faced and artless young lady who loves him."

The openness was unexpected. Not that it had been lacking from their interactions – it never had – but there was a great deal more of it this time, and it went deeper. Which made it most affecting.

"I thank you for giving me so much credit," Elizabeth said with feeling. "Your kindness is all the more appreciated, seeing as you knew nothing of me until a few weeks ago. I might have been yet another self-serving creature who had pursued him for his name and fortune."

Lady Rosemary chuckled and patted her hand.

"You might have, but there was little cause to fear that you would be so. Over the years, he has had more than enough practice in detecting deceit and avarice. For my part, I was reassured as soon as I made your acquaintance."

Unwittingly, Elizabeth cast her a questioning glance, which her friend must have noticed, for she explained with a faint smile:

"Your heart is in your eyes, my dear. So there is a vast deal of reassurance in the way you look at him when you think no one is watching. And the same can be said of the way he watches over you, all the while flattering himself that he is perfectly discreet about it, I imagine," Lady Rosemary said with mild amusement as the heat of a blush crept into Elizabeth's cheeks. Her host patted her hand again and warmly concluded, "No one who has seen the pair of you together can doubt that yours is a marriage of affection. If they still doubt it, they are blind, mean-spirited or severely misguided. But any which way, they are not worth your notice. There. Now, would you care for another cup of tea?"

The cheerfully matter-of-fact end to the heartfelt conversation seemed exactly calculated to set her at ease, so Elizabeth settled a look of gratitude upon her friend.

"I thank you. For the tea – and everything else. But perhaps I should go and wait for Georgiana. I expect she will return home with a heavy heart… It might help if we have the chance to talk in private. That is, if she is willing to speak of her friend's distress and disappointment…"

She might not, Elizabeth inwardly acknowledged. Georgiana was uniformly unwilling to say much about anything, let alone discuss something so personal. Even so, she had to try.

"Well, all you can do is try," Lady Rosemary said, as though she had guessed her thoughts. "Yes, Georgiana will be saddened on her friend's account. They were very close. But she is deeply devoted to her brother, so his happiness is paramount to her. As for Miss Endicott, she will recover," Lady Rosemary added with a sympathetic quirk in her lips. "I shall not say this to Georgiana, for she is too young to believe me, but you will see my meaning. I have every confidence that Beatrice Endicott will soon forget her disappointment, because she is not so much in love with Darcy as with being in love. That is my opinion, and I have seen my share of the world and its follies. Like many of her age and disposition, Miss Endicott has found delight in dreaming of the day when she would marry her Prince Charming. It was highly predictable that she should have cast Darcy in that role. He is her best friend's brother, kind, handsome and amiable to a fault. But she will grow up, as all of us are wont to do sooner or later, and will come to see the world as it is, not as she would wish it. And then she will look around and, in due course, fix her affections in their proper place."

Elizabeth thanked her friend for that final effort to set her heart at ease. But later, as the carriage was conveying her apace towards Berkeley Square, she could not help thinking that Lady Rosemary's talk of girls growing up and learning to see the world for what it truly was savoured strongly of disappointment.

For the first time in their acquaintance, it occurred to her that she might have reason to feel sorry for her friend. Lady Rosemary was wealthy, glamorous and independent, she belonged to the highest circles and always appeared to enjoy life to the full. She never gave the impression that she was wistful and lonely, but… perhaps she was. Elizabeth had no notion whether her friend's marriage had been a happy one or not. Nor did she know why Lady Rosemary had not remarried. Until now, their connection had been amiable and open, but not so close as to permit enquiry into such private matters. Yet that might change as of today. Their friendship had certainly grown closer. So perhaps she *could* ask more personal questions now, and offer a sympathetic ear, if Lady Rosemary should ever feel inclined to talk about her sentiments and wishes.

It was a pity that she seemed to harbour no romantic interest in Colonel Fitzwilliam, Elizabeth reflected. Their exchanges were lively and sporting, but evinced nothing more than the friendly rapport she had with Darcy, which was indeed too bad, for the colonel and Lady Rosemary seemed made for each other. The close similarity in temper and manner was plain for all to see – not to mention that, in a prudential light, it would be an excellent match for him. As a second son, the colonel should choose a lady of fortune, and in that regard, much like in many others, Lady Rosemary was an unrivalled catch.

'Heavens! I am beginning to sound just like my mother!' Elizabeth chastised herself with a rueful smile, then sobered. This was not the time for matchmaking – and she would be better advised to watch out for such schemes closer to home.

⊚⊚ ⊚⊚

Georgiana had already returned. Elizabeth could ascertain as much within moments – a flow of softly played notes reached her as soon as she stepped into the house. Doubtlessly her sister would not appreciate the interruption. Even so, once Thomas had assisted her in removing her outdoor apparel, Elizabeth made her way towards the music room.

No sooner had she pushed the door open than the piece was brought to an abrupt halt. Georgiana glanced up, murmured a subdued greeting, then lowered her eyes to the music sheets, but did not recommence playing, which was just as well.

After the briefest of deliberations, Elizabeth decided against crossing the room to join her at the pianoforte. Standing beside the young girl – towering over her – was hardly conducive to speaking heart to heart. So she opted for one of the sofas.

"Will you sit with me?" she asked, gesturing towards the empty space beside her, and eventually Georgiana did as bid, although with visible reluctance.

It would have served no purpose to resort to bland civilities and enquire if she had enjoyed her call in Portman Square, so Elizabeth said instead, "Thomas has taken your purchases of fabrics to your rooms. A pity that you did not have the time to choose blue ribbons, or the cashmere shawl you spoke of. We could go back in the morning, if you wish," she suggested by way of a friendly overture, but Georgiana shook her head.

"I thank you, no. That will not be necessary. Besides, I have made different plans for the morrow."

"With Miss Endicott?"

"No. I am going riding with Miss Bingley and her brother."

Elizabeth pursed her lips.

"Oh. I was not aware that Miss Bingley was fond of the activity. What of going for a ride with your own brother?" she suggested with as much diplomacy as she could muster, yet that effort was lost on her young sister.

Georgiana's swift retort held a noticeable hint of petulance:

"I would certainly prefer it. But he cannot seem to find the time these days."

There was some truth in that, Elizabeth inwardly acknowledged. Of late, Darcy had set aside the habit of early morning rides in favour of watching over her as she battled with the episodes of nausea. A faint quirk tugged at the corner of her mouth. She loved him dearly and his tender care was much appreciated, but she could certainly dispense with the mortification of having him standing by that confounded bowl with her. He would be much better employed in resuming his rides with his sister.

"That might be the case," she owned, sparing Georgiana the details, and merely added, "Not for long, though. 'Tis a passing phase, I assure you."

"I am relieved to hear it," the young girl replied, yet there was no measure of relief in her crisp tones.

Elizabeth did not pursue the matter. There was a more important topic that begged to be introduced, so she proceeded with some caution:

"Georgiana, do you enjoy spending time with Mr Bingley and his sisters?"

"Of course," the retort came without hesitation. "Why would I not? They are very pleasant people, and some of my brother's closest friends – and therefore mine."

"There *is* a longstanding friendship between Mr Bingley and your brother," Elizabeth quietly conceded, "but it does not follow that the others—" She stopped short, cleared her voice, and then changed tack. "Lady Rosemary and I fear that Mr Bingley's sisters might have their own motives for—"

"Is that how you spent your time today, discussing my friends and their perceived motives?" Georgiana cut her off with singular boldness for one who was uniformly timid and subdued.

Yet, however unexpected, that did not deter Elizabeth from her purpose.

"Yes, in part," she nodded. "I should not wish you to be deceived by false professions of regard. You see, I have had sufficient reasons to think them disingenuous, but today Lady Rosemary opened my eyes to another possibility, and we both think you should be on your guard—"

"Should I!" Georgiana exclaimed, and it was a splutter, not a question. "I am much obliged, I'm sure, but Lady Rosemary no longer seems infallible, and I would be all the more indebted to her if she were not so free with her advice. As for *your* words of caution, give me leave to say that you are a fine one to talk about wilful deception," she finished in a low hiss, her thin voice little short of vitriolic.

Elizabeth's eyes widened at the surprise attack.

"Pardon?"

"Pray spare me the show of ignorance and injured dignity," the young girl shot back, her stare unblinking and ice-cold. "Let us speak without disguise, for once. You might as well learn that I am no stranger to the unsavoury particulars of your marriage. I know all there is to know about the unfortunate... rushed... patched-up affair! In your quest for an advantageous match, you have orchestrated a compromising situation and used my brother's honourable nature against him. And here we are: you gained what you wanted, and I must call you my sister. Worse still, each and every day I must endure the heartache of seeing my brother in your power. With your dark arts and allurements, you have contrived to twist him around your little finger – *him*, the most astute and sensible of men! I have lost him to you, and I have also lost my closest friend, who can scarce bear to see me now, let alone come to this house nearly every day, as she used to. So I would rather not lose any more friends on your account, if it is all the same to *you*," she spat, eyes brimming. Then, with a strangled, "Excuse me," she leapt to her feet and ran out of the room.

⌘

Stunned disbelief was Elizabeth's first response. Anger came second, but she could not stay angry with the outspoken girl for very long. Soon, her ire was directed towards the true sources of the malice: Mr Bingley's sisters. Georgiana's own relations – the supercilious ones, that is to say – might have added their prejudices to the mix, but it was plain to see that the chief culprits were Miss Bingley and Mrs Hurst. Elizabeth could easily detect their malevolence in Georgiana's reproaches. Those offensive words were theirs, much as they had come from the young girl's lips. The vipers had dripped their insidious venom in Georgiana's ear while she was alone in town, and presumably added to it afterwards, whenever they could devise an opportunity for private conversation. They had taken advantage of their privileged position as longstanding friends, whom Georgiana would naturally trust. They had played on the girl's affection for her brother and made her anxious for his fate – and hers – at the hands of a newcomer painted as a scheming Jezebel, who had ensnared him with her wiles and cunningly trapped him into marriage.

Georgiana must have received little, if anything, by way of antidote to their poison. Seemingly, their malicious representation of the scandal was all she had, and it was easy to see why: loath to injure her with talk of Wickham, Darcy must have cloaked many of the pertinent details under a discreet silence. As to married life and the happiness that came with it, what brother shared such confidences with a sister who was more than ten years his junior? And what young and timid sister dared quiz her much older brother on personal matters?

Lady Rosemary had declared earlier that those who had seen the pair of them together and still doubted their mutual affection must be blind, mean-spirited or severely misguided. If Georgiana was misguided, that was through no fault of hers. Those harpies were to blame, and they had caused more damage than they had imagined. Given her secret history with Wickham, how distraught the girl must be if she was made to think that her beloved brother had been caught into a snare as wicked as the one she had so narrowly escaped!

The notion brought Elizabeth to her feet, yet halfway to the door she drew to a halt. Not because she knew she would not be welcome in Georgiana's chambers or wherever else the girl might have sought refuge. That was neither here nor there. They *had* to talk. The question was how to go about it.

The obvious answer came to her in a trice: she should speak with her husband first – they ought to deal with this together.

He should be home soon. He had been obliged to call upon Lord Malvern to discuss a set of unforeseen developments in their joint affairs, and Elizabeth hoped that the matters would be resolved to their mutual satisfaction. But then there was the invitation to

Lady Dalrymple's house for dinner – nothing but an inconvenience, given the pressing concerns at home. Yet there was no avoiding it now. Not at such short notice.

So the home concerns would have to wait until the morrow. And perhaps it was not such a bad thing after all. It *would* be useful to have a few more hours to ponder on ways to address the issue – decide what she should say, and how. For tact was of the essence.

As she retraced her steps towards the sofa, Elizabeth grimaced, knowing full well that tact could only go so far. However sensitively she might put it, her husband would be livid to hear that, thanks to Miss Bingley and Mrs Hurst, his sister thought her false and him beguiled beyond redemption. As for Georgiana, the young girl would distrust and resent her all the more if she appeared to have gone tattling to Darcy.

With a huff of exasperation, Elizabeth lowered herself into her seat. This was a difficulty she could have done without – and yet another reason to prevent a closer connection with the Bingleys. Goodness, to think that the pair of gorgons might have become Jane's sisters! Or Georgiana's.

Elizabeth leaned back, her countenance set into lines of stern determination. Praise be, Jane was safe from them. And so help her, they *would not* hold sway over Georgiana for much longer, either!

Chapter 30

Darcy returned so late from Malvern House that he barely had the time to retire and change his apparel. For her part, Elizabeth was a great deal more advanced in that regard. She had gone up the best part of an hour earlier, had bathed and donned an elegant dress, then sat at her dressing table for the most exacting stage in the preparations.

While Sarah was putting the finishing touches to a very flattering hairstyle, a quiet knock sounded at the furthest door, the one that led to the corridor. Oddly enough, it was Georgiana, who had never sought admittance into Elizabeth's rooms before. But the turn of the young girl's countenance gave a fair indication as to what had brought her, so Elizabeth turned in her seat and glanced up at her lady's maid.

"Will you give us a minute, Sarah?"

Her expectations were confirmed as soon as they were left alone. Still standing by the door, Georgiana muttered without looking up, "I came to apologise for my outburst. It was… I was uncivil. I should not have spoken thus."

"I would much rather know what you are thinking," Elizabeth replied, and meant it. "Do come in," she urged. "Will you not sit down?"

"I thank you, no. I should…" Georgiana's voice trailed off as she gestured vaguely towards the door behind her. And then she raised her chin and met Elizabeth's gaze at last. "Have you told my brother?"

'*Ah. Now we come to the point,*' Elizabeth reflected, not entirely surprised that this should be the girl's main concern. But all she said was, "No. And I do not intend to."

Georgiana's tense shoulders slumped as she exhaled in manifest relief, only to eye her with renewed suspicion when Elizabeth added, "But I must and I shall speak with him about Mr Bingley's sisters and their role in our disagreement. You were given a misleading account,

Georgiana," she resumed, when the young girl made to interrupt. "If you wish to hear the truth, you should ask your brother."

The young girl gave a quiet little snort.

"That is a singular suggestion. Sadly, it goes against everything I have been taught, and I am not in the habit of taking liberties. 'Tis not my place to hold my brother to account."

"Nor is it to judge him," Elizabeth observed, and at that Georgiana seemed to have forgotten about the need to keep her voice down so that she would not be overheard from the adjoining chamber.

"I am not judging him!" she heatedly protested.

"No, you are judging *me*. But my alleged ability to lead him by the nose does not speak well of him either, does it?" Elizabeth softly teased, then sobered. "I wish you were not made to fear for his happiness," she earnestly added. "We *are* very happy, and deeply attached. You may not believe me – after all, you scarce know me, and have no just cause to trust me. But I hope you will, in time. I—"

She stopped short when the door to her husband's bedchamber opened without warning – both of them had long dispensed with knocking on that particular door, as was the case with its counterpart at Pemberley – and Darcy walked in, resplendent in his evening apparel.

"Elizabeth, would it be—?" he began, but did not finish, once his gaze fell on his sister. Astute as ever, despite Georgiana's recent opinion to the contrary, he must have sensed some of the undercurrents, for he arched a brow and darted his eyes from one to the other. "Is anything the matter?"

A reply along the lines of *'No, nothing at all,'* would have gone against the promise she had made him: that she would not present him with civil and compliant falsehoods for the sake of harmony. So Elizabeth cast him a warm smile and, finding the right balance between diplomacy and candour, she gave a flourish of her hand and airily assured him, "Oh, rest easy, 'tis nothing that cannot wait until the morrow."

⚬⚭ ⚭⚬

The Dowager Viscountess Dalrymple liked to entertain on a larger scale than Elizabeth had expected, and among the lady's many guests she encountered some whose society gave her no pleasure.

Miss Bingley was of the company. So was her sister and Mr Hurst, but not the ladies' brother. Mr Bingley must have been engaged elsewhere. Lady Rosemary certainly was – she had been asked to dine at Devonshire House, Elizabeth had already learnt as much that morning – which was a pity, for her friend's presence would have made the evening a great deal more enjoyable. Even so, Elizabeth played her part with her usual aplomb, exchanging civil nothings at dinner and later in the drawing room, once the ladies had retired and left the gentlemen at their brandy and port. All in all, she could congratulate herself on her performance – not least her success in keeping an even mien around Miss Bingley and Mrs Hurst when a modicum of conversation with them could not be avoided.

Yet some time later, when Elizabeth sought a few moments' rest from the chattering ladies, young and old, and withdrew with a fresh cup of tea to one of the sofas scattered about the place, she found with a flare of vexation that her equanimity was about to be tested. Mrs Hurst approached and availed herself of the spare seat beside her, then pressed her arm with a falsely solicitous, "My dear Eliza, we cannot have you sitting here all alone and neglected. I thought I should come and keep you company. So, dare I hope that you are having a tolerable evening?" she intoned, her air leaving Elizabeth in no doubt that she dared hope the opposite, and moreover that the detestable woman had joined her for the very purpose of making her evening intolerable, if she could.

Refusing to oblige, Elizabeth smiled brightly.

"Oh, much more than tolerable, I thank you. I am having a remarkably pleasant time."

"I am thrilled to hear it," Mrs Hurst disingenuously claimed. "But what a pity that Georgiana is not here to experience the same delights! I thought she would join you."

"You did? Then I am sorry for your disappointment, but I daresay this is nothing out of the common way. Georgiana rarely dines in company."

"Oh, I did notice that," Mrs Hurst replied, "but I imagined that things were about to change, in view of Lady Rosemary's pronouncements this morning. You know, that Georgiana must learn to move in a variety of circles, so that she might make a suitable match."

"Yes, things must change, and they certainly shall," Elizabeth declared, almost beginning to enjoy the game of thrust and parry. "But it is too soon to talk of Georgiana's marriage. She is full young."

"True," Mrs Hurst retorted. "So, are you daunted by the prospect of superintending her coming out?" she asked, changing tack, but Elizabeth had no difficulty in parrying that feint either.

"Oh, I doubt I will have much to do with it. I should not be surprised if Lady Malvern steps into that role. As you may imagine, I have no experience in such matters," she smiled sweetly, "and I still have a great deal to learn about the ways of the *haut ton*. But, to my good fortune and Georgiana's, we have a great many relations and friends who are disposed to offer assistance."

"Indeed, and I hope you count me among them," Mrs Hurst had the audacity to utter. And then she added with a gay little laugh, "But you are too modest, my dear Eliza. You should not be so severe upon yourself. You seem to have a natural talent for adjusting to your new life. Almost as though you were born for it. I have watched you finding your footing among the upper echelons, and I am delighted to say that I never saw you falter. Take Lady Rosemary, for instance. In that regard, your forbearance is beyond admirable. I must confess myself exceedingly impressed."

The fulsome praise could only serve to put her on her guard, but Elizabeth knew better than to reveal as much. She matched Mrs Hurst's false gaiety with blatant good cheer of her own.

"Forbearance?" she chuckled. "I have no need of forbearance, I assure you. Lady Rosemary is excellent company, and a very dear friend."

Mrs Hurst's smile widened.

"How very enlightened of you! Once again, my compliments. I will own that you never cease to surprise me. Given your conventional upbringing, I never imagined you would take so readily to the permissive ways of the *ton*."

The swordplay was growing increasingly tiresome, so Elizabeth gave a careless little shrug.

"You speak in riddles, Mrs Hurst. But I daresay this is part of your enduring charm."

"Why, thank you," the other beamed, then leaned closer until Elizabeth could feel the feathers of the woman's turban brushing against her temple. "My apologies for resorting to veiled comments,"

Mrs Hurst murmured. "There is little risk of being overheard, I grant you, but one never knows who might be listening, and it would not do to speak too freely of such things in unmarried ladies' hearing. Naturally, I was referring to Lady Rosemary's liaison with Mr Darcy. The pair of them were practically inseparable at one time."

The vicious stab found her unprepared. Much as Elizabeth sought to repel the malevolent attack by preserving an air of amused indifference, the control must have slipped by a fraction, for Mrs Hurst gave a quiet gasp of feigned distress and horror.

"My goodness! You did not know!" she whispered, vainly striving to conceal her wicked satisfaction. "I spoke out of turn. Oh, this is in every way horrible. I am beside myself – utterly distraught! My dearest Eliza, I beg you to forgive me…"

Elizabeth could scarce hear her as disjointed thoughts chased each other in her head: *'No! This is false! It must be. A falsehood… naught but the grossest falsehood! Monstrous… Evil… The vilest, basest lie!'*

"Think nothing of it," she said at last, forcibly shaping her lips into an insouciant smile, but her foe would not be silenced.

"How can I?" Mrs Hurst quietly spluttered. "My dear friend, you *must* allow me to apologise – nay, to abjectly beg your pardon! I simply thought you had discovered the truth for yourself, or that your husband had told you." She shook her head and tutted, her mien a picture of compassion that formed a stark contrast with the dark glee in her eyes. "He *should* have made a clean breast of it, if you ask me. That was badly done, badly done indeed. Mr Hurst never conceals his peccadilloes."

Her lips frozen into the same smile, yet her mind in chaos, Elizabeth barely restrained the urge to bid her hold her tongue. The smug whispers were distracting her – keeping her from thinking clearly. What *was* the repulsive woman's game? There was but one logical conclusion: Mrs Hurst must be as dense as she was fiendish, otherwise she would have grasped by now that slandering Lady Rosemary and Darcy was the surest way of ruining her own social ambitions. Once they learnt of the calumny, they would ensure she was snubbed by all their influential friends and relations. She would be censured and despised as a peddler of venomous falsehoods!

Unless…

The path of reason led to the abyss. Elizabeth reached the brink and stood staring into the darkness: Louisa Hurst need not fear the lash of public ridicule if what she said was true.

She blinked. Winced too, perhaps – she could not tell. Elizabeth was but vaguely aware that her ears were ringing as she forced the corners of her lips to curl up again, and squared her shoulders for the performance of a lifetime.

Her pain was her own affair. She *would not* collapse into a heap of misery before Mrs Hurst, Miss Bingley and their friends! She would present herself as the embodiment of nonchalant composure, and the devil take all those who were of a mind to hurt her!

So Elizabeth turned her head and looked her opponent in the eye.

"I never was one to dwell on the past," she said, shrugging with perfect indifference. "The present and the future are far more engaging. Still, let me set your troubled heart at ease. You need not fret. I *was* informed of that particular detail. And found it of no consequence."

The full set of false claims must have rung true, for Mrs Hurst's countenance mirrored surprise, suspicion, then surly disappointment.

"I see," she muttered. "That is a relief. I am very glad to hear it."

The rewards of the successful performance were cold tea and a narrow escape from humiliation. All that remained was to keep up the pretence for the rest of the evening.

❧ ❧

And that was precisely what she did. Once the gentlemen came in, Elizabeth stood to meet her husband halfway across the room, then chose to lean on his arm for the duration and partner him at whist when the card tables were laid out. Mrs Hurst's purpose had been to cause trouble. She would be delighted to find signs of disharmony between the pair of them – so she should be obliged with none. But the effort was past bearing, and the experience phantasmagoric. The countless pier glasses that adorned Lady Dalrymple's drawing room showed glimpses of someone who had borrowed her features: a young woman with her head held high, laughing and chatting with every appearance of gaiety – while on this side of the looking glass there was emptiness and heartbreak.

The parable of the Spartan boy and the fox sprang to mind, and Elizabeth's lips quirked into a faint grimace. Perhaps she ought to ask her father if the Bennet blood had received some small infusion from that part of the world.

And then she closed her mind to reflections that might sap the little strength she had, and channelled all her efforts into the final stages of the performance.

She only faltered once, in a brief moment of quasi-privacy, when Darcy returned with their refilled glasses and, screening her from the rest of the company, he offered hers, settled an unbearably warm look upon her and murmured, "You are so beautiful tonight."

He lightly stroked her arm, and for the sake of her composure, Elizabeth was glad of the long kid gloves. She lowered her eyes to conceal her tears and resolutely blinked them back as she whispered, "Thank you."

Chapter 31

The dressing room was quiet. The storm was within. Never in her life had she been so wretched. Nor had she ever felt so lost. Lost and alone.

Sarah had long gone – had assisted her with preparing for the night and left her. Yet Elizabeth remained where she was, finally at liberty to give free rein to the tempest of emotions she had struggled to suppress, and utterly defenceless before the rising tide of misery.

Of all the people in the world – kindly people, or malicious, or indifferent – her husband was the only one whom she had imagined she could fully trust. Her safe haven. Her partner in life, in every sense of the word. How could she possibly trust him still?

The other betrayal – Lady Rosemary's – paled in comparison. Elizabeth choked out a muted, bitter laugh. Her one friend in town, her only real friend, was worse than a sworn enemy. At least her enemies were honest in their dislike. Even Miss Bingley and Mrs Hurst. Whereas Lady Rosemary and her show of friendship… What did she hope to gain? Darcy's approval? His revived affections?

She would not – *could not* believe that the liaison was continuing at the present time. For all the insidious mistrust, Elizabeth could not make herself believe that there was duplicity in her marriage. She could not doubt the love – the closeness – the ardent desire. Her husband *was* hers completely – for now. While she had the bloom of youth, and was carrying his child, and they were caught in the first flush of passion.

But what of the years to come? What of the time when she would become a matron and begin to resemble her mother in looks, if not in manners?

She flattered herself that she could show far more decorum, and in time she might acquire some town polish, but not a vast deal of it. She might improve her mind so as to speak more knowledgeably about art and music and current affairs, she might learn to move with greater ease in his exalted circles but, much like her mother, she was and would remain a country girl at heart.

What if that was not enough?

That very morning, Lady Rosemary had declared her to be just what her husband needed: a fresh-faced and artless young girl who loved him – and the remark had seemed cordial, supportive and heart-warming at the time. But what if it had not been intended as a compliment? What if it had been a veiled way of saying that Lady Rosemary regarded her as an inexperienced country girl – his country wife, who would be content to keep house and raise his children at his country estate, while his erstwhile paramour might endeavour to provide him with stimulating company in town?

Anger swelled, but with it came a crippling sense of insecurity. Never in her life had she felt inferior to anyone, not while she had been an unmarried girl at Longbourn, and least of all since she had become Darcy's wife. She had rejoiced in the luxury of looking down on the likes of Miss Bingley and Miss Prescott. She could easily tolerate their malice – laugh at it – even allow herself the unholy satisfaction of revelling in their envy, for she was the one who had gained what they all coveted. Spiteful cats had never caused her to doubt herself, had never made her feel inferior – inadequate.

Yet she could not say the same of Lady Rosemary. The more she dwelt on it, the more she loathed the notion that, in comparison to that statuesque and highly sophisticated woman, she appeared as a *gauche* country miss – the genteel version of the fresh-faced milkmaid. Was that what Lady Rosemary had in mind, a Hertfordshire milkmaid, when she had avowed herself pleased with finding her young and fresh-faced? Pleased with finding her naïve, that is to say. Easily outmanoeuvred. Not a threat. No competition.

Did Lady Rosemary imagine that, before long, Darcy's marriage would go the same way as most of the marriages of the *ton?* The few months that Elizabeth had spent in town had been enough for her to discover that infidelity was not the exception, but the norm. Evidence abounded all around. The late Duke of Devonshire's *ménage à trois.* Lady Melbourne's constancy to her lover, not her husband. Her daughter evincing the same. Lady Oxford's offspring, collectively known as the Harleian Miscellany on account of their different parentage. Lord Paget abandoning his wife and children to elope with Lady Charlotte Wellesley, sister-in-law to Lord Wellington, and a mother of four.

Yes, she had heard the rumours, and Mrs Hurst was right in one regard: her upbringing was too conventional for her to condone the ways of the upper echelons. So she had silently pitied and despised them, but not for one moment had she feared that she and her beloved husband might become like them: distant, indifferent, leading separate lives.

She had taken on the world at his side. Had felt secure in his arms, in his home. Secure in their happiness – their own private fortress. And had remained oblivious throughout to the enemy at the gate.

Anger swelled again, and this time it was directed inwards. To think that she had often disdained Jane's generous candour! Her own wilful blindness was a vast deal worse. With infinite conceit and folly, she had always prided herself on her discernment, yet her errors of judgement had come thick and fast. She had trusted Wickham. Had found Mr Bingley amiable, and the perfect match for Jane. Had imagined that Georgiana was merely shy and reserved around her, and had failed to detect the simmering resentment and the active dislike. And she had seen a close friend in Lady Rosemary – the worst misjudgement of them all.

Eyes narrowed, Elizabeth stared at the guttering candles. She was no match for that poised and handsome woman. That woman his own age, who belonged in the same circles – most certainly not a country miss eight years his junior. If he should begin to draw comparisons – and why should he not? – it would not be Lady Rosemary who would be found wanting.

And what then? If he discovered he had made a poor bargain in choosing her – if she failed him in some fashion, failed to rise to the challenges presented to the mistress of Pemberley – if he wearied of her unsophisticated sameness – would he seek out Lady Rosemary again?

She flinched. Why ever had he not married Lady Rosemary while he had the chance?

Elizabeth sighed, weary to the bone. Weary of harrowing questions at the end of an exhausting evening. A needlessly exhausting evening – she could see that now. Aye, she had staged a good performance, but what of it? She could not continue in that manner, make her appearance at Lady Melbourne's musical *soirée* in a fortnight, greet

Lady Rosemary amicably and pretend that nothing was amiss, while everyone around them knew all that there was to know about their unwholesome trio – had always known, and likely snickered behind her back the entire time. And she the only one left in the dark!

Elizabeth curled her hands around the edges of the dresser in so tight a grip that her fingers ached. How *could he* leave her unprotected before their scorn? The least he could have done, the very least, was to disclose his history with that woman! As for allowing, nay, encouraging that *'close friend of his family'* to assist her in society… Heavens above! *What* was he thinking?

The violent flare of indignation revived her flagging spirits like a fiery potion. It was a bitter brew, but it gave her strength for what must come.

She drew a steadying breath and used it to blow out the candles, then unerringly made her way to the closed door.

～～

Elizabeth found her husband leaning against the headboard of the large bed, book in hand, his dark-coloured robe in sharp contrast with the snow-white linen. Darcy glanced her way as she stepped in, and set his book aside.

"I was wondering what was keeping you," he said, reaching to turn down her side of the counterpane. "Come, my love. Come to bed. You need your rest. 'Tis very late."

Aye. So it was: late. Too late for a restful, happy night. How was it possible that his gentleness should work to soothe and break her heart at the same time?

Elizabeth closed the door behind her until the latch engaged with a muted click, and advanced towards the towering piece of furniture, but stopped short of it and lowered herself into the wingchair beside the bed.

"Are you unwell?" she heard him ask, concern in his voice and countenance, as he stood, tightened the sash of his robe, then came to crouch beside her and reached to hold her hands. "You look very pale. Shall I fetch you some of those biscuits?"

Elizabeth shook her head. She did feel queasy, but this was nothing like the well-omened nausea of the last few mornings. It would not be cured with Mrs Blake's crackers.

"Mrs Hurst spoke to me this evening," she began in a strained monotone, then forced herself to say the cursed words, "of a past liaison between you and Lady Rosemary—"

She stopped short when Darcy's head snapped up, and even in the poor light of the solitary candle she could see him blanch. In dismay? Anguish? Anger?

He made to speak, but Elizabeth was there first:

"Did she lie?"

It was a wild hope, surging from his strong response and her sudden guilt. Had she been too quick to take the word of a known foe and believe the worst, on account of her own subconscious self-doubt? For, after all, one might ignore but could not entirely forget that country girls of fifty pounds a year and few accomplishments were a poor bargain for gentlemen of breeding and substance, who could have married into the best houses in the land.

The hope vanished as soon as it came.

It was shattered with just one quiet word:

"No."

The breath she had been holding left her lungs in a forceful rush, and Elizabeth slumped back in her chair as the hold of his hands on hers tightened into a fierce clasp.

"My love—" Darcy began, but she forestalled him, not in the least disposed to hear whatever hollow words he was about to offer.

She met his eyes and rasped, "Were there others?"

Under her intense scrutiny, his countenance settled into lines of discomfort as Darcy brushed the back of her fingers with his thumb and answered her question with another:

"Elizabeth, what would you have me tell you?"

"The truth. It is a simple question: were – there – *others?*" she enunciated, her voice crisp, as she drew her hands away and folded them together in her lap.

Darcy held her gaze, his mien solemn.

"No man should relate his past exploits to his wife."

Elizabeth flinched. There: she had her answer. How missish and unworldly of her to even ask! Of course there had been others! He was no schoolboy. He was nearing *thirty!* That particular aspect of his life – it had not crossed her mind to consider it until then, and she cursed Louisa Hurst yet again, this time for forcing the notion into her head, along with mental images, no less hideous for her inability to picture the other female faces that had preceded and succeeded Lady Rosemary. Other fashionable ladies of the *ton?* Kept women? Courtesans? Any and all of the above – and if so, how many?

She did not ask him that, afraid to hear the answer. Instead, she retorted, "Perhaps I should rephrase my question: are there any others with whom I have associated, or am likely to do so in future?"

The answer was another quiet, "No."

It brought little comfort.

"Thank goodness for small mercies," she tersely observed. "I should be loath to keep entertaining your acquaintances with the spectacle of the naïve wife unknowingly befriending her husband's former conquests."

At that, Darcy made to speak again, but she would not have it.

"*Why* did you not tell me?" she hissed. "I should have imagined that I deserved this much: to hear it from *you*, not gleefully and maliciously sprung upon me by Louisa Hurst, halfway through a social engagement!"

The bitter, long-withheld reproach was still gushing out when Darcy gave a murmur of deep contrition and raised his hands to her shoulders to draw her close. But Elizabeth would not permit that either, so he let his hands drop – only to flinch when she spoke of Mrs Hurst and her deliberate malice.

"That woman should be muzzled and kept on a leash!" he burst out, savage anger in his eyes.

"Yes. And I daresay I should like to see that," Elizabeth shot back. "But I wish I had the truth from *you*."

"*So do I*," he said with fervour. "Elizabeth, I was not—" He broke off and ran his hand over his mouth and chin, then shifted from his crouch to sit on the floor, beside her wingchair. "I tried to tell you," he wearily resumed. "A number of times. The latest this morning. But then you looked at me and smiled as you do when you are bent on mischief and teasing, and you were so happy… I… I could not bring it up," he finished with a sigh.

Elizabeth winced and briefly closed her eyes, as if to shield them from the morning's brightness. That joyous moment – she could remember it in exact detail. Yet now all the details painted a wholly different picture. His unease. His hesitation. His contrition, which had seemed excessive at the time. The tension giving way to resignation.

A self-deprecating huff left her lips. So, that was yet another instance where she had mistaken the matter. Her archness had not prompted him into sharing everything there was to be said. It had achieved the opposite.

She frowned.

"I cannot thank you for the attempt to spare my feelings. It went awry. And it is openness I favour."

"I know," he said, tracing the contours of her armrest, then drew a deep breath and sought her eyes again. "Elizabeth, I know I should have mentioned it on the day you met her. Not doing so was a severe misjudgement. But there was not much to tell. No, that was badly put," he amended. "Rather, there seemed to be no way of telling you without making far too much of it. And the more enjoyable and helpful you found her acquaintance, the more there was to lose once I brought up the past. The distant past," he said with emphasis, reaching for her hand once more, and this time Elizabeth did not oppose him, too caught up in what he had just said.

"Distant?" she echoed. "How distant?"

"More than five years ago. Even so, it might have altered your perspective and caused you to keep away. Which would have been a pity, because she genuinely *is* supportive and kind—"

"Is she!" Elizabeth exclaimed with renewed bitterness and a disbelieving snort.

It did not deter him.

"Yes," Darcy insisted. "And she has been acquainted with my relations for long enough to know that some of them would be cool and condescending, and that others in their circle would follow suit and close ranks against you. So you needed a friend. Preferably an influential one."

"And did you not imagine that the neat arrangement would be ruined once I heard about your history with her from another source? I daresay that a fair number of your acquaintances must have noticed your overt partiality at the time when the pair of you were '*practically inseparable,*' as Mrs Hurst had the goodness to put it."

A knot formed at the corner of Darcy's jaw as he exhaled.

"More fool me, what I did imagine was that they all saw it for what it was. Not partiality, Elizabeth. Not in that sense," he said, and there was something in his voice that softened hers by a degree when she asked, "Is there any other?"

His gaze still locked with hers, Darcy nodded.

"I think so. And I need you to believe that it was not some… tawdry entanglement," he resumed with energy, releasing her hand to give a quick, dismissive gesture. And then he looked away. "I sought her out because we had something in common. Her husband had just passed away after a long and horrible illness. My father was reaching the final stage of his. His health had been failing for some time, but the last few months were…" He swallowed hard. When he resumed, his voice was low and strained. "We came to town so that he might have his physicians close by, but there was no cure, and he knew it. So did I. And Georgiana. Father had asked me to prepare her, and…" He gave a faint, despondent shrug. "I did as best I could. But she was at school, thank goodness, so she was spared the worst of it."

Whereas he had not been spared at all. Elizabeth had already guessed as much, but now she could see it clearly in his haggard countenance. The pain was there, fresh and raw, just as it must have been before the passage of time could begin to soothe it. He was reliving the old anguish, and her heart went out to him. She could not help it, that surge of aching tenderness, and she made no attempt to stem it. She shuffled out of her wingchair and came to sit beside him on the floor. And when he wrapped his arms around her and drew her close, her heart twisted in her chest, for more than one reason.

She did not have the leisure to tease them apart, those reasons, and carefully explore them, because he spoke again.

"We all knew it was only a matter of time. He had already grown very frail and weak, and was almost constantly in pain. Dr Graham was here at all hours, but there was nothing he could do, just stupefy my father with laudanum. Towards the end, even that came to be useless. The laudanum scarcely did its office, and there was no relief to be had. By then, the worst part was not that the end was coming, but that it was not coming fast enough. And that I was pondering on ways of hastening it… and ending his suffering."

Tears rolling down her cheeks, Elizabeth put her arms around his waist and held him, just as he held her, while the harrowing confessions were whispered into her hair in a voice so ragged that he barely sounded like himself at all. She did not interrupt, but listened in silence, letting him speak – letting the poison come out.

And come out it did, in yet another noxious rush:

"That was the time when Rosemary was… a lifeline. A dose of sanity. She understood. She had borne the same while she had nursed Sinclair," he said, and the hoarse murmur brought a sharp stab of pain, deadlier and more immediate than poison.

The name had rolled so easily off his lips! Not the title, just the name, with all its heartrending intimacy.

The stab that followed a fraction of a second later was one of guilt. For, having learnt about the horrors of his father's illness, it was odiously self-absorbed of her to find the worst pain in the instinctive mark of intimacy, and the fact that *the other* had been at hand to comfort him, not she, at the time when he had been in the direst need of comfort.

The question burned on the tip of her tongue and it was callously ill timed, yet Elizabeth could not hold it back:

"Was that when the pair of you…?"

She could not finish, but there was no need. He knew her meaning. Naturally.

"No. Later, once my father had been taken home to Pemberley and laid to rest. I returned to town for Georgiana and…"

And had found an empty house in mourning, from which he had been driven away by loneliness and grief, to seek solace elsewhere.

Her face was averted, so Darcy could not have seen her flinch, yet he instantly resumed, as though he had guessed her thoughts and her aching need for reassurance.

"It was not— It was short-lived. A brief episode, if you will. Very brief, and certainly not public. But…"

But it had not remained as private as he had imagined. Was that what he had been about to say? For that was the fact of the matter: even if the *'episode'*, as he called it, had escaped public scrutiny, it had drawn notice close to home – had drawn the suspicious gaze of his best friend's sisters and had fuelled their jaundiced speculations. He should have credited that loathsome pair with a keen sixth sense, if nothing else!

She forbore to point that out – by now it must have been plain enough to him already – but remained still, her head on his chest, the steady rhythm of his heartbeats and the soft murmur of his breathing the only sounds that she could hear, until Darcy pressed his lips to her hair and spoke in a sorrowful whisper.

"I am grieved... shocked... that you were ambushed in so heinous a manner. I have always known that Bingley's sisters had none of his generosity and kindness – that they were self-absorbed and shallow and plagued by delusions of grandeur – but I was not expecting vicious cruelty. Nor did I imagine that, despite due discretion, an accurate guess was made as to—" He broke off and cleared his voice, then swiftly resumed, "Forgive me. That savoured strongly of deceit, and deceiving you was never my intention. I never meant to keep the truth from you, nor cause you pain – you know that, do you not? I am only seeking to explain why I thought I had sufficient time to decide when and how it should be made known to you so as to cause the least—" He heaved a deep sigh and pressed his lips to her hair again, before he choked out with anguished fervour, "I wish to God that I had found a way of telling you weeks ago! But I feared you would grow uneasy at finding her a permanent fixture in my aunt's circle, and you already had enough reasons for unease, real reasons, from my relations and their confounded clique. It seemed foolish and unhelpful to make you wary of one of the few people whom I could trust to show goodwill and lend assistance. Same as in Georgiana's case, I thought there was merit in you getting to know her first and forming your own opinion freely, without preconceptions." His shoulders rose in a sudden shrug of frustration, and his tone of voice grew acidly self-critical. "The glaring flaw in that plan struck me eventually. You would have never drawn that comparison. So my delay in giving you all the facts, however old and immaterial, smacked of concealment and duplicity."

'Oh, what a tangled web we weave!' Elizabeth might have scoffed a short while earlier, when she was still sustained by anger. But all her anger had been smothered by oppressive heartache.

Learning what he had endured – what his father had endured – tore at her heartstrings, but she never would have shied from that knowledge. She would have readily shared his anguish over his father's fate – shared it readily and devotedly.

The rest, however...

The rest was a dark shadow that could not be pushed away. That truth, once learnt, could not be forgotten. Not even if she quitted the haunts of the *bon ton*, hid at Pemberley, and never laid eyes on Lady Rosemary again...

"Which was precisely what she hoped for!" Elizabeth gasped, unthinkingly speaking her thoughts aloud, once several pieces of the hated puzzle had suddenly fallen into place.

Yet the forming picture was for her eyes only, which was no wonder, for she had yet to mention everything else that had come to pass on this wretchedly eventful day.

Her exclamation made her husband start.

With a disconcerted, "Pardon?" Darcy drew back to search her face.

"I think I can guess Mrs Hurst's game: she would have dearly liked to see me turning tail, and Lady Rosemary out of their way," Elizabeth began to explain, glancing up but briefly. It was hard enough to say the name, without meeting his eyes as she did so. And then she forced herself to say it again. "Lady Rosemary suspects Mrs Hurst and Miss Bingley of slyly seeking to promote a match between Georgiana and their brother. She made it clear enough to them this morning, when we came across them at *Harding and Howell's*, that she was minded to oppose their schemes. She dropped a few broad hints to that effect, and also taunted them with Lady Melbourne's *soirée*, to which they had not been invited. I can only conclude that they were hoping to drive us from town and continue to work upon Georgiana in your absence, to persuade her that she would be happier with them than at home. It seems to me that they have already been busy in that respect while we were away."

"Have they!" Darcy spluttered. "Busy doing what?"

Elizabeth gave a disdainful shrug.

"Oh, their usual tactics: twisting the facts, mixing honey with poison. I think they gave your sister an unflattering version of events. About the scandal in Meryton, I mean."

His countenance darkened.

"What did they say?" he asked, and Elizabeth shrugged again.

"I have no notion. Georgiana and I have not had the chance to cover the details. But I know she is troubled."

His brows still quirked into a frown, Darcy nodded.

"I noticed. Earlier this evening, when she was here. So this was the matter you were speaking of? The one that could wait until the morrow?"

"Yes. But now it seems that it can barely wait that long. Georgiana has made arrangements to go riding with them. I think she should sit with you instead, so that you might make her see that Miss Bingley and Mrs Hurst are not to be credited with good intentions. As for their brother—"

Darcy gave a small gesture of unconcern.

"I expect they hatched their schemes without him. He has no thoughts of courting Georgiana," he declared with no little confidence, and Elizabeth's eyes widened.

"Mr Bingley has spoken to you of this?"

He grimaced.

"After a fashion."

"But... would you have even wished to have him for a brother?"

"Perhaps. I know not." He shrugged. "I have not given it much consideration. Georgiana is full young. There is plenty of time for her to ponder on her choices."

"True..." Elizabeth said, averting her gaze as the inescapable heaviness of heart steered her thoughts away from his sister's choices – and drew them back to his.

She absently smoothed the lace of her dressing gown, her stare vacant, her mind's eye fixed on the shadow that was now stretching darkly over a place where there had been nothing but light.

"Will you tell me something?" she asked after a long silence, and found that her sombre tone brought a fervent ring to his whisper when he promptly answered, "Anything!"

She was not as prompt in voicing her question, but took her time, and chose her words.

"You said it was short-lived, your... association," Elizabeth finally began, only to falter as she came to the last word and inwardly chastise herself for taking so long, and still not choosing better. Association! How ludicrously prim and *gauche!* But be that as it may. She could not have used Mrs Hurst's sordid word again.

She opened her lips to resume, but Darcy spoke first:

"Elizabeth, it was—"

She did not wait to find out whether or not he was about to give her the exact duration, but forcefully shook her head and squeezed his arm to stop him. She did not wish to know! – she *did!* – she could not tell... and it was yet another torment to be assailed by such conflicting sentiments!

Even so, Elizabeth forced them down as best she could, so that she might give voice to a couple of her most tormenting thoughts:

"What I meant to say was that I cannot possibly imagine anyone more eligible, so… why did the pair of you not marry?"

The words tumbled out, and even as they did, she wondered how she was to bear it if he were to say that he *had* offered – and had been refused, for some unfathomable reason.

The matter remained undecided when he replied, "Because neither one of us wished it."

"You discussed it, then."

"Only to dismiss it."

"Why? It would have been a splendid match."

"Yes. And also a mistake."

From the moment when she had blurted out her most difficult question, Elizabeth had found herself enfolded once more in his embrace, her head resting on his shoulder, but now she shifted slightly and raised her eyes to his as she quietly said, "I do not follow."

Darcy's hand came up to brush a stray lock from her face before he made his answer:

"Strong-willed people are a good match only if they value the same things in life. Which she and I do not. Her life is in town. She relishes the fast pace, the influential salons, the frisson of high politics and power. She thrives among the fashionable set, whereas I can just about bring myself to tolerate them for brief periods of time, and only out of necessity. So there was every chance that an alliance between us would have led to estrangement or resentment or both. We would have traded a good friendship for a bad marriage – or at least a fraught one. There would have been advantages, of course – the obvious ones derived from her rank and fortune, and the ways in which she would have assisted Georgiana – and, all things considered, I might have found it a risk worth taking. But it was made clear from the start that she would take no risks of the kind. So yes, it was a short-lived association," Darcy concluded, for some reason choosing to make use of her *gauche* euphemism, "and it ended by mutual agreement for the sake of our friendship. And that is all there ever was to it."

He tightened the hold of his arms around her and pressed his lips to her brow when Elizabeth chose to lean into him and rest her head back on his shoulder. But her foremost aim had been to avert her eyes.

All that there ever was to it? No, not all. Not by a fair margin.

The harrowing experience that Lady Rosemary had supported him through had bound them in the most intimate ways. In ways that went a vast deal further than physical intimacy.

A few moments earlier he had insisted that theirs had not been some tawdry dalliance, and then had done his utmost to persuade her of that fact. Now that she was thoroughly persuaded, Elizabeth could only think, *'Would that it had been a mere dalliance, and nothing more!'*

A mindless flare of passion, soon spent and soon forgotten, she could have understood and easily dismissed. For it would have been as lacking in significance as the casual encounters – the trifling exploits which, as he had put it, no man should relate to his wife. But this was a connection that ran deep. A strong bond of confidence and affection. An unbreakable bond. And, for his sake, perhaps she should not even wish it broken.

Sadly, she could not find it in her to be as selfless as that.

How was she to ever learn to look beyond it? To know that this bond existed – and not mind? Not fear it a little? Not care that they shared memories of their time together? A Rosemary to remember…

A shiver coursed through her at that intrusive thought, and Elizabeth could not but suspect that she would need many years' worth of wisdom before she could begin to conquer it.

"You are cold," she heard him whisper, and was glad of his misapprehension. "You would be more comfortable under the counterpane."

But she shook her head and whispered back, "Not just yet."

Darcy made no protest, and she was glad of that as well. Instead, he reached behind them and drew the quilt that lay at the foot of the bed, then draped it over her and enfolded her in his embrace again. And silence reigned unbroken for a fair while, until he asked in a strained whisper, "What are your thoughts, my love?"

Her thoughts…

Elizabeth grimaced. Her thoughts were unbefitting any rational, self-respecting woman who valued honesty and honour – and she was suitably ashamed of them. For her overriding thought was this: she would have been much happier not knowing every facet of the truth. If his past had no bearing on their future, then she need not know it. She would have preferred to be spared that burden.

Yet if she were to make this tardy and pointless admission now, after demanding and receiving complete candour, he would be justified in saying that there was no pleasing some.

So she nestled her head against his neck and, instead of mortifying thoughts, she equably offered a question that troubled her not at all, for she already knew the answer:

"And Miss Endicott? Was she an option because she could have been moulded into the role, and the match would have pleased your sister?"

She felt his arms grow rigid and heard him sigh, doubtlessly at learning just how much intelligence had been forced upon her in a single day, but he did not comment on that. He stroked her hair and answered simply, "Yes. Just so."

'And I?'

The question sprang to mind and flared up like lit touchpaper – yet remained unspoken. She fancied she knew the answer to that, too. There was no need to request avowals. The feel of his arms around her was just as soothing, if not more. So she closed her eyes, and endeavoured to close her mind to questions for a while.

Chapter 32

Cosy darkness enveloped her as Elizabeth stirred and stretched, then nestled against her husband with a soft, contented little murmur. It came as second nature to her now, burrowing into his embrace, which was no wonder. Not once had she slept alone after the first ten nights of her married life – or nine and a half, if one was to be punctilious about it.

She could dimly sense the light clasp of his arms around her waist, and snuggled closer to the source of warmth and comfort. Yet as her head came to rest on his shoulder, a curious thought formed at the back of her foggy mind: it was odd that they should be abed…

Odd… yes… but why?

The bemused question pulled her out of sleep. The fog cleared, and she remembered everything. This was not like their other nights, from the time when life was blissfully simple and all was right with the world.

She heaved a deep sigh – and that was when she discovered that her husband was not asleep either. A light kiss was pressed to her brow, and Darcy's voice rumbled softly in the darkness:

"Talk to me."

Elizabeth tilted her head back and peered at him, but all she could distinguish was the contours of his face, not his expression.

"How long have you been awake?" she whispered.

"A while."

"What time is it?"

"I don't know."

She reached up and stroked his cheek, only to find her fingers twined with his and carried to his lips. Then he lowered their joined hands to his chest and urged again in a low and almost pleading murmur:

"Talk to me. No wall of silence, remember?"

Of course she did. How could she forget? The recollection of that glorious morning of joy and perfect harmony flooded through her, yet brought a dull ache to her heart. She had told him then that she expected future storms and troubled waters. But she had not expected *this*.

The treacherous tightness in her throat was sudden and vexing – beyond vexing – and, lips pursed, Elizabeth decided that mutinous muscles with a will of their own *would not* hold her to ransom.

She swallowed hard and forced herself to whisper, "No, nothing of the sort. 'Tis just that… I cannot talk a great deal of sense at the moment."

"I do not want you to talk *sense*," he countered. "I wish you would speak your mind. You need not spare me your reproofs. But I cannot bear your silence."

Elizabeth's hand twisted under his, so that she could stroke his fingers.

"I am not biting back fresh reproofs, Fitzwilliam. I understand. This belonged in the past – the whole of five years ago – and you wanted it left there—"

"Yes," he rasped. "Elizabeth, if I could go back—"

"Shh… I know, my love. I know," she said in a soothing whisper. They could not go back, more was the pity. There was nothing for it but to tend to their scrapes and wend their way forward. So she resumed, "What is left of my anger is reserved for Mrs Hurst and Miss Bingley. And much as I detest letting them claim any measure of victory, I have no wish to hold out simply to spite them. I am weary of malice, and I would rather go home."

"Oh… Very well, if you— If you wish," he sombrely replied, then cleared his voice and added, "For how long? Or is it too soon to know?"

His odd manner perplexed her, as did his questions.

"Well, I thought we might stay for as long as it pleases us, but—"

And that was when he stunned her with a relieved, "So, you are not aiming to go by yourself?"

"Of course not! Why ever would I?" she exclaimed, and felt him shrug, before he raised his hand and gave a vague gesture.

"Because of… all this. And also what you said the other day about Longbourn being a very busy place while your uncle and his family are visiting."

Touched, Elizabeth shook her head and tutted.

"Now which one of us is not talking any sense?" she chided softly. "I meant I would rather we returned to Pemberley, not Longbourn."

"Oh," he repeated, his tone markedly different, and Elizabeth chuckled.

"Oh, indeed," she teased and stretched up to brush his lips with hers, then pointed out, "In view of a certain ceremony last December, should it not go without saying that Pemberley is my home?"

"By the same reasoning, so is this house. Which must account to some degree for my confusion," Darcy said in a matching tone, but when Elizabeth spoke again, she chose candour over levity.

"This is a beautiful house, and I imagine I will grow attached to it in the fullness of time. But it is Pemberley that feels like home."

"Then let us go home. Would that we never left!" he whispered, his voice rife with feeling, as he weaved his fingers through her hair.

His lips caressed her cheek in their slow glide towards the corner of her mouth – too slow, to Elizabeth's way of thinking, so she did not wait, but turned her head to meet him in a long, healing kiss. And in a flash, what had begun with all the gentleness of a tender reunion became avid and urgent – a feverish hunger. A desperate need for each other, and for the way they were.

She wrapped her arms around him to bring him very close, and revelled in his fierce clasp when he crushed her to his chest.

Yet the shadows lingered – and in the end she drew her fervid lips from his to bury her face into his neck and gulp back the tears which, much like the abiding shadows and the rush of pernicious mental pictures, would not obey her will, and could not be suppressed.

⋆⊙⊙⋆

The note was handed to her when they came down for breakfast, both weary, both pale and drawn.

"This has just come for you from Gracechurch Street, ma'am," Peter informed her, and Elizabeth murmured her quiet thanks as she broke the seal and unfolded the short letter.

"Nothing amiss, I trust," Darcy offered, once he had dismissed the footman, and she shook her head.

"No, nothing. This is from Jane," Elizabeth explained, her countenance brightened by the welcome surprise. "She writes that she had decided to come to town on the spur of the moment when my aunt and uncle were ready to return, and is wondering when we might meet. You will not mind, will you, if I were to forgo breakfast and go to see her now?"

"No, of course not," Darcy replied, pressing her hand. "Let me order the carriage."

"Thank you. I expect I shall only be gone for a few hours."

"You need not rush back. Take as long as you wish. Our scheme was thwarted anyway."

Elizabeth cast him a faint smile. It had been a thoughtful scheme – a means of providing them with an occupation, lest they spend the day fidgeting about the house and treading on eggshells around each other, after the previous evening's heartache and dismay. He had suggested a drive to Kew as a distraction, and hopefully as a chance to speak with Georgiana and correct some of her misapprehensions. But they had awoken to a dreary morning – dull, leaden skies and unremitting rain – which had at least presented them with one silver lining: the wet weather had also done away with Georgiana's plans to go riding with the Bingleys. Thus, there had been no need for Darcy to ask her to cry off, nor had he been rushed into a difficult yet mandatory conversation.

Over and above her eagerness to see Jane, Elizabeth could be nothing but glad that her husband and his sister would now have the entire morning to themselves. Their discussion ought not be rushed, and it *should* be private. She had never seen much merit in claiming a share in it in the first place. Spending the morning with Jane and Mrs Gardiner would be a vast deal better – a profound relief, in many ways. The timing of Jane's unexpected arrival in town was most fortunate indeed. Almost as though her beloved sister had foreseen just how much she would need her.

But that fanciful notion savoured excessively of self-absorption, so Elizabeth discarded it at once. Jane must have come to town for reasons of her own. All that remained now was to muster some degree of patience, travel to Gracechurch Street and learn what those reasons were.

"So… you are engaged?" Elizabeth stammered, setting her cup of tea down with a quiet clatter as she endeavoured to digest Jane's momentous intelligence: three days prior, Mr Vincent had made her sister an offer of marriage!

"Not as such," Jane murmured, only to confuse her further.

"Not as such?" Elizabeth echoed, nonplussed. It was an odd response to a question commonly answered with a *'Yes'* or a *'No.'*

She darted her eyes from her sister to her aunt, and found that Mrs Gardiner was perfectly placid – a clear indication that no part of this was a surprise to her. And then Jane finally resumed and threw some light on the perplexing business.

"He did not wish for an immediate answer. In fact, he was adamant that I should consider the matter while I was away. Our dear aunt had already suggested I return with them, you see," she added, reaching out to affectionately press Mrs Gardiner's arm, "and arrangements had been made for my uncle to escort me back to Longbourn in a fortnight, when he is due to travel to Birmingham. It seemed… a good opportunity for reflection. And for my part, I am doubly glad of the chance to speak with you before making my decision."

"With me? Oh, Jane, I cannot presume to advise you," Elizabeth replied, daunted by the prospect of having a say in something of so personal a nature.

"No, that is not what I was hoping for," Jane promptly countered as she shook her head. "Not advice. Just that we might talk about this."

"Of course," Elizabeth whispered, overcome with compassion at the thought of her dear sister's struggles between common sense and an aching heart. "Let us talk of anything you wish, and I will listen. But first, pray set my mind at rest and tell me that nothing has changed from the last time we spoke, and you are not considering the match simply because it would make Mamma happy!"

"You may rest easy on that score," Jane declared firmly. "I am not swayed by Mamma's wishes. And before you ask, she knows nothing yet. It would have been both unkind and unwise to share this with her before leaving Longbourn. But as to changes from the last time we spoke…" She sighed, then raised her head to lock her gaze with Elizabeth's. "I cannot claim that there are none. For one thing, my sentiments have changed. I think… I believe I have grown to care for him… very deeply…" Jane faltered, then gulped. "I love him, Lizzy," she confessed – an explosive statement delivered in a whisper.

Elizabeth's eyes grew impossibly wide.

"You do?"

"I see what you are feeling," Jane replied with a self-conscious quirk in her lips. "You must be surprised, very surprised. You would be in the right to think me fickle, having seen me languishing about and sighing for Mr Bingley—"

"Of course I do not think you fickle! You have pined for him for long enough," Elizabeth exclaimed, her energetic protest nearly drowning out her aunt's, spoken just as swiftly, but in a calmer tone. "Besides," she argued, "you had only known Mr Bingley for a month—"

"Five weeks," Jane corrected her, and Elizabeth gave a little shrug.

"Five weeks, then," she conceded. "Whereas Mr Vincent has been at Netherfield for...?"

"Three months and a half."

"Quite. And you said so yourself: during that time, the pair of you have met often and spoken at length of weighty matters. You saw Mr Bingley at just a handful of gatherings, you dined with him, stood up with him on occasion, played at whist and spoke of commonplaces. Not the same, is it? And if we go further and begin to compare one man with the other – or rather a grown man mindful of his duties and a pleasure-seeking butterfly, here one moment, gone the next..."

"You do not mince your words," Jane quietly remarked, her gaze fixed on her fingers as she nervously smoothed a fold of her gown.

Elizabeth gave a vague gesture of agreement.

"He injured you," she said by way of justification. "Be it through carelessness or deliberate inconstancy, Mr Bingley injured you, and I cannot forgive him. Oh, Jane," she tenderly exclaimed, reaching out to clasp her sister's hand, "it would be such a relief to see you free of him! Yes, I will own that I *was* surprised to hear that you have formed an attachment to Mr Vincent – you were adamant that there was naught but camaraderie between the pair of you, nothing romantic. But I am ever so happy for your sake! If there is anything I can say for Mr Bingley, 'tis this: giving up the lease on Netherfield was the one good thing he has ever done, and he has my gratitude for that. If the place had remained in his possession, his hold on you would have endured. So yes, I am grateful that he severed all his ties to Hertfordshire, and Mr Vincent came to live there in his stead. Had Netherfield stayed empty, you would have known no better.

You would have clung to your recollections of the most amiable man of your acquaintance. And I say thank goodness that he cannot impose upon you any longer with his facile charm. The measure of a man is in his deeds, not his jovial manner. We can both think of at least one other example in support of that."

Jane cast her a mildly reproving glance.

"Oh, Lizzy, surely you are not comparing Mr Bingley to Mr Wickham!" she softly chided, and Elizabeth felt compelled to apologetically press her hand.

"Forgive me, but yes, on some points I do. And I am most certainly comparing Mr Vincent to—"

She broke off, startled by the avowal she had very nearly made.

It was her aunt who finished her sentence for her:

"To your husband?"

"Yes," Elizabeth owned, the surprise in her voice mingled with a new ring of conviction.

She recognised it now, that instinctive sense of the familiar and the reassuring that she had experienced at Longbourn on the evening when she had made Mr Vincent's acquaintance. He did remind her of her husband, and her brow furrowed as she sought to make sense of that.

Yet she could not. Not fully. She could not list clear similarities. It was everything and nothing: their reserve; their mien and manner of address; a certain something in their air, and in Mr Vincent's turn of countenance as he had followed Jane with his eyes from a distance.

When that last notion came to her, Elizabeth paused and pondered on it with no little interest. Yes, that *was* exceedingly familiar. It brought to mind the way Darcy had kept watching *her* whenever they had been in company together in the first weeks of their acquaintance. And that was later shown to be an unwitting sign of his growing attraction.

It was a heart-warming thought, and not just because it evoked poignant recollections. It boded well for Jane's future, too. If Mr Vincent's manner stood testament to his own attraction – if her sister was to be as cherished as she was – then Jane *would* find happiness at last.

Elizabeth stroked her sister's hand and pressed her lips together in a wry grimace as she silently chastised herself for not drawing all the parallels a great deal sooner.

She, of all people, was best-placed to do so. She had not been singled out with telltale signs of partiality either – not at first – yet, with hindsight, the hallmarks were there. She *should* have recognised them in another.

She cast a self-conscious glance towards Mrs Gardiner.

"You noticed too? Oh, dear. Now I feel quite foolish. I must admit that I was rather slow in making the connection. But, in my defence, I have only spent one evening in Mr Vincent's company – and not a quiet evening, either. Most, if not all, of our Hertfordshire friends were also in attendance."

Mrs Gardiner nodded, an understanding smile at the corner of her lips.

"Precious little insight can be gained over the course of a single evening, and a busy one at that. Merely the obvious, perhaps – such as the gentleman's reserved nature. But your uncle and I were privileged to have better opportunities for observation. And I believe it is safe to say that, much like your husband, Mr Vincent has a way of going about his business unobtrusively yet with great diligence, and does his best by those entrusted to his care. It was a pleasure to see him with his little girl, for instance. He is most affectionate and mindful of her welfare and comfort, just as Mr Darcy is with his sister. Which, by the bye, leads me to think that your husband would likewise make an excellent father."

Cheeks tingling with the heat of a sudden blush, Elizabeth gave a murmur of agreement and busied herself with retrieving her half-empty cup of tea as she wondered just how much her perceptive aunt had noticed. Had Mrs Gardiner guessed her secret already?

She took a sip of the now lukewarm beverage, and chose to let the matter rest. It was decidedly too soon to share her happy tidings, but above all, she would not steal her sister's thunder. Today was Jane's day – a time when they should speak of her beloved sister's tidings, and not hers.

"Well, thank goodness for new beginnings. I am so happy for you, Jane!" she said warmly, so as to bring the conversation back to its proper path.

Yet, to her surprise and concern, Jane flinched.

"Thank you," she replied in a low monotone. "But this is not— Not easy, is it? Nor as simple as it seems."

"Why not?" Elizabeth asked, her concern mounting.

"Because he *had* a wife, and he loved her – worshipped her," Jane brokenly whispered. "How shall I bear to be compared with a picture of perfection? Or endure the notion that he married me just so that Ella has a mother?"

"Is *that* how he put it?" Elizabeth exclaimed, making no effort to conceal her surprise and indignation, and at almost the same time Mrs Gardiner gave a murmur of dismay, which went to show that although Jane had told their aunt of Mr Vincent's proposal, this was the first time that she was sharing her anguished thoughts, and her reservations.

She went on to do so as she answered Elizabeth's question:

"Not in those words, no. He was very kind, very gentlemanlike, but he did not speak to me of love, Lizzy. He spoke of second chances, for both of us. And perhaps that should suffice… I daresay it *would* suffice many," she despondently said, then looked up and her forced composure crumbled. "But not me," Jane declared with quiet yet fierce energy. "It would not be a second chance for me. It would be another heartbreak. A lifelong heartbreak, in this case – and I could not bear it. Frankly, Lizzy, I would much rather beg the favour of ending my days at Pemberley, once I helped raise your children and grandchildren. I simply cannot bear unrequited love again!"

"You must not speak of begging favours," Elizabeth earnestly countered. "You know how happy it would make me to have you with me every day! But I wish you to have more than placid contentment. I wish you to find happiness too."

"Yes, well…" Jane sighed, but Elizabeth would not allow her to continue in that vein.

"What if Mr Vincent has his own concerns of a similar nature?" she suggested. "You said you told him everything. Have you considered that he had merely spoken of second chances because he is as daunted by *your* first love as you are by his?"

Her countenance alight with hope, Jane sat up and the corners of her lips curled up into a smile of tenderness and compassion.

"You think he might be?"

Carefully balancing her teacup so that she could reach out and clasp Jane's hand again, Elizabeth tentatively offered, "It *is* a possibility. So I think you should return to Longbourn and… look into it."

"It would explain why Mr Vincent insisted you take some time to consider the matter, rather than give him your answer then and there," Mrs Gardiner speculated, then patted Jane's knee. "For what it may be worth, dear girl, I agree: you *should* go home and see where you stand. And perhaps put your young man out of his misery," she added, only to bring her hand to her lips with a rueful little chuckle. "I beg your pardon, that was presumptuous. After all, Mr Vincent appears to be but a few years my junior. But that aside, I do believe you should return to Hertfordshire as soon as may be. I will speak with your uncle when he comes home this evening and we shall make arrangements—"

"Oh, I wish we had the chance to speak of this at Longbourn and save him a needless journey," sighed Jane, then glanced apologetically at her sister. "Forgive me, Lizzy, that was badly put. I should have been sorry to miss the chance of seeing *you*, but Uncle Gardiner must have his hands full now, and having him escort me hither and thither—"

"Nonsense, my dear," Mrs Gardiner affectionately chided. "Of course he will oblige you in so significant a matter."

"But there is no need to trouble him. Surely my husband and I can take you to Longbourn in his stead," Elizabeth swiftly intervened.

Yet no sooner had her relations thanked her for the offer than she began to see the glaring flaws in such a plan. They could not convey Jane to Longbourn on their way to Pemberley. Their return home would have to be postponed, for she could not possibly put so many miles between her and her dearest sister while Jane's happiness was hanging in the balance. And if everything went well – if a wedding was coming – then she would certainly wish to be at hand and share in her sister's joy.

She could order the carriage and drive Jane back, of course – but it would be unfair to ask Darcy to join them and leave Georgiana to fend off Mrs Hurst and Miss Bingley by herself – that is, assuming he could impress her with the full belief that they must be kept at bay. As for bringing her along to a place that was within a mile of Wickham... No, that was out of the question.

So Darcy would be required to remain in Berkeley Square. Elizabeth saw that now, and the realisation instantly brought to mind the previous evening and his ill-concealed dismay when he had misunderstood her meaning and imagined that she wanted to quit town and go to stay at Longbourn – without him.

She had disabused him of the preposterous notion, and she had no wish to resurrect it. This was not the best of times for them to be apart…

The sting of tears found her unprepared. Pressing her lips together, Elizabeth leaned forward to avert her face from her relations under the flimsy pretext of making room for her teacup on the table, and for a few brief moments flattered herself that she had schooled her features into a semblance of composure.

Yet she soon found that it was her turn to be disabused of preposterous notions.

"What is it, Lizzy? Are you unwell?" Mrs Gardiner asked.

"A little. A sudden headache…" Elizabeth dissembled.

She should have known better. Excuses of that nature were meant for strangers. Bound by the unwritten rules of polite intercourse, strangers were obliged to pretend that they gave credence to civil falsehoods. But affectionate relations obeyed different rules – and Elizabeth's sister and her aunt were quick to demonstrate that.

"Oh, Lizzy, don't!" Jane pleaded, edging closer to clasp both her hands in hers. "Don't hide behind fabrications! Not from me – us. You never get headaches! Something is amiss. What is it?"

"What distresses you, dear girl?" Mrs Gardiner gently pressed her for an answer too.

"Let me share your troubles, Lizzy! You listened to mine…"

"And *that* is the material point," Elizabeth said with no little difficulty. "You have troubles of your own. Today is not about me…"

"Why ever not?" Mrs Gardiner insisted. "Talk to us, Lizzy! If nothing else, you might feel better if you unburden yourself…"

Elizabeth choked out a muted sound of disagreement. She highly doubted that she would. She fought to stem her tears – blink them back – as she inwardly railed against her new and frustrating inability to keep a tight grip on herself and her emotions. But her emotions raged and the tears welled up beyond control. Persistent blinking achieved nothing. It merely made the tears spill over her cheeks.

"Lizzy, you are frightening me!" Jane gasped. "What is the matter?"

"Talk to us, Lizzy," Mrs Gardiner urged again.

Oh, how she wanted – *needed* – to speak out! Her dearest sister, her wise and decorous aunt – throughout her childhood and unmarried years, they had been her mainstay. Her only source of female guidance and comfort. And that much was true: for better or worse, she desperately needed to unburden herself.

And she did. Before she knew it, everything came out: the malice; the truth; Lady Rosemary; the bond forged between Darcy and that woman – that flawless woman who belonged in his world, and was so frightfully capable and strong!

"I am being unreasonable, I know," Elizabeth said at last, her voice raw with tears, as she furiously dabbed her eyes with her aunt's handkerchief, which had somehow made its way into her hand. "This... all this... is firmly in the past... and I should leave it there. But I cannot!" She crumpled the kerchief into a ball of fabric and brokenly whispered, "I cannot help it... I *am* doing my best to set this aside... put it from my mind... but it will not go away. I picture them together... And I cannot bear it..."

"No, of course not. I know. I understand," Jane murmured, wrapping her arms around her in a warm embrace – and as she rested her cheek on her sister's shoulder, Elizabeth silently chastised herself for thoughtlessly adding to Jane's wariness of a future with Mr Vincent.

"Forgive me," she rasped. "I should have known better than to tell *you* this... and put notions in your head."

"Oh, hush," Jane chided. She pressed her lips to the back of Elizabeth's muslin cap, then resumed, a hint of archness in her voice, "What, you think it has not crossed my mind, just because you are a married woman and I am not? I may be fairly naïve, Lizzy, but I was not born yesterday. Nonetheless, dearest, listen," she urged, clasping Elizabeth's shoulders and putting distance between them so that she could look her in the eye. "Listen, Lizzy: should you not be glad that your husband had someone to comfort him through the worst of his grief?"

"*Glad!*" Elizabeth echoed, and could not quite help the sudden flare of vexation. No one but Jane would be so saintly as to view things in such a light!

She dried her eyes and mumbled, "You have always put me to shame with your goodness, and this is no different." With a deep sigh, she dropped her hands into her lap and acknowledged, "You are in the right, of course. For his sake, I should be glad. But I have been nothing of the sort. I was – I *am* – distraught and horribly jealous that it was she, not me, who was there to comfort him."

"Aye. But nevermore. Your husband will now turn to *you*, and you to him, in times of grief and times of joy," Mrs Gardiner finally chose to speak and offer her own words of wisdom. "I know that peace of mind does not come easy – but then, nothing worth having ever does. Life is short, and it does not offer many blessings. This will sound sententious, I know, but we should treasure the blessings we are given, and not waste time and energy on prophecies of doom," she said, enveloping her nieces in a smiling gaze that was nothing short of maternal, then her air grew cheerfully matter-of-fact. "Now bear with me for one last truism, and then I shall be done: a modicum of faith goes a long way. I say have some faith in the men you love, and moreover in yourselves. So, they both encountered paragons at some time in their lives. Well, what of it?" she shrugged. "You had it from the man himself, Lizzy: he had no desire to marry Lady Rosemary. He married *you* – and until yesterday anyone with eyes in their head could see that the pair of you were exceedingly happy. As for Mr Vincent, he strikes me as a gentleman of sense and feeling, so I imagine he would not do something quite so foolish as to squander a second chance at happiness. And on this note, we shall have to reconsider the travel arrangements – for, as I see it, neither one of you should be away from home."

Chapter 33

Much as she would have wished to support her dearest sister at this time of momentous decisions, Elizabeth could not argue against their aunt's kind wisdom. Aye, both she and Jane should be where their heart was, so that they might find their way, and mend everything that was in need of mending.

Thus, it was not long until she alighted upon the most sensible solution: the Darcy carriage should convey Jane to Longbourn on the following morning, with a footman in attendance.

"Promise you will write as soon as may be!" Elizabeth urged, clasping her sister's hand, and her eyes misted as she hoped for happy tidings, and joyous preparations, and a wedding.

She steadfastly refused to dwell on the opposite – yet silently vowed to use all her powers of persuasion to entice Jane to Pemberley, at least for the summer, should it not be her sister's lot to find happiness in Hertfordshire.

The journey back to Berkeley Square seemed to take an age.

But at long last there she was, in the spacious entrance hall, with Thomas at hand to receive her outdoor garments, and Mr Howard hovering at a respectful distance.

"Has Mr Darcy gone out?" Elizabeth asked, and the butler was quick to answer.

"No, ma'am. I believe he is in his study."

It was all she needed to know.

She went directly, and found him not at his desk, but gazing out of the window that overlooked the gardens.

He spun round with a start, and his sombre countenance brightened into a tentative smile. Yet what she had in mind was a different sort of greeting.

Elizabeth crossed the room with quick, purposeful footsteps, and did not break her stride until she stood before him. And then she lost no time in twining her arms about his neck, and raised herself on tiptoe to press her lips to his.

A fraction of a second later, she was ensconced in his embrace, and an overwhelming sense of homecoming spread through her, loosening every form of tension and filling her heart with joy. This was where she belonged. *This* was home: beside him. She loved him. Trusted him. Their union was the greatest blessing she could hope for. Her aunt was in the right: blessings should be treasured. It was naught but unmitigated folly to look into his past and dredge up reasons to make herself unhappy over concocted prophecies of doom.

"I missed you," she breathed against his lips – which was absolutely true, but also quite absurd; she had been gone for less than four hours.

But when he tightened his hold and choked out, "And I you," she could not find anything absurd in it.

Nor could she doubt that this was a blissful homecoming for him too, and that he had ached for it as much as she. So she weaved her fingers through his hair and pressed herself against him, forcing aside uncertainty and folly and old shadows, until every coherent thought grew meaningless and hazy, and nothing mattered but their closeness, and the wild kisses that took her breath away.

Neither one drew back when they stopped for air. Her limbs fluid, Elizabeth leaned her head against her husband's chest and remained thus, relishing the tight clasp of his arms. She gave a soft sigh of contentment when she found that his hold did not slacken. It was precisely what she needed. She had no wish to be released.

As their ragged breaths slowed to a quiet murmur, wisps of thought swirled up, still far from coherent, yet their tenor was triumphant. She had prevailed over old shadows, for once. And if they should seek to intrude upon even more intimate moments, as they had on the previous night, then they would have to be driven back – again and again and again. There was nothing else for it.

Somehow, the prospect no longer seemed so daunting. This first victory made her bold, and more than a little giddy. So giddy as to archly muse on their inconvenient location – for, if they were in their own apartments, not his study, she would have been very much inclined to test that particular resolve.

But then she raised her head to press her lips to the corner of his jaw and told herself that there was a vast deal to be said for patience and an early dinner. It would not be the greatest hardship to wait a few hours more.

With that, Elizabeth forced herself to remember the world beyond the four walls around them. She stroked the unruly locks at his nape and asked, "Have you had the chance to speak with Georgiana?"

"Mmm?" Darcy mumbled, his mind quite obviously elsewhere. And then he seemed to gather his wits together. "Oh. Yes. We spoke."

"And?"

His lips tightened into a grimace.

"She has a better understanding of things now. I daresay there is no risk of Bingley's sisters imposing upon her any longer," he said darkly, and Elizabeth stroked his hair again.

"That is a relief. But I expect she was quite shaken. Come to think of it, I have not heard her in the music room when I came in. She must be still upset. 'Tis not like her to neglect her daily practice."

"No, it is not," Darcy concurred and sighed. "She went up to her chambers a while ago. Well... I thought I should give her some time to herself. I hope she will come down when she is ready."

Elizabeth nodded. Many ills were cured in time. With any luck, this would be no exception.

"I beg your pardon, it was remiss of me not to enquire after your relations," Darcy said, disrupting her musings. "How did you find them? I trust they are in good health."

"They are, I thank you." Praise be, everyone's health was good, if not everyone's spirits, she mused, then resumed, "But that reminds me: I offered Jane the spare carriage. She needs to return to Longbourn sooner than she had arranged with our uncle, but he had already taken time away from his business, and I fear that he would struggle to accommodate her. This would not cause you any inconvenience, would it?"

"No, of course not," Darcy assured her, and pensively added with a gesture towards the papers that lay scattered on his desk, making it look a great deal less tidy than usual, "There are a few matters that should be addressed before we leave town, but not many. In fact, I would have dealt with them this morning, if..."

His voice trailed off, but Elizabeth easily grasped his meaning. He would have seen to his correspondence already, were he not so distressed by the state of affairs between them.

Her heart brimming with a poignant mixture of love and compassion, Elizabeth pressed her lips to his once more. But what was meant as a brief and light offer of comfort came to be neither brief nor light. It swiftly turned into yet another flare of passion. Into an elated celebration, too – because the state of affairs between them was so markedly changed.

"Goodness, we are behaving like a pair of besotted newlyweds," she said with a breathless little laugh when Darcy's lips left hers to wander towards the hollow underneath her earlobe.

"So?" he chuckled in his turn – a low, throaty sound which she found quite as delectable as the host of feather-light kisses he had just begun to trail down the side of her neck.

"Nothing. 'Tis… as it should be," she said, a slight catch in her voice. "Still, you were saying something…"

"Was I?"

"Your papers?"

"What of them?" Darcy asked in a ragged whisper, sounding very much as though he was picturing his letters of business flying off his desk, so that it might be put to a use that had nothing in common with the one for which it was intended.

The notion set her cheeks ablaze – it was shockingly immodest. It was also shockingly appealing… Was his door perchance fitted with a lock?

Elizabeth might have asked that daring question, had he not raised his head to capture her lips and render her dizzy with another long, ravenous kiss.

And then, of the pair of them, it was he who came to his senses. To her disappointment, Darcy tore his lips from hers, but still held her close as he spoke with obvious difficulty – in an effort, she suspected, to distract himself from enticingly immodest possibilities:

"Those papers… Yes, I— They do need some attention… A few decisions to be made, some letters to write, a brief meeting with my man of business…" He cleared his voice and resumed, his tone more decisive, "All this could be resolved soon enough, so we should be able to leave for Pemberley in a day or two. If your sister is at liberty to remain in Gracechurch Street till then, we could travel together and take her to Longbourn on our way. Would you not prefer that?"

"I would," Elizabeth smiled at this fresh proof of his thoughtfulness. "But Jane had some tidings for me this morning – and now I hope you will not think that I am sporting with your patience if I confess that I had a change of heart and I would rather we did not leave town as yet."

"It makes no difference to me if we leave in two days' time or later," Darcy replied, just as she thought he would, and then followed that with an equally predictable, "What did your sister have to say?"

Elizabeth saw no reason why she should not tell him.

"Mr Vincent has made her an offer of marriage."

"I see," he said, greeting the intelligence with little surprise, if any. "Of course you would wish to attend the wedding. When is it to be?"

"Nothing is decided yet. Not even if there will *be* a wedding."

That did put a puzzled quirk in his brow.

"She does not wish to marry him?"

"She does. But she fears the dangers of an unequal marriage."

Darcy gave a quiet snort of disbelief.

"What is suddenly so dangerous about making a life at Netherfield?"

"Netherfield has naught to do with it," Elizabeth began to clarify her earlier choice of words. "It is a comfortable home, I grant you, and if that were everything she had ever wanted, the decision would have been an easy one to make. What she fears most is unequal affection, not the disparity in their circumstances. She had barely recovered from her heartbreak, and dreads rushing headlong into—"

Elizabeth did not even notice the slip of the tongue – not until Darcy cut her off with a swift and wary, "Heartbreak? What heartbreak?"

Flustered, she pressed her lips together.

"I should not have brought it up. Jane begged me to keep her secret, and it was hers not mine, so… I promised I would. Well, I suppose it makes no difference now. Much water has flown under the bridge, as they say across the Channel. But Mr Bingley broke her heart. It took her a long time to recover."

Darcy's arms fell from around her without warning, and Elizabeth found herself released from the tight embrace. Instead, his hands came up to clasp her shoulders and knead them with his fingertips, as though to comfort her. Yet, if anything, it was he who seemed in greater need of comfort. His countenance had frozen into horror, and when she pressed him to tell her what was amiss, his only answer was a faint, "Oh, Lord…"

"Fitzwilliam, *what* is the matter?" Elizabeth insisted in acute concern and raised her hand to stroke his cheek, only to see him flinching at the touch.

She bit her lip and let her hand drop. But, with a lightning-fast motion, so abrupt that it startled her, Darcy released his grip on her shoulders, caught her hand and brought it to his lips. He bowed his head, and remained motionless for a long moment. And then he lowered their joined hands and swallowed hard.

"This could not have come at a worse time!" he groaned. "After yesterday, you needed no fresh reason to—" He broke off and squeezed her hand almost to the point of pain. "But I should not— I cannot keep the truth from you. Elizabeth, your sister's heartbreak was not Bingley's doing. It was mine."

Her eyes widened into utter shock.

"*Yours?* How?"

"He did not return to Hertfordshire because I advised him against it."

"*Why?*" she choked out in a strangled whisper.

Darcy's reply was barely above a whisper too.

"I thought her indifferent." His voice gathered strength as he resumed, "I watched her closely, yet saw no symptom of regard."

With an indignant splutter, Elizabeth wrenched her fingers from his clasp and drew back. But for a quick move, as though to steady her, Darcy did not seek to detain her, and when she stopped to glare at him from two paces, he crossed his arms over his chest, his gaze clouded with contrition.

It could not appease her. It was belated, and of no use to anyone.

"What business had *you* to be the judge?" she fulminated. "Or Mr Bingley to take your view as gospel truth in so personal a matter?"

The thought of Jane suffering for months on end fuelled her anger at the pair of them and the damage they had caused with their blindness. She was so incensed that she could scarce heed him when Darcy made his answer:

"Bingley has always been exceedingly modest, with a stronger dependence on my judgement than on his own," he offered, but that was just as unlikely to appease her. It was a pitiful excuse, and did not speak well of either him or Mr Bingley.

And then another notion dawned, and Elizabeth gasped.

"Did you also advise him to give up the lease on Netherfield – and then claimed to have no knowledge of it?"

"No, I most certainly did not!" Darcy exclaimed, as though the mere suggestion was insulting – and, upon reflection, so it was, Elizabeth allowed.

She had accused him of outright deceit, and could not but feel ashamed of it already. She made to apologise, but he spoke first:

"However ill you think of me just now, you must believe that there was no duplicity—"

"I know," she intervened. "'Tis not your way, and my accusation was uncalled for."

Arms still crossed over his chest, Darcy raised his hand to give a faint gesture of acceptance.

"You are angry, and with good reason. I can only assure you that there was neither duplicity nor malice. Over the years, watching over Bingley has become somewhat of a habit. He had lost his head over a handsome woman before. But this was different. His partiality for your eldest sister was beyond anything I had ever witnessed in him. So yes, I did make it my business to observe her too, and just as carefully. It was plain to see that Bingley's attentions pleased her, but she did not encourage him with any sign of affection. I was—"

Whatever he was about to add remained unspoken when Elizabeth gave a bitter huff. Seemingly, her friend Charlotte had a much better understanding of the world than she. Months ago, Charlotte had declared that few had heart enough to be really in love without encouragement, and if a woman was too skilful in concealing her affection from the man who had inspired it, she ran the very real risk of losing him.

Her words had been proven eerily prophetic.

"I see your meaning," Elizabeth muttered, compelled towards fairness, for it *would* have been unfair to blame the man she loved for an error that was but marginally his. "I would have thought that *you* of all people would recognise reserve and understand the wish to guard one's feelings from the world's scrutiny," she could not help pointing out, a quirk in her brow. "Still, my childhood friend Miss Lucas had also remarked on the lack of encouragement, although she knew Jane's disposition a great deal better than you do. My friend warned that Mr Bingley might never do more than admire Jane in silence, if she did not help him on. Yet Jane did help him on, as much as her nature allowed. It was for him to give himself the trouble to ascertain her feelings, not you or Charlotte or anyone else."

Darcy exhaled.

"Thank you. That is… very generous," he said, relief in his voice and countenance, and came closer – close enough to take her hand. "Even so, now it is for me to tell him what her feelings are."

"*Were*," Elizabeth corrected him with some emphasis. "There is no point in raking over the ashes now, when she is in love with Mr Vincent."

"Is she really? She was in no haste to accept him," Darcy observed, but Elizabeth would not have it.

"That has naught to do with Mr Bingley!"

"Who, then?"

Elizabeth's lips tightened and she looked away.

"Mr Vincent's late wife, if you must know," she murmured, and flinched as she revealed the crux of her sister's troubles, which bore at least one stark resemblance with her own. "The bar was set so very high. Coming a poor second is a daunting business, and Jane fears it even more than—"

She broke off and bit the corner of her lip, but Darcy seemed to have no difficulty in guessing what she had stopped short of saying. With a sharp intake of breath, he released her hand and wrapped his arms around her.

"*You* have nothing to fear," he declared, his voice fierce, his eyes intent on hers. "Elizabeth, you are second to no one! Never were and never will be. My love, you must trust me on this, if nothing else!"

"I am making reasonable progress," she said, smiling through fresh tears as she twined her arms about his waist, and he gave a shaky chuckle, his gaze warm with tenderness and unfettered joy.

Darcy bent his head to press his lips to her brow.

"Are you? Thank goodness for that, then," he said – and Elizabeth wholeheartedly agreed.

Thank goodness for that, aye. And for him.

She was still nestling in his embrace when Darcy spoke again, his voice a low rumble in her ear as she rested her head against his chest.

"I must seek him out and tell him, Elizabeth. Bingley deserves to know."

She raised her head then, so that she might look him in the eye.

"You want to make amends for steering him away in the first place, and it does you credit, but it was he who chose to give her up. Frankly, I question both his strength of character and the depth of his devotion. If he truly cared for her, he would have stood his ground. You would have," she said simply – an instinctive declaration of love and trust. "But he cut and ran. Moreover, in all the months that we have been in town, not once did he enquire about her—"

"He did. He asked *me*," Darcy countered. "And he is as devoted to her as ever, I assure you."

Elizabeth's brow furrowed.

"Did he tell you that?"

"Not in so many words, but there was no need," Darcy replied with an uncomfortable grimace. "His proverbial zest for life and his carefree good humour have gone out of him. Not to mention that he used to be here at all hours, yet now he can scarce bear to see me."

"Because he resents the advice you have given him?"

"Because I am happy and he is not. And you remind him of your sister."

Disconcerted by the revelations and the sudden surge of pity, Elizabeth could only murmur, "Oh…"

She sighed, her heart aching for Jane, for Mr Bingley – the latest addition on the long list of those whom she had misjudged – and even for Mr Vincent, although she barely knew him. But, given all that Jane had to say about him, he, too, deserved better than to be denied his second chance at happiness.

If only they had spoken of this sooner, she and her husband, and brought everything into the open before it had come to this! But she had endeavoured to shield Jane and keep her secret, as Jane had begged her to, and all the while Darcy had sought to do his best by his friend. Yet all those good intentions had caused naught but heartache, and the age-old proverb had been proven true: hell was paved with good intentions.

Whichever man Jane chose, the other would suffer. And being asked to choose would make her wretched, too. Nevertheless, no one had the right to decide for her.

So aye, Mr Bingley *should* be told.

But only if Jane was in agreement.

⚬⊙⊙⚬

Elizabeth allowed her husband to escort her to the wingchair by the window and help her sit, as though she were made of spun glass.

"Rest a little," Darcy coaxed, "while I tell them to bring the carriage round again," and she did not gainsay him, although she felt in no need of rest.

She had already spent the best part of the day sitting – in her aunt Gardiner's parlour; in the carriage, on the way to Gracechurch Street and back – and at the moment she would have been far more inclined to pace about the room in agitation.

As soon as the door closed behind him, Elizabeth stood and began to do just that.

After some absurdly long deliberations dominated by his insistence that she did not tire herself with several journeys between Mayfair and Cheapside, they had settled on the one solution that was acceptable to both: he would accompany her when she returned to Gracechurch Street to speak with Jane, as he strongly felt that he should make his own apologies for his misjudgement and his interference. And then, if Jane granted her permission, he would go in search of Mr Bingley.

Beyond that, neither one of them could plan. Nor was there any point in speculating. Yet the futility of it was no deterrent as Elizabeth kept pacing back and forth across the room.

Soon enough, however, her unprofitable employment was brought to an end by a timid knock. At her invitation, the door opened and Georgiana ventured in, her footsteps hesitant and her mien that of a chastened schoolgirl facing the headmistress.

Whatever the young girl had been told that morning had not fallen on deaf ears, that much was clear from Georgiana's manner, so Elizabeth cast her an encouraging smile as she mildly informed her, "Your brother will return directly. He has only just stepped out."

"I know. I caught a glimpse of him as I was coming down," Georgiana murmured, smoothing the fringes of her shawl with small, nervous gestures, and eventually summoned the courage to glance up and carry on. "It was you I was looking for. Peter said I would find you here, and I wanted…" She flinched as her voice trailed off. And then she clasped her hands together, drew a deep breath, and a forceful rush of words burst forth. "My brother spoke to me this morning and gave me the full story. He told me that Wickham was to blame for everything – *again!* I knew next to nothing, and I believed the worst. So gullible and witless! And abominably rude to you… My brother did not take me to task for it – and if he knew, he would have. Thank you… He said you were exceedingly kind, and you are. Kinder than I deserve. Thank you for keeping your word and not telling him that I was so horrid. I should have had the decency to tell him myself – what I said – how I acted. But I dared not distress him further. I have given him too much pain already with the disharmony I caused between you. He was in the lowest spirits while you were away. But he looked no different when he left this room just now. Grim-faced… Distraught… So I fear that the pair of you are still at odds, and I'm sorry – so sorry! I never meant to make him wretched! And yet I hardly ever seem to do anything else!"

The last couple of words were half-lost into a muffled sob, and her eyes filled with tears. So did Elizabeth's as she closed the remaining distance to wrap her arms around her anguished sister, only to find with some astonishment and deep compassion that, far from rejecting her and her impulsive gesture, Georgiana clung to her and wept brokenly, piteously, violent sobs racking her whole frame.

"Sh-sh-sh, do not distress yourself. This was not your doing," Elizabeth said, stroking her hair. "You have not caused disharmony between us, and your brother is not wretched. He is concerned about a different matter – an old misunderstanding that needs to be addressed. We were about to go and seek to fix it. He rushed out to order the carriage. That is all."

The young girl's sobs had subsided as she listened.

And then she whispered, "Truly?"

"Yes, truly."

Georgiana exhaled, yet kept her head on Elizabeth's shoulder, and her arms around her waist.

"Can you forgive me?" she asked at last, still not drawing back to meet her eyes.

"Of course. 'Tis others who hold the lion's share of the blame, not you. Grown women, moreover, who should have known better. Besides, you love your brother dearly, as do I, and with that in mind, I think the pair of us should be able to forgive each other a great many things, as and when the need arises," Elizabeth chuckled softly and dropped a kiss into her sister's flaxen ringlets, touched by Georgiana's newfound openness and her unspoken need for affection, and just as glad to see an end to the hostilities.

They would go home to Pemberley, and start again. But first there was one more crucial thing to wish for: that, one way or another, Jane's happiness would be secured as well.

⋙ ⋘

Mrs Gardiner's parlour was very quiet. The moment was too fraught for idle conversation. Because – after a taxing interview with Elizabeth, followed by some deeply awkward minutes once Darcy had been allowed to join them – Jane had agreed to see Mr Bingley. Darcy had hastened to Mayfair to track him down and fetch him. And now he was in the adjoining room, speaking with Jane.

A glance at the clock on the mantelpiece told Elizabeth that a mere quarter of an hour had elapsed since Mrs Gardiner had closed the door between the parlour and her sitting room as a sign that she understood their need for privacy and silently sanctioned it, and then had returned to her seat on the sofa to feign interest in her needlework.

For her part, Elizabeth had no such means of employment, and neither did her husband. Darcy had just posted himself at one of the windows, something which Elizabeth had long learnt to recognise as his habit whenever he was preoccupied or troubled – and it was no wonder that on this occasion he was both. It was only due to Jane's angelic goodness that she had granted her forgiveness for his interference, and he knew it. Even so, *that* conversation had been awfully difficult. And goodness only knows how Mr Bingley had received the tidings. One thing was certain: when the pair of them had finally made an appearance in Gracechurch Street, they both looked uneasy and grim.

Another glance at the clock only served to show that the arms of the timepiece were moving unspeakably slowly. Elizabeth sighed and looked away. And yet she could still hear it, the maddeningly objective tick-tock that obeyed its own rules and cared not one jot for people's wishes, their troubles or their whims.

She glanced up and cast her husband a faint smile when, presumably prompted by her sigh, Darcy left his post and came to sit beside her. He covered her hand with his, and their eyes met to exchange matching looks of concern. Then he leaned back into the seat and, still holding hands, they waited... and waited... almost as though they were sitting just outside a sickroom where an examination was conducted, expecting the physician to come out any moment now, to let them know whether or not there was any hope.

The feeling was nothing short of eerie.

And then, all of a sudden, there was movement – footsteps – voices.

But they were not coming from the nearby sitting room.

The unexpected burst of activity was in the entrance hall.

A furrow in her brow, Mrs Gardiner set her needlework aside, yet before she could rise to her feet and seek to discover the cause of the disturbance, the door of the parlour was flung open and Mr Bennet came in without waiting to be announced.

"Papa! What brings you here?" Elizabeth exclaimed, leaping from her seat, just as the door behind her opened and her sister joined them, drawn by the commotion. Darcy rose too, as did Mrs Gardiner, and the latter asked, an anxious ring to her subdued voice:

"Not bad news, Brother, I hope...?"

"What else, my dear?" Mr Bennet said bleakly, making no attempt at equivocation. "Not the worst, rest easy. No one is in any danger to life and limb. 'Tis Lydia. She has eloped. With Wickham," he imparted, his eyes coming to rest on Darcy – the one most likely to understand the implications.

Elizabeth gasped, her horrified glance darting from her father to her husband, then her sister, and she saw Jane blanch.

It was only when she followed Jane's fixed gaze that Elizabeth learnt why her sister looked so stricken. There was more to it than the ghastly tidings. Mr Vincent had just walked into the room.

Chapter 34

"As you are here, I take it that they are not headed to Scotland," Darcy said – the first to speak after the dreadful announcement.

"They are not," Mr Bennet confirmed. "Vincent's men have made enquiries at several inns and toll houses on the way to the North, but no such people were seen to pass through. The one good fortune of the day was that he chanced to be at Longbourn this morning, when the mischief came to light, so his men's efforts saved me the inconvenience of rushing up and down the country on a wild goose chase. They soon learnt that a couple answering Wickham and Lydia's description had driven southwards in a hired chaise. We traced them easily to the Tyburn turnpike, but no further. They were last seen at the *White Hart*, where they dismissed the chaise and removed into a hackney coach."

Mr Vincent showed no inclination to contribute to the narrative. Having greeted the assembled company with a restrained bow, he lost no time in approaching Jane.

"They *will* be found," he said, his voice firm yet low, as though his words were meant for her alone. "Have no fear. This will be set to rights as soon as possible."

"Thank you," Jane murmured, a patchy blush spreading over her pale cheeks.

Across the room, Mr Bennet resumed speaking:

"The number of the hackney coach could not be discovered. The proverbial needle in a haystack," he scowled. "Which is why we abandoned that fruitless exercise, and Vincent suggested we involve his erstwhile batman in the search."

This time, the gentleman pressed Jane's hand in reassurance and stepped forth to have his say.

"Sergeant Rolfe is discreet and entirely trustworthy. More to the point, I have good reason to think that he will not disappoint. Ever since he quitted the army, that is precisely how he made a living: from finding people who do not wish to be found," Mr Vincent pithily explained.

"So, Darcy, I was hoping you might know a thing or two of the rogue's old haunts, so that Rolfe could be told where he should begin," Mr Bennet intervened. "We stopped in Berkeley Square on the way, and discovered that the pair of you were here," he said, encompassing his son-in-law and his second daughter in a weary glance – only to quirk a brow and splutter, "Ah. And so is Mr Bingley. Well… that is a surprise."

Pressing her lips together in no little vexation, Elizabeth inwardly allowed that Mr Bingley was duty-bound to eventually make his presence known. He could not very well lurk in the sitting room indefinitely, despite his understandable unease at intruding upon a moment such as this – to say nothing of his disappointment that his portentous interview with Jane had been interrupted. So Elizabeth did not wonder at his bleak air of discomfort. Yet, at this point, she could spare but little sympathy for Mr Bingley. It was her sister who deserved the greatest share. Acute mortification seemed to stifle Jane like a heavy pall. As for Mr Vincent, his dismay – sharp, raw and beyond concealment – earned him a great measure of Elizabeth's sympathy as well.

It was Mrs Gardiner who broke the short and awkward silence. She spoke to perform the introductions – a mandatory task, but not in the least likely to dispel the awkwardness. Quite the reverse. The oppressive discomfort grew into a thick mist, invisible yet suffocating, as the gentlemen exchanged stiff bows, and Mr Vincent laboured to school his countenance into blandness.

Mr Bingley made no such effort – or if he did, his efforts failed him. Yet it was Mr Vincent's ashen face and the look in his eyes that spoke volumes to Elizabeth, and the old sense of the familiar struck her more forcibly than ever when she saw him struggling for control and seeking to resume the original discussion, as though he were not so shaken.

"If we might return to the matter in hand, knowledge of Wickham's old haunts would be of use to Rolfe," he said, his voice growing steadier as he continued, "Does anything spring to mind, Mr Darcy?"

"Not about his haunts, no. I thought too ill of him to keep track of his pursuits. But I can think of someone who would be all too glad to aid and abet him: a Mrs Younge in Edward Street," the answer came in a few terse words, which made Elizabeth cringe.

She had already heard that name on the day when her husband had disclosed Wickham's sins against his sister. Mrs Younge was the perfidious companion who had colluded with the rogue to bring about Georgiana's ruin.

And then Darcy spoke again, filling her with an unbearable sense of shame and obligation when he urged, "In fact, I think we should investigate the place directly. Time is of the essence. With any luck, we might locate our quarry without Sergeant Rolfe's assistance."

Elizabeth raised her eyes to his at that, and clasped his hand, painfully aware of what he had just shown himself ready and willing to endure for her sake. Not only the disgrace that Lydia's folly had forced upon them all, as though that were not bad enough, but also the revolting prospect of meeting, cajoling, perhaps even bribing that vile woman whom he abominated and despised!

"I am distraught that you should have to do this," she murmured for his ears alone, and could scarce be comforted when Darcy whispered back, "Think nothing of it! Elizabeth, I beg you would not distress yourself. It must be done. I imagine that—"

Whatever he was about to add remained unspoken, for Mr Bingley saw fit to join them and cut in:

"Might I be of assistance, Darcy? I would very much like to help in any way I can. What would you have me do? Name it, and it will be done!"

Elizabeth frowned, irked by his intrusion – and, truth be told, by his request as well. Mr Bingley's wish to help was commendable, and it was to his credit that her youngest sister's infamy and her family's dishonour did not make him turn tail and run, but none of the others were in need of precise instructions.

She barely suppressed a huff. What else did she expect of someone who lacked the confidence of his own judgement?

"Pardon?" Elizabeth heard her husband say, and she could not tell with perfect certainty if he was as put out as she, or merely disconcerted. "Ah, yes, there is something. You can take my carriage and fetch Fitzwilliam. Seek him at home. If he is not there, my uncle's people will know where you can find him. Then join us in Edward Street, at number thirty-four. Look for a large, three-storied house. If our searches take us elsewhere, I will be sure to leave a footman waiting for you with directions," Darcy said, but it did not seem to be what Mr Bingley wished to hear.

"Oh? I was thinking you might want me to come along and lend a hand, but… Very well. I did say I would do whatever is needed, so I will fetch Fitzwilliam if you require his presence."

"I do not require it, as such. Knowing him, he *would* wish to be involved. Never mind, though. One of my people can convey the message," Darcy replied with a vague gesture, but Mr Bingley shook his head.

"Nay, I see your meaning. That would delay matters. At least I can gain admittance where a footman would not. I shall go directly, and meet you there. At number thirty-four, you said?"

Darcy nodded by way of both thanks and confirmation, and turned away as he resumed, "So, I imagine you would choose to wait here for now—"

"Frankly, yes, I would," Mr Bingley cut him off for a second time, only to grow beet-red and flustered when it belatedly occurred to him that Darcy's words were meant for Elizabeth, not him. He cleared his voice and stammered, "I will see you in Edward Street as soon as it can be arranged."

At any other time, Elizabeth might have reflected on his plight with no little compassion, for this was shown to be a most challenging day for Mr Bingley. But, all things considered, it was a wretched day for everyone. So she left Mr Bingley to bid his adieus and make his exit, and kept her eyes trained on her husband as he softly spoke:

"Pray do not fret, and seek to rest. You have taxed yourself too much already. All will be well, my love, one way or another. I cannot say as yet how long this will take, but I shall not stay away a moment longer than strictly necessary. I hope that a message can be conveyed to Georgiana to let her know that we are detained. Not the particulars, perhaps," he grimaced. "At least not yet. But she should know that we will be late."

"Oh, yes, of course. I will ask my aunt to send someone at once," Elizabeth assured him – and suddenly she was aghast to find herself shockingly like her mother: volatile, irrational, incapable of self-restraint. It was a frightful sensation, that rising tide of senselessness and ungovernable panic, yet she could not fight it, and soon lost the will to try. She gripped his hand and fervently entreated, "Promise me – you *must* promise me that you will not do anything foolish! I will not draw an easy breath unless you promise me that I need not fear for your safety!"

Goodness, she verily sounded like her mother, too!

Any moment now, she would begin to speak of tremblings and flutterings, and tell him that her nerves were torn to shreds! But that was neither here nor there, Elizabeth decided, and breathlessly repeated, "Promise me that you will not put yourself in harm's way, Fitzwilliam!"

Of the pair of them, Darcy was the one with sufficient sense as to maintain some decorum and not kiss her in her aunt's parlour and in her relations' presence. The passion was confined to his ardent tones when he promptly made his answer in a low and fervent murmur:

"Good Lord, Elizabeth, why would you even think that I would risk what we have for the likes of *him?* A reckoning is long overdue, I grant you. But rest easy, my love. I will not call him out."

⋄⋄⋄

Mrs Gardiner's parlour was quiet once more, ever since the gentlemen had laid the battle plans and set out on their mission. A messenger had been dispatched to Berkeley Square with a few tactful lines for Georgiana, and another brief but far more revealing note had been sent to Mr Gardiner at his warehouse. Then there was naught to do but wait, speak in hushed tones and seek to comfort each other.

As Elizabeth knew full well, it was her sister who was in the direst need of comfort. Arms wrapped around herself and pale as a sheet, Jane sat on the edge of the sofa staring blankly into space, her desolation plain for them to see. But there was little succour that Elizabeth and her aunt could offer apart from sweet tea, which Jane would not touch, and gentle words, which could not soothe her.

For quite some time, she did not even seem to hear them. But she flinched when Mrs Gardiner said, "Let us not dwell on the worst that could happen. If Mr Darcy is correct in his assumption and this Mrs Younge is the one whom Wickham relied upon to shelter them, then they might be found in time, before Lydia is utterly ruined. If she is returned to us before any real harm is done, then this could be hushed up—"

"Should we not send an express to Longbourn?" Elizabeth said swiftly. "I should not wish to give Mamma false hope, but there will be no chance of hushing anything up if she shares the whole story with all and sundry."

"She will not. Mamma must have taken to her bed at once," Jane spoke for the first time in many minutes, her tone of voice eerily flat, and however perturbed by her air of unnatural detachment, Elizabeth found merit in that comment.

Jane was probably right, she inwardly allowed. In all likelihood, their mother was now seeking solace in smelling salts, nerves, tears and lamentations of regret, while keeping her state in her bedchamber in a bid for sympathy and attention. So the unhappy tidings would go no further than the servants and Mrs Phillips. Mrs Hill would keep the servants in check. As for Mrs Phillips, she had a little more restraint than their mother – or rather, a better sense of self-preservation.

Yet the meagre reassurance that stemmed from such reflections could no longer hold Elizabeth's interest when Jane leapt to her feet, the disquieting blankness in her countenance giving way to pure anguish.

"I wish with all my heart that poor Lydia is found," she exclaimed. "It would be a wretched fate indeed to pay with a lifetime of misery for a moment's folly. She made a frightful error, but she is young, barely more than a child. I have no such excuse for my poor judgement!"

"Jane, you cannot possibly compare—" Elizabeth countered with energy as she left her seat to clasp her sister's hands. "You have done nothing wrong!"

Jane winced.

"You did not see his face, Lizzy," she mournfully whispered. "He came to me – he loved me enough to come to me, although he knew full well that our entire family must partake of Lydia's disgrace. Even so, he assisted Papa in the search... came all this way for my sake – and found me in cosy conversation with Mr Bingley!"

"You must not lose hope!" Elizabeth earnestly urged her. "If he came to support you in our time of trouble, you must believe that he loves you enough to hear what you have to say."

"I... I tried to have my say," Jane disclosed, her eyes brimming. "Just for a few seconds, I could speak privately with Frederick— with Mr Vincent," she needlessly amended, "and I told him that

I *had not* planned this. That I did not travel to town so that I might meet with Mr Bingley. I—" she faltered, and drew a shuddering breath. "It made no difference. I could not even tell if he believed me! He merely said that I should not make myself uneasy… that it was of no consequence… Of no consequence!" Jane brokenly repeated, tears rolling down her cheeks. "And then he told me that I should not consider myself under any obligation – that I should disregard what he said a couple of days ago – and at that very moment Papa said he was ready to set off. I barely had the chance to stammer that I could not disregard it, but that was not enough… It was a foolish thing to say. I did not see it at the time… and now I cannot put it from my mind. It made me sound as if I *was* speaking out of obligation. I should have said that I had not the slightest *wish* to disregard his offer of marriage! If I were not such a hopeless ninny, I should have given him a sign… any sign. I should have done *something!* At the very least, I could have held his hand. No, that would have been just as useless," she retracted, prey to unabated agitation. "It could have been misconstrued as pity. What I should have done is take him aside the moment he stepped through that door and tell him that *he* is the one I love – the one I wish to marry. If he will have me."

Elizabeth eyed her with no little astonishment.

"So… your mind was made up, even then?" she asked, and Jane sighed in unconcealed exasperation.

"Oh, Lizzy, I told you this morning what my only fear was: that he did not love me enough. As soon as I saw him walking into this room, I knew that my fear was unfounded." She winced and clasped her hands together. "Oh, I should never have agreed to see Mr Bingley! But it seemed cruel to him and churlish to your husband to refuse, and—" Jane heaved a deep sigh as she gave a vague, despondent gesture. "He has been in my thoughts for such a length of time… I needed to know how much of that was him, and how much an image I painted in my imagination."

"And?" Elizabeth and Mrs Gardiner prompted in one voice.

Lips twisted into a grimace, Jane darted her eyes from her sister to her aunt.

"I can see it now: my sentiments for Mr Bingley bore all the markings of a schoolgirl's infatuation. I should have had more sense at two-and-twenty, but—"

"You should not be so severe on yourself," Mrs Gardiner said with great gentleness. "Such is the way with one's first attachment: it possesses a particular charm, which dazzles the eye and gilds every flaw."

At that, Jane settled a solemn look upon her aunt.

"Did you see flaws in Mr Bingley?"

"Jane dear, I have just met the gentleman," Mrs Gardiner said mildly. "The material point is, did you?"

Kind-hearted as ever, Jane gave a little flourish of her hand that seemed to say *'No matter.'* But in the end she chose to share her thoughts with her dearest relations.

"I... Well, I could not help thinking that he could have spoken less of Mr Darcy's role in our estrangement, and more of his own."

Elizabeth's eyes widened.

"He blames my husband?" she spluttered.

"Not entirely, no," Jane hastened to reply. "You must not think too ill of him, Lizzy. Do make allowance for his circumstances," she generously argued in defence of her irresolute suitor. "So far, he has spent his life being his father's son – Mrs Hurst's and Miss Bingley's younger brother – Mr Darcy's callow friend. Is it any wonder that he has yet to learn the habit of responsibility? He is still trapped in adolescence... whereas I am not. Not any longer. If he had stayed with me— Nay, even if he had left Hertfordshire but kept the lease on Netherfield and returned to me today, I do believe we could have been happy as we grew into adulthood together. A dollhouse sort of happiness perhaps, yet gratifying all the same, because neither one of us would have known any better. But... now I do know better. I *am* grown up already, and playing house is no longer as appealing as it was. I need more, and I need it to be real. I need to be Frederick's partner in life, not a placid figure in a dollhouse."

Her eyes misting, Elizabeth nodded. A dollhouse arrangement was a poor substitute for a true union. She was about to wrap her arms around her sister and say as much, when Jane glanced out of the window and gasped.

"Goodness, can it be? Look, Lizzy! *Look!* 'Tis Lydia and Mr Wickham!"

Chapter 35

With a flurry of skirts and a rapid staccato of footsteps on the floorboards, Elizabeth and her relations darted out of the parlour and rushed to open the front door without even waiting for the knock, let alone the servant assigned to that duty. They breathed sighs of relief when they were given proof that they had not been suffering from some collective delusion. Lydia was indeed standing on the threshold. But when Mrs Gardiner opened the door fully, they also discovered something else: that a redcoat looked much the same as another when his back was turned. The officer they had espied from the window as he had assisted Lydia out of the hackney coach was not Mr Wickham, but Lieutenant Denny.

Lost for words, Elizabeth stared. Her aunt and her eldest sister were faring no better. It was Lydia who broke the stunned silence:

"Good gracious, you look as if you have just seen a ghost," she chuckled. "I am very much alive, I assure you, and so is Denny. Do you suppose we might come in?"

The brazen flippancy of the remark only served to increase Jane's bewilderment, but it had a contrary effect on Elizabeth and her aunt. Brow arched, Elizabeth stepped out of the way. As for Mrs Gardiner, she settled a long, stern gaze upon her unrepentant niece and motioned the newcomers within with a stiff gesture and a crisp, "By all means."

Of the pair of them, it was Mr Denny who had the grace to show some embarrassment about Lydia's nonchalance and lack of manners as he bowed to Mrs Gardiner.

"Regretfully, ma'am, I must decline. I wished to ensure that Miss Lydia arrived here in safety, but duty calls, and I must away."

"So soon?" Lydia pouted, possessing herself of his arm, but the lieutenant patted her hand and cast her an apologetic smile.

"I fear so. I should not leave Chamberlayne to hold the fort for very long, lest Mrs Younge and her minions be moved to help Wickham escape—"

"He is still there, then? At Mrs Younge's house, in Edward Street?" Elizabeth cut in.

"The very place," Mr Denny confirmed, with no little surprise at her good information. "So, you knew where he was hiding?"

"My husband made a guess," came Elizabeth's laconic answer, and then she saw merit in elaborating: "I expect he is there now, along with my father and several others. They left some three quarters of an hour ago."

Lydia released Mr Denny's arm to smother a giggle in her fist, and Elizabeth could not suppress the urge to glare at her. Whatever did she find quite so diverting in this ignoble circumstance of her own making?

"Wickham is having a goodly number of unexpected visitors today. Oh, I would have given anything to see his face when he laid eyes on Mr Darcy," Lydia chortled, and this time Elizabeth did not feel so inclined to censure her, but grudgingly allowed that the notion *was* darkly satisfying. "I hope Chamberlayne has a good memory, so that he can give me a faithful account of the entire business when I see him next," Lydia added, and Mrs Gardiner could not fail to respond to that, no doubt reminded, along with her two eldest nieces, that they, too, would appreciate a full account of everything that had come to pass on this most eventful day.

"We should not loiter in the doorway," she said with determination. "Come, Lydia. And you likewise, Mr Denny, if you wish. By the sound of it, Lieutenant Chamberlayne shall not miss you, if he is already assured of plentiful assistance. Perhaps you would like a cup of tea. And *we* would very much like to learn what happened," she pointedly declared, her gaze travelling from one source of information to the other.

"Of course, of course," Mr Denny muttered, then gave an uneasy gesture in his companion's direction. "Nevertheless, I think I should leave it to Miss Lydia to tell you all there is to know. I should rejoin the others. I am more likely to make myself useful there."

"Indeed," Lydia beamed, surprisingly disinclined to detain him now. "Go, go, and tell Papa how you charged headlong at Wickham to come to my rescue. He will like that above all else," she declared.

Then, once the officer had bidden his adieus and returned to the waiting hackney coach, she gaily waved him off and, without waiting for the conveyance to vanish around the corner, she bounded into her uncle's house, untamed and unabashed. "Come, let us sit," she said, sweeping into the parlour as though she owned the place. "I have such a tale to tell! But first you must give me your good wishes. Denny and I are to be married!"

⁂

"No, dear girl, first you must tell me something else," Mrs Gardiner solemnly said – the only one to recover from the surprise of Lydia's announcement. "Let me ask, are you well? That is to say, are you unharmed? Has Mr Wickham… injured you in any way?"

"Has he forced himself upon me, you mean?" Lydia voiced the question that her aunt could not bring herself to ask quite so directly, thus demonstrating that Mrs Gardiner's efforts towards delicacy had been entirely lost on her. "No, he has not," she vouchsafed the answer that her aunt and sisters had been praying for, only to find that Jane, who was sitting beside her on the sofa, leaned closer and clasped her into a tight embrace.

"Thank goodness! Oh, thank goodness," Jane murmured, dropping a host of little kisses into her disarrayed ringlets, and the fiercely protective outburst, testament to Jane's affection and utmost relief, made Lydia's lips curl up into a startled and rather foolish grin.

She returned Jane's embrace and a couple of her kisses, then patted her shoulder in something like impatience.

"There, there. No harm done, I tell you. Come now, are you trying to choke me? I can scarce breathe as it is," Lydia chided with an uneasy chuckle, but reached out to seek and hold her eldest sister's hand when Jane drew away. "I suppose I have that woman to thank, Mrs Younge," Lydia resumed with a grimace and a shrug. "She showed us up, then said that it had been a while, and she hoped I would not mind if the pair of them should have a little chat. I had no notion what they had to natter about, but they took their time. He came back eventually with some port and two glasses and a maid on his heels, bearing luncheon on a tray, but we had scarce finished eating when Denny and Chamberlayne burst in, sabres at the ready! And what a sight that was! If they were unknown to me, I should have been frightened out of my wits, but as it was—"

"How did they know where to come? And indeed that they were needed?" Elizabeth intervened, too keen to hear the salient points to have much patience for Lydia's effusions.

"Denny had stayed with Wickham at Mrs Younge's house before, when they had come to town to amuse themselves. So he knew that he should look in Edward Street first."

"They went there together to drink and gamble and goodness knows what?" Elizabeth exclaimed. "Are you telling me that Mr Denny is as depraved as Wickham?"

"Depraved!" Lydia snorted. "Lord, Lizzy, the things you say! Have a care, lest you grow as priggish as Mary. Of course Denny drinks and gambles and whatnot! He is a military man. What would you have him do in his spare time, read from Fordyce's sermons? Now hush, quit your quibbling and listen. I am coming to the best part," Lydia commanded, releasing Jane's hand to emphasise the brusque request for silence with a peremptory gesture, her forefinger in the air – and, however irked by her tone and manner, Elizabeth merely scowled as she complied. "As it turned out, Denny had always had a *tendre* for me," Lydia announced with boundless satisfaction, then shook her head. "The foolish man! He should have spoken sooner, and then I would not have given Wickham the time of day. Well, never mind that now. So, this morning he grew alarmed when he discovered that Wickham had absconded and was last seen riding out of Meryton with me—"

"But... you do not ride! Do you? When have you learnt?" Jane queried, a furrow in her brow, and Lydia rolled her eyes.

"I have not. Wickham hired just one horse and I rode in front of his saddle to the *Cross Keys*, if you must know. But the material point is that this morning Denny began to piece everything together, so he asked Colonel Forster's permission to go with Chamberlayne, track down Wickham and come to my rescue. Have you ever heard anything more romantic?" she cried, her triumphant glance darting to each of them in turn.

"Romance aside, it would have been a kindness to let your father know where you might be found, rather than leave him to fret and flounder hopelessly," Mrs Gardiner observed.

Lydia squared her shoulders and defensively retorted, "He did send a note to Longbourn! He said so. Well, I expect Papa had left already," she shrugged in callous unconcern, which could not fail to rouse Elizabeth's indignation.

"Lydia, have you any—?" she exclaimed, rounding on her thoughtless sister like a fury, but Jane laid a quelling hand on her shoulder and asked, "What exactly *did* Mr Denny piece together?"

"Oh, you know, Wickham railing against Mr Darcy, how he had deprived him of this, that and the other," Lydia said with a careless wave of her hand. "And then a few nights ago he had boasted to Denny over brandy that it would not be long until he was paid a goodly portion of what he was due. He said that Darcy would soon find his luck running out, and would have no option but to open his purse strings and part with a pretty penny for the sake of his family's good name."

"What was he planning?" Elizabeth gasped in horror.

"Blackmail," Lydia hissed. "Wickham meant to ask your husband to pay him fifteen thousand pounds to marry me," she imparted, cold fury in her eyes.

It made for a startling picture, that look of livid anger in a countenance that had heretofore reflected nothing stronger than childish petulance. It made her appear grim, and aged her by a decade. Not a pleasant way to grow up, Elizabeth mused, and reached to press her youngest sister's hand.

Yet building bridges was a frustrating business, she discovered, when Lydia snatched her hand away and snapped, "Don't you dare pity me, Lizzy! 'Tis not as though you have not misjudged the man as well."

'At least I have not eloped with him!' Elizabeth bristled, stung. Even so, she gathered her wits and kept that ungenerous thought to herself. Not only because it would have been a spiteful thing to say. But also, had she not acknowledged as far back as November that she had come frightfully close to entrusting Wickham with her fate, and that it was only by pure chance that her eyes were opened to what he truly was?

So, instead of sharp retaliation or resentful silence, Elizabeth opted for a mild chuckle and a little teasing.

"Oh, nothing of the sort, I assure you. If anything, I am rather envious. I was priced at a mere ten thousand."

"What?" Lydia spluttered.

"Last autumn, after the scandal, he asked for ten thousand pounds to marry me."

"Did he, now! Humph! Charming, that is. You never said."

Elizabeth bit her lip. No, she had not shared that revolting information with her mother and her younger sisters, and now she wished she had. But who in their right mind could have imagined that Lydia would still place her faith in Wickham, after everything else that was said about him at the time?

Reproaches would not serve though, so Elizabeth saw sense and asked pertinent questions:

"How did you learn the details? The exact sum and everything? Did Wickham confess?"

"No," Lydia said tersely. "He told me that we could not go to Gretna until he settled his affairs in town. I only found out what his *'affairs'* were when I read the letter he wrote for Mr Darcy. Denny found it on him, once Wickham was trussed up."

"Trussed up?" Elizabeth echoed, chortling with dark amusement.

Lydia gave a forceful nod.

"Aye. Like a chicken. Or a big, ugly turkey. Denny and Chamberlayne secured him to the largest chair in the room, then searched him for concealed weapons. That was when they found the letter. He tried to hop about and free himself when our backs were turned, but that gained him nothing. All he did was fall over, chair and all, and finished by looking utterly ridiculous, helpless and useless and with his legs in the air," Lydia said with a snort of contempt mingled with angry satisfaction. "But I am getting ahead of myself. The best part was Denny storming in with his sabre drawn. The most glorious sight that ever was seen!" she enthused, clasping her hands to her chest. "Chamberlayne was nothing to him – nothing! He is lanky and awkward and not handsome at all! He can wield a sword, I grant you, but it was Denny who appeared as the very picture of an angel of vengeance."

Her more mature and sensible relations exchanged brief glances, but this time did not interrupt her besotted effusions.

Lydia chose to change the tone herself. Her dreamy gaze gave way to fresh anger as she growled, "My only regret is that he did not skewer Wickham! You will never guess what the rat did, so I will tell you: when they burst in, he leapt to his feet and pulled me from my chair, and for a moment I thought he aimed to drag me from harm's way, but no, nothing of the sort from the likes of *him!* He used me as a *shield!*

Can you believe it? He used me as a shield as he retreated to escape into the bedchamber!"

"And?" Jane breathlessly prompted as the other two leaned forward in their seats, leaving Lydia in no doubt that she had their full attention. So she lengthened the pause for effect, her eyes twinkling mischievously.

"I bit him," she finally revealed with savage glee. "I dug my teeth into his hand until I tasted blood. It did the trick. He loosened his hold, and I could wriggle free. After that, it was the work of a moment for Denny and Chamberlayne to subdue him. They aim to take him back to the regiment, for Colonel Forster to mete his punishment, but Denny did not think that I should travel with them. Then he remembered making your acquaintance last Christmas," she said to Mrs Gardiner, "so we went and found a hackney coach. And on the way here he proposed! I accepted him, of course, although the location left much to be desired," she said with a little moue of discontent. "He might have chosen a better place to make his avowals, but I daresay it could not be helped. Now, me, I would have preferred we carry on to the North for, after all, I was cheated of the delights of a journey to Gretna, and I told him so. But he chuckled and said he hoped I would be satisfied with Brighton, and that he would much rather start on the right footing with Papa." She grimaced and, to Elizabeth's renewed vexation, she dismissively declared, "That is a foolish thing for him to fret about, for of course Papa can have no objections. Still, I shan't be sorry to be married from Longbourn and have Denny's fellow officers form a guard of honour, with their sabres drawn. And I shall like Brighton beyond all things! Good gracious! Who would have imagined, when Colonel Forster said that the regiment would be encamped near Brighton for the summer, that I should go with them as Mrs Denny? Mrs Denny! How droll that sounds! And how droll indeed, Jane, that I should be married before you! As for Kitty, she will be green with envy when she hears that I am to spend all summer in Brighton! And I shall not breathe a word till the last moment that I intended to take her with me all along! Oh, what a good joke!" she chortled. "This is how it will be: I shall tell Mamma, so that we may lay our plans and get the maid to pack Kitty's trunk overnight, and when I come to bid my adieus Mamma will bluster, 'Heavens, Kitty, you are not even dressed for the journey yet! Make haste, make haste, don't keep your sister and Mr Denny waiting! Bless me, girl, you will tear my nerves to shreds!'" she mimicked so faithfully that Elizabeth lost the battle against a traitorous smile.

Lydia was incorrigible! Wild, noisy, thoughtless and fearless as always. Through a happy accident of fortune, she was not to become Mrs Wickham – and for that, she and her relations should give daily thanks. As for Mr Denny, Elizabeth could only hope that the lieutenant was endowed with forbearance and good humour, for he would soon discover that he had his work cut out for him!

The urgent note had brought Mr Gardiner home, but he had not tarried long. He had merely come to offer comfort, stopped to rejoice in fresh details about the gratifying outcome, so much better than anything they could expect, then turned his gig about and went to join the others in Edward Street.

The wait seemed terribly long for those condemned to maddening inaction in Mrs Gardiner's parlour, with little else to do but tap their feet and wander back and forth from their seats to the window.

Yet their patience was finally rewarded about an hour later.

Sounds of activity could be heard in the entrance hall, with Mr Gardiner urging his impromptu guests to make their way within, and Mr Bennet quipping, "Well, this is the first time that I travelled with military escort, but I imagine it shan't be the last."

Elizabeth and Jane exchanged hopeful glances at the remark. Their father's inclination to make sport was a sure sign of his revived spirits, and thus an indication that nothing had gone wrong in the encounter with Wickham.

Mr Bennet's quip meant a great deal more to Lydia. No sooner had he uttered the words *'military escort'* than she leapt to her feet grinning from ear to ear and rushed to the pier glass to pat her ringlets into place and pinch her cheeks – a wasted effort on both counts, for her hair would not be tamed, and her cheeks were already flushed.

Jane remained where she was, but her forbearance seemed to be gained with a struggle. She shuffled forward till she was perched on the very edge of the seat, and fixed her gaze on the closed door as she strained to listen and pick out other voices – or rather, one voice in particular, Elizabeth assumed, and reached to press her hand.

Yet when Mrs Gardiner went to open the door that led into the hall, it was only their father and Mr Denny who made their presence known. They ambled in and the officer bowed, whereas Mr Bennet greeted his sister, then his gaze found Lydia and he muttered, "Ah. And there is the prodigal."

If that was an invitation to filial remorse and profuse apologies, it remained unanswered. Her air not in the least repentant, Lydia glanced from Mr Denny to her father, and all she said was, "Well?"

Her manner, so thoughtless and undutiful yet so in character, provoked her father into a half-resigned, half-exasperated snort.

"Yes, yes," he snapped, "I have given him my consent, and you are to marry. It was either that or locking you up for the rest of your life. Frankly, I am most grateful to Denny here for sparing me the confounded inconvenience of the latter." But when he turned to the gentleman in question, his voice grew suitably solemn as he added, "Not to mention the great debt of gratitude for your quick thinking, sir, and your noble intervention."

"Pray do not mention it, Mr Bennet. I think we can both agree that it was not so much noble as self-serving," Mr Denny said with a sheepish smile for him and another one for Lydia. "Needless to say, I consider myself fully recompensed."

Mr Bennet quirked a brow at that, but had the good grace to let it pass without comment. For her part, Elizabeth found the exchange nothing if not reassuring. So, there might be hope for Lydia after all. It was plain to see that Mr Denny held her in his affections. The love of a good man might help her mend her ways. Either that, or he would remain blissfully blind to all her flaws, and she would run rings around him. But there was no way of knowing. Only time would tell.

"So, there we are," Mr Bennet said in lieu of any disparaging remarks about his own daughter, much as Lydia deserved them. "With you and Darcy welcomed into the fold, I can only hope that my other girls will favour a physician, a man of the law and a vicar. Then I daresay that we might collectively rejoice in having a recourse against most things in life."

Elizabeth chuckled softly and made to speak, but Jane was there before her.

"It pleases you to jest, Papa, and I am glad to see you restored to excellent spirits. But pray tell us, what news from Edward Street? Is everyone safe, and everything as it should be?"

"Yes, my dear," Mr Bennet confirmed with an airy gesture. "All is well, never fear. The others will return directly. They went with Vincent to take Wickham to the docks."

"The docks!" Elizabeth exclaimed. "Why there, of all places?"

At almost the same time, Jane gasped, "Mr Vincent has gone to the *docks?* At this time of night?"

In truth, *'night'* was an exaggeration. Dusk had barely begun to fall. Yet Mr Bennet forbore to point that out, and merely said, "He did not go alone. Between them and their footmen, they form a large enough party, so rest easy, they shall not be set upon by ruffians. As for why there, Lizzy—"

"But Mr Vincent *is* aiming to return here, is he not?" Jane spoke over him – a breach of manners which, until that day, she would have deemed unthinkable.

Mr Bennet's lips twitched as he let that pass as well.

"I should very well think so," he retorted. "It would be a poor show to leave the others to make their way back by hackney coach. Now then, as for what took them to the docks," he resumed, "Wickham was given three choices: the debtors' prison for a lengthy sojourn which Darcy declared himself all too happy to arrange; the Peninsula under Colonel Fitzwilliam's command; and, last but not least, Vincent offered to have him enlisted as a marine and sent to East India. Not surprisingly, the reprobate chose the latter, and I shall not cavil. I certainly wish him as far away as possible. So returning him to the regiment in Meryton was out of the question," he grimly added. "No one wants him there, except perhaps Colonel Forster, who must be eager to vent his fury over the disgrace Wickham has brought upon him and his regiment. Sadly, desertions from the militia are not dealt with as harshly as those from the regulars, so Colonel Fitzwilliam has undertaken to write to Colonel Forster as soon as may be, and reconcile him to the notion that a duly severe punishment will be meted out in a different manner. And on that note, rest easy, sir," he said to Denny. "I have every intention to go and see him myself on our return to Hertfordshire, and have my say on the matter, lest Fitzwilliam's missive arrive too late for comfort. It would not do for you and Mr Chamberlayne to bear the brunt of your colonel's ill-humour in the meanwhile."

"That is very thoughtful, Mr Bennet, but quite needless, I assure you," Mr Denny replied with somewhat of a wicked grin. "Colonel Forster is a reasonable man who understands the subtleties of a punishment to fit the crime. You might find it illuminating to hear that he once told us how much he detests any and all voyages by sea."

"Indeed," his fellow officer chimed in, and Elizabeth glanced towards the doorway, whereupon she found that, while her papa was speaking, the rest of the party had quietly filed into the room – Lieutenant Chamberlayne, her uncle, and one other, whose prompt return she should have expected: Mr Bingley. And, judging by his countenance, he was painfully aware that in the last ten minutes Jane had mentioned Mr Vincent twice, yet not once had she enquired after *him*.

꧁꧂

The only source of light in her uncle's study was the flickering of the fire in the grate, Elizabeth found when she stepped in with a tenderly spoken, "Oh, Jane! You should not be sitting in the dark."

Suddenly brought from her reverie, her sister murmured, "Yes, I suppose I should have lit the candles, but…" She shrugged as she dried her eyes with her fingertips – a gesture which Elizabeth did not miss, however quick and surreptitious. Then Jane glanced over her shoulder with an apologetic grimace. "I lost track of time, it seems. Forgive me for tarrying so long. Do you need me?"

Elizabeth cast her a warm smile.

"Always. But that is not why I came. Our aunt wishes to know if you would like a bite to eat. There is a light repast laid out in the parlour. I told her I would ask. It was a good excuse to see how you were."

"Pray do not fret over me, dearest. I am well enough," Jane claimed, yet Elizabeth unerringly saw it for the valiant falsehood that it was.

She could not doubt that her sister was far from well. Likewise, Elizabeth knew without being told that the repast was of no interest, and that Jane had no wish to rejoin the others, all the while striving to conceal her heaviness of heart. Because Mr Vincent had yet to return.

Mr Bingley had left. He had solemnly excused himself, once Jane's unspoken message had inadvertently yet ever so forcefully hit home. Her countenance shrouded in compassion, she had followed him into the hall and, at her suggestion, they had retreated to Mr Gardiner's study to speak in private of everything that had been left unsaid.

It must have been a harrowing adieu.

Jane might wish to unburden herself in her own good time – but, for now, Elizabeth did not press her. She merely approached to hold her sister in a comforting embrace, and they remained thus, staring silently out of the window, as the late evening darkened into night.

There was little to see. The steady stream of carts, coaches and people had dwindled to a trickle. Fewer and fewer vehicles trundled past the carriage discreetly emblazoned with the Darcy arms, which had been stationed at the door ever since it had conveyed their father and Mr Bingley to Gracechurch Street, awkward as that shared journey must have been for both.

But then, some time later, a large conveyance drew to a halt behind it, and the tension in Jane's frame told Elizabeth that the newly arrived coach had captured her sister's full attention.

Jane leaned closer to the window and stared. Elizabeth did likewise. And their suppositions were confirmed when the nearest door opened and Darcy emerged, followed closely by Mr Vincent. They paused and lingered, talking. What was still left to talk about?

Elizabeth had no answer to that question. Yet she was quite certain that the same notion flashed through Jane's mind as well as hers when the men stepped apart, and only one of them – Darcy – could be seen bending his steps towards the house, whereas Mr Vincent turned to speak to his coachman. And the door of the carriage remained open wide.

"He is *not* leaving!" Jane gasped, unconsciously gripping Elizabeth's arm with such force that she winced.

Yet, just as suddenly, Jane loosened the tight hold, spun round and darted to the door.

Caught slightly off guard, Elizabeth followed a couple of seconds later, and reached the entrance in time to see her sister rushing past Darcy with somewhat of a nod, to arrive at Mr Vincent's side and visibly startle him with her presence.

It would not do to stare, so Elizabeth looked away. Yet as she descended the short flight of steps and approached her husband, she could not help darting the odd glance towards the other couple, and saw Mr Vincent reaching into his conveyance for a carriage rug, which he draped around Jane's shoulders. And then, a few moments later, they climbed into his coach and closed the door behind them, presumably to speak without fear of interruptions.

There was much to be said for privacy, wherever it might be found, and under different circumstances Elizabeth might have suggested that she and her husband have their own private conversation in their own carriage. But, as it happened, she knew her uncle's study to be unoccupied, so she reached for Darcy's hand, cast him a warm smile of welcome, and simply said, "Come."

Mr Gardiner's room was just as Elizabeth had left it – dark and quiet – and she was glad to find it so. With a small sigh of contentment, she nestled into her husband's embrace as soon as the door was shut.

"Is it done, then? Has Wickham set sail?" she asked, her cheek resting on Darcy's lapel, and he gave a mirthless chuckle as he pressed his lips to her muslin cap.

"No, that would have been a great deal too easy. He sails Tuesday week."

"Tuesday *week*?" Elizabeth echoed, drawing back to stare at him. "But what if he—?"

"Oh, he *will* be on board, never fear," Darcy spoke with grim satisfaction before she could even finish her question. "Fitzwilliam undertook to make sure of it, and gleefully too. He said that the task was its own reward. Besides, Wickham is under no illusion as to what will befall him if he should ever seek to cause us so much as a hint of trouble. Until today, he was blissfully unaware that I had purchased a great many of his debts. Now he knows that it would be easy work indeed to have him grow old in Marshalsea. With that in mind, I trust he will heed me."

"He should thank his stars for your forbearance," Elizabeth muttered. "You could have had him thrown into the debtors' prison without delay."

Darcy gave a faint gesture of agreement.

"That may be so, but there is much to be said for Vincent's solution. Many will draw an easy breath knowing that Wickham is halfway across the world."

Not least Georgiana, Elizabeth was quick to grasp. And then her thoughts flew to her eldest sister.

"What was Mr Vincent saying, once he had brought you back?" she could not help asking, gesturing over her shoulder as she explained, "We saw you from that window. Was he taking his leave?"

"No. He asked me to give him a moment. I suppose he was—" Darcy cleared his voice, then quietly resumed. "Whatever he was thinking, I doubt that leaving was a real option. I imagine he needed to know where he stood, and learn that sooner rather than later. Stoicism can only stretch so far."

A tender smile tugged at Elizabeth's lips.

"You should know," she whispered, and Darcy gave a strained chuckle in response.

He fell silent for the briefest moment. And then his question came without preamble:

"Bingley is no longer here, is he?"

Elizabeth shook her head.

"He left a while ago."

A sigh was his only answer, just as Elizabeth had expected.

For her part, though, she did have something to say.

"Fitzwilliam, you must not blame yourself," she urged, reaching up to stroke his cheek. "You may be assured that Jane does not. Nor I."

"But Bingley does, and rightly," Darcy countered with great sadness. "I should have left him be last autumn. And failing that, today."

Her hand sliding to his shoulder in a light caress, Elizabeth imparted, "Jane reproached herself as well, for agreeing to see him. But I think 'tis high time for blame to rest in its proper place," she earnestly argued. "You gave a piece of ill-informed advice. It was Mr Bingley's choice, and his alone, to heed it in preference to his own judgement. Much was said of his natural modesty, I know. And what then? Were you to be his keeper for all time, and guide him on every matter? If he would not choose his *wife* without your blessing, how is he to be trusted with any decision of import? I feel for him in his disappointment, I do, and your distress and guilt over your role in the affair pains me all the more, but you must allow me to believe that Jane deserves better. She deserves a husband she can rely upon."

This time Darcy's response was a grimace and a tilt of his head, so she continued:

"Whenever lesser men are disposed to do women an injustice – and, truth be told, they often are – they speak of females as mercurial creatures of caprice, who scarce know what they want and change their minds from one hour to the next. But you shall not be surprised to hear that we tend to grow up with a fairly good notion of what we wish for in life. The difficulty lies elsewhere: in not having the power of choice, merely that of veto, and above all in wishing for more than we can reasonably hope to find in a man of flesh and blood. Love. Tenderness. Esteem. Compassion. Patience. Strength, when the circumstance requires it. Comfort, whenever we are in need of such. If we knew anything of passion, we would certainly wish for that as well. And because I never was one for moderation, to all these I would have added yet more: humour, common sense, and the constant improvement of his mind by extensive reading," she said, and saw him smile at that teasing reference to a distant time.

Her heart aglow with all manner of blissful recollections, Elizabeth reached up and brushed the hair from his brow, then wrapped her arms around his neck.

"So my point is this: some of us are blessed with unimaginable fortune. Not only do we find everything we had ever wanted but, against all odds, we are given more than we could wish for," she whispered, and stood on tiptoe to press her lips to his.

Epilogue

"Oh, *Rufus!* " little Emily Gardiner cried in exasperation when, yet again, he was the first to reach the ball, easily caught it in mid-air and ran off with it to the far end of the lawn.

Picking up her skirts, Emily darted after him in hot pursuit, and the other children followed. Older than her and able to run faster, her brother Edward soon outstripped her, as did Ella Vincent, but that did not put them at any advantage in persuading Rufus to relinquish his prize.

His posterior in the air and his docked tail wagging, the terrier chewed on the leather ball, dropped it but briefly to bark in greeting, then hastened to retrieve it and, leaping to and fro, he evaded Edward and Ella with no difficulty whatever, scampered off to Hetty, the Gardiners' eldest, and dropped the ball at her feet.

Much too good-natured to take offence at the favouritism, Emily grinned and piped up, "He does not understand the rules of rounders, does he? He thinks we are playing with him, and wants you to throw again."

"You might as well, Hetty," Edward shrugged. "He shan't let us finish the game. A pity, because we were winning. Ah, never mind. Throw it to me," he cheered up as he began to run further afield. "But throw it low, and let us see if he can catch it."

Quick to find ample promise of amusement in the new game, Hetty did as bid, and before long Emily and Ella joined them in the merry frolic, and the midday air rang with squeals of laughter and excitable barks.

The only one to wince at the gleeful racket was Mrs Bennet.

"Oh well, at least they are running out of doors, for once," she sniffed.

As for Elizabeth, she gazed upon the children's antics with an incongruous mixture of resignation and delight, only to dart her eyes towards her husband when his warm hand covered hers and he asked, "A game of quoits perhaps? What say you, will that do?"

Tenderness filled her heart and overspread her countenance at finding him so quick to sense her longing for brisk activity and ease of movement. Yet, to her way of thinking, the disport that he had suggested was too tame and static – all in all, a poor substitute – much as Kitty, Miss Flora and Miss Lyle were clearly finding it to their satisfaction. The young ladies' brother and Georgiana did not seem to disdain it either. The pair of them had obligingly made up the numbers in the children's game, but had thought better of joining the little ones in their romp with Rufus, and had chosen quoits instead.

Elizabeth was of a different mind. So she twined her fingers around Darcy's and chuckled softly, "No, it will not, but I thank you all the same. I *would* stretch my legs, though. Shall we take a turn around the garden?"

"Of course," he said and rose from the picnic rug, just as Mrs Bennet tutted.

"Oh, you and your walks, Lizzy! Mind you do not overexert yourself. And you are not even wearing boots, but those flimsy slippers. What if you should catch a chill from the wet grass?"

"The grass is dry," came Darcy's terse retort, and for the sake of his imperilled equanimity – and hers – Elizabeth was glad to see her father breaking off his banter with Mr Kettering and Mr Lyle in order to lend assistance.

"My dear madam," Mr Bennet drawled, "need I point out that Lizzy is a full-grown woman of above one-and-twenty – a wife, moreover, and soon to be a mother? Surely she can be trusted to choose her own footwear by this stage."

The intervention earned him a glare and a "Humph!" but Mrs Bennet reserved that treatment for her husband. She still stood in enough awe of Darcy as to grow silent – or at least as close to grudging acquiescence as she would ever come.

While Mr and Mrs Gardiner took to pacifying her mother with sweetmeats and conversation, a tactic they had perfected over time, Elizabeth took her husband's proffered hand and stood, albeit with rather less agility than she should have wished, and they wandered off together, arm in arm.

"You were in the right, the grass *is* dry," she impishly murmured as soon as they had gained some distance, and Darcy had the good grace to look contrite.

"Forgive me," he whispered back. "I should have held my tongue."

Elizabeth chuckled mildly and patted his arm in reassurance.

"I have been telling myself that for many a year. Believe me, I know that it is more easily said than done. She means well and I love her dearly, but I do wish she would not lavish me with quite so much attention. She would drive me to distraction if she were to stay until the babe is born."

The overabundant flow of motherly advice on all things pertaining to her *'delicate condition'* had been a constant source of friction throughout her relations' sojourn at Pemberley, but that aside, it had been a delight to have them come and stay for the whole of August and most of September. Not her uncle, naturally – Mr Gardiner's affairs would not permit him such a lengthy absence, so he had only joined them a se'nnight prior. As for Lydia, she had sent word that she was much obliged for the invitation, but her husband could not be spared from his duties, and she was not going anywhere without her *'dearest Denny'*. Still, judging by her letters, her extended stay in Brighton was no hardship. She had written of innumerate balls and assemblies, of sailing trips and wild exploits on land, and boastful as Lydia was by nature, Elizabeth could readily believe her when she declared herself *'sublimely happy'* and wrote that she was having *'the most magnificent time'*.

Jane was exceedingly happy too, and she showed it just as openly, yet without any of Lydia's *panache* and parade. As was her wont, Jane's happiness glowed in her countenance, in her every word and gesture, and she had no use for hyperboles.

To Elizabeth's added joy, Jane's happiness was frequently before her eyes. Within weeks of their wedding, Mr Vincent had relinquished the lease on Netherfield and had brought his wife and daughter to live at Baybrook Hall, his newly purchased estate in Staffordshire which, among its many virtues, had the great merit of being less than twenty miles from Pemberley.

So now Netherfield lay empty and, to Elizabeth's mild vexation, Mrs Bennet often spoke of her hope that a single gentleman of good fortune might come to reside there and, with any luck, take a fancy to Kitty.

"Or even Mary. Who knows? Stranger things have happened," Mrs Bennet had been heard to say.

How Mary felt when her mother spoke thus can only be imagined, but Kitty showed nothing but indifference at the rosy speculations whenever they returned to revolve around *her*. Elizabeth had some suspicions on the matter, yet kept her own counsel and merely suggested that Kitty remain at Pemberley to keep Georgiana company and assist with the new arrival. Kitty had accepted with alacrity, Mr Bennet had agreed, and all had been arranged to satisfaction, without the slightest reference to Kitty's interest in Mr Webb, the vicar of Kympton. In due course, something might arise from that quarter. But it was too soon to tell.

Elizabeth's lips twitched at the thought that, once she had ambled down that road, she might seek to play matchmaker for Mary and Mr Hewitt, the amiable owner of the bookshop in Lambton.

But it would be exceedingly vain of her to take any credit for Charlotte's upcoming marriage. In truth, she had done nothing but invite her friend to Pemberley. When that letter was written and sent, she had not even heard of Mr Kettering's nephew, let alone made the gentleman's acquaintance. How was she to know that Major Aubrey would sell his commission and come to live with his uncle to lend a hand in the management of Clifton, which he stood to inherit? Or that he would become so taken with Charlotte?

Nay, she could take no credit, but would reap the rewards. Her dear friend would come to make a life in Derbyshire as well! Elizabeth's only regret was that she was in no state to travel halfway across the country to attend the wedding. It was to be held in a month's time, and even that fast-approaching date barely seemed close enough for Mr Kettering. Warmed by the hope of dandling his first great-nephew on his knee, the dear old gentleman had spent the best part of September teasing Major Aubrey, nudging him to propose and threatening him with disinheritance *'if he should be a damned fool and drag his heels about it.'*

It would be such a joy to have Kitty and Mary likewise settled within easy distance of Pemberley! Although not so much for their mother and father… Their dear papa would find amusement in his books, as ever. But how would their mother occupy her time between journeys north? Perhaps, for now, it would be a kindness to let her indulge dreams of Netherfield and its future tenant, whoever he might be.

As to the gentleman of good fortune who had taken possession of it last year at Michaelmas, only to give it up on the following quarter day, little was known of him but the content of a note and a very short letter.

The note had been delivered to Berkeley Square on the morning after the fateful day in Gracechurch Street, and merely announced that Mr Bingley had left town.

The letter was but marginally longer. It had come to find them at Pemberley some six weeks later, once they had returned to the North after Lydia's wedding, and Jane's. It had been sent from Gibraltar, and was the sort that anyone might read – that is to say, if they could decipher the script, for the penmanship was a frightful challenge. But, that aside, it contained no intimate details, no explanations, no reproaches. It only revealed that Mr Bingley had embarked on a long journey with no fixed destination, and finished with the promise that he would write again from wherever his travels might take him. If he had written, his next letter was yet to reach them. Elizabeth could only hope it would – and, for his sake and no less her husband's, that Mr Bingley was safe, and that he would find his peace.

There was no indication that his sisters would find theirs. Peace – much like goodwill, decency and kindness – seemed to be missing from their vocabulary. But rumour had it that they were currently gaining a better understanding of other concepts, such as *'exile'* and *'rusticating.'* Mr Hurst had apparently arranged a long sojourn in Scarborough for them, and claimed that the air of the metropolis was proven injurious to their nerves. Presumably Mr Hurst's own nerves were recovering nicely in their absence. But that was mere conjecture. To date, no letters had arrived at Pemberley from Mr Hurst, his wife or their sister. Not that the Darcys wished to receive any communications from that quarter.

Lady Rosemary was a wholly different matter in every way – so, with that in mind, Elizabeth had made it her business to begin a correspondence, which she maintained with some unease, but no less determination. As yet, it was impossible to tell if they were ever to rekindle their untroubled friendship. For now, exchanging letters was infinitely preferable to meeting face to face.

Loud barks disrupted Elizabeth's musings, and she darted her eyes across the lawn to see Rufus still prancing merrily around the children. She shook her head and smiled.

"He shan't know what to do with himself when they are gone."

The only one who seemed to have lost interest in gambols was Ella. She wandered off, bending down now and then to pluck tiny daisies from the grass. Once she had gathered a fair number, she ran to Jane with a cheerful, "We can make another daisy chain, Mamma! I gathered as many as I could. Do you think we need more?"

How strange that sounded, Jane being called '*Mamma*'!

Yet no sooner had that thought crossed her mind than Elizabeth ruefully chided herself for still finding it strange, although she must have heard the appellation on Ella's lips dozens of times already. If it sounded odd to her, it must be doubly so for Jane. Or perhaps not. Jane had always been maternal, even towards Lydia and Kitty when they were little. How could she not lavish motherly affection upon the angelic and tender-hearted daughter of the man she loved?

Another look in their direction revealed Jane naturally falling into that role. She released her husband's arm to guide Ella to a sunny spot further along the path, and there they sat, nestled close together, scattering the small flowers on their laps, so that they might choose the ones with the longest stem. This was no new amusement. Elizabeth had often seen them plaiting summer flowers into crowns. Yet the picture they presented was as endearing as ever, so she kept glancing at them from a distance as the pair chatted with great animation and their daisy chain took form.

The third in the family scene was silent. Mr Vincent was merely sitting beside them on the grass, attracting no notice with either word or gesture. Yet when Elizabeth chanced to dart her eyes towards him, she was compelled to look away, lest she trespass on the intensely private moment.

She already knew that he was devoted to her sister. But as he sat watching Jane at work, cheek to cheek with Ella, her arms encircling his little girl and her gentle hands guiding the small fingers, his mien and his rapt gaze spoke of a mix of sentiments that ran a vast deal deeper than devotion.

Heaven help him – heaven help them all – when Jane would be exposed to the pain and peril of the childbed!

But that thought came far too close to home, so Elizabeth promptly silenced it.

And then another notion sprang to mind, making her lips curl up into a smile. Now, there was a sterling reason to feel grateful for her mother's lengthy visit: her mamma stood as living proof that the Bennet women were resilient. There was much to be said for that heartening perspective.

"Shall we go this way?" she indicated the short flight of steps that led to the ornamental gardens. "I think I should like to sit for a little while."

"Your back?" Darcy asked, quick to understand her current and highly frustrating limitations, and Elizabeth nodded with a faint grimace, then chuckled.

"Which is precisely why I am suggesting we hide behind some obliging shrubs. I should be loath to let Mamma see me and give her enough reason to point out that she knew better all along."

Darcy's reply was a twitch of his lips and a roll of his eyes as they ambled towards the nearest bench. It was pleasantly secluded.

"The grass may be dry but the stone *will* be cold," he wryly observed and sat, gesturing towards his lap. "What of this arrangement?"

"Hmm, I imagine it will serve," Elizabeth retorted, but the wide grin she flashed him gave the lie to the teasing understatement.

In truth, the arrangement was very agreeable indeed – and all the more so when he took to kneading the taut muscles in the small of her back with gentle yet insistent pressure, the work of his fingers loosening the tension and alleviating the dull ache. With a soft purr of contentment, she nestled closer, and Darcy dropped a light kiss on her temple.

"Better?"

"Much better."

"Shall I go on?"

"If you would…"

"Of course."

Elizabeth leaned her head against his shoulder, relishing the soothing ministrations that brought a great deal more than physical relief. A wonderful sense of peace filled her heart to overflowing – one of the glorious sensations that were part and parcel of their marriage, and as familiar to her by now as the elation that she invariably found in his embrace, or the surge of possessive joy, shockingly close to gloating, that he sent rushing through her with or without reason at deliciously unpredictable times of day.

Yet this time it was entirely predictable, so Elizabeth had no cause to wonder at the exhilarating rush that rose and spread to every fibre of her being. What came as a surprise was that it seemed to somehow reach the babe as well, and urged the little one into a sudden somersault.

"Oh," she quietly exclaimed, darting her eyes to the rounded swell that vigorously moved from side to side, very much with a life of its own. She cradled it and raised her head to share the wondrous moment with her husband, her astonished delight softening into tenderness when she saw him stare back in awe mingled with panic.

"Is that—?" Darcy broke off and swallowed hard. He cleared his voice, but it still rang with both awe and panic when he spoke again. "Is that meant to happen?"

Elizabeth smiled and reached out to clasp his hand in reassurance.

"I believe so. Mamma and my aunt did say that the movements will become most noticeable. But, for all their words of wisdom, I will own that I did not expect quite so much energy," she added, and her warm smile widened. "Someone must be growing eager to join the others in chasing after Rufus and playing games of rounders."

Darcy choked out a strained half-chuckle in response. But then, as though on cue, another energetic movement followed the first, and a tight knot formed at the corner of his jaw.

"Is it very uncomfortable?"

Elizabeth shook her head.

"Not at all. 'Tis wonderful," she whispered.

Without a word, Darcy drew his hand from hers to curve it gently around the shape of their unborn child with excessive and decidedly uncommon caution for one who had done so dozens of times already, ever since her condition had begun to show. Under his warm hand, the babe moved again, leisurely this time, in a sort of a rolling wriggle. The sensation was exquisite.

Elizabeth turned her head to brush his cheek with her lips, then nestled once more against him, her fingertips lazily tracing circles over the back of his hand.

"Well, I think we can conclude that if this is not the son and heir, 'tis a very boisterous daughter," she observed, and Darcy smiled.

"Good. I hope all our daughters take after you."

Laughter in her eyes, Elizabeth glanced up.

"You say that now, but should you not be careful what you wish for? I am prepared to wager that you have not considered the surfeit of wilfulness and the squabbles that are bound to come from that, nor the tree-climbing and the muddy petticoats. To say nothing of suitors."

Darcy's lips found hers for a long, unhurried kiss, before he drew back and gave a rueful chuckle.

"I will own that I am not looking forward to the last part. But let us take it one step at a time."

The End

ABOUT THE AUTHOR

Joana Starnes lives in the south of England with her family. Over the years, she swapped several hats – physician, lecturer, clinical data analyst – but feels most comfortable in a bonnet. She has been living in Georgian England for decades in her imagination, and plans to continue in that vein till she lays hands on a time machine.
She loves to look for glimpses
of Pemberley and Jane Austen's world,
and to write about Regency England
and Mr Darcy falling in love with Elizabeth Bennet
over and over and over again.

You can connect with Joana Starnes on
Facebook: www.facebook.com/joana.a.starnes
Instagram: www.instagram.com/joana_starnes/
Website: www.joanastarnes.co.uk
Twitter: @Joana_Starnes

Or visit
www.facebook.com/AllRoadsLeadToPemberley.JoanaStarnes
for places and details that have inspired her novels.

Printed in Great Britain
by Amazon